Praise for THE SILENCE OF SIX

A YALSA Quick Pick for Reluctant Readers

"Suspenseful . . . Along with pleasing fans of Cory Doctorow's *Homeland* and like 'hacktion' thrillers, this offers sobering insight into how fragile our privacy really is." —ALA *Booklist*

"Teens who are, or wish they were, wired to the teeth will appreciate a thriller that speaks their language."
—*The Bulletin of the Center for Children's Books*

"The suspense is palpable in this tour de force mixture of mystery and computer technology that takes readers inside the weird world of hackers and top level secrets. A classic puzzler with a twenty-first century twist."
—Michael Cart (*Booklist* columnist)

"An entertaining and exciting book with non-stop action. . . . [A] hard-to-put-down read." —TheExaminer.com

AGAINST ALL SILENCE

AN SØS THRILLER

E.C. MYERS

ADAPTIVE BOOKS

An Imprint of Adaptive Studios

Culver City, CA

Visit us on the web at: www.adaptivestudios.com

Library of Congress Cataloging-in-Publication Number:
2016938462

ISBN: 978-0-9960666-9-3
pbk (B&N) ISBN: 978-1-945293-31-3
pbk ISBN: 978-1-945293-47-4
Ebook ISBN: 978-1-945293-02-3

First paperback edition, 2017

Printed in the United States of America.

Designed by Torborg Davern

Adaptive Books
3578 Hayden Avenue, Suite 6
Culver City, CA 90232

10 9 8 7 6 5 4 3 2 1

ALSO BY

E.C. MYERS

FAIR COIN

QUANTUM COIN

SOS: A Prequel to The Silence of Six

THE SILENCE OF SIX

To the NSA, GCHQ, BND, and all the other Big Brothers.

Now we are watching you. Do the right thing.

AGAINST ALL SILENCE

AN SØS THRILLER

FOR THE FIRST TIME IN HIS LIFE, MAX STEIN WAS IN A line that was moving too fast. He was one of hundreds of passengers proceeding steadily in a long, zigzagging path toward the security checkpoint at Charles de Gaulle Airport. He hurried to catch up to a man in a gray Armani suit who had suddenly gotten five feet ahead of him.

Max turned to the red-haired woman behind him with a toddler in a sling on her back.

"*Après vous.*" Max gestured them ahead of him.

She smiled. "*Merci.*" As the mother stepped past him with a folded umbrella stroller and a large tote bag, her little boy scrunched his face and grinned at Max.

"Pro tip: People with little children are easiest for pickpocketing," Enzo murmured beside Max. "They are already distracted."

Max stared at his pale, freckled friend. "Don't you dare. You're already going to get in trouble for sneaking into this line without a boarding pass."

Enzo shrugged. "I am a kid. I make the stupid mistake. 'I did not know! Honest, it not happen again!'" He said that last part with wide eyes and an exaggeratedly naïve voice. "It is their fault for not paying attention. *Imbéciles!*"

Max shook his head, but he was flattered that Enzo had wanted to see him off right up until the last minute.

"Mentioning 'mistakes.'" Enzo tapped the woman on her shoulder. She turned and he held up a small round tin of caramels. "*Excusez-moi, mademoiselle. C'est a vous?*"

"Oh! *Merci! Merci!*" she said. Her son took the container from Enzo and shook it happily. And noisily. "They are his best snack," she explained slowly in English with a heavy French accent.

Enzo dropped back to stand beside Max, unsuccessfully trying to hide a self-satisfied smile.

"You stole candy from a baby. That's low," Max whispered.

"And I gave it back. Victimless crime. I like to keep in practice." He glanced behind them.

"Worried someone saw you committing your 'victimless crime'?"

"No. I am wondering who else you will invite to go ahead of you." Enzo nodded at the mom. On her back, her son squirmed and kept turning his head to look from side to side. "At least you have improved the view. Ooh la la."

"E, don't be a stereotype. And she was only the second one."

"Number three, counting the mean granny you held the door for when we arrived." The elderly white woman had marched past without even acknowledging the gesture, not that Max had needed thanks. It was just a nice thing to do.

Max pressed his lips into a tight smile. "If I can leave France knowing I taught you to be a gentleman—"

"You know what happens to gentlemen? They miss their flights." Enzo scratched his left ear, pushing up a tuft of spiky brown hair. "Unless you do not wish to leave?"

Max hefted his heavy backpack on his shoulder and stepped forward, looking straight ahead. "I want to leave. I just don't want to say good-bye."

"This is not good-bye. It is 'see you online.' We can keep in touch, even without Panjea." Enzo nudged Max playfully.

Max slapped his hand to the left back pocket of his jeans. He held out his hand, palm up, to Enzo.

Enzo stuck out his tongue and held up Max's cell phone. Max snatched it back.

Even though he trusted Enzo implicitly, it still made him nervous to lose control of his phone for even a short time. That could be all it took to turn your helpful tool into one that helped someone else instead.

Max had been living with Enzo Beaumont and his parents, Alicia and Ophélie, while attending his fall semester of high school at Lycée Jules Verne in Paris. The women had treated

Max like a second son, and in the last four months, he'd gained a brother in Enzo.

The exchange program had been a perfect escape from Max's hometown of Granville and the wild ride his life had become since he and his friends had taken down Panjea last year. Enzo's joke about the now-defunct global social network only reminded Max of what he was returning to.

His old paranoia was already kicking in. Was he imagining it, or had that tall blonde woman in the line across from them been listening closely to their conversation? She kept sneaking glances their way.

Max hadn't been in the news in Europe as much he had back in America, but if you read the right websites, followed certain blogs, you might know who Max Stein was or even recognize him in an airport. Enzo had already known everything about him by the time they met—everything *public* anyway, which felt like more and more every day. But Max simply considered that basic required research; it was perfectly natural to search for information on the American teenager coming to live with you.

Enzo had been excited to have an "infamous hacker" living in his own home, even if they had to share his small bedroom, and was eager to learn anything Max was willing to teach him about computers—that is, hardly anything at all. Max and the younger boy had bonded quickly, finding they had plenty in common as only children with unusual hobbies.

Max didn't find it easy to make new friends—not real ones,

the kind you could trust with your life. His best friend, Evan Baxter, had died the previous year, taking his life in a very public way. He had entrusted Max with information that launched him on an investigation of Panjea. The social media giant had been collecting information on its users and manipulating the way they voted in the recent presidential election—and killing anyone who discovered their secrets.

Max had two regrets about the part he'd played in exposing the company. The first was that Panjea's mastermind, Kevin Sharpe, had succeeded in getting his candidate, Angela Lovett, elected. Though Sharpe had been charged with conspiracy and murder, his old boss had granted him a full pardon for his actions as soon as she entered office.

Many criticized President Lovett's decision, while others praised it as a savvy political move: getting Sharpe out of the headlines, making him a brief blemish on her administration rather than a shadow cast over her entire term. Her approval rating barely dropped two percentage points.

From all accounts, Sharpe had fled the States and disappeared, perhaps as a condition of his release, perhaps to get a fresh start. Or maybe he feared someone would take justice into their own hands.

Max's second, larger regret was that Evan had chosen to kill himself in order to get the world to pay attention.

Make that three regrets: A year later, and everything Max and his hacker friends had fought for had been for nothing.

Not entirely for nothing. Max had met Penny and Risse

Polonsky, and they had become real friends.

And now Max had Enzo too, and the Beaumont family. With them, he could just be himself. He didn't have to pretend to be the good son, or the popular soccer star, or the doting boyfriend, or even some hotshot hacker. Or what the media made him out to be: a social-justice warrior. He was just an eighteen-year-old kid enjoying his last year of high school.

Naturally, even that was just another act.

"Online isn't as good as real life," Max said. His geek card could be revoked for saying that, but he now believed it was true. "That's why I'm going home. My dad loves Christmas, and it wouldn't be the same without him. But I'm still going to miss you and your moms."

"Just because you're going home, that does not mean you have to stop looking for *your* mother," Enzo said. "I will keep looking here, whatever you need. If she is in France, we will eventually find her."

Max eyed Enzo. The kid had an uncanny way of reading people, another thing they had in common. You couldn't be a good social engineer or a good pickpocket without understanding other people. So naturally Enzo understood that Max was having a hard time leaving because he hadn't accomplished what he'd *really* come here for.

"Thanks, but we should have found her by now," Max said.

Four months of research and weekend trips and tracking down cold clues that ended in dead ends. Max had finally admitted to himself that it was a fool's errand, and even though it had been a private mission, Max was still embarrassed that he had failed.

What kind of hacker couldn't track down their own missing mother?

"Maybe you should have asked your friends for help," Enzo said.

"I did. I asked *you*."

Enzo smiled. "But I am no Dramatis Personai."

Max heard the wistfulness in Enzo's voice and shook his head. "This is too personal. Plus I don't want to get in any deeper with them if I can help it."

Max had retired his old handle, 503-ERROR. It was too well known and carried too many expectations; without a true leader, Dramatis Personai had started looking to Max for guidance. Serving that role and the heavy responsibility that came with it made him uncomfortable.

The line had slowed down, but every step was still taking Max farther away from a place that unexpectedly felt as much like home as his house in Granville. Despite Enzo's reassurance, Max knew he would never have as good a chance at locating his mother once he left France.

"How are you doing on time?" Enzo asked.

Max turned on the phone that was still in his hand. "Flight leaves in two hours." He noticed a new email with an update on his flight's status.

A major winter storm was blanketing the midwestern

United States in snow. Those things always rippled through the airline system, causing delays and canceled flights, especially in the week leading up to Christmas.

Max quickly typed in his twenty-character password while Enzo watched carefully, still trying to crack it. He thumbed open the email. Just a gate change.

"It's still on schedule," he said.

While in Paris, Max hadn't been checking his encrypted email account as often as he used to. He hadn't quite disconnected from online life, but he had more than enough to do in the real world. As he scrolled through a slew of unread messages—so much for inbox zero—the old stress crept back with a familiar tension in his neck and a dull throbbing behind his eyes.

He could only turn down so many interview requests, media opportunities, and invitations to join rallies or support petitions about personal privacy and internet freedom. He believed in those causes, but it seemed everyone wanted him to step up and take charge for them. They talked about the importance of individuals, but Max hardly felt like a person anymore.

Hadn't he given up enough already?

He kept scrolling down the list of emails—until he saw the one message he wanted to read, the one he'd been waiting for.

Penny had cut off communication a couple of months ago, right around the anniversary of Evan's death. Her last email had said she was working on something important, but Max wondered if she'd just needed a break like he had.

He worried she needed a break from *him*.

Granted, their history was . . . complicated. She had sort of been Evan's girlfriend, mostly online, and now she and Max were dating. Also mostly online.

Being eight hours away from each other didn't make their relationship conventional or convenient, but like Enzo had said, the internet made it easy to stay in contact, and they were used to living their lives through a screen anyway. If anything, it made the experience more intense more quickly; things had heated up during their last in-person meeting.

But it seemed like that had scared them both a little. Without discussing it, they had backed off. They hadn't made any other plans to get together in real life. Then Max had departed for France, and school and his search for his mother had taken center stage, while Penny grew more distant and focused on whatever she was working on.

"I should have kept your mobile. What about 'being more present'?" Enzo said.

"Sorry." Max shut off his screen. It hadn't taken long at all to fall back down the rabbit hole. "Penny emailed me."

"Finally. What did she say? Did she send a picture of herself?"

Max shook his head. "I haven't opened it yet."

"Read it!"

Max switched his screen on and tapped Penny's email to open it. He smiled at the subject line. They always used spammy fake headlines when they wrote to each other.

From: p-squared@freemail.net

To: maxwell.stein@freemail.net

Subject: Re: CONGRATULATION! Trip Grand Prize!!!

Max,

Please come to Berlin at once if convenient. If inconvenient, come anyway. Ada Kiesler would like to meet, and we have a mutually beneficial proposal for you.

See you soon!

<3 <3 <3

Penny

Max stared at the screen in disbelief.

"What?" Enzo asked.

"She wants me to come to Berlin . . . to meet Ada Kiesler."

"Ada Kiesler? The woman who leaked those emails from VT?" Enzo asked.

"Or tried to." Max looked around. He had no reason to worry about someone watching them, any more than everyone was being watched all the time these days. But Kiesler's name might set off red flags if anyone overheard them.

Even with Max's attempts to distance himself from controversies about the abuse of technology to monitor and control private citizens, Max knew all about Ada Kiesler's situation, if only because she had been in the headlines enough to take some of the media attention away from Max.

Until last winter, Ada Kiesler had been Assistant Vice President of Verbunden Telekom AG. VT was the largest media company in Europe, one of the top three in the world. It had a monopoly on providing internet and voice services in Germany, and it often faced accusations of attempting to dominate the internet on a global scale, which VT embraced in its slogan: "Giving the World a Voice."

Surprisingly, the primary critic of VT's aggressive tactics had been Kiesler herself. As AVP, she often advocated for an internet protected from overbearing corporate and government influence—one that could be trusted to serve public interests alone.

Instead of firing her, VT's press machine had spun it that Kiesler's continued employment demonstrated their fair and open policies and their willingness to consider alternative business models.

Then, last December, the online news site *Der Fenster* had published a dozen emails from top-ranking executives at VT that revealed corrupt, even criminal, practices of manipulating financial markets to force their competitors to accept buyouts.

"She is in hiding?" Enzo said.

"At the Chilean Embassy in Berlin," Max said.

A moment later, Enzo voiced the question Max kept asking himself: "What does she want with you?"

Max shrugged.

In general, Europe did not do much to protect whistleblowers. When Kiesler leaked those emails, she had faced criminal charges, prompting her request for asylum at the Chilean Embassy. Meanwhile, her bosses and colleagues had been under public scrutiny for less than twenty-four hours—all the time it took for *Der Fenster* to retract its story and apologize for publishing sensational news without fact-checking first. No other news outlets had been willing to publish the thousands of emails and documents Kiesler claimed she possessed, which she said would expose VT's far darker business dealings.

"That's so badass." Enzo grinned. The boy's open admiration bordered on hero worship, which bothered Max. He nudged Enzo lightly in the side with his elbow.

How had Penny gotten involved with Kiesler? Was this the special project she'd been working on? And why did she need him to come there?

Despite himself, he was intrigued. Max liked puzzles, and this had the makings of a big one.

"You are going, yes?" Enzo asked.

Max gestured around him. The line had kept moving along, and they were almost at security.

"No. I'm going home."

He reread the email. It had arrived six days ago. Too bad he hadn't found it sooner; he could have fit a quick trip in. But would he have?

He typed out a quick response.

From: maxwell.stein@freemail.net
To: p-squared@freemail.net

Subject: Re: Re: CONGRATULATION! Trip Grand Prize!!!

Pen,

Berlin?! Why didn't you tell me you're in Europe? I just
got this, but I'm on my way home for Xmas. In fact, I'm at
the airport. I'm so sorry, but I can't make it. :(

Please give my apologies to Ms. Kiesler(!!!!). And good
luck with whatever's going on . . . Let's catch up soon?

Hugs,

Max

His thumb hovered over the Send icon.

Max could maybe switch to a later flight to California, grab
another one to Berlin for not too much money. It was only a
few hours away. But his dad was waiting for him to come home
so they could buy and decorate the tree together.

With just the two of them, Christmas could have been a
depressing reminder of the absence in their lives, or even
worse—just another day. The first year after Lianna Stein left,
holidays had been empty, bitter occasions. But Bradley Stein
had rallied and worked harder to make them special, as if
doing the work of two parents, and he pulled out all the stops
at Christmas.

The house was always full of the aroma of baking ginger-
bread, stockings were hung by the chimney with care, and
all that. His Christmas gifts were also way too extravagant.
Max had gotten his first laptop at six years old, the year after

his mom had disappeared. In some ways, he'd been looking for her ever since, and that mission had helped steer him into hacking.

There was no way he could miss Christmas at home. Max sent the email.

"A shame," Enzo said. "Berlin is a great city, especially during Advent. We went on holiday there three years ago. The women are gorgeous."

"You were what, twelve?" Max asked.

"You don't have to be a painter to appreciate fine art," Enzo said.

"Whatever that means."

Another email popped onto the screen. *That was fast.*

But it wasn't a reply from Penny—it was an error report that his message could not be delivered.

"My email bounced," Max said.

Max's skin crawled. His last text to Evan before he died had bounced too. He'd been too late to save him, and Max couldn't ignore the feeling that he was failing another friend when she needed his help.

"Okay?" Enzo asked.

Max cleared his throat. Nodded.

"Good. You are next."

Max and Enzo kissed each other's cheeks and then Max rubbed the boy's spiky head one last time for luck. Enzo backed up, thumb and pinky out to mime a cell phone. *"On s'appelle?"* he mouthed. He turned and worked his way to the back of the line.

The security agent, a man in a black suit, gestured Max forward.

"*Bonjour*," Max said.

"*Bonjour*," the man said in a bored voice. He took Max's American passport and opened it. "Did you enjoy your stay?"

"So much I wish I didn't have to leave," Max said. It felt odd not having Enzo close by; they'd been practically inseparable. Max glanced behind him. Enzo was still hanging around by the back of the line, while the female security agent there watched him warily.

The man straightened and scrutinized Max's passport. He looked up at Max and scrutinized *him*.

"Maxwell Stein?" the man asked.

"That's right." Max felt his shoulders tighten. Something wasn't right.

Max had been one of the best soccer players at Granville High not just because he could run fast, but because he had good spatial awareness of where the team members and the ball were at all times. That skill was shifting into high gear now. He noticed four airport police officers approaching from four different directions, and he was certain others were behind him and closing in. He had the uncomfortable feeling that *he* was the ball on their playing field.

"Is there a problem?" Max asked lightly.

The man snapped Max's passport shut. "Pardon. Stay right here."

The man left and consulted another officer by the full-body scanner. Max adjusted the straps of his backpack and flexed his calves. He could get past them, he might even be able to outrun them. But they were armed, and where would he go?

This was probably just some misunderstanding. He hadn't done anything wrong—not lately, anyway, nothing they would care about—but if he ran, he would look guilty of *something*, and they would come after him.

He glanced over his shoulder. Naturally, Enzo had picked up on the fact that something was happening. Another officer stood an arm's length away from the boy.

Enzo's eyes asked a question. Max shrugged. He squeezed his cell phone tightly, hands shaking with anxiety and adrenaline.

His phone!

Max held it slightly away from his body and glanced down at it, so it wouldn't be obvious that he was using it. He probably should be firing a quick text to his dad, but it was more important that he password-lock it so—

"I'll take that." A hand eased Max's phone away from him. *Shit.*

"Please come with us." The officer held Max's arm in a firm grip and handed his phone to her partner.

"Am I under arrest?" Max asked.

"We have a few questions for you."

"I haven't done anything." Max pulled, but it felt like his arm was in a vise. "What is this about?" he asked more loudly.

"Max!" He turned and saw Enzo edging away from the guard near him, his own cell phone already out and recording.

Max forced a smile and shook his head as the second officer roughly grabbed his other arm, and they marched him past the security checkpoint through a narrow door marked DOUANE. He was pulled through a series of stark white corridors. Most of the doors had signs marked PRIVÉ and SÉCURITÉ—but Max had rarely felt less secure than he did now. The officers spoke to one another in soft, rapid French that Max couldn't follow. He gathered he was in trouble.

Sorry, Dad, he thought. *I may miss Christmas after all.*

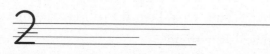

THE INTERROGATION ROOM, AS MAX THOUGHT OF it, didn't look anything like the ones he saw on television and movies. There was no one-way mirror, no cameras watching him or bright lights shining in his face. It was just a cramped, windowless conference room with a square wooden table and four uncomfortable plastic chairs. There was a half-full water cooler by the door without any cups. Detention at Granville High was worse.

But after he'd been sitting alone for two and a half hours without speaking to anyone, the room felt as bad as any prison.

One of the fluorescent lights overhead blinked every five seconds and was starting to give him a headache.

Max considered the possibility that this was a new, subtle form of torture and wondered how much more trouble he could get into if he climbed onto the table and tried to remove the bulb.

A key slid into the lock, and Max jumped off the table and scrambled back into his seat. A woman walked in. She had black hair, an unseasonal tan, and a smart navy blue suit that made Max feel like a slob in his Disneyland Paris T-shirt, jeans, and green hoodie. She studied him for a moment, eyes narrowed, and then looked up at the flickering light. Max swept his arm across the table to erase the telltale footprints of his canvas sneakers.

She sat across from Max and slid a bottle of water over to him. She wore no ID and didn't seem like the other police officers. *Their boss?* He took the bottle and twisted the top off, breaking the seal. So probably not tampered with, then. He was thirsty, but he managed just a delicate sip of the cool, refreshing water before he asked, "Who are you?"

"You are Maxwell Stein," she said with a heavy French accent.

Max nodded. He rattled off his Social Security number.

"That isn't necessary. We already know all about you, *503-ERROR*." She emphasized his handle as though she was expecting him to be stunned or impressed.

Despite his forced bravado, Max was scared, but he also knew there were two ways to play this: He could reveal how frightened he was and do his best to cooperate, or he could give in to righteous indignation and show them he was no pushover. Whatever they were detaining him for, which seemed related to his now-infamous, quasi-illegal online persona, they couldn't treat a private American citizen this way.

On the other hand, he'd heard that French police had

once detained a six-year-old girl for three days, because they thought her passport was a fake. That was cold.

He was pretty sure they couldn't keep him without telling him why, but he wasn't up on international law. All he knew about France's legal system was that their prisons were supposed to be particularly bad. He swallowed.

"Oh, good, so you know how to Google. If you know everything about me, then you hardly need me here to answer your questions." Max stood.

The door opened and a wiry black man entered, carrying Max's backpack and laptop bag. He dropped the bags onto the table, and Max glimpsed the gun holstered under his left arm. The man stood by the door.

"I'm Bujold, principal controller of the DGDDI," the woman said. "French customs."

"Okay."

"What are you doing in France?" she asked.

"Right now I'm trying to leave. My flight just left, so thanks for that."

Bujold pressed her lips together.

Max sighed. "I was participating in a cultural-exchange program. I studied at Lycée Jules Verne last semester."

"We're more interested in your extracurricular activities," she said. "You've been traveling a lot."

Telling them about his efforts to track down his mom was way too personal.

"Just sightseeing," Max said.

"Mm-hmm." She reached into her blazer, and Max tensed. Instead of a gun, she drew out a cell phone. *His* cell phone. It was plugged into a portable battery, and the screen was still active, so they'd probably already searched it and downloaded his data. Maybe they'd even added some of their custom features by now.

The phone wasn't loaded with anything more sensitive than Max's school assignments, but it always angered him when authorities felt they were entitled to pry into his life.

"How did you enjoy Berlin?" she asked.

"I've never been," Max blurted out. "What's in—? Oh."

Ada Kiesler was in Berlin, holed up in the Chilean Embassy. Penny was there too.

Bujold rested his phone on the table. She slid his backpack closer and unzipped it. She started pulling items out of it: rolled T-shirts, balled-up socks, his boxer shorts—all clean, at least. He had packed the bag so tightly and carefully, it was obvious that they had already examined his belongings, so this was all some performance for his benefit.

"Three hoodies?" She raised an eyebrow.

"I get cold easily, and they're really comfy," Max said. "Feel them. They're soft."

Just as Max had framed his idea of an interrogation room from media, movies and TV often portrayed hackers as kids in hoodies sitting in dark rooms in front of glowing computer screens. Sure, Max fit that profile, but he didn't pull up his hood while he was hacking.

He did *once*, but only because Evan jacked up the air conditioning in his room due to his hatred of sweat and pretty much all bodily excretions. Especially the sight of his own blood. Max shivered.

"You okay there, *monsieur*?" she asked. The way she used the salutation somehow showed the exact opposite of respect for him.

"See? Just cold." Max tucked his arms in at his sides.

Bujold pulled a small box wrapped in sparkly pink paper from Max's backpack. She shook the box gently.

Bujold pulled out three more boxes: a small square in plain brown paper, a long rectangle covered in purple unicorns, and a picture frame box wrapped in the cover page of *The Granville Herald*.

"What are these?" Bujold asked.

"Souvenirs. Gifts. They're personal."

She held up the square box. "We have to open them."

"Can't you run it through the X-ray scanner?" Max asked.

"Or you could tell me what's inside."

"That's a mug. For my dad."

She carefully peeled back the paper.

"What are you doing?" Max asked.

"Confirming what you said."

She opened the box, preserving the paper expertly; she must be a hard person to surprise at Christmas.

"A mug," Bujold pronounced. She held up a blue mug showing the character Tintin and his white dog, Snowy. Max's dad had read those comics with him when he was a kid. Max had always wanted to travel the world like the intrepid young reporter, but his first globe-trotting adventure hadn't turned out so well.

She opened the pink wrapping paper on the first box and pried open the lid. She pulled out a laptop sleeve decorated with a circuit board showing the Paris Métro map.

"Pretty. For your girlfriend?" Bujold asked.

"I don't know," Max said.

"You don't know who it's for?"

"I mean, I don't know if she's my girlfriend."

Bujold winked. "I get it. What's her name? Penelope Polonsky? She was involved in that whole . . ." She waved her hand, to indicate everything that had gone down with Panjea last year. Penny hadn't drawn as much of the media attention, by design, so these guys likely didn't know that she was a hacker too, and she had been a key member of the hacktivist collective Dramatis Personai.

"What's she up to these days?" Bujold asked.

"I don't know," Max said truthfully.

"I find that hard to believe."

"She kind of does her own thing. We haven't spoken in a while. That's why I'm not sure about whether . . ." He gestured at the gift he'd bought for Penny, to indicate all his uncertainty over their current status as a couple.

"She's been making some interesting new friends." Bujold's eyes didn't leave Max's face. She was fishing for information.

"If that's what this is about, I only just saw her invitation to Berlin. Since you've read my emails, you know I turned it down. I've never met Ada Kiesler. I don't know what she could want with me, and I don't know how Penny's involved. I only want to go home."

They stared at each other.

"Don't worry, we'll wrap these for you again." Bujold turned her attention to another box. She carefully unwrapped and opened it. Her face lit up. "Marsupilami!" She pulled out the stuffed toy, a yellow monkey with black spots and a long tail. She stroked its plush fur.

"Is that what it's called?" Max asked.

"You didn't know? Who's it for?"

"I bought it because it's cute," Max said.

That toy was for Penny's fifteen-year-old sister, Risse, but they shouldn't have any idea that she existed, and Max wanted to keep it that way.

Max picked up the last present—the one he had brought with him from home. "This is a framed photo of me and my dad. I was hoping to find my mom while I was in Paris, okay? I was going to give it to her. It didn't happen."

Bujold took the wrapped frame from him gently and returned it to his bag. "Okay. Thank you, *monsieur.*"

"Call me Max," he said.

She smiled. "There's just one more thing you can help us with, Max."

She slid his laptop bag closer. "We need to see what's on your computer."

Max really did feel a chill now. "Why?"

"To find out if you're a cyberterrorist."

Max snorted.

"Did I say something humorous?" Bujold asked.

"Cyberterrorism isn't an actual *thing.* It was made up by the media."

"So says the cyberterrorist."

"What have I supposedly done?" Max asked. He gestured at his stuff strewn across the table. "Let's put it all on the table. I don't like games."

That was the first lie Max had told her. He loved puzzle games, and he was very good at them. But not when the deck was stacked against him. They were withholding information from him, hoping that he would slip up and reveal information they thought he was withholding from *them.* This could go on all day, or only as long as their patience lasted.

"You're required to tell me why you're holding me," Max said.

She shrugged. "Your name has an alert in our security system."

Max blinked. "I'm on the no-fly list?"

"We're waiting for information from the TSA, but you're on at least one of your government's many watch lists."

"What for?"

"You tell me. However, our cyber division was already familiar with your background, so we can imagine what you've been up to."

"Actually, I've given up hacking. White hat or otherwise."

"I find that hard to believe."

Bujold unzipped the bag and pulled out Max's laptop. She turned it to face him and opened the screen. "If you haven't been breaking the law, why protect your computer with such sophisticated encryption?"

Max suppressed a laugh. There was nothing sophisticated about it. Anyone could encrypt their computer in the same way using simple, free software, but few people bothered. Even basic encryption was enough to protect your private information from hackers or government snooping.

"You can want your information to be secure even if you have nothing to hide," Max said. "Everyone should do it."

She scoffed. "It must be hard going through life paranoid about everything."

"It isn't paranoia if people really are after you." Max spread his hands to indicate the room. "Even when you haven't done anything wrong. Considering my government murdered six people last year, you'll forgive my distrust of authority."

She nodded. "Please enter your password."

Max grimaced. "Nope. You know enough about my personal life from your databases."

"It's only a matter of time before we crack it, but your cooperation could save you some time here."

"Am I under arrest?" Max asked. "If so, I should be allowed to communicate with my embassy. I should get a phone call. But no, you're holding me illegally, and you don't even know why. I demand to be released immediately."

"You *demand*?" Bujold slapped his laptop shut and stood, tucking it under her arm. "Get comfortable. You aren't going anywhere for a while, Max."

Someone knocked at the door. The security officer waited for Bujold to nod her permission before he opened it. One of the customs agents, a heavyset man in a light blue short-sleeved shirt, entered.

"What?" Bujold snapped.

The agent glanced at Max and said something to Bujold. She looked astonished.

"Excuse me." She hurried out of the room with Max's laptop, followed by the customs agent and the security officer. Once again, Max was alone.

She returned a few minutes later, clearly annoyed. She put Max's laptop down on the table in front of him.

"I'm still not going to help you," Max said.

She stared at him for a long moment before finally saying, "You have friends in high places. An American representative is on his way here to vouch for you."

"Who?"

"Kevin Sharpe."

Max bristled at the mention of that name. "Sharpe is in Paris? He's no friend of mine."

"Then you owe him. He's pulling some strings to have you cleared for travel."

"That doesn't make any sense." How had Sharpe found out that Max was here? And how did he have any strings left to pull? The man had left his position—and his country—in disgrace.

Most importantly: Why would Sharpe help Max?

He scowled. "It's more likely that Sharpe put me on the list himself."

"Apparently this is all just a mix-up. We don't know why your name is triggering a security alert, but it's possible our screening program was hacked." She narrowed her eyes.

Max held up his hands. "Don't look at me!"

"No, I doubt you would have wanted to put your name *on* a watch list. We're looking into what happened. This is a serious concern if we have a breach."

Some hacker had added Max to a TSA watch list? That was a terrible prank. Who would do that? Who *could* do that? Someone he had crossed in Dramatis Personai? Even with all their skills, only a handful were capable of something on this level, and Max counted them among his real friends.

"You said Sharpe is coming here? To see me?" Max asked.

"So I was informed. Sit tight. Can I get you anything?"

"If I'm not under arrest, am I free to go?"

She frowned. "You can't fly as long as this restriction is placed on your record in the database, but technically you don't have to stay in the airport, no."

"Then I'm leaving." Max stood and started shoving his things into his bag, torn wrapping paper and all.

Mistake or not, his flight had already departed. If his name was cleared, he could get his ticket changed, but he had no intention of waiting around for Kevin Sharpe. This stunt seemed designed to keep him in Paris and at Sharpe's mercy, and whatever Sharpe wanted in return for a favor with the TSA had to be bad news. Or perhaps the man was seeking revenge for Max's part in exposing his crimes and destroying his career.

"I can't stop you, but I strongly advise you to remain here until the matter with Mr. Sharpe is settled," Bujold said.

"Nope. I'm out of here. Now." Max zipped his backpack closed.

But where should he go?

Penny. If Sharpe was in Europe, he had to warn her. Maybe she could help Max straighten out this mess. If a hacker had put him on a watch list, a hacker could take him off it.

Bujold led Max back through the hall he'd been practically dragged through before. It was a lot shorter than he'd remembered. Airline employees turned to stare at him as he walked past.

Soon they were standing outside the security checkpoint, where this all had started. Max saw Enzo standing there, between his mothers, Ophélie and Alicia. Enzo held a white sign that said 503-ERROR. Their faces all brightened when they caught sight of him, and Max had to squeeze his eyes shut to hold back the tears.

"Sorry for the trouble, Max." Bujold gave him a stern look. "But I do hope this really was just a misunderstanding."

She turned and headed back to the security offices. Max walked toward the Beaumonts.

"Max." Alicia pulled him into a warm hug that somehow made him feel safer than he had felt in years. She still smelled like cinnamon, from the scones she'd baked that morning.

Alicia Beaumont was a foot and a half shorter than Max and looked like an older, plumper version of her son—pale, freckled skin; pink cheeks; wild, curly brown hair. She reminded him of a hobbit, and that meant comfort.

Ophélie Beaumont, on the other hand, was almost as tall as Max, with brown skin and glossy black hair. She was less touchy-feely than her wife, but she patted Max on the shoulder supportively.

"What are you doing here? You had that important meeting you couldn't miss," Max said. Ophélie was still dressed in her lavender suit and high heels, with her leather briefcase slung over one shoulder.

She shrugged. "I missed it. We had to come as soon as Enzo called. Are you all right?"

"I am now. Sorry to trouble you all."

"It was no trouble. You're family," Alicia said.

"Yeah!" Enzo hugged him and then handed him the sign that said 503-ERROR.

"Cute." Max tucked it away in his bag. So much for secret identities.

"What happened, Max?" Ophélie asked.

"I promise you, I didn't do anything wrong," he said.

"Of course not. You're a good boy, just like Enzo," Alicia said.

Enzo smiled angelically.

"A better boy than Enzo, if we're being honest," Ophélie said.

"*Quoi!*" Enzo said.

His mother was no fool. She might not know about Enzo's pocket and lock-picking hobbies, but she knew he was up to *something*. To their credit, the couple didn't pry as long as he didn't get into trouble, but Max knew if Enzo did need them, they would have his back no matter what.

Just like they had supported Max. He had wanted to make a good impression on his host family. Start over. Be someone new. But as soon as he'd arrived in their home, he had come clean about his own criminal past.

He had downplayed his role a bit, but even they had heard about Panjea. Alicia managed her own catering service, and Ophélie was a graphic artist at a Paris ad agency, so social networking was an important part of their business. The deal was that Max wouldn't do any "hackery," as Alicia called it, while he was living with them. That was no problem, since Max had planned to avoid that sort of thing anyway. Now he worried they would think he'd been lying to them.

"They said this was all a mistake. Something in their passenger database got screwed up. But I can't fly home until it's sorted out," Max said.

"What?" Enzo said.

"That's terrible," Ophélie said.

"We've already called the American Embassy. They'll do

something about this," Alicia said.

That was supposed to sound reassuring, but Max was just as worried about how his own government would handle him in this situation.

"Of course we're glad to have you back with us, and you can stay as long as you like," Alicia said.

Ophélie nodded.

"But I hate to think about your dad missing you for Christmas," Alicia continued.

"Dad! I have to let him know what's going on," Max said, reaching for his phone.

"I called Brad while you were being questioned. And I texted him as soon as they told us you were being released," Alicia said.

"Oh. Thank you." Max felt the tears coming on again.

"I know how I would feel in his place. I know exactly, because I was just as worried about you." She sniffed.

"Excuse me?" A tall man with red hair and shockingly blue eyes edged into view, clutching a small voice recorder.

Great. A reporter. It must be a slow news day.

"Excuse me, Mr. Stein. '503-ERROR'?" the reporter asked.

Max glared at Enzo. The boy's mouth rounded into an *O*.

"Why did the *douanes* detain you?" The reporter shoved his recorder in Max's face.

"Uh. As far as I know, it was just a clerical error." Max tried to sidle away from him, but the man smoothly shifted to keep him in range.

"So this isn't related to any computer hacking? Is this connected to Panjea?" the reporter asked.

"*Everything's* connected to Panjea, wasn't that the idea?"

The reporter chuckled indulgently. "Did you enjoy France?"

"Very much so. Which is fortunate, since I can't seem to leave." He took another step back from the reporter and bumped into Ophélie.

"And what did you do while you were visiting in Paris?" the reporter pressed.

"No further comments. Yes? Thank you," Ophélie cut in. She took Max's arm and steered him toward the exit, leaving the stunned reporter behind.

"Let's get you home," she said in a low, firm voice.

Home. It wasn't Granville, but it still made Max happy to have somewhere to go where people cared about him.

They hurried down the busy corridor toward ground transportation.

"What an amateur," Enzo muttered.

"Who?" Max asked.

"That reporter."

"Why do you say that?"

"He forgot to switch on his recorder."

Max thought back. His unsettled feeling grew as he realized Enzo was right: the red light that indicated the device was recording hadn't been on. It could have been an honest mistake, or . . .

Max glanced back. The red hair bobbing among the crowd,

keeping pace with Max and the Beaumonts, was easy to pick out.

"He is persistent though," Enzo said, looking behind them too.

Max walked faster.

Was the redhead even a reporter? He obviously wasn't worried about being spotted—either because he had the advantage over Max, or because he wanted to intimidate him. The man could be one of the French customs agents, hoping Max would reveal his plans to them. Or maybe someone Sharpe had sent to keep tabs on Max until he arrived.

Which reminded him: Max shut down his cell phone and pulled out the battery and SIM card. When they passed a trash receptacle, he tossed the phone in. It thunked hollowly at the bottom of the metal bin.

"What is going on?" Enzo whispered. His mothers were just ahead of them now, blissfully unaware of the drama unfolding behind them.

"I'm not sure. Just taking precautions."

"You think someone is tracking you?"

Max sighed. He'd come to France to escape this nonsense, but it had finally caught up to him. "Of course I'm being tracked. A better question is: Who's tracking me this time?"

3

ALICIA BEAUMONT FAWNED OVER MAX IN THE backseat of the taxi. Enzo sat on Max's other side, Ophélie in the front passenger seat directing the driver to their apartment.

"There's a fresh bûche de Noël at home," Alicia said.

"A what?"

"A 'Yule log,'" Alicia translated.

Max pictured a log crackling in a fireplace like the one on TV every year.

"It is a traditional dessert," Enzo said. "Very delicious!"

Thanks to Alicia, Max had put on at least five pounds in France, even though he'd been keeping up with his morning five-mile runs.

"That car is still following us," Enzo whispered.

Max twisted around in his seat. The silver hatchback had kept a few cars behind them all the way from the airport. For a moment, headlights illuminated a red halo around the driver's head. The "reporter" who had questioned Max.

Alicia turned too. "What is so fascinating back there?"

They were halfway back to the Beaumonts' place, and now that Max was certain they were being tailed, he couldn't let this go on.

He cleared his throat. "I appreciate you coming to pick me up and . . . everything. But as long as I'm stuck here a little longer, I thought I might visit a friend in Berlin until I can fly home."

"His *girl*friend, Penny," Enzo chimed in with a singsong voice.

The glow of the phone screen from the front passenger seat blinked off, and Ophélie tipped her head to the right to exchange a meaningful look with Alicia.

"Wonderful! You can fly out of Berlin Tegel Airport," Alicia said. "After you're cleared to travel. But in the meantime, Berlin is so beautiful at this time of year. You will love it."

"I wish I could go with you," Enzo said.

"That wouldn't be very romantic." Alicia wrinkled her nose.

"No, but it would be so great to meet—" Enzo stopped himself. "Max's girlfriend."

Ophélie gave her son an odd look.

"This is sudden, Max," she said.

"I didn't know Penny was in Europe until today, and she wants me to meet someone who's kind of a big deal . . . Ada Kiesler."

"Kiesler?" Alicia said.

"Right?" Enzo said. *"Incroyable!"*

"That's the woman who accused VT of market manipulation, yes?" Ophélie asked.

"How does your girlfriend know her?" Alicia asked.

Max shrugged. He really didn't have that many details. Or *any* details. Plausible deniability.

"This is a chance of a lifetime! Can I go with Max?" Enzo pressed his hands together in supplication.

"Absolutely not," Ophélie said.

Nice try, kid, Max thought. But even if his parents gave Enzo permission to tag along, there was no way Max would drag him into this, whatever *this* was.

"Oh, Mère! S'il te plaît?" Enzo asked.

"Well, why not?" Alicia said. "Kiesler is risking her freedom to do the right thing."

"You think so?" Ophélie pushed her mouth to the side. "On the contrary. She's a criminal."

Uh-oh. Max hadn't meant to start an argument between his host parents.

"It would be good for him to meet someone who's standing up for her beliefs," Alicia said. "Look what a good influence Max has been."

Enzo winked at Max.

"Laws exist to keep society functioning, and she broke them. Now she's hiding from justice," Ophélie said.

Whoa.

"Enzo's on holiday, so he won't miss school . . . ," Alicia said.

"*Oui.* Classes. I would not want to miss them," Enzo said.

Alicia smiled. "And I can take a few days off from work to go with him. They won't miss me in the shop."

"Eh?" Enzo said. "*Maman?*"

"A little vacation. Just the three of us!" She clapped.

This was getting out of hand. Apparently Ophélie thought so too.

"No!" she shouted. The car swerved to the left, and the driver swore in French.

"It could be dangerous," Ophélie said softly.

"Dangerous?" Alicia laughed. "The worst danger is having too much fun. Maybe staying out late, sneaking drinks at the beer garden. We used to be young, no?"

Ophélie gave Max a knowing look in the rearview mirror.

He cleared his throat. "Um. She's right. I don't think you should come. Either of you. Sorry, Enzo."

Enzo looked down at his hands folded in his lap. "But I could help."

"What do you mean? What's going on?" Alicia asked.

"The situation with Panjea . . . It was worse than I described," Max said. "People died. My friend died. When you get mixed up with powerful and ruthless corporations, you can get hurt. That's what makes someone like Ada Kiesler so brave. That's why she has to hide. And I'm afraid there's some risk involved in going to meet her." He looked at

Ophélie. "You've been doing some research on me."

"Yes, but I have been since before you arrived." Ophélie glanced at her son. "I saw an article about you open on Enzo's computer after we learned you would be staying with us."

"*Houp!*" Enzo said. "I was not so good about security before I met you, Max. But of course, you should not have looked, *Mère.*"

"And you still let me into your home?" Max asked.

"I don't like what you do, but I didn't want to hold it against you before meeting you. It's too easy to form opinions about people from what you see on television, online. You, Max, are wonderful, and I'm so glad you came to live with us. 503-ERROR, I am not so fond of."

Me neither, Max thought.

Alicia faced Max. "What happened? How did people die?"

It all finally came out. Ophélie had known most of it already, but she hadn't heard Max's side of things, and Enzo never tired of hearing him talk about his "adventures"— adventures Enzo was sure he wanted to share.

Alicia looked shaken. "Well, Ophélie is right—"

"As usual," Ophélie said.

"I mean, what you did and who you are now are different things. I think you were very brave, and you were brave to tell us the truth when you came here. And I am grateful that you told us the rest, to keep Enzo safe. This new information doesn't change anything between us," Alicia said.

Max relaxed.

"But it does seem like answering this call for help may be trouble, and the timing is suspicious considering what happened today."

"I'm wondering about that too." Max glanced out the back window. The hatchback was still there, four cars behind.

"The silver car?" Ophélie said.

Max's eyebrows shot up. "Yes. It's been following us since the airport. The red-haired man who questioned me is driving."

Max had assumed Ophélie was more focused on her phone and work than her immediate surroundings, but she obviously noticed a lot more than he thought, at least where her family was concerned.

Alicia laughed. She stopped when no one joined her.

"You aren't joking?" She turned, and Enzo pointed out the car following them.

Ophélie leaned toward the driver and whispered something. The taxi picked up speed and began maneuvering aggressively between cars. The distance between them and the hatchback increased.

"We'll take you to the train station, Max," Ophélie said. "But I'm not even sure that *you* should go to Berlin. There must be some authorities you can turn to for help. Maybe the embassy . . ."

"I can handle it," Max said. "Probably. I'm just going to see Penny, meet Kiesler, hear what they have to say. Like Enzo said, it's the chance of a lifetime. Then, hopefully, I'm on a plane back to California, home in time for Christmas." And things would go back to normal, whatever that was.

"It would be nice to have company on that long train ride, no?" Enzo asked.

Max nudged him with his elbow. "It would, *ami*. But you're still sitting this one out." Max cared about the younger boy and his mothers too much to drag him into an unknown situation like this. He couldn't stand it if his new brother got hurt because of him.

Alicia nodded. "That does sound best."

"But you'll check in with us regularly," Ophélie said. "As long as you're in Europe, we're responsible for you. We are your guardians."

"We love you, Max," Alicia said. "If you need anything, let us know."

Max blinked and swiped a hand across his eyes. "Will do."

4

MAX CLOSED HIS LAPTOP AND RUBBED HIS WEARY
eyes. They stung, which meant he was long overdue for a
break. He blinked to clear his vision and then turned his head
to look out the wide window at the beautiful view that he'd
been missing.

From the high-speed train, the German countryside was
zipping by a little too fast to truly appreciate anyway—like
watching a movie on fast-forward. You got the gist of it in a
fraction of the time, but it wasn't relaxing. The endless parade
of picture-perfect rolling hills, snow-capped mountains, and
open fields dotted with sheep made him think of a looping
slideshow of laptop wallpapers, only the resolution seemed
worse than what he saw on his screen. Barely HD.

When he started thinking that the world in front of him
was less real than the one on his computer, he definitely had

been spending way too much time staring at a screen.

Max pulled his hood back and smoothed down his hair. He hated conforming to the pop-culture stereotype, but it was drafty by the window. Besides, he hadn't been hacking—aside from borrowing Wi-Fi access via an unsecured hotspot on a computer in first class, one car up. The owner of the machine labeled "Gérard Depardieu" was lucky that was all Max was interested in, because he had easy access to everything.

There were a handful of other tempting targets in the vicinity, likely belonging to commuters between Paris and Berlin, but Max didn't have time to play around—and business machines were usually better protected than your average consumer's laptop. Usually.

Max pretended to stretch his arms, using the motion to peek over the seat in front of him and casually check his surroundings. The seats directly in front of him were empty. An elderly East Asian couple sat across the aisle from him, the woman reading and the man watching a video on a tablet with a pair of large over-the-ear headphones.

Max had checked every car of the train after he boarded and made sure the redheaded reporter hadn't followed him on; under Ophélie's instructions, the taxi driver had lost the silver hatchback. He'd also parked very briefly between a large truck and the sidewalk to allow Max to slip out of the car and into the train station without being observed.

Something in Max's shoulder clicked, and he turned the fake stretch into a real one. He had a bad habit of hunching over his laptop, face pressed close to the screen until he was practically falling into the virtual world. It was terrible for his posture, but his subconscious ruled when he was online.

As he looked around, the glass door at the front of the car slid open—he imagined the whoosh of a *Star Trek* turbolift whenever they opened, though they were silent—revealing a woman with a blonde ponytail and a long blue peacoat. They made eye contact for a moment, and she looked startled. She hesitated for a split second before stepping through the doorway and hurrying down the narrow aisle.

That was weird, Max thought. It was almost like she hadn't been surprised to see him—rather she was surprised *he'd* noticed *her*.

Aside from the Beaumonts, no one should have known Max was here or where he was going. He was now well outside the jurisdiction of French customs, so was she working for Kevin Sharpe too?

He tried to shrug the woman off as no one to be concerned about—for the moment. After Panjea, it had taken Max a long time to get over the feeling he was being followed. In fact, he hadn't really relaxed until he'd come to Europe. The events of the last twenty-four hours had put him back on high alert; in this state, he suspected everyone's actions and motives.

It isn't paranoia if they're really after you.

With a sigh, Max opened his computer again.

After he'd gotten it back from French customs, he'd gone over it carefully to be sure they hadn't loaded any programs to snoop on him. Which, of course, they had.

What was surprising was that they weren't too bad. There were a couple of programs installed so clumsily they must have been placed that way intentionally for him to find. He'd also found and disabled the scripts they'd tried to hide that would let them trace his computer and log keystrokes—likely an attempt to get into his encrypted drive.

He'd combed through the whole machine, even the encrypted drive, looking for anything out of the ordinary. He knew the system so well, and he had such a good memory, that it was easy to tell exactly which files and folders they had accessed. And he was certain they'd copied over everything they could see.

In the end, he'd wiped the unencrypted drive and started over from scratch. It was the only way to be sure.

Confident that his computer once again was secure, Max had spent most of the train ride reading up on Ada Kiesler. A few articles in the last couple of months had mentioned that she couldn't be reached for comment. Even restricted to the Chilean Embassy, Kiesler had been keeping the discussion going about Verbunden Telekom's questionable practices through blog posts, video messages, and chat threads. But none of those sites had been updated in the last month. After participating in an "Ask Me Anything" at Reddit, Kiesler had effectively gone dark—or perhaps been silenced against her will. As far as anyone knew, she was still safe at the embassy.

Max had just been assuming he would find her there, but Penny hadn't specified where the meeting would take place, probably expecting Max would contact her when he got her invitation. His big plan was to show up at the embassy and ask to see Kiesler. If that didn't work, plan B was Christmas shopping and eating. Food was supposed to be great in Berlin.

His stomach rumbled. He had filled up on leftover scones this morning, but that had been almost eight hours ago, just before boarding the train. Being shadowed by strangers made him hungry. He needed caffeine even more.

Max logged into an encrypted chat program. Of course Penny wasn't signed in. He hadn't seen her online in months. He hadn't been worried that something was wrong, because he knew her sister, Risse, would tell him if she was in trouble.

Since getting Penny's email, he had done something he had avoided doing before: checking for traces of her online, looking through forums, catching up on hacker boards, visiting her alias social media accounts—trying to build a profile of her activities that would link her to Ada Kiesler.

She was good, *the best*, because he had come up with absolutely nothing. He didn't even know what her online handle might be since she'd handed over full ownership of Double-Think to Risse. Penny might have been operating primarily off the grid, or she was carefully covering her tracks. Or maybe she was working on something so private and off the beaten path that no one knew about it. Max was getting more and more intrigued, despite his commitment to Not Getting Involved.

There was one person who must know what Penny was up to: Risse.

Max packed up his laptop and stood, doing another quick survey of the car. Absorbed in their phones, tablets, computers, nobody seemed interested in him. He hadn't been the only one ignoring the view outside.

One person was looking out the window: the woman from first class, now sitting in the last row. Why would she come back to economy for the same view in a less comfy seat?

He moved toward the back of the car slowly; on his feet, the swaying of the train was more pronounced, making for unsteady footing. He had transferred at Mannheim to Eurail's high-speed InterCity Express, which traveled up to 186 miles per hour. It was amazing that he could make the trip from Paris to Berlin in only nine hours.

Max watched the woman from the corner of his eye. She didn't pay him any attention as he passed and exited, tapping the glass door to slide it open. *Whoosh.*

Max let the door close behind him and paused between the two train cars for some privacy; the doors on either side of him were transparent, but the noise of the moving train was louder here, which would help prevent anyone overhearing his conversation. He fished out his cell phone, a cheap replacement he'd picked up at a shop in Paris Nord Station.

Max ran the Cryptalk app to encrypt his call and dialed Penny's number; having a photographic memory came in handy when you had to keep throwing your phone away and didn't want to keep a list of contacts.

He wasn't surprised when the call immediately went to voice mail: *Hi, this is you-know-who. Leave a message about you-know-what, and I'll do the thing.*

The sound of her voice alone made Max smile, making him realize how much he missed her—how badly he wanted, needed, to talk to her. Whatever was going on in Berlin, it was worth the trip to see her before he went home.

He disconnected without leaving a message and dialed Risse.

She picked up after the second ring. All he heard was air and the distant clacking of a keyboard.

"Hello?" No answer.

"Risse. You there? Hello?" Maybe she'd accidentally answered the call . . .

Or she was in trouble. Max's pulse sped up.

"Risse?" he whispered. "You okay?"

"I'm giving you the silent treatment," she said. She kept typing.

Max stifled a laugh. "Uh. Why? Come on, Risse. Don't be—" *Childish.* That would go over well. "Mad."

"How do you like it when someone ignores you?"

Not this again. "I wasn't ignoring you. I've just been busy. There's a lot going on with—"

The door behind Max whooshed open. The woman from first class shuffled past Max toward the adjoining car.

"*Entschuldigung*," she said. So she was German, or spoke it fluently. He stared after her until the door closed and she disappeared from view. She left behind the heavy aroma of cloves.

"Someone's tracking me, Risse," Max said.

"Duh. The question is: *Who's* tracking you? And why?"

Max smiled. He quickly caught her up on the events at the airport.

"You're on a TSA watch list? I bet I could get you off that if you want. Penny hacked into their fancy 'Secure Flight' system within weeks of its activation."

"Of course she did. Thanks for the offer, but wait on that for now," Max said.

"You should have called me," Risse said.

"They didn't give me a phone call. I wasn't technically arrested."

Risse blew a raspberry. Max pulled his phone away from his ear.

"I mean after you were released," she said.

"I'm calling you now! You know I can handle myself."

She snorted. Risse knew how valuable her skills were. "That you think that makes me even more worried about you."

"Seriously. That thing at the airport was just a mistake."

"You don't really believe that, do you? Sloppy, Max. All that time offline must have dulled your instincts. There's no such thing as a coincidence for people like us. Someone wanted you to stay in Paris."

"Well, too bad for them, because I'm on a train to Berlin."

"So that's what that noise is."

He peered through the glass door. The German woman, who he thought of as "Clove" because of her perfume, was nowhere in sight. "But now that you mention it, I think a woman on the train is watching me."

"Tell her you have a girlfriend."

"Not like that! At least, I doubt it's like that."

"Good."

"You'd rather she be interested in me for some nefarious purpose instead?"

"Definitely. Hey, why are you going to Berlin? Get a lead on your mom?"

"No such luck. I'm meeting up with Penny and—" Encrypted call or not, Max didn't want to say Ada Kiesler's name. "Her *friend*."

"Pen's in *Europe*?" Risse sounded shocked. "Okay, now it makes sense. I figured as much, given the time stamp on her texts, but she keeps strange hours when she's working."

"You didn't know she was here either?" Max asked.

"I haven't heard from her much. She's working a job, but she only checks in to make sure Mama and I are all right. And she's been transferring money to me every week." Risse paused.

"From something illegal?" Max asked.

"You know that's a relative term for her."

That was another long-standing argument between Max and Penny. The law was much grayer for her. She was the best hacker he knew, and she could make money from her talents in any number of ways, above and below the law, and every-thing in between.

"She disappears into her work like this. Even living in the same house sometimes I don't know what she's up to. But it isn't like her to keep me in the dark on purpose." Risse sounded upset.

"I'm sure she has her reasons."

"Which doesn't mean they're good ones," they said together, and laughed.

"But she contacted *you*," Risse said.

"You know how overprotective your sister is of you. She just didn't want you to get involved."

Max felt the same way about Risse. He hadn't even men-tioned her existence to Enzo, and Max trusted him as much as he trusted anyone.

It was petty, but he also felt better that Penny hadn't been communicating with Risse either, though he was jealous of those precious text messages to check in. It meant things were probably fine between Max and Penny, and she was just too busy with whatever mysterious thing she was working on.

"Listen, I'd better go," Max said. "I need some food in me."

"Okay," Risse said. "But don't keep being a stranger. I'm counting on you to tell me what Pen's up to. You can call even when you don't need something. Wild idea, I know."

He sighed. "I'm sorry. My life's been complicated."

"Which is code for: I'm being a dumbass."

"Risse!"

"Max, you can leave hacking behind. I even sort of understand why you want to. But you can't ditch us like your other friends."

"What?"

"Courtney. Isaac. Do you really think you can't be friends with them just because you aren't playing soccer anymore?"

"It's comp—" Max shook his head. "I *am* being a dumbass. Right now my life is a puzzle I need to figure out for myself, all right?"

"You two are so perfect for each other," Risse muttered.

"What?" Max asked.

"Forget it. Max, I love you, but you can be really frustrating sometimes." She paused. "Since it makes you uncomfortable to talk about your *feelings*, let's drop it for now. Wait. You're going to *Berlin*?"

"Yeah?"

"I've been keeping an eye on chatter in the DP boards."

Knowing her, she was archiving everything people said online too, though that was explicitly prohibited. Given enough data about DP's anonymous users—the times they went online, the way they wrote, the causes they supported—it was often only a matter of time before you could figure out who they were in real life. Risse would only use that information for good, to protect her own identity and the people she cared about.

"Someone was looking to hire hackers a few months ago,"

Risse said. "But this was the unusual thing—they needed them to be local to their marks, and they had an interesting list of locations. Berlin was one of them. A half dozen other places in Europe too, including Great Britain and Lille, France. South America. Several in the U.S. and Amsterdam. Canada, even. It was the kind of posting that set off all sorts of red flags, and twenty-four hours later, the posts were gone."

"You think Penny bit?"

"I don't know. This sounded like some kind of nation-state thing, like, NSA level. She's very careful about the jobs she picks."

"Speaking of being careful, watch it with DP, Risse."

"Don't you start worrying about that too. Everyone's been on their best behavior lately. You should be happy. You really helped shake things up."

"It's just a lot to take on, if you're becoming their de facto leader." She had taken over the DoubleThink identity, and no one had ever known it had once been shared by the two sisters.

"You've been a good influence on me. I've talked to some people on private channels—"

"Really private, or quote-private-end-quote?"

"I believe very strongly in online privacy, Max."

"*Your* privacy. But you wouldn't be a good leader if you didn't worry about the group's activities. I bet you've researched everyone by now."

"STOP already did a lot of that work for me," she said. Max felt a jolt at the mention of Evan's online handle. "But I pride myself on being very thorough. I mostly want to make sure Vic isn't sneaking back in under another name, after going ghost because of his involvement with Panjea."

Max wondered if Vic had really gotten away, or if he'd been one of the last silenced by Sharpe and his agents. The former CEO of Panjea and wannabe hacker had been a patsy, but he'd also known too much that would have made it impossible for President Lovett to sweep things under the rug.

"I'm also on the lookout for moles and government agents. I have one person I suspect of being from law enforcement, because he was a lot easier to research than the others," Penny said.

"A carefully planted fake identity."

"Bingo. Too carefully planted, and over-watered. But there could also be a long-standing member who's been flipped to the dark side."

"You're the perfect person for the job of keeping everyone honest."

Dramatis Personai had wanted *him* to lead them, but he'd walked away. They were really much better off looking to Risse for guidance. He didn't have his own act together enough; he had no business telling other people what to do. Especially when he wasn't sure that a group like Dramatis Personai should even exist anymore.

The hacking collective had proven to be a powerful force for good, but hackers were too unpredictable and quick to take extreme action, without thinking through the outcomes.

"Max, just remember you can call or chat me anytime. Be safe," she said.

"Thanks, Risse. Take care of yourself."

Max tucked his phone away and continued down the train to the dining car. Risse was right: He should have called her sooner. She and Penny were totally different people, but sometimes they felt like two sides of the same coin. On the phone they even sounded alike at first.

Despite the smackdown she had delivered—which he deserved—talking to her had raised his spirits. He was touched that she'd been working to prove his innocence, even while she was angry with him.

Having just hung up the phone with Risse, Max was stunned to see her behind the counter in the Bordbistro café car. A slightly older version of her, with piercings in her right eyebrow and left nostril and a tattoo of a compass on her clavicle. But the resemblance was uncanny; she even had her black hair in Risse's trademark pigtails. Somehow she made them look . . . sexy?

Oh, that's so wrong, Max, he thought.

"Hullo," she said with a thick French accent.

"Hi," Max said, averting his gaze. Just the smell of rich coffee and cooking food made him feel more awake—and hungrier. He picked up a paper menu and studied it while using the opportunity to look at the other people in the café car. The only passenger who stood out was Clove—because she was standing at the counter right next to him. Technically, this time he had followed *her*. Coincidences happen, especially when you were on a train with a limited number of places to go.

"Can I help you?" Not-Risse asked.

"Coffee," Max said. "Café Americano. In the biggest cup you have. And a sesame bagel with Nutella."

"Nine euros," she said.

Max counted out the money.

"Are you a student?" Clove asked Not-Risse.

"Yah."

"What are you studying?"

"Architecture." She handed Max a paper cup of coffee and passed him a small pitcher of milk.

"How about you? Are you in university too?" Clove asked Max.

He was so surprised that she had spoken to him, he automatically answered to be polite. "Not yet. Next year."

"What do you want to study?" She blew on her coffee and took a sip.

"I don't know."

"No?" she asked.

"Maybe law." That had just popped into his head, but Max hadn't given much thought to his future profession. For a while he'd figured he could just get by on a soccer scholarship, but he'd let that idea go. He could study computers, but that was like the difference between reading a book for fun and having it assigned in class. And what could he learn? He could probably get a job in IT even without going through college at this point—if any company trusted him enough. Why not law?

She smiled. "A lawyer. That is good."

"Like, a civil lawyer." Max ran with it. "Looking out for the public good, maybe for a nonprofit company." Like where his dad worked.

"Good," she said again. "You are American."

That wasn't a question, and her curiosity was putting Max's guard up, so he countered with a question of his own. "What do you do?" Max asked. She looked a little too old for college.

"Freelance." She tossed back her hand dismissively. "I travel a lot."

Freelance? Travel? *She's a spy!* Max thought.

Not-Risse wrapped up Max's bagel and placed it with a container of Nutella in a paper bag. As he left, Clove nodded at him and smiled. Max gave her a casual wave and hurried back to his seat. A short while later, she passed him and disappeared back into the first-class car.

What was that all about?

Max set up his laptop again. As he chewed his bagel, he started pulling up maps of Berlin. Just in case.

5

MAX QUICKLY DISEMBARKED HIS TRAIN AT BERLIN Central Station and hurried down the busy platform toward the exit. As he walked, he pointed his cell phone at the domed roof, which the internet had informed him was composed of 11,800 unique glass panels. The intricate grid was stunning even at night, but Max wasn't interested in taking a picture; instead, he was using the selfie camera to spy over his shoulder.

He scanned the bustling crowd behind him until he spotted Clove. There she was, exiting from a first-class car, a cell phone pressed to her ear. She didn't bother looking around her, but followed the flow of the crowd along the platform in Max's direction. He snapped a couple of pictures of her, hoping that this time, he really was imagining things.

Max lowered his phone and focused on weaving through the crowd to make himself a harder target to follow. Finally, he reached the open area at the main part of the station. The cluster he was in paused to gape at the massive Christmas tree stretching up and up and up, nearly to the ceiling, topped by a giant silver star. Max pushed on toward the Washingtonplatz exit, and soon he was stepping out into his first Berlin night.

The view drew him up short. Berlin had even fewer high-rise buildings than Paris—in general, skyscrapers were more scarce in Europe than in the U.S.—so the historic city sprawled against the horizon as far as he could see. What Berlin might have lacked in a skyline, it made up for in *lights*; the glimmering and golden windows, streetlamps, and spotlights were like an inverted star field, with the inky night sky above.

Max turned slowly to take in the entire view. The train station behind him shined like a crystal palace, its windowed façade decorated with the outlines of glowing blue stars of all sizes, framing the tree still visible through the glass. To the east, Berlin's famous TV tower, one of its tallest structures, was fully illuminated by bright, white spotlights that gave it an eerie, ghostly presence.

In the distance, a large Ferris wheel sparkled as it turned lazily. Before him, the river Spree added to the magic with shimmering reflections of lights from the bridges spanning it, the train station, and passing cars. At this time of year, Berlin was every bit the "city of light" that Paris was famous for being. But Max also remembered that where there was light, there were shadows, and Berlin was better known for being the capital of spies and secrets.

Max pulled up his hood, adjusted the straps of his backpack, and set off down Washingtonplatz. He continued to force his way past slow-moving pedestrians, tossing apologies behind him as he went. *Bump. Verzeihung!*

Max took a left down a one-way street and picked up his pace. A light, frigid rain sprinkled against his face and coated him with dampness, feeling like cold sweat on his skin. His toes began to freeze in his canvas sneakers, and he nearly slipped on the slick pavement.

He took another furtive glance behind him via his cellphone camera and couldn't believe it when he spotted Clove trailing him about thirty feet back, her peacoat open and flaring behind her dramatically like a cape. Just his luck that real female spies wore sensible shoes instead of impractical high heels like they did on TV. She was still talking to someone on her own cell phone. Max looked around, wondering whom she was speaking with.

There! A gray Volvo MPV was cruising slowly down the street, keeping pace with Max. He saw the telltale glow of a cell phone, which illuminated the driver's face—not the redheaded man Max had encountered at the airport, but a Caucasian with a ponytail and a scraggly mustache and beard.

Well, crap. He had to give this guy the slip.

Max turned onto Friedrich-List-Ufer street and broke into a light jog. Tires squealed behind him, but the backed-up traffic around the station was working in Max's favor. He easily raced past the slow-moving vehicles on the small road. After being cooped up on trains for nine hours, it felt good to be moving again, though his legs were stiff from sitting for so long.

When he hit the intersection with Rahel-Hirsch-Strasse, he faltered only a moment before continuing on, dodging between cars across two lanes. Horns honked and people shouted angrily at him in German. *Verzeihung!* Max had only learned a handful of German words, but he was glad "sorry" was one of them. He was getting a lot of use out of it already, after only a few minutes in Berlin.

Max paused on the other side of the street, with a footbridge stretching before him over the Spree and into a little park. From there, he could follow pedestrian paths to the Tiergarten, the park that he had pinpointed as the best place to lose his shadows before proceeding to the Chilean Embassy. Max had planned out a route that avoided roads for motor vehicles, so the Volvo wouldn't be able to follow him.

Max turned to look back across the street. He couldn't make out the gray car among the sea of headlights, but incredibly, he hadn't shaken Clove. She was jogging down the sidewalk, heading straight for him. Not subtle at all, but he had to hand it to her: not many people could keep up with Max in a race. Not that she could catch him.

Max spun and made for the park.

His phone vibrated in his back pocket. *Really not a good time, whoever you are,* he thought. He was running along a little dirt path now. He concentrated only on his breathing, the feel of his soles hitting dirt, the sound of his footsteps. His breath puffed in front of him. It was a cold night, but Max was overheating from running with a heavy bag on his back while wearing a thick sweatshirt and jeans. Perspiration and rain dripped into his eyes. He pushed himself to go faster. An echo of his footsteps pounded along behind him, and he knew it was Clove.

What did she want? He glanced behind him. She was still the same distance away; she didn't seem to be trying to catch him. Rather, she was content to match his pace. She clearly didn't mind that he knew she was following him.

The path ahead curved, and he ran parallel to a road for a moment. Headlights swept over him, and he blinked and squinted to get a look at the car—the gray Volvo!

Of course. The driver was still in contact with Clove, so she was directing him to where Max was. Did they plan on grabbing him?

He caught a glint of something in the driver's hand, aimed at Max. A shiver ran down his spine, and he cut hard to his right.

A dirt path angled away from the road, and Max followed it. The Volvo's motor roared. He panicked for a moment. He had to get to the larger park, where its cover of trees would keep him out of sight of the car, and get away from Clove, but there were no more paths leading in that direction.

Screw it. "*Where we're going, we don't need roads,*" Max thought.

Once again, he darted across a lane of traffic to a tree-lined island, then raced across another lane going in the opposite direction. A car screeched to a halt a couple of feet away from Max, its driver leaning on the horn. Max kept going, his heart pounding and his legs shaky from the close call. If he kept this up, he'd end up saving his pursuers the trouble of killing him.

Trees. A small paved plaza, with a few couples strolling in the soft moonlight who turned to look at Max curiously as he sprinted by. More trees. Another street. More cars.

Finally Max reached frost-tipped grass, crunching under his feet and brittle like hay. The Tiergarten park. He glanced over his shoulder and saw Clove still in hot pursuit. Seriously, what did she want with him?

Max ran across the open lawn of the Platz der Republik, his chest burning from sucking in freezing air. His thin canvas sneakers provided little warmth, and the cold ground soon numbed his toes.

The majestic Reichstag building, the historic seat of the German Parliament, rose on Max's left, windows gleaming in the night, mounted with a dome lit up as bright as day.

Max's phone vibrated again. He slowed long enough to work it free from his pocket and nearly dropped it. It was Penny. He answered it.

"Hey," he said breathlessly.

"Max! Finally. Where—Are you okay?"

"Kind of," Max gasped.

"Are you running?"

"Yes!" Max sucked in a painful breath. His lungs were like ice cubes. "So, I'm being followed. Trying to lose them." He coughed.

"Oh, Max. I just got off the phone with Risse. She told me you're coming to Berlin."

"I'm *in* Berlin," Max said. He assessed his surroundings. "Tiergarten. About to cross Scheidemannstrasse."

He dove into the road. Honking horns drowned out whatever Penny said.

"—was that?" she asked.

"Just crossed Scheidemannstrasse!" *Barely.*

"Are they still following you?"

Max peeked behind him. Clove was farther back now, a couple hundred feet, but she wasn't struggling at all. Unlike Max. She would outpace him eventually, if he didn't shake her off. As long as she had him in view, he couldn't escape her partner in the car.

"Yup," he said.

"What do they look like?"

"The one on foot is a blonde woman. German. Athletic. Very athletic. Any idea who she is?"

"Could be anyone." Penny sounded worried. "How do you know she's German?"

"She was on my train. She asked me questions about school and where I'm from."

"Think she knows who you are?"

"Maybe. She said she's a freelancer who travels a lot. I'm

more worried about her friend in the gray Volvo. Black hair in a ponytail, mustache, and beard. He might have a gun."

"Aargh. You've got to lose them, Max."

"Working on it!"

"If they know who you are, they may be trying to find out what you're doing here. You can't lead them to the embassy. You can't be seen anywhere near Ada Kiesler. It's bad enough anyone knows you're in Berlin."

"Well, then where do you want me to go?" Max asked. He finally passed into the treeline, but without leaves for the winter, they weren't providing as much cover as he'd been counting on. The lack of a clear path would slow down Clove, but that was slowing down Max too.

Penny was silent for a moment. "'Go West, young man.'"

"What?" *Whatever.* Max cut to his right and continued pushing his way through the trees. The slower pace was helping get his second wind. He didn't usually sprint for such long distances, and he'd covered many times the length of a soccer field already. "What am I looking for?"

"Big gold column with an angel on top. You can't miss it."

"The Victory Column?" Max huffed. "I don't really have time for sightseeing right now."

"It's the perfect place to get away from pursuers. The column is at the center of a big roundabout. Don't try to run across it—there's five lanes of traffic. You get to the middle through a pedestrian tunnel. If you're coming from the east, you should see two entrances on either side of you."

Max kept running. He didn't look back, but the distant snapping of branches and rustling foliage told him Clove was behind him, though he was putting some distance between them. He heard snatches of her shouting in German.

"I'm almost there." Ahead, the Victory Column rose up out of the night, glowing almost supernaturally with golden floodlights. On top, he saw the back of Victory herself, wings spread behind her. "Where are the stairs?" he asked.

"Look for two small temples—there should be one on each side of Seventeenth of June Street. Both will lead to the same main tunnel to the Column. When you come up the stairs, head around the Column's base and take the stairs down on the opposite end. They lead to two more tunnels. If you take the one on the left, wait for me to drive by. I'm in a pink-and-gray smart car."

"Of course you are," Max said.

"Oh, would you rather take a taxi?"

"No, no. I like pink very much, Penny."

The path opened up and Max saw a squat, rectangular structure with four square columns to the right of Strasse des 17. Juni. Its mirror image faced him on the left. He veered north to the closer one.

The building looked like a temple entrance to a dungeon in the *Legend of Zelda* games. A small white sign beside the stairway read TUNNEL ZUR SIEGESSÄULE.

"Siegessäule?" Max butchered the word.

"It means 'victory column,' and 'Goldelse' is the German

nickname for the gaudy cake topper on it. That's what you want. Go! I'm almost there, Max!"

Max pounded down the flight of stairs, then turned left and headed down another short flight. The opening to the tunnel stretched before him, dark and foreboding like the maw of some kind of creature. He caught a sour whiff of urine. He raced inside.

Bright lights along the walls illuminated the dimly lit tunnel. It smelled like a public bathroom, and coarse graffiti decorated the worn walls. He imagined it was quite full of tourists during the day, but right then, he seemed to be the only one down there. If he wasn't already running, he would have hurried out of there as soon as he could.

Just inside the tunnel, a black glass panel in the wall lit up as Max ran past it, exploding in a dancing light show of pixels like a bright shadow trailing behind him. Some kind of art installation to liven up the poorly maintained tunnel. *Neat*, Max thought, when he had recovered from the surprise.

His heavy footsteps echoed, bouncing off the tunnel walls so it sounded like there were feet pattering all around him. Very disorienting, and harder to tell if there was anyone else inside. Another tunnel branched to his right and continued up ahead. He assumed that led to the other temple he'd seen.

As he paused, he heard steps descending those stairs. He didn't wait around. He went full tilt to his right, and soon he was racing up the exit to the circular plaza around the Victory Column. He allowed himself one glance at the large statue above, and realized that all tourists were treated to this view up Goldelse's skirt. Then he took off again, following the decorated base and heading for the stairs leading down to the other set of tunnels.

"I'm heading down the other tunnel," he panted. "Taking the one on the left."

"Almost there," Penny said. He heard cars honking in the background from his phone.

There was a fifty-fifty chance that Clove would take the tunnel on her right, and then they would get away. But when Max emerged from another identical temple, he saw the gray Volvo idling in front of it on the street's shoulder. The driver spotted Max and once again raised something black, while lowering the driver-side window.

Max turned and took the stairs back down dangerously fast, three at a time. Something flashed behind him. He jumped the last five stairs and hit the ground running, his feet temporarily numb from the shock.

"Penny, change in plan! I'm taking the tunnel on the right. Pretty much now!"

"Crap. Okay. Okay! I'll be there. Good thing this road is just a big circle. I'll bring the car around, but if we miss each other, you'll be on your own until I can turn back."

Max ran back down the way he'd come. As he passed the tunnel from the Victory Column, he glimpsed a figure— Clove. She was *fast*.

Max hurtled past her and heard her steps behind him, now

much closer on his heels. No escaping her now, unless Penny was where she said she'd be.

He ran up these stairs three at a time, fingers grazing the railing. One misstep and he'd be down and out. Clove was right behind him.

"Where are you, Penny?" Max muttered. Across the roadway, the Volvo lurched forward into the traffic circle, cutting off a red Volkswagen. *Damn.*

He heard Penny before he saw her. Horns went off and people shouted, and he turned to see a tiny, cute pink-and-gray car racing along the roundabout toward Max, cutting across multiple lanes to the right. It was slowing down too, which was why the other drivers were so pissed. But . . . it wasn't stopping.

"Run!" Penny said. He heard her through his phone and the open windows of her car as she pulled out of the roundabout and started down Strasse des 17. Juni two feet from the sidewalk.

"Jesus, Penny," Max said. He followed the pink-and-gray car, drawing up alongside it and reaching for the passenger-side door. He stretched his arm way out—his fingers grazed the cold handle twice. He caught hold, pulled, and his arm was nearly yanked out of its socket. He let go and squeezed his fingers, stumbling a few feet behind.

"Unlock the damn door!" he said.

"Oops. Sorry!" Penny said. The door clicked.

Max caught up and tried again, lifting the handle and

popping the door open. He shrugged out of his backpack and tossed it into the footwell. Then he put on a final burst of speed and threw himself into the seat. Penny jammed the brakes for a split second, causing the door to slam shut, then floored the accelerator. They zoomed away. In the passenger-side mirror he saw Clove standing by the street, bent over with her hands on her knees. So she was human after all.

"That was so badass. I've always wanted to try that trick with the door," Penny said.

"This . . . is . . . a . . . clown . . . car," Max gasped.

"That had better be a funny German word that means 'thank you.'"

"Yes." He concentrated for a moment on breathing, then remembered to buckle in. "Thanks."

"You're welcome." Penny sped up the car and it vibrated ominously.

"Is this thing safe?" he asked.

"Shut up about my car. It's a rental," Penny said. "Her name is Bessie, and she's very sensitive."

Max looked at Penny.

He hadn't seen her since the summer. Her blonde hair had grown long enough for her to style it in a French braid, which was draped over her left shoulder. Under a red peacoat, she wore a tank top that had STEMPUNK spelled out in illustrated gears, cogs, and pipes.

"What?" she said.

"I missed you."

"Max?" Penny said.

"Yes?"

"Two quick things. First—" She leaned over and kissed him, then returned her attention to the road.

"Ah," Max said. "What's the second thing?"

"You said you were followed by a gray Volvo?"

"Yeah."

"Change that to the present tense. We aren't out of the woods yet."

Max glanced in the passenger-side mirror and saw the gray Volvo moving up behind them, weaving through cars to keep them in its sights. He turned and stared through the small back window of the car.

"He picked up Clove," Max said.

"Clove? You introduced yourself?"

"That's just what I call her. She smells like cloves."

"There's another traffic circle coming up. We'll lose 'em there."

"How?" Max asked.

"By doing something dangerous, illegal, and stupid. But that's pretty much my standard MO. Hold on, cute."

Penny turned the car into the roundabout and sped past the first turnoff. Then she yanked the wheel to the right, and the car shuddered, almost tipping, as she headed into oncoming traffic.

"Oh, shit!" Max said.

She continued the turn to the right, cutting across the pedestrian crossing, fortunately empty of pedestrians—and just barely wide enough for the compact car to clear the posts and pylons meant to prevent cars from doing what they were doing.

She whipped the car around to the left, and Max could have sworn the vehicle tipped onto its two left wheels for a moment, before she neatly slid in between two cars coming off the roundabout and matched their speed.

Max glanced in the mirror and saw the Volvo keep on past. But it was a roundabout, so they'd be back around in a moment.

"Oh, shit," Max said again. "That worked."

Penny was hunched forward in her seat, concentrating on the road, her hands clenched around the wheel. She began a series of maneuvers, taking streets seemingly at random to lose the car tailing them. After they had crossed over the Spree for the third time, she relaxed.

"Now, you were saying?" Penny flipped her bangs back with her right hand.

Max grinned. "I really missed you."

"Copy and paste. You must have a lot of questions."

"So many. But mostly I just want to kiss you again."

Penny smiled. "After we meet with Ada, there will be much kissing." She frowned. "Specifically, you and I will be kissing. You'd better not kiss Ada."

"Deal. And when will that be?"

"We'll be at the Chilean Embassy in twenty minutes."

Max settled back in his seat, suddenly exhausted as he crashed from the adrenaline rush. But he couldn't relax, because now his heart was beating fast for another reason: He was about to meet Ada Kiesler!

PENNY PARKED ON MOHRENSTRASSE IN FRONT of a closed bookstore, opposite a six-story building with floor-to-ceiling windows and a façade in the Belle Époque tradition that Max had seen all over France. Two silver-and-blue police cars took up parking spots flanking the entrance, and a couple of policemen guarded the main doors.

A half dozen people clustered around a lamppost on the sidewalk.

"What's that? The Ada Kiesler fan club?" Max asked.

"No, those are the loonies who think she should give herself up and go to prison. The 'Free Ada' protesters are sensible enough to go home for dinner."

"Ah." The protesters weren't marching or shouting. They were mainly bent over their phones, which cast their faces with a ghostly white glow. "I'm beginning to doubt their commitment to Sparkle Motion."

Penny snorted. "Here, put this on." She passed Max a rubber mask.

Max held it up and suppressed a shudder. It was the grotesque face of a hairy goat-man with horns: the Krampus, a disturbing Christmas figure popular in Germany.

"Uh. Why?" he asked. "Are we going to rob the joint?"

"Your face is too recognizable. We don't want anyone to know you're visiting Ada. It's for your protection."

"What about you?"

Penny grinned. She removed her glasses and hung them from the neck of her shirt. She pulled on a rubber mask of her own.

"Boo!" she said.

Her face was all red eyes and a gaping mouth, with big rotting teeth and a ghastly, enlarged tongue lolling out. The mask had six horns, twisted and gnarled, and the head was covered in matted black-and-gray fur.

"Ugh," Max said. "Are you supposed to be a literal internet troll?"

"Close." Her voice was muffled behind the rubber and fabric. "I'm a Perchta! The goddess of light and dark."

"Okay." Max pulled the mask on, his nostrils filling with the suffocating smell of latex. His vision was narrowed to only what was directly in front of him. "This is so gross."

"Ready?" Penny asked.

"I guess so."

"Let's go."

Penny got out of the car and grabbed a messenger bag from

the back. Now he saw the rest of her outfit. With her snug jeans and thigh-high black boots—not useful for running, if it came to that, but otherwise he had no complaints—the mask looked even more incongruous, and oddly more terrifying.

Max slung his backpack over his right shoulder and followed his creepy goddess across the street to the building at number 42.

As they passed into the pool of orange light from the streetlamp, some of the protesters gasped and pointed. A couple of flashes went off, and one woman followed their progress with her cell phone.

"See?" Penny said. "Surveillance everywhere. Everyone's a photographer and reporter. Other people are part of the problem."

They stopped in front of the double doors, and Penny tapped on the glass. It was dim inside, enough so that Max was startled by the phantasmic reflection of his mask with its pale, wrinkled face and sharp, yellow teeth.

But after a moment, a security guard slowly approached them. Max glanced back nervously at the police officers watching them, then looked away. He couldn't decide whether to be impressed that they hadn't batted an eye at him and Penny walking up in Halloween masks, or critical that they showed so little interest in keeping watch.

Above the entrance, the coats of arms of the Peruvian and Lichtenstein Embassies were mounted. Higher up, outside a second-floor window, hung a red, white, and blue flag with a single white star—the Chilean flag. Their coat of arms was fixed beneath the base of the flagpole, but Max couldn't make it out.

The front doors unlocked and opened. The guard yelped when he looked up and saw Penny and Max's masks.

"*Guten Abend. Entschuldigen Sie bitte, dass ich Sie störe,*" Penny said. She pulled up her mask so the guard could see her face. "*Sprechen Sie Englisch?*"

"Yes . . ." The guard still looked freaked out. He had one hand on his holstered gun, and he was glancing back and forth between Penny and Max to the police officers, who were standing by and grinning.

"The building is closed," the guard said.

"We're here to see Ms. Ada Kiesler in the Chilean Embassy. We should be on the visitor list."

The guard sighed. "Names?"

"Emmie Steed and Charlie Bartowski."

"Wait here." The guard closed and locked the doors.

A few minutes later he returned. "Okay. Come on with you." The guard held the door open wider and ushered them in. Max pulled off his mask and blinked sweat out of his eyes. Penny took his free hand and squeezed gently.

After sending them through a full-body metal detector and having their bags examined halfheartedly, the guard pointed them to the elevator, which they took to the second floor. The reception desk was unstaffed that late, so they waited in the hall outside a door with the coat of arms of Chile. It featured a white star on a blue-and-red shield flanked by a deer and a condor, both of which were wearing crowns. A scroll displayed their motto: POR LA RAZÓN O LA FUERZA.

"By reason or force," Max translated. His high-school Spanish was much better than his spotty French and nonexistent German. "Hmmm."

The door opened, and Penny put on her glasses. A portly white man with thinning hair greeted them. The sleeves of his checkered button-down shirt were rolled up.

"Hello! Welcome to Chile," the man said.

"Sorry to disturb you so late," Penny said.

The man shrugged. "Where else should I be?" He leaned in and gave Penny a quick kiss on both cheeks. Then he turned to Max and extended his hand. Max shook it.

"I'm Sebastián Ortiz Molina, Chilean legal attaché." He smiled.

"I'm Penny Polonsky. This is—"

"Maxwell Stein," Max said.

"Please, may I see your passports?"

Max fished in his backpack and produced the small blue folio. "Shouldn't the guard have checked these?"

"I'm handling this myself, given the sensitive nature of the situation. As per Ms. Kiesler's instructions, I listed you under different names for security." He handed back their passports. "All seems to be in order. Just one more thing, if you will indulge me. You have phones?"

Max and Penny showed him their cell phones. Max noted

enviously that Penny had a new crypto phone that hadn't come out in the U.S. yet.

"I will lock them in our hidden safe here. It blocks all microphones and signals. They will be quite secure."

Max tightened his hand around his phone. "Señor, if it's just the same, I don't like to let my phone out of my sight. I'll remove the battery though."

Penny nodded. "Me too."

Sr. Ortiz studied them for a long moment. "As you wish."

Max quickly pried off the back of his phone and removed the battery. Penny's phone should have been trustworthy with all its privacy protections, but she followed suit.

Sr. Ortiz nodded. "*Gracias.* Please, come with me."

Max and Penny exchanged bemused looks and followed the man into the embassy suite.

"Your country is doing a great thing, granting Ms. Kiesler asylum," Penny said.

"That's . . . what's your expression? Above my pay grade. I find her charming, brilliant, and interesting, as well as beautiful."

Sr. Ortiz continued leading them down darkened hallways, decorated in the Chilean colors of red, white, and blue.

"We have her situated in a back office, near the kitchen," Sr. Ortiz explained. "Away from windows, as an additional security precaution."

He knocked on a narrow door that looked like it led to a supply closet, then opened it a crack.

"You have visitors, Fräulein," Sr. Ortiz called.

"Great! Please send them in, Seb!"

Sr. Ortiz ushered Max and Penny through the door, but he didn't follow them in—probably because the room was smaller than Max's bedroom at home, maybe fifteen by twelve feet total. It looked like an office break room that had been converted into sparse living quarters; in fact, there was still a compact microwave, a water cooler, and a vending machine in one corner. Max had always wanted a vending machine in his room.

The mottled gray tiles were covered with a fraying throw rug, and one wall had been decorated with maroon curtains, but he could tell there were no windows behind them. Bookcases lined another wall, stuffed with books, magazines, and newspapers, and an elliptical machine was against the opposite wall, facing a thirteen-inch tube television. A small round conference table in the center of the room held a laptop with a separate mouse and keyboard. Four black metal folding chairs were arranged around it. Chinese-takeout containers littered the table.

Ada Kiesler had been living here for a year?

A slight woman put down a book and rose from a beat-up green suede couch in the corner, which had a folded blanket and a pillow on one armrest. It took Max a moment to recognize her, but there was no mistaking the streak of premature white in her dark brown hair, tucked over her left ear, and the rose-tinted round sunglasses perched on her nose.

He also recognized her resonant voice instantly, from the online presentations and podcasts he'd listened to in which Kiesler had discussed netiquette and online privacy. It was eerie to hear her addressing him in person. "It's really you," she said.

"I think that's my line, Ms. Kiesler," he said.

"Please call me Ada. May I call you Max?"

He nodded.

"I'm a big fan of your work," she said.

"Ditto," Max said.

She gave him a wide smile. "I'm not quite what you were expecting, right? I wish they'd stop using those five-year-old pictures of me on the news," she said. "Most days I don't even change out of pajamas. One of the few pleasures in working from . . ." She looked around, then shrugged. "Exile."

As a businesswoman in the tech industry, Kiesler always had dressed for the part, with smart suits, carefully applied makeup, and high heels. She looked entirely different in a black track jacket, gray tank top, and yoga pants. Her customarily bobbed hair had grown long enough to pull into a high ponytail.

She was still clearly a leader—her self-confidence and capability showed in the way that she carried herself—but she looked more like a normal person, someone Max could picture himself hanging out with.

Standing before him, she looked much shorter than on TV, but most people were short compared to Max. Max started to extend his hand, but he quickly withdrew it when she moved in for the European double kiss.

Oh, okay, we're doing that, he thought as he returned the gesture. Her perfume or shampoo was vanilla scented.

"It really is an honor, Ada," he said.

"The honor's all mine."

Ada turned to Penny and smiled. "And it's lovely to finally meet you, PlusGood. Penny." Kiss, kiss.

Max hadn't realized that Penny had already debuted with her new handle, +g00d.

"Wait, you haven't met before?" Max asked.

"Not in person," Ada said.

Now Max knew why Penny had been uncommonly silent since they had arrived. She was starstruck. He wondered if Ada's invitation to Max had been an opportunity for Penny to meet her hero face-to-face.

"We both like keeping a low profile, and if I came and went all the time, people would start asking questions," Penny said.

"You haven't kept a low profile lately, Ada," Max said.

"No, I haven't!" She laughed. "I'm so, so glad you both came to see me. I wasn't sure you would."

"It was a hard invitation to pass up," Max said. Since Ada had moved into the embassy, her visitors had been few, but impressive, including notorious whistle-blowers like Daniel Ellsberg and Thomas Drake. "I actually wasn't able to accept at first, but my stay in Europe was unexpectedly extended."

Penny's face flushed. Max cocked an eyebrow at her. Did

she know something about that incident with the TSA watch list? He'd have to ask her about that later.

"Have you eaten?" Ada gestured toward the table with the remains of her dinner.

"I'd just like some water." Max was thirsty from his impromptu run earlier.

"Please, make yourself at home, such as it is. I've certainly tried to," she said.

While Ada and Penny settled on the couch, Max went to the water cooler. He picked up a clean mug from the shelf next to it. It was black ceramic with Verbunden Telekom's logo: a lopsided *V*, with a vertical upward stroke on the right that was crossed to form the *T*. The horizontal line was an arrow pointing forward.

"We can order something else if you like. There's an amazing Thai restaurant nearby," Ada said.

"You get room service?" Max filled the mug and chugged it all. He refilled it and then picked up a plastic cup advertising the 2012 Summer Olympics to fill for Penny.

"One of the few perks of not being able to leave this room." At his questioning look, she went on. "I'm under protection of the Chilean Embassy, for which I'm very grateful. But they haven't given me license to wander around freely, not even in the rest of the embassy. They don't quite know what to do with me, but I think having me here makes them feel important. In some ways, I'm a political prisoner, even though I can leave at any time. Until they decide I'm more valuable to them out there than in here."

"That . . . sucks," Max finished. That was an inadequate way to describe her situation. He thought he had it bad because he couldn't go home for Christmas, but she was spending the holiday here, probably alone. And she might never be able to go home again.

"Indeed it does," she said.

He realized he didn't even know whether she had a family waiting for her somewhere; the media had picked apart her life, but there hadn't been a lot to find before her tenure at Verbunden Telekom.

He joined the women on the couch and handed Penny her cup of water. She took it with both hands and smiled her thanks, then seemed to forget she was holding it.

Her short fingernails were bright purple. Each nail had white dots or dashes painted on it. Morse code? From the pinky of her left hand to the right, it read: dash, dot, dot, dot dash dot, dot dot dash dot.

T-E-E-R-F? No, wait, he was reading them backward. From Penny's point of view, the word on her left hand was FREET. That didn't make much sense either. The right read: dot dot dot dot, dot, dash dot, dot, dash.

HENET. FREET HENET? Oh! *Free the net.*

"This place wasn't so bad as long as I could keep conducting my business online. It's actually kept me incredibly focused and productive. But last week, VT disabled all internet service from the Chilean Embassy. They claim there's a 'network problem' that they can't fix, but nothing electronic comes in, nothing goes out." She tilted her head. "Or rather, it's all getting intercepted and never reaches its intended destination. Folks around here are calling it the Berlin Firewall."

"So that's why you haven't been online," Penny said. "They're trying to prevent you from releasing more information about them."

She already had opened her laptop and plugged it into the same network jack Ada's equipment was connected to.

Ada nodded. "And pressure the embassy to ask me to leave. Seb—Sr. Ortiz—is insulted and angry. He's been threatening to make this an international incident, but officially VT is not at fault. We're under a siege of sorts, but so far he and his staff have been holding strong. I don't know if that will last. How long could you go without internet access?"

"Three days," Max said instantly. That was his limit when Courtney had challenged her classmates to disconnect and turn off their devices.

"Three hours," Penny said.

"How can VT get away with this?" Max asked.

"They can do whatever they want, and this is the least of their infractions," Ada said. "VT's business model treats broadband internet as a privilege, when it should be considered a basic utility, like electricity and water."

Max nodded. Internet access was a modern necessity, especially for people who essentially lived their real lives online. Ada seemed pleased that he agreed with her.

"So you can imagine how frightening it is that they own and operate the internet in Germany, as well as a large portion of the European Union. And increasingly all over the world. That's why I'm here, Max." She spread her arms wide to indicate the small room.

"Okay, this firewall they've set up around the embassy's network is pretty sophisticated. High-level hacking. I can't believe they would have anyone on staff capable of this," Penny said.

"Neither would anyone else. That's what makes it so sneaky. But VT has outsourced dirty work to hackers before," Ada said. "There's a lucrative online market where hackers offer their services for extralegal jobs and do things like sell zero-day exploits to the highest bidder."

"The Curtain," Penny said. Ada looked at her sharply.

Max was startled. He knew Penny had been a hacker for hire since well before he'd met her, but he thought she'd limited her activities to discovering bugs and selling them to software companies, like a digital bounty hunter. Had she been finding work through The Curtain too? Was that how she'd connected with Ada?

The Curtain was a black market—*the* black market today—that was hidden so deep in the Deep Web, it was practically its own entity. Like some of the notorious dark markets before it, Silk Road, Evolution, and OpenBazaar, it had risen to be the preeminent site for illegal transactions of all kinds. It went way beyond selling drugs or forged documents, offering everything from organ trafficking to hired assassins to trading in sex.

The Curtain was the internet's worst kept secret. But just

because you knew something existed didn't mean you could find it if someone didn't want you to, or do anything to shut it down. The location of The Curtain and its organizers, especially its purported founder known only as the Wizard, had proven to be especially difficult to pin down. Even Dramatis Personai hadn't been able to penetrate its mysteries.

Penny typed for a little longer. "I don't think I can get around this. I might not be able to even if I were logged in directly at VT." She was clearly frustrated and disappointed in herself. "As an internet service provider, naturally VT can limit or disable connectivity through their management software. But this wasn't done through the system. Something else is blocking access."

"Something physical?" Max asked. "Did they cut the lines?"

That was a low-tech, brute-force method, but if the right trunk line was interrupted, it could cause a huge amount of trouble for the maximum number of people—and it couldn't be fixed without digging up and laying new wire. The jerks who did that kind of thing weren't hackers except in the literal sense, using sharp tools instead of sharp wits.

"No. Or rather, I think there's a physical component— they would have to have access to the connection somewhere in the building, or at a nearby junction—whichever internet exchange accepts and passes on the data coming from this building. Data packets are going out, but they aren't reaching their intended destinations."

"So we're connected to the internet, but all the traffic is

being blocked?" Ada asked.

"Right. Or redirected," Penny said. Her eyes moved back and forth quickly behind her yellow computer glasses. She was churning all this information around in her head, using her talent at free association to look for connections that often weren't apparent to Max. When she and Risse were working on something together, it was like she doubled her processing speed—watching them figure something out was like watching a telepathic tennis match, as they rapidly lobbed ideas back and forth.

"Redirected? So it isn't a firewall at all. It's more like a black hole," Ada said.

"Or a wormhole. Which begs the question: Where is all that information going?" Penny closed her laptop with a huff.

"Thanks for trying," Ada said.

"Oh, I haven't given up. I just haven't figured it out yet," Penny said.

Max bet Penny just needed time to talk the problem out with Risse before they arrived at a solution. They were an incredible team, which is why it was so strange that Penny had insisted on going solo on this.

"That attitude is why I love working with you. I'm glad you're on my side," Ada said.

Max agreed. Penny's skills would make her a formidable threat if she ever used them for evil instead of niceness.

"But you must still have some connections to the outside world," Max said.

"Oh, I can get news from papers and television, but that's so slow compared to social media. Have I missed anything important?"

Max laughed. He told her about the interrogation at the airport, the redheaded man following him, and finally his narrow escape from Clove and her mysterious accomplice in the Volvo.

"Oh, dear. I was afraid my invitation would put you in danger," Ada said.

"You were? Why?" Max asked.

Ada closed her eyes for a moment.

"I know everyone thinks I'm a fugitive from justice, but that isn't the real reason I came here for asylum. At least it isn't the whole reason."

"But there are cops waiting to arrest you outside," Penny said.

"Prison is the best-case scenario."

"What's the worst?" Max asked.

Ada took a deep breath. "The moment I walk out of this building . . . the moment I show my face outside . . . I'm dead."

7

"DEAD?" PENNY ASKED.

For such a heavy word, it hung in the air between them for a long time.

"You think VT would have you killed over this? With the world watching?" Max asked.

"I believe they would, but this goes much deeper than my former employer." Ada pressed her lips together. "I should have been more forthcoming with you, but there was no way to deliver this information except in person. Now I'm afraid I've made you both targets too. I'm sorry to put you in this situation."

"We're here now. Why don't you start by explaining what you say you've involved us in?" Max said.

"All right." Ada folded her legs beneath her. "As you would expect, VT monitors everything transmitted through their services. Of course, the revelation that a company is collecting customers' information has lost its shock value, because everyone does it these days. But what *should* get people's attention is that VT has been so successful at preventing me from releasing the information *I've* collected about *them*."

Max nodded. He, like everyone else, hadn't been able to download and examine the documents Ada had released before the links disappeared. The initial article also hadn't connected the dots the way Ada was doing now—and then it too had been redacted, seemingly voluntarily by the paper *Der Fenster.*

Kevin Sharpe and Panjea had resorted to good old murder to deal with those who could expose them, but VT was powerful enough to pressure major news outlets to bury stories they didn't want published, and simply cut off Ada's communication channels to silence her just as effectively.

"How can they have that much influence?" Max asked.

"We think of the internet as a virtual space that's all around us. Like air." Ada spread her hands. "But the internet also has a very physical presence."

"Data centers and IXs," Penny said.

"Yes. In the real world, the internet is actually made up of unassuming buildings that store hard drives with everyone's data and the internet exchange points that allow them to communicate with each other, like a telephone switchboard. There are also the fiber-optic cables that connect them all together—the true 'World Wide Web.' VT has been quietly acquiring as many internet exchange points as they can."

She was talking about the so-called backbones of the internet, on which the whole system relied. When you sent an email, it was transmitted as light signals along fiber-optic cables to the closest IX and then redirected along the fastest route possible to its destination—which wasn't necessarily the shortest *distance*. The invitation Penny had emailed Max had likely traveled all the way to the U.S. and back again, even though they were both in Europe, but it still took much less time than the blink of an eye. IXs made it all possible, acting just like giant versions of network hubs in homes and offices.

"Wouldn't people notice? VT would be charged as a monopoly," Max said.

"European company, European laws. All our major tele-communication companies are monopolies, with close ties to the government. So far no one has noticed this activity but me, or if they have, they aren't interested in exposing it. VT isn't buying large companies, Max. Your average person never even thinks about IXs, and they certainly couldn't name one. These are comparatively little businesses who contribute to the over-all infrastructure of the internet. By design, individually they don't matter; if one fails, the others pick up the slack. But con-sider what it would mean if one entity owned them all."

"So how much of the internet does VT control?" Max asked.

"About seventy-three percent of all internet traffic."

Max whistled. That one company had access to seventy-three percent of the information and transactions passing through the internet was terrifying to him.

"As well as forty-five percent of cloud storage via various content delivery networks," Ada added. "They've been purchasing key data centers around the world as well."

"Whoa," Max said. "That must take some serious cash."

"They also stand to make a nice profit, if they sell unlimited access to their information to government agencies. Not just sharing private information, but allowing them to delete data without leaving any trace that it was ever there," Ada said.

"You have proof they're doing this?" Max asked.

Do I really want to get dragged further into this mess? he thought.

He was already in it—so was everyone else in the world. The difference was that he was no longer oblivious to what was happening, and he was one of the few people in a position to do something about it, though damned if he knew what that was.

Ada reached into a pocket of her track jacket and pulled out a nickel. She twisted it a certain way, and it separated into two halves. She showed him a microSD card nestled inside. She clicked it back together again and handed it to him.

"This is everything I originally released to *Der Fenster*, which was promptly scrubbed off the internet in the wake of their retraction. Right now, there are only local copies of it for safekeeping with people I trust, since we can't rely on the cloud." She tipped her head toward Penny.

People often said that once something is online, it will always be online. That was true for a lot of things—mostly the embarrassing stuff you wished would go away—but actually stuff vanished all the time. Valuable stuff like articles and journals images and sound clips and videos.

When websites folded or servers crashed, when the money ran out, important pieces of history, written in ones and zeroes, were lost, sometimes forever. A lot of people had been working on archiving content on the internet, an incredible task the larger it grew, but VT had accomplished the opposite: a way to remove information.

Being able to share anything on the internet was what made it such a powerful tool—for good or evil—but the ability to erase it was even more formidable. VT could not only revise history, but in a real sense it could shape the future into whatever it wanted, by affecting the ways people could communicate in the present.

"Any time we try to repost these files anywhere, they disappear within minutes," Penny said. "We've also been reluctant to try posting everything, because VT doesn't yet know the extent of what Ada collected on them."

"This is why you're here? To help Ada get this information out?" Max asked.

Penny nodded.

She had hesitated to get involved in this kind of thing before, concerned about protecting her secrets and Risse, but this was almost reckless. She had really taken it hard when the world had collectively shrugged at the revelation that members of the U.S. government had been using Panjea to monitor and manipulate the public. Even before updating its terms of service to safe-guard customers' private information, the social network had been signing up new users and winning back old ones.

Max was content with what he'd managed to accomplish, but Penny was convinced they could have done more and that it was a mistake to give up the cause now.

I've created a monster, Max thought.

Max didn't know if this situation was something they could actually change. For all its flaws, people depended on the internet too much; for many of his friends, the internet was their whole world. If it couldn't be trusted anymore, at all. . . . How could they fight that, without their most valuable asset? Their only asset?

"No wonder you finally came forward, Ada," Max said.

"This isn't why I released their information. I've known about this stuff, bits and pieces of it, for years. I'm—I *was* AVP, after all."

"You knew about what VT was doing?"

"I helped develop this strategic plan, and I was quite proud of it. Once upon a time, I actually believed that monitoring everything was the only way to protect us. I changed my mind in light of all the abuses of citizens' rights around the globe. I hoped to use my position to stall VT's progress from within. Meanwhile, I was gathering information—this time, monitor-ing everything for the right reasons. Blowing the whistle was the nuclear option if I failed to stop VT using the right chan-nels."

"So this is some kind of redemption thing? Why reveal it now?"

Ada smiled. "Because of you, Max."

"Me?"

"What you did with Panjea was amazing. You inspired me. I was starting to lose my resolve. I had collected all this evidence, but it never felt like the right time to release it. I wasn't sure if I could. The longer I delayed, the stronger VT became. Even as I despaired that I couldn't stop VT on my own, you gave me hope that one person can make a difference."

Max's face burned with embarrassment. "I wasn't the first to do something like that, and I had a lot of help." He smiled at Penny.

"I could use your help now," Ada said. "Since I've been studying the data I stole, I've discovered another, even more criminal activity at VT. I didn't know anything about it while I worked there; big hitters would have to be involved to hide it from me for so long."

"This is why you're afraid for your life?" he asked.

She nodded.

"What is it?"

She took a deep breath. "I believe VT is supporting The Curtain."

Max stared at her blankly until it sank in. "Say that again?"

"I believe that Verbunden Telekom, or at least certain high-ranking people there, have been committing a significant portion of the company's resources to running The Curtain."

"That's . . . huge." Once again, words failed Max.

Penny gave him a look that seemed to say, *See? I told you this was important.*

"The Curtain itself is huge," Ada said. "It would need serious support to stay in operation, and at the moment, nothing remains online unless VT allows it. You said it yourself: VT needs a lot of capital to buy out a controlling majority of the internet. Well, The Curtain holds almost as much in annual revenues from illegal sales as Amazon does. We're talking upwards of eighty billion dollars."

Max blinked rapidly as he processed that. "Wow. But are you sure they're connected?"

"That's another area where I could use your help," Ada said.

"Oh." Max's excitement deflated.

"I was first tipped off when I noticed that certain divisions at VT were hiring hackers online. If you review the files I took and read between the lines, it's plain that something's going on, but they have been very good at covering their tracks."

"So, you don't have any actual evidence yet, but VT thinks you do. Is that enough reason for them to kill you?"

"With so much money on the line? And VT's reputation? Someone must think it's important enough. My gut tells me this goes all the way to the top. It would have to."

"To the CEO? What have you got on him?" Max asked.

"Nothing. Richard Rhone keeps to himself. So much so that he hasn't even been seen in public in thirty years. I don't know anyone who's met him in person. Only a few people have ever heard his voice."

"Are we sure he's alive? Or ever was alive? Sounds like a ghost," Max said. "How can he run a company like that?"

"He communicates everything through his personal assistant. She must get her orders from someone. She's rarely seen either, because by all accounts, she hardly ever leaves his side."

"What's your move? What can I do?" Max asked.

"I may not have found proof that VT is running The Curtain yet, but I don't need to in order to stop them. We can do that with the files we already have, by continuing to pressure VT as publicly as possible. If we can weaken their hold on the internet, maybe The Curtain will fall too. I can't get the word out or keep on them from in here. Especially without internet access. But *you* can."

"You already have Penny helping you."

"Penny likes operating behind the scenes, and no one does it better. This requires a leader. Someone with people skills and connections. Someone who can work openly and honestly, instead of in the background. Someone like you, Max." She shook her head. "Not someone *like* you. You're the only person for the job."

"I totally agree," Penny said. "You already have the megaphone, Max. You just have to use it. You're practically the face of internet freedom, you know? You could call any reporter right now, and they'd give you an interview."

Max chewed the inside of his cheek. He was both flattered

and frustrated that he had come all the way to Europe to avoid getting dragged into other people's fights, and yet here he was.

Once again, someone wanted to use Max to accomplish what they couldn't. Even if it was for a good cause, it still felt like he was no closer to finding his purpose. Could it be that he was only meant to be a tool, accepting his programming from others like a glorified computer?

No. The decision was up to him, and Max did have his own goals. Working with Ada wouldn't get him any closer to home or help him to find Lianna Stein.

"I have to think about this," Max said.

Ada looked surprised, but she quickly hid it and smiled. Penny didn't try to hide her disappointment.

"Of course. I would be worried if you didn't. This kind of work. . . . It isn't the sort of thing you jump into blindly," Ada said.

"Thanks for understanding," he said.

"I do understand, Max. Only . . . don't take too long to decide? I don't think we have a lot of time. VT has a good lead, not to mention nearly unlimited resources. And I'm rather exposed here. It's only a matter of time before the Chilean government decides that I'm worth more to them as a bargaining chip than as a refugee," Ada said.

"I'll let you know soon. How will we stay in touch?"

"Until Penny and her team can get us back online, I'm afraid we'll have to risk meeting in person. It's the most secure way to communicate with my limited options. But do be careful.

If anyone finds out you were here, you'll become a target too."

Ada walked Penny and Max to the door, thanking him again for coming to hear her out. He promised to look over the files she'd given him and consider becoming her spokesperson.

He was startled when Ada knocked on the door— shave and a haircut—and a moment later the door was unlocked and opened by Sr. Ortiz. He hadn't realized that they'd been locked in this whole time. Had Ada meant she was literally a prisoner?

Penny stayed behind to chat privately with Ada for a moment before joining Max in the hallway. Just before the door closed behind her, Max saw Ada's calm façade slip, giving him a raw glimpse of her fear and loneliness.

Sr. Ortiz locked Ada in and then led them back the way they'd come.

Max pulled on his Krampus mask with a resigned sigh. "Thanks, Sr. Ortiz."

"*De nada*," Sr. Ortiz said.

When Max and Penny returned to street level, they found the crowd of protesters had finally dispersed, but the building was still under police watch. Max scanned the area, alert for a potential assassin hunting Ada.

An officer called out to them in German.

"I didn't catch that," Max whispered.

"He wants to have a word with us," Penny said.

"We haven't done anything," Max said.

The beefy officer, who looked more like a bouncer at a club

than a policeman, gestured at their masks. "Take them off."

They're worried Ada is trying to sneak out of the embassy.

"I think we'd better," Max said.

He and Penny lifted their masks, and the guard scrutinized them. Then he nodded and waved them on.

No one else was around, so Max pulled off his mask and stowed it in his backpack while they walked to the car. "Sheesh," he said. "You okay, Penny?" She was still strangely silent.

"You have to *think about it*?" she said. "Max, I vouched for you. I thought you'd be all over this."

"Penny, come on. You know how I feel about being in the spotlight."

"We aren't asking for a lot. Just do some interviews, write some blog posts. Tweet. You could make a real difference without doing a hell of a lot."

"At what cost?"

Penny stopped short. "You're kidding. Ada gave up everything to expose VT: her job, her reputation, her freedom. Her life is in jeopardy. And you're still hung up on not getting to be a 'normal teenager'? Whatever that's supposed to be!"

"You know: going to parties, getting drunk, getting laid."

"Woo. Sign me up for all that." She rolled her eyes. "Honestly, Max."

"Well, look where Ada's sacrifice got her, and it still isn't over. She'll probably end up in prison, and for what in the long run? Penny, there are real, serious, and lasting consequences to the choices we make—even on the side of justice. Sometimes people die."

"I know that." She swiped the back of a hand across her eyes.

"Sorry, I know you do." He reached out to put a hand on her shoulder, but he hesitated. "You say it's just a blog post here, an interview there, but that's still me putting my neck out. Pulling my family and friends into something that's way bigger than all of us. And I have to weigh the danger against the potential for doing good.

"Remember when I was chased from my train? That's the kind of thing I'm talking about. I don't want to live that way anymore, Penny. Or should I call you 'PlusGood'? So much for your vow to work more openly as Penny Polonsky. A bit hypocritical to expect me to be the face of this thing while you're still hiding behind a handle."

Penny sighed and looked down. "Touché."

"Then there's the small matter of my being detained by French customs agents, so I missed my flight and ended up being free to come to Berlin. You wouldn't know anything about that, would you?"

"Nope," Penny said.

"Really."

She grimaced. "Okay, guilty. But I didn't think it was going to be such a big deal."

"*Penny.*" Max was horrified. "How could you?"

"They should have been able to sort it out right away."

"Four hours is not 'right away.' And my name is still on the list."

"I'm a hacker," she said. "I do whatever gets the job done. I know how much you hate attention, and I'm sorry our efforts to make the world a better place interfered with your holiday. But if you don't like it, I won't bother hacking the list again to remove your name."

Max's shoulders drooped. "I don't want to do this, Penny."

"I'm just saying: If you can't stomach our methods anymore, there's another way. If you decide to step up."

He had meant he didn't want to argue with her, but he also didn't want to get involved in their mess, which he was convinced there was much more to than he'd been told.

"I hardly think I'm the best spokesperson for the Free Internet movement," he said.

"You'd be surprised how damned charming you are. You convinced me to help you last year, and no one is more selfish than me."

"I thought you volunteered because of Evan's endorsement."

"Like I said." She winked. "Charming and *cute*. Hey, if I hadn't signed up, you'd be back in Granville instead of in one of the most romantic cities in the world with a hot girl." She smiled hopefully. "I'll make it up to you somehow."

"You did say something about kissing . . . but we need to talk about this." Max looked around. "Maybe somewhere else, huh?"

"Where do you want to go?"

"I'm hungry," he said. "Should we look for that Thai place Ada mentioned?"

"I have a better idea," Penny said.

"I'm worried."

"No, trust me. We're near a famous Christmas market that's supposed to be fantastic."

"As long as they have food."

"So much food! It's just a few blocks away."

"Lead on, Macduff."

"That's supposed to be '*Lay* on, Macduff.'" She blushed. "Which sounds kind of naughty. Oh, Shakespeare. You saucy fellow."

"Heh, 'shake spear' too. I know a made-up name when I hear one."

"Maybe he was a hacker too," Penny said.

"No, just a hack."

Penny grabbed Max's hand and led him through the quiet Berlin streets toward the brightly lit square. They joked around, falling into their old familiar patterns, but he knew they were forcing it to keep things normal. Whatever that meant.

Penny snuggled close, but before Max could enjoy it, she murmured, "Don't tell me someone's following us."

Max listened. Distant footsteps were keeping pace with theirs. They could be echoes, but. . . . He pretended to trip and caught himself, disrupting the pattern of their steps. There was no corresponding delay at first, but then the footsteps paused and shifted to mirror theirs. It sounded like they belonged to two people.

"Someone's following us," Max said.

"I asked you not to tell me that. What do we do?"

"Keep walking. Could be another couple out to visit the Christmas market. Let's see if they're going the same way, then try to get a good look at them."

She squeezed his arm. They continued to walk and fake being happy tourists, eyes looking straight ahead with their attention squarely behind them.

No, things had never been anything like *normal* for Max and Penny, but he'd been enjoying what they did have—and considering everything they could have together one day. But now he couldn't help worrying that even if they survived this adventure, their relationship might not.

GENDARMENMARKT WAS FILLED WITH TWINKLING golden lights. Nestled among a columned concert hall and two identical domed churches, a small city had sprung up of pointed white tents topped with eight-point stars. A sparkling tree towered over the square, which even this late in the evening was crowded with people wandering around and admiring the wares offered at the many craft stalls.

"My dad would go bananas over this," Max said.

Penny paid the nominal entrance fee for both of them, while Max casually watched the street behind them for their "echo"—but no one appeared. Before they passed through the glowing arch into the market, Max paused to photograph its lit sign reading WEIHNACHTSZAUBER GENDARMENMARKT.

He checked the picture on his phone. "WeihnachtsZauber?" Max sounded the word out, poorly.

Penny raised her gloved hands, fingers spread. "It means 'Christmas magic'!"

Penny grabbed him in an embrace. He was surprised by her sudden, open display of affection, until she whispered, "Just trying to get a better look at the suspicious couple behind you on our left. The short white dude with brown hair and the bald black dude with the goatee."

"Why are they suspicious?" No one else seemed to be taking much of an interest in them, with the gaudy splendor all around. Max and Penny were just two more tourists out of the tens of thousands who visited the market.

"They're shopping kind of funny. They're together, but they aren't speaking to each other, and they look at every stall exactly the same way. Watch. Artoo walks slowly along the stall while Threepio picks up an item on the end and scans the crowd while pretending to study it."

"Artoo?"

"I can give people nicknames too! He's the shorter one, obviously."

"Obviously."

"Look. Threepio hands the item to Artoo and moves on to the next stall, and then they switch tasks."

Max turned his head slightly to watch from the corner of his eye as they performed this strange ritual.

He looked away. "That's creepy. They're acting like robots—"

"Programmed to mimic humans."

"Which is why those nicknames." They grinned at each other.

Max liked it when they were on the same wavelength like that, the way she and Risse were. The way he and Evan had been.

"How'd you notice what they're doing?" Max asked.

"I notice people. You're great at reading individuals, but I pay attention to crowds, how the parts work within a larger system. That's one of the reasons I was interested in Dramatis Personai. You know how I feel about groups."

He nodded.

"But gatherings like this are fascinating, almost like we're all running the same intuitive algorithm, something deep in our code. Those two don't fit the behavioral model you'd expect for this setting," she said.

Leave it to Penny to think of people in terms of computer programs. Although Max did it too, in a sense; humans were often the weakest part of any secure system.

"Then we don't fit in here either. If they're watching us, we should go. Or split up," Max said.

"Nope. They'll split up to follow each of us, and what good is that? Let's play the happy couple on holiday for a while and look for the right opportunity to shake them. They won't try anything in such a public, crowded place."

"Okay."

Penny started to pull away, but Max held on.

"Hey, we need to make this look good." He closed his eyes and rested his chin on Penny's head.

"If you insist." She hugged him more tightly. "Mmmm."

When they finally let go of each other, Penny rubbed at her eyes with the back of a gloved hand. "Damn. Cold air always makes me tear up."

Max blinked a couple of times. "Winter allergies are the worst. Pine needles and candy canes get me every time."

"Well . . ." Penny linked her right arm through his left and leaned into him. "Shall we?"

They strolled slowly past the booths, checking out the knit things and sculpted things and even some 3-D printed things. Everything smelled delicious: roasting chestnuts and baked pastries and sizzling meat.

Max caught periodic glimpses of Artoo and Threepio; they were always three or four booths away.

It wasn't long before Max and Penny had grabbed a regional delicacy called a "flame cake" that resembled a little personal pizza: fresh thin bread topped with sour cream, bacon, and leeks. It was one of the best things Max had ever eaten. You couldn't go wrong with bacon.

While they drank steaming cups of nonalcoholic "glow wine" in souvenir cups commemorating this year's market, they stopped to watch a glassblower. She worked the melted glass with her delicate tools like it was taffy, pulling the fragile threads and twisting and folding them to create a reindeer. It was mesmerizing.

"Isn't it odd that we ended up hanging out so far from home?" Max said.

"We were long overdue for a romantic night out. Though I didn't expect it to be a double date." She rolled her eyes in the direction of the men keeping tabs on them. Max drew her away from the glassblower's stall.

"I want to travel all over the world. Maybe that's one of the reasons I jumped at this job," Penny said.

"What *is* the job?" Max lowered his voice.

"What we told you. We're trying to get the message out." Penny sipped her glow wine and avoided looking at him.

"Come on, Pen. There's more to it than that. Calling you in to do tech support because the internet's down is overkill, like hiring Ellen Ripley to take care of a rat infestation."

Penny raised an eyebrow. "Thank you?"

"You know what I mean. Why are you really here? How did you get connected with—" He stopped himself, remembering that they were in public now. He nodded toward the stage near a snow-covered fountain, where a jazz band was playing Christmas music with lots of brass—perfect for drowning out conversation. They headed for it and worked their way closer to the front row of onlookers.

"Now. What are you and Ada really doing?" he said into her ear.

She bopped her head in time with the music. "I can't tell you unless you promise to help us."

"That's insulting."

"*I* trust you. You know I trust you with my life, and Risse's." Penny touched his arm. "But this isn't up to me. I'm not the one calling the shots here."

Max drained his cup and let the cinammony brew warm him up.

"But it's something big?" he asked.

"It's the biggest. There's a lot at stake here, Max. More than you can imagine. Think about it: We're fighting for the internet. That's . . . *everything.*"

Not everything, Max thought. *What about us?*

Max noted that Artoo and Threepio were closing the distance on them, pushing their way through the crowd. Trying to overhear their conversation?

Max reached for Penny's hand. "Are you sure we can trust her?"

She let out a puff of breath. "I trust someone else who supports her. You remember H8Bit?"

"I haven't heard that handle in a long time."

H8Bit had already been a legendary hacker when Max was a kid. His MO was hacking into websites and reducing them to blocky pixels, like a retro video game. Max still remembered the thrill he'd felt when he saw the text that faded in after loading the page: YOU ARE BEEN PIXELH8TED.

H8Bit always struck for a purpose. In one case, an Arkansas school had suspended a kid for publishing their budget on his blog for a social-studies project, which showed it had diverted money away from their library and computer center to renovate the football field. *Bam!* Pixelh8ted.

He had done the same thing to a restaurant that kicked

out the family of a boy with Down syndrome, and a theater chain that advertised it only showed movies with white people in them. Which admittedly was most movies, but still.

"H8Bit was amazing. His best hack was when he took down that webhosting site WebBuddy—"

"Because of those sexist ads with blondees in bikinis! Those always pissed me off," Penny said.

Every time a site was Pixelh8ted, it drew the attention of the media, which led to everyone trying to visit it at the same time—often causing the sites to crash. It was an ingenious way of performing a denial-of-service attack, by getting regular people to swamp the servers with site requests. WebBuddy and all the sites they hosted were down for almost a full day.

In fact, that attack had been the inspiration for Max to get into the DDoS game and assume the handle 503-ERROR. H8Bit had kind of made him.

"Wasn't H8Bit in Dramatis Personai back in the day?" he asked.

"He was one of its founding members. He dropped out before the group really made its name."

"Then he disappeared." Max had assumed that with more hackers using the internet to strike for justice, H8Bit had felt like he was no longer needed, or had started using another handle. "How'd you find him?"

"Evan left me H8Bit's PGP key in that posthumous data packet."

"Oh," Max said.

Penny had never let him watch the video message Evan had recorded for her, which he was certain she had managed to archive; the one Evan had sent Max disappeared as soon as he'd played it, though he'd tried everything he could think of to recover it. Even with Max's photographic memory, he wanted to be able to see his friend again, even in a recording.

Penny hadn't told him what Evan had left her, until now. He'd only assumed Evan had sent her something useful. After months of puzzling over the files Evan had downloaded to his phone, Max had realized that Evan had given him the keys to the kingdom of conspiracy blogs: backdoor administrative access to Fawkes Rising.

Evan had hacked into the blog to write a post asking the question, "What is the silence of six, and what are you going to do about it?" When Fawkes found the deleted draft after everything went down with Panjea, he had contacted Max to tell him.

They figured Fawkes Rising had been one of Evan's backup plans in case he couldn't interrupt the presidential debate with his cryptic video message and horrifying live suicide. Then Fawkes had requested an interview with Max. Already burned out on publicity, Max had turned him down.

Not long after that, Fawkes disappeared under mysterious circumstances. His friend "Bob" took over the site until he went into hiding, claiming he feared for his life. Once the site had been dark for a while, Max had used Evan's access to poke around its files, but he hadn't turned up anything, and he was already deep into his search for his mother with no room for another potentially deadly mystery. He still wondered why Evan had thought access to the blog would be useful to him.

"H8Bit had become a kind of mentor to Evan in the year before he died," Penny said. "He's the one who set up that barcode on Evan's grave and hosted the files for Evan. Guess where?"

"WebBuddy," Max said.

Penny tapped her nose.

"So you've been talking to H8Bit, and he's been working with She-Who-Shall-Not-Be-Named," Max said.

The band onstage ended their song, and the crowd broke into enthusiastic applause. After the band began their next song, a catchy upbeat version of "Greensleeves," Penny responded.

"Ada needed someone with serious skills to get to some of the more sensitive files at VT."

"Again, hiring a hacker like H8Bit for that kind of thing is overkill. Something else is going on," Max said.

"Some people won't settle for less than the best." She winked. "As for H8Bit, Evan trusted him, and his recommendations have never let me down." She elbowed Max and smiled.

"Yeah." Evan had gone to great lengths to bring Penny and Max together to expose Panjea. But had he also anticipated them getting romantically involved?

No one had known Max and Penny better than Evan, so

he must have at least considered the possibility. On the other hand, Evan had a lot of blind spots in dealing with other people, especially on an emotional level; it might never have crossed his brilliant, analytical mind that his two best friends might hook up . . . let alone so soon after his death.

Penny seemed to deal with any guilt or discomfort she felt about it by avoiding talking about Evan as much as possible. It was unusual for her to bring him up like this. For a long time, Max couldn't help but bring up Evan often; he thought they should talk about him. More and more lately, he wondered if the main thing he and Penny had in common was Evan, and what that meant about their relationship.

"So if Ada already has what she needed from VT's servers, what are you doing there?"

"Not me, Max! Please. *Emmie* is consulting for them."

Emmie Steed was one of Penny's fabricated online personas—a hot computer engineer who had the uncanny ability to gain access to male-dominated companies and social functions.

"H8Bit set that up too. Officially, I'm doing pen testing at their various sites. In the wake of their recent data breach, they're finally getting serious about security," she said.

Pen testing—penetration testing—was when someone was hired to break into a building and its systems to look for weaknesses. Appropriately enough for someone with her name, Penny was very, very good at it.

"But that was an inside job," Max said.

"Yes, it was, but VT hasn't revealed publicly that You-Know-Who had help from one or more hackers. She couldn't have collected all those files over such a long period of time—she was primarily a paper pusher with limited security clearance of her own. Emmie is looking for holes in their system hardware and wetware and helping plug them."

"And while you're there, you're trying to figure out how to get her back online. Maybe use their systems to distribute their own files?"

"Correct!"

"Uh-huh. As Enzo would say, '*Mon oeil!*'" Max pulled down the skin under his right eye with his index finger. "I don't believe you. What are you really doing?" He was getting tired of asking, but he knew she was hiding something.

"You'll just have to trust *me* for now," Penny said.

Normally that would be a given, but Max was having a harder time with it now that she was keeping a secret from him—and from her sister.

"Who's Enzo?" Penny asked.

They wandered away from the band and back to the stalls, while Max told Penny about his time in Paris living with the Beaumonts. They looked at handmade jewelry and ate candied apples, and he showed her pictures of Enzo and his mothers on his phone.

"They seem nice," Penny said thoughtfully.

"You miss your family," he said.

"Yeah."

"How long have you been in Berlin?"

"A few months."

So pretty much since she'd cut off communication with Max.

"If your work here is so important, why didn't you ask for my help sooner?" Max asked.

She laughed. "Because I didn't want to have the argument we just had."

"Still would have been nice to hear from you. All this time, we could have gotten together sooner."

"We were both in Europe for a reason. We would have just distracted each other," she said.

"You're probably right." Max leaned down and kissed her. "Like this?"

"Mmm-hmm," she said. "What were we talking about again? Never mind." She kissed him again.

That did the trick. Max was certainly less interested in talking, especially about Ada, and he certainly didn't want to mention Evan again right now.

A camera flashed. Max turned. Artoo was holding a camera and snapping shots of the market. It was a real camera, with a serious zoom lens, not a cell phone like most tourists would probably use. He had almost certainly gotten a photo of Max and Penny, though he was pretending to be interested in anything and everything but them.

Max took a step toward Artoo. Penny grabbed his arm and pulled him around to face her.

"What are you going to do? Fight him for his camera?"

Max gritted his teeth. "I don't know! I'm tired of being followed."

"Me too. It's time we go."

Max bristled. "I'd rather find out who they're working for."

"Later. Come on, I know the perfect place to help us disappear."

Max followed Penny back the way they had come, moving past the stalls without stopping and weaving among tourists against the flow of pedestrian traffic. Max sneaked a glance behind him, pretty sure that Artoo and Threepio knew they'd been made. They were still following; just as Max thought they'd lost them, the men would round the corner, hands in their coat pockets. Max wondered what else might be in them.

Someone brushed against Max with a gentle bump. He pulled away from Penny.

"What?" she asked breathlessly.

"I think I was just robbed." He checked his own pockets.

Enzo had tried to teach Max how to pick pockets, but the lessons never took. Max's fingers just weren't nimble enough, and he was too tall to avoid being noticed in most situations. But Enzo's patient instruction had made Max wiser to the tricks and techniques pickpockets used to divert attention from what they were really doing. The art of social engineering and intrusion in secure computer systems wasn't so different from lifting a man's wallet from one pocket while "accidentally" bumping into him. At least in theory.

Max scanned the area. A towheaded boy of ten or eleven pulled up the gray hood of his jacket and disappeared into a crowd.

"You can catch him!" Penny said.

"It's okay. Nothing's missing." He patted his pockets again to be sure. Everything was still there: His wallet in the front right pocket of his jeans, his cell phone in the front left, his passport tucked into the inside pocket of his jacket.

"The files!" Penny whispered.

Oh, crap. Ada's files!

Max hooked a thumb into the small coin pocket of his jeans. He pulled out the fake nickel concealing Ada's memory card and double-checked to make sure it hadn't been swapped for a real nickel.

"Whew. I guess I overreacted," Max said.

"You're high-strung. For good reason." She looked behind them. "Where'd those guys go?"

Max looked, but Artoo and Threepio were gone. Had the kid just been a diversion while they sneaked away? But it wasn't like Max and Penny had been following *them*.

"I guess they decided to call it a night. The market's about to close anyway," Penny said.

"Or they're going to ambush us." He pointed to the tent next to them, which sold knit hats with animal faces. "Here's our exit."

"What? That isn't—"

He pulled Penny into the stall with him, and they ducked

under a display counter.

"*Was zur Hölle?!*" the shopgirl shouted.

Max pulled up the thin fabric at the back of the tent and Penny scooted through the opening. He slipped out behind her, and they found themselves on the street just outside the market. They hurried away, taking the long way back to their car, looking for Artoo and Threepio lurking ahead of them and listening intently for footsteps echoing behind them.

"Do you have a place to stay tonight?" Penny asked softly.

"Oh. I hadn't actually given that any thought. I guess I'll try a youth hostel?"

"Not this late, during Christmas week. I'm at the Park Inn, courtesy of VT," Penny said. "Easiest commute ever, since they own the building, which is also their corporate headquarters. I suppose . . . you could come over. If you want."

"That'd be great. Thanks." He disguised his enthusiasm by mumbling.

Preoccupied as Max was by thoughts of what might happen back at Penny's room, he soon returned to mulling over the meeting with Ada, what special project Penny and H8Bit were working on, and their various pursuers with their mysterious agendas. Talk about killing the mood.

He also kept thinking about the encounter with the young pickpocket. It wasn't until they were standing next to Penny's car that he remembered his backpack. He slipped it off his shoulders and rummaged through it.

"What is it?" she asked.

"The pickpocket. I forgot to check my bag."

"Oh! Good thought. Anything missing?" Penny asked.

He felt a bulge in a small side compartment he remembered being empty. He opened the flap and froze. "No. Actually, it looks like he *left* something for me."

"Is it ticking?" Penny leaned closer.

Max pulled out a sleek black smartphone. It didn't have any markings on it to identify the carrier or manufacturer, so it was probably a disposable pay-as-you-go one like Max's burner.

"That's a nice phone," she said.

"It isn't mine."

Max hesitated for a moment before pressing the power button. It prompted him for a password. Without knowing whom the phone belonged to, he couldn't even begin to guess the code. He pressed his thumb to the biometric pad on the front while he thought—and the password prompt faded to reveal the home screen.

"It thinks it's your phone," Penny said.

"That's freaky."

He flipped through the menus and checked out the installed apps. Nothing that identified the owner; it wasn't even registered to any email or social media accounts. No stored contacts. Nothing that looked overtly suspicious either—other than the phone itself.

"What do I do with it?" Max asked.

"I'd get rid of it. Someone's probably using it to track you."

He turned it over. The back was a smooth piece of molded plastic held in place with four tiny screws. The battery on this phone apparently was not a user-replaceable part, so he couldn't fully deactivate it.

Max looked around, feeling panic rise in him as if he were holding a bomb that could go off at any moment. The Spree was just a few blocks east of them.

"I'm gonna dump it in the river," he said.

The phone vibrated in his hand, and he almost dropped it from shock. A moment later it rang, blasting Beethoven's "Ode to Joy" at full volume. It sounded even louder echoing down the otherwise quiet street.

"What the—?!" Max said. He pressed a button that muted the call and stared at the screen. The number of the incoming call was blocked.

He looked at Penny. She shrugged.

Max slid the green phone icon to the right and lifted the phone to his ear.

"Hello?" he asked.

"*Guten Abend*, Maxwell. It's been a long time."

That voice. Max had never expected to hear it again.

"Sharpe," Max said. "I told you never to call me here."

Penny's eyes widened.

"Amusing." Sharpe's flat tone said otherwise. "I've already gone to some trouble to contact you, and I don't have time to waste."

Penny's astonishment had turned to anger. She clawed her

hands in front of her like she wanted to strangle someone.

"Then let me save you some time by hanging up now," Max said.

"You have no reason to trust me, but here's some free advice: Don't share all the details of our conversation with Penny."

"You're watching us." Max looked around, expecting to see Artoo and Threepio lurking in the shadows of a nearby building.

"Not anymore, thanks to you." Sharpe laughed. Max was surprised he had a sense of humor, as skewed as it was. "But someone dangerous has taken an interest in you, which is why I had to sneak this phone to you so we could talk. If only you'd waited for me in Paris."

"I don't need your advice, Sharpe. In fact, it isn't worth much to anyone anymore, is it? Didn't Lovett fire you?"

"That's *President* Lovett, and don't forget who put her in that office." Sharpe sounded defensive. Max had hit on a sore subject. Good to know—Sharpe had a big ego, which had been bruised when Lovett had distanced herself from her former campaign manager.

"Learn from my example. No matter how much you think you know a person, no matter how strong you think your relationship is, everyone has their own agenda, and they will throw you under the bus if they think it will help them," Sharpe said.

Max half turned away from Penny and lowered his voice.

"I trust Penny with my life."

"Then you must have a death wish."

"You know what? Don't worry about me sharing this conversation, because it's over," Max said.

"Your girlfriend is mixed up in something far worse than what we were doing at Panjea. Has she told you what she's doing at Verbunden Telekom?"

Max glanced at Penny and took a couple of steps away from her. She looked confused. Max held up a hand. *Wait.*

"What are you talking about?" Max whispered.

"That got your attention. Despite our history, I'm not your enemy. Nor am I the enemy of America, or freedom, or any of that good stuff. I run—used to run—a *security* company. All I'm interested is in protecting people from the real threats out there. Cybercriminals and unethical hackers. Terrorists and traitors. People like Ada Kiesler."

"So you know I've just met her," Max said. He again checked over his shoulder. Where were they? He studied the cars parked along the street. Empty, he was fairly sure. Penny gave him an impatient look. He didn't blame her; he didn't know why he was still listening to Sharpe either.

"Why else would you be in Berlin?" Sharpe said. "Kiesler's activities are undermining internet security and disrupting people's confidence in the companies and governments that are safeguarding them. We've seen how damaging that can be."

"And how little they deserve our blind trust in them."

"Well. Be that as it may, if there's any truth to Kiesler's allegations about VT, I need to know about it. The U.S. is closing in on a long-term business partnership with both VT and the German government."

"You want a copy of her files?" Max said. He covered his coin pocket with one hand, worried that it was stupid to be walking around with an unencrypted memory card containing them.

"That would be a start. If she's right, those files will do much more than discredit VT. If they prove that the U.S. has been supporting their activities, it would damage President Lovett's reputation and prevent her from doing her job effectively, or at all."

"I have no love for Lovett, but why are you still looking out for her?"

"It isn't the president I'm trying to protect, but the nation. Not only that, but the integrity of the internet itself. A controversy like this would be a major setback in our negotiations to establish new security protocols around the globe. Whatever it may look like, VT is building a safer, more reliable, and more useful internet."

"And making a nice profit, while also selling out their customers' privacy to U.S., U.K., and German intelligence agencies. Hey, let's get to the point so I can refuse and resume the awesome date I was on. What do you want from me?"

Sharpe wouldn't be contacting Max unless he wanted something. The man wasn't interested in serving the best interests of anyone but himself, regardless of his insistence that he was trying to protect Lovett, the U.S., and the internet—by his own admission. He had to have his own angle in all this.

"I need to know *everything* Kiesler has on VT and how and when she intends to release it," Sharpe said. "Not only the files she previously released to *Der Fenster*—of course I have those already."

"Why not wait for them to be public and read them with everyone else? Oh, because it might expose Lovett. Let me guess: You want me to help cover all this up."

"This isn't a cover-up, it's damage control. I'm expecting you to help conduct an independent investigation of the extent of VT's allegedly criminal activities, while defending your own damn country." Sharpe was barking like a lecturing military general. Where did he get off being so self-righteous when he personally had done more damage to his country than anyone?

Max narrowed his eyes. "Why should I trust you?"

"You shouldn't. I don't trust you. But alliances have been built on shakier ground. All I'm asking is that you consider my request and remember what I told you about your good friends. If you can review the files yourself, go ahead, and if you see anything I need to know about, pass that information on. And as a gesture of good faith . . ."

The phone beeped in Max's hand. He checked the screen and noticed a text-message notification in the top left corner, from a blocked number.

"What's this?" Max asked.

"Information *you've* been looking for. No strings attached, but I believe you'll do the right thing when you start digging deeper."

Max swiped down to reveal an address: 15 Place Saint-Étienne, Floor 2, Strasbourg, France.

"What am I supposed to find there?" Max asked.

"Good chat, Maxwell. You'll probably discard this phone, but for what it's worth, I assure you it can't be tracked, even by me. It's the best way to reach me, any time. Either way, I'll be in touch later. Now go find your mother."

Sharpe hung up.

"My mother?" Max said.

"Max?" Penny tapped his arm. Max jumped, aware that he was squeezing the phone and had been staring at his reflection in its glossy screen for some time. The address was burned into his perfect memory. 15 Place Saint-Étienne, Floor 2, Strasbourg, France.

Damm it. Sharpe had offered the only thing that would have convinced Max to listen to him.

Max held up a finger and mouthed, "Hold on."

He continued walking toward the Spree, Penny trailing behind him, until they reached Oberwasserstrasse. He tossed the phone into the narrow canal there. It barely splashed when it hit the dark surface of the water and disappeared from view.

"What did Sharpe want?" Penny said.

Max hated himself for not telling her everything—yet—but

she hadn't come clean with him either. Yet.

"He gave me an address for my mom," Max said. "She's in Strasbourg, France."

"That was a long conversation just for him to give you an address."

"He likes to hear himself talk."

"But why did he help you?" Penny asked.

"I don't know. It could be a trick."

"Of course it's a trick."

Max was certain that Sharpe was a murderer, no matter what the American legal system said. But that didn't mean he couldn't be honest in his current dealings with Max, especially if it aligned with his interests. There was no reason that Max couldn't use Sharpe, while making him think he was using Max. He didn't trust Ada Kiesler much either right now . . . and he was even beginning to doubt Penny.

"It's the only lead I've gotten on my mom in the six months I've been here," he said.

"How did Sharpe get information that we couldn't dig up?" she pressed. "I think he's bluffing."

It was when Sharpe's old associate Vic Ignacio had shown Max video footage of Lianna Stein that Max had gotten his first inkling that his mother was still out there, somewhere in France.

He'd searched for information about her on the internet periodically in the years since she'd left, but if she had been online at all, it was with an alias that he couldn't trace back to her. However, with Panjea's shady resources and the full support of his crack team of Dramatis Personai hackers, Vic might have been able to track her down through other methods, like facial recognition—and he absolutely would have shared that information with his boss. In fact, Sharpe had probably told Vic to look for her in the first place, as a way to get to Max.

If Max went to Strasbourg now, he would be doing exactly what Sharpe expected him to do. No strings attached? There was no such thing; those "strings" were often lines of computer code that could break, destroy, and even end lives. Chasing down this lead was like agreeing to help Sharpe cover up the U.S. government's relationship with Verbunden Telekom.

"He's playing you, Max. I don't know why. But he clearly knows how to get to you," Penny said.

"It's my *mom*, Penny," Max said. "What would you do?"

In the end, that was the only argument that mattered.

Penny sighed. "Okay, but let me dig around on my own first, maybe save us the trip." She wiggled her fingers in front of her like she was typing at a keyboard.

"Us?" Max said.

"Naturally, I'm coming with you." Penny folded her arms across her chest in a challenge.

Max grinned. "Even better."

She led the way back to her car. Max trailed just behind her, the smile fading from his face. For all Penny's suspicions about Sharpe's motives, Max was startled to find himself doubting hers. Why was she going all the way to Strasbourg with him when she was in the middle of something so important that she couldn't even be straight about it with her boyfriend? She would certainly have confided everything in Evan by now.

God. Was he jealous of Evan? Maybe it wasn't guilt that had been holding him back from fully committing to their relationship; maybe he'd been trying to compete with what Penny and Evan had shared. Maybe Max was worried that she didn't yet consider him to be her equal.

Don't be stupid, Max. She wants to go with you because you're important to her too. Don't question it.

Those were Max's thoughts, but he heard them in Evan's voice. That was new and disturbing.

It was probably good advice, except that one of Max's most useful qualities was that he questioned *everything*. Which didn't rule out enjoying more time with Penny, as long as he stayed on his guard. That was the hardest part, because he'd always felt like he could trust her completely, and he didn't know how he could act normally around her until they could both be completely honest with each other.

He hurried to catch up with Penny and then took her hand in his. He had his doubts about her, but at least she still considered them to be an "us."

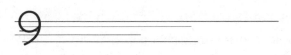

9

MAX AND PENNY HUDDLED IN THE BUSY, SNOW-covered square across from 15 Place Saint-Étienne in Strasbourg, France. They had been staking out the building all afternoon.

The seven-hour drive from Berlin had been uneventful, if cramped for Max. They were fairly certain they hadn't been followed, a lucky break considering how easy it was to spot Penny's colorful vehicle on the road.

Max had been worried about crossing the border back into France, but his passport and visa checked out as usual; perhaps the border-control officials weren't on the alert for him yet, or they were only monitoring to make sure he didn't try to *leave* France. Getting out again could be tricky.

Whatever Max had thought might happen with Penny last night in her lavish Berlin hotel room had been totally derailed by Kevin Sharpe's call. Penny had headed straight for the queen-size bed—and sprawled out on it with her laptop. By the time Max had closed and locked the door and followed her inside, she was already preoccupied with her "digging."

Penny's online research quickly verified that the second floor of 15 Place Saint-Étienne was a rental property, but she couldn't find any information about its current resident. No searches for Lianna Stein or her former name, Monroe, turned up hits with Strasbourg, France. Penny even scoured surveillance photos of the area, street views on maps, and tagged tourist photos on the off chance one of them had captured a picture of Max's mom. She was very thorough—but Max had been too, and he'd had Risse helping him. None of their previous investigations had turned up anything, until this address.

The ground floor of the timber-framed house was dedicated to an organic-food restaurant, and the upper four stories seemed to be private apartments. The curtains on the second-floor windows were drawn. Penny had walked by the building when they first arrived and taken a snapshot of the intercom and its directory of tenants; strangely, the name on the second floor had been peeled away. No help there.

The sun set around 4:30 p.m., and as the streetlights came on, the second-floor windows remained dark. Those curtains hadn't so much as twitched the entire time they'd been watching.

Penny giggled.

"What?" Max asked.

"That statue of the flute boy in the fountain? It's called 'Der Meiselocker.'" She laughed again.

"Is that German?"

She nodded, reading from her phone's screen. "It was a gift."

"But why is it funny?"

"'Der Meiselocker' translates as 'The Tits-Charmer.'" She cracked up again. "I should get a selfie with him and send it to Risse. Oh, man. You should see the statue they traded for it. It was a naked dude with a fish in his hand. I am not making this stuff up." She held up her phone to show him the screen.

Max sighed. They'd clearly been sitting there for too long. Penny's brilliant mind was broken.

Max had had enough anyway. He certainly had heard everything he could stand about Strasbourg and the historic downtown area they were in, situated in the "Grand Island" surrounded by two branches of the river Ill. He now knew more about seventeenth-century architecture than any eighteen-year-old should. He didn't care about all the tourist destinations only blocks away that he didn't have time to visit. He was there for just one reason.

"The only suspicious thing around here is us." Max had taken a couple of runs around the block, both to keep warm and to keep an eye out for anyone watching them watching the house. If Sharpe was trying to trick or trap them, he was doing an excellent job at hiding it. For all they knew, the man himself was waiting in there for them.

"I told you we should have put a cup out with a sign that says, 'Need money for bandwidth,'" Penny said.

"I'm going in," Max said.

Penny checked the time on her phone. "It's only six o'clock. She might not be home from work yet."

"Then I'll have plenty of time to look around. If my mom lives there, she won't mind me letting myself in."

Hopefully she would be so happy to see him—after the shock wore off—that she wouldn't sweat the small points of how he'd gotten there. But while Max's dad was the most laid-back, supportive person he knew, the mother he vaguely remembered had been a stickler for Every. Little. Thing. Max could practically hear her repeating her favorite phrase, "The devil is in the details," better than he could recall the sound of her saying, "I love you."

"Coming?" Max asked. He tried not to betray how much he wanted Penny to say yes. He had played out this scenario with his mom a dozen different ways, but never with Penny at his side. Now that the moment had finally arrived, he was glad Penny was there, in case things didn't go as well as he hoped.

Would Lianna welcome her son, or had she completely written him off by now? How would he handle it if he was rejected—again?

"You just try to leave me behind." Penny rubbed her gloved hands together to warm them up. "But how do you plan to get inside?"

"I'm flattered that you think I have a plan. . . . Um, like

you said, people are coming home from work right now. I'll pretend I've lost my key?"

"They probably know everyone who lives here. Same reason we don't want to just ring all the buzzers." She tipped her head back and squinted, thinking. "We could just ask about who lives on the second floor. Maybe she even eats at that restaurant. You have a picture of her?"

In the last five hours, Max had imagined his mother eating in the organic-food restaurant, people-watching from the window seat; she'd always been a bit of a health nut. He'd imagined her walking down the street. Getting a cup of coffee at the shop on the corner. Sitting and reading next to the "Tits-Charmer" fountain.

Max smiled. *Okay, maybe that's a little funny.*

"What's with the creepy smile?" Penny asked.

He picked up his backpack and crossed the flagstone square to the street. After months of searching the internet and asking people if they knew his mom, he was too close to finding her to literally sit on the bench. He was tired of being on the sidelines—he wanted to be in the game.

Penny caught up with him at the private entrance of the building, panting out little clouds of breath. "At least it'll be warm inside. If we can get inside. Don't tell me you're going to use a credit card to break in."

Max studied the door to the upstairs apartments. It was painted TARDIS blue and had a wrought-iron grate in front of its window. He crouched and examined the lock.

"This looks old enough for that to actually work." He tried turning the cold knob in the center of the door first. You never knew with "historic" buildings like this, but it was definitively locked.

Max swung the bag on his right shoulder to his front and unzipped a side pocket. He pulled out the cloth roll Enzo had given him before he left for Berlin. He unrolled it and selected two of the shiny lockpicks.

"I thought your door-opening tool of choice was an axe," Penny said, referring to his attempt to free her from a locked office at Panjea with a prop axe from *The Lord of the Rings*—notably a very successful attempt, for all her kidding. "When did you learn to pick locks?"

"I'm versatile," Max said. "Enzo's into locksport. It's kind of like hacking into systems to challenge yourself, and because you can."

He fiddled with the slender tools, realized he was using the wrong end of one of them and turned it around, hoping that Penny hadn't noticed. She snorted.

"Stop looking over my shoulder. Make sure no one's watching us." He switched the hands in which he was holding each tool and started again.

"Because glancing around furtively while your friend pokes at a lock doesn't look suspicious," Penny said. "Make it quick. There are a lot of people around."

Max was as surprised as she was when the lock clicked almost immediately. He palmed the tools, turned the knob, and opened the door. *Old lock.* He grinned.

"Voilà!" he said.

"Beginner's luck." She had him there. Penny sauntered past him into the dimly lit foyer.

Max glanced behind him at the street, amazed no one was stopping them, and followed her inside. He closed out the cold and bought them some privacy while they got their bearings, stamping their tingling feet and rubbing their hands to restore circulation.

The narrow hallway was decorated with a strip of green Persian carpeting and an antique side table with a trendy vase and a round mirror. Penny flipped through the stack of envelopes on it, arranged by floor and the tenant's name.

"Second floor . . . Lee Hardy," she said. "Who's that?"

"You got me." The letter was official-looking, from the European Court of Human Rights.

"Should I . . . ?" she asked, picking at one corner of the sealed flap.

"That would be illegal."

"Ha." Penny replaced the envelope with a little pout.

They were way past illegal now. No gray areas involved with breaking and entering.

Max headed for the narrow staircase at the end of the hall. They clomped up the steps as softly as they could, but the aging, creaking wood loudly announced their presence. They reached the second-floor landing and faced another door.

Max pulled out his lockpicks.

"Why don't you try knocking first?" Penny said.

"Oh. Yeah," Max croaked, his throat dry.

Whether he was faking his way into a secure facility, playing in a big soccer match, or asking out a girl, Max had always managed to stay frosty under pressure. The fact that he had to concentrate on keeping his hands from shaking and that his legs felt like they might give out showed just how nervous he was.

As important as this was to Max, he was only now discovering how badly he wanted to see his mother again—and that a tiny, stupid part of him actually wanted to walk away.

Perhaps he had only wanted to find her because it was just another puzzle to figure out—a challenge that he hadn't been able to rise to without help.

Max rapped his knuckles softly against the door.

"Try again, Max," Penny said.

He knocked harder. And waited.

And waited.

Then he jumped as Penny jabbed her thumb against the doorbell, and an irritating, clanging buzz sounded throughout the apartment. No response. She jiggled the doorknob in frustration.

"I know you remember everything, but are you sure this is the right address?" she asked.

"It's definitely the address and apartment number Sharpe sent me. But what if his intel is old? If Mom did live here, she could have moved in the last year. Maybe that's why her name isn't downstairs."

"So you're up, Houdini. Dazzle me." Penny crossed her arms.

Max knelt before the door and wiped his sweaty palms on his jeans. This lock looked new. It was all shiny bronze, no scratches around the keyhole. He was relieved to see the name SCHLAGE etched above the keyhole.

"I've practiced on this brand," Max said. But Schlage made a number of different locks, and some were tricky. He hadn't advanced past the most basic single-pin mechanisms yet.

Max selected the L-shaped torsion wrench and a hook pick and started testing the lock. He heard Enzo's voice describing how to probe the tumbler inside and guide the pins into place so he could turn the plug. "Just point and click." Easier said than done. Defeating physical security like this required the same kind of concentration and trial and error that defeating virtual security did, only he didn't have months to work his way in.

Twelve minutes later, dripping sweat, hands trembling from exertion, Max rotated the wrench in his left hand, and the plug inside the lock turned.

He clambered to his feet and brushed nonexistent dirt from his knees. He turned the knob and the door opened.

"Open sesame," Max said.

"Wow," Penny said. Max smiled. It wasn't often he was able to impress her. "Can you teach me to do that?"

"Sure. I mean, there's an art to it, but locks like this one are pretty basic."

She raised an eyebrow. "Easy there, tiger. Don't get carried away. It did take you twelve minutes."

The door wide open, Max hesitated before crossing its threshold. Penny nudged him over it, then slipped inside and closed the door.

"Let's make this quick," Max said.

He opened the door to his left and found a dark bedroom with the shades drawn. He took a few steps inside, feeling like entering this intimate space was more of a trespass than entering the apartment itself. The bed was made and looked picture-perfect, like something out of an IKEA catalog, with way more pillows than any bed needed and extra sheets and a duvet with an abstract gray-and-black pattern swirling over it. Was this his mother's style?

The floral scent—honey and lavender?—brought Max back to his childhood, watching his mother get ready for work in the morning. She had never worn much makeup, but every day she spritzed on the same perfume—this perfume. The sensory memory helped him recall his mother more vividly than he had been able to in the last thirteen years. But that didn't guarantee that she lived here.

He breathed in the familiar smell and sneezed three times in a row. He wiped his sleeve across his nose, then picked up a hairbrush on the dresser. The golden strands tangled in its bristles dashed his hopes. His mother's hair was black.

Professional clothes hung in the closet, suits and blouses and dresses neatly arranged by color. Shoes lined the floor, similarly arranged.

He opened the blinds beside the bed and looked out onto a courtyard behind the house. The snow was disturbed by tracks, the imprints of shoes and paws leading to and from distinctive yellow patches. He shut the blinds and left the bedroom.

Max found Penny sitting at a steel-and-particleboard computer desk in the spacious living room/kitchen, typing on a beat-up old Lenovo laptop.

"What are you doing?" Max asked.

"What I do best," Penny said. She mashed the keys like a deranged pianist for a few seconds. "There. I'm in the Pentagon."

The Windows login screen showed the truth: a long string of asterisks filling the password field. Username: Lee.

"Stop goofing around and help me look for clues."

"I *am* looking for clues. I already explored everything but the kitchen. The apartment's pretty, but it's small, and there's practically nothing here. Generic art on the walls, boring furniture, no personal photos. No books—never trust someone who doesn't own books, even classics and bestsellers just to pretend they read."

That didn't sound like his mother. She had loved reading. Most of the books in Max's house had been hers—and he'd read them dozens of times. His clearest memories of her were them reading together at bedtime.

It was so strange that he couldn't remember everything about her, when he could recite a forty-two-character string of numbers and letters flawlessly after merely glancing at it.

"It's like no one lives here," Penny said.

"Except for the computer and a telltale hairbrush in the bedroom."

"I mean 'no one' in the metaphorical sense. I've been in hotel rooms with more personality."

"So maybe she doesn't like *stuff*."

"Or she wants to be able to leave at a moment's notice. Or already *has* left," Penny said.

"Let me take a crack at this password while you investigate the kitchen," Max said.

He sat down in front of the computer and pondered the login screen. He cracked his knuckles and rested his fingers on the keys. The keyboard had the AZERTY layout used in France and Belgium.

Penny called from the kitchen. "Two plates, two bowls, two mugs in the cupboards. No silverware—just a pile of disposable chopsticks from takeout and a spork, of all things."

"Any tea?" Max asked.

"Hold on . . ." Max heard a cupboard open. "Yes! Oolong." Mom's favorite.

"Okay," Max said. He cleared the password field and started typing. Penny came up behind him and flipped his hood over his head.

"That's better," she said.

He pushed the hood back.

His first guess at the password failed. So did the second.

"Third time's the charm." He hit Enter. Still locked.

"Hmmm. I wonder . . ." Max tried the three passwords

again, this time typing with the classic American QWERTY layout in mind.

The password screen disappeared and the desktop appeared: a picture of a fluffy gray kitten.

"What was it?" Penny asked.

"Dad has a simple system for generating passwords, which uses your birth date to shift the letters in the alphabet so any word you type looks like it was randomly generated. I use it too. I don't know how long ago he was using that method, but I tried it with Mom's birthday, November 16. But I had to use the American keyboard layout. She must have changed the settings and you can't tell when you're only seeing asterisks in the password field."

"What base word did she use?"

His first two guesses had been her own name, then Dad's. Max swallowed. "Maxwell."

"D'awww . . . ," Penny said.

The older computer took its time loading icons, and navigating the system was painfully slow. The hard drive clicked and whirred, noisy compared to the solid-state drive Max had in his machine. But he worked quickly to assess the system for any interesting data—and he was pleased to see it was reasonably secure.

"Is that her cat on the wallpaper?" Penny asked. "I didn't see"—she sniffed—"or smell one anywhere."

"Mom's allergic to cats, so we never got one. This looks like a LOLcat, without the meme text." Max opened the documents folder. "Here, look at this." Penny leaned on his shoulder to read the screen. "I don't see anything unusual."

"That's just it. Just like her apartment, there isn't anything personal on here. But aha! Here's a hidden, encrypted folder. Good for you, Mom."

Max closed the window and opened a web browser—an open-source search engine. *That* was surprising.

"You're giving up already?" Penny asked.

"I don't need to break into her private files. I just wanted to confirm that she lives here, and it looks like she does. Now I want to know *who* she is." Max typed in "Lee Hardy" and "Strasbourg."

He pieced together his mother's life one link at a time. As Lee Hardy, she was president and co-founder of Monde Libre, a nonprofit human-rights organization that supported victims of human trafficking throughout the European Union. She had been in Strasbourg for three years, but apparently had lived in Paris before that, where she had produced documentary films about France's homeless population.

"My mom's a hero," Max said.

"Guess it runs in the family," Penny said.

Max looked for recent images of his mom online, finding surprisingly few for someone in such a prominent, respected position. One photo showed her giving a presentation at a tech talk just three months ago; her hair was blonde and styled in a short bob.

Max stared at her face, reconciling it with the fading image he'd had of her for years. Then he became preoccupied when he saw another photo of her holding hands with a heavyset, silver-haired gentleman.

A crash at the door made him jump. He and Penny whirled around to see a man in a blue uniform and peaked cap rush inside and point a gun at them.

"*Police! Ne bougez plus!*" the man yelled. Another officer joined him, also armed. "*Ne bougez plus!*"

"Oh, shit." Max slowly raised his hands.

10

YOU HAVE THE RIGHT TO ANSWER QUESTIONS OR *the right to remain silent.*

Ha.

At the police station, Max was presented with a paper acknowledging that he knew why he was being detained—breaking and entering, suspicion of burglary—and that he knew his rights. Max signed, then exercised his right to explain that he was Lee Hardy's son and she wouldn't mind him being in her apartment.

Since they had different names and he was unable to provide his mother's contact information, other than the address at which he'd been arrested, the police didn't believe him. Instead, they called his dad in the U.S.

Max wasn't allowed to speak to him, so he didn't have a chance to apologize for making him worry, for disappointing him, for ruining Christmas. Given his own past, his dad wouldn't be as upset about Max getting arrested as he was about the reason for it. Max hadn't told him about searching for his mother. *What must Dad be thinking now?*

Max had plenty else to deal with himself. The police notified the embassy of Max's arrest and put Max in a cramped and cold holding cell while they "continued the investigation" and made arrangements for a judge to set a trial date. They said they would try to find him an English-speaking lawyer. But it didn't sound like they planned to try very hard.

Max assumed that Penny was being treated similarly, though it would be worse for her due to her distrust of authority figures. With good reason: She had a lot to hide. And she probably wouldn't cooperate in contacting her mother, who hadn't the slightest clue that Penny was in Europe.

It only took the French police three hours to realize who they had in custody and demand to know what "noted hacker" Max Stein was trying to do with Lee Hardy's computer. For the second time in as many days, Max was asked to log in to his laptop and phone. He refused and wondered if he would ever get out of here. They could only hold him for twenty-four hours, he thought, but he only knew enough about the French judicial system to have little faith that they had his best interests in mind.

After seven hours in detention, Max was convinced that Kevin Sharpe had set him and Penny up after all—and worse, had done something to his mother to get her out of the way.

But why have them arrested? To stop them from helping Ada Kiesler? Where was Lianna Stein? Was Sharpe seeking revenge by tormenting Max with doubt about what had happened to her?

That question, at least, was answered when the door to his cell opened, and his mother walked in.

They stared at each other, and the moment seemed to stretch. Max forgot where and when he was. The years between them faded away like wet tears on a pillow, and he was a five-year-old boy again. Without knowing how he got there, he was up and at the door, hugging her. *Being hugged.* At last.

Then she held him at arm's length, and they got a good look at each other. He would never again forget how she looked: older, yes. Different from how she should. She was a foot and a half shorter than him, which would take some getting used to. But this was Lianna Stein. Mom. The one person in his life who could do no wrong.

Until she did.

He opened his mouth and tried to speak, but he couldn't form the word. He cleared the thickness from his throat and tried again. "Mom."

"Maxwell! Oh, honey, it's really you. You're so tall!"

Her voice. How he'd missed hearing her say his name.

She wouldn't let go of his hands, and he didn't want her to. Her hands were smaller than they'd seemed when he was five, but their touch still made him feel safe and cared for and loved. Her honey-and-lavender scent tickled his nose.

"What on earth are you doing here?" she asked.

"In prison or in France?" he said. "It doesn't matter; same answer. I was looking for you. Instead, *you* found *me*." Just like he'd always wanted.

She smiled.

"I tried to tell the cops we're related, but . . ."

"They're being extra cautious because of some disturbing messages I've received."

"What? Like, threats?"

She shrugged. "It comes with my line of work. So I left town for a few days and met with some clients in Germany while the police kept an eye on my apartment. During their rounds, they saw a light on upstairs, knew I was away, and assumed you were burglars. When they called to tell me whom they had arrested, I tried to explain that you're my son, but they insisted I identify you in person. I hurried back."

"Thanks."

"I pulled some strings—some big ones—and you're free to go. Obviously I'm not pressing charges, but the police are charging you anyway. Possessing lockpicks with intent to commit a crime is, shockingly, illegal."

"So what happens now?"

"They're keeping your passport, and you're released on bail—under my supervision. You can't leave France." Lianna hesitated. "That'll be rough on your father, I know."

"How long do I have to stay?" Max asked.

"The judge set the trial for January 10."

"*January?*" Max sighed. He wasn't just going to miss Christmas, but New Year's and the start of the new term.

"On the bright side, that gives us more time together." Lianna stepped out of the cell and held the door open for him. "This isn't how I imagined our reunion would be."

"Me neither," he said.

He'd always imagined, *hoped*, that he would come home from school one day and his mom would be there, like she'd never left. Usually a glass of milk and plate of cookies was involved, because why not? His idea of what having a mother was like had been shaped more from thirteen years of TV and movies than from his actual experience of five years, most of which he'd forgotten.

Over the years since she'd left, he'd revised his expectations to a letter waiting for him when he got home. A postcard. Finally, it had been easier to cope by not rushing home after school. Instead, he spent his free time at Evan's house, pretending Mrs. B. was Max's mom too, or hanging at the bookstore, or hacking at Denny's. He'd started running, taken up soccer. Bradley Stein had retreated more and more into his work when his son basically disappeared too.

Max couldn't say all that to his mother. Not yet.

She shrugged. "Then again, consider your parentage. I met your father in jail. Did he ever tell you the story?"

"A couple of times." A couple *thousand* times. But Max never tired of hearing about it.

Bradley and Lianna been arrested at the same political

rally. His dad couldn't remember what they'd been protesting at the time, but he could recall every detail of what they'd said in the cell packed in with twenty other people before Lianna's parents—who were much wealthier than his own—had posted her bail. He usually said it had been the second best night of his life. Ask about the first at your peril.

The police clerk handed him his belongings—absent his passport and lockpicks. He immediately made sure that Ada's fake nickel was still there, but he would have to wait until they left before he checked for the memory card inside. If it was missing, there wasn't much he could do anyway. It might even be a blessing if it got out through some other way, sparing Max a tough decision and an even tougher road if he allowed himself to get swept into her and Penny's mission.

"Oh! Penny!" Max said. He couldn't believe he'd nearly forgotten her in the shock and excitement over seeing his mom.

"What penny?" Lianna said.

"My, uh, friend Penny was arrested with me. Can you help spring her too? Her family isn't around to bail her out."

"I'll see what I can do." Lianna went back to the front desk and called over an officer.

"Hey, what took you so long?" Penny said, from right behind Max.

Max spun around. She was holding an open bottle of Orangina and a bag of chips.

"Penny! How'd you escape?"

"They let me out hours ago. I hung around to see if there

was anything I could do to help you." She fell quiet, looking over Max's shoulder.

"Is this your friend?" Lianna said, coming up alongside Max.

"Yeah," Max said.

Penny smiled. "Penny Polonsky. Nice to meet you, Mrs. St—Hardy?"

"Call me Lee." Lianna went in for the double-cheek kiss, which Penny managed gracefully.

"Penny Polonsky," Lianna said. "Perfect name for a super-hero in disguise."

Penny glanced at Max.

"I didn't tell her to say that." He turned to Lianna. "I said something similar when we first met. I guess she didn't need your help, but thanks for trying."

Lianna nodded. "They only have *you* on video picking that lock, Maxwell. Penny was technically an accessory, but Monsieur Roy, my landlord, doesn't care about that," she said.

"Do you think the police asked him to press charges against me to keep me here? For some reason they think I'm a threat to national security." They had no idea Penny was the hacker they should be worried about.

"I'm afraid he's always had it in for me, and this is one way to make my life difficult," Lianna said. "Shall we get out of here? You two must be exhausted."

"I found us a hotel," Penny said to Max.

Lianna's eyebrows shot up. She looked from Max to Penny.

"Maxwell is staying at my place, but we have plenty of room for you too, Penny," Lianna said brightly. "Oh, you know. You've seen it already." She puffed out a cheek.

Things suddenly felt extremely awkward.

"Thank you, but I'll be all right," Penny said. Staying with Max and his mother was clearly the last thing she wanted to do. "You two have a lot to catch up on. I have to head back to Berlin for work in the morning." She avoided looking at Max.

Technically he had to go with his mom, since he'd been released to her custody. But the prospect of spending all that time alone with her, so soon. . . . He saw the same uncertainty he felt in his mom's face. He definitely wanted Penny around for moral support and as a buffer between them.

"Come on, Penny," Max said. "Didn't you want to check out Strasbourg's famed Christmas market?"

"I do. It's the oldest one in France. The Christkindelsmärik dates back to 1570," Penny said.

"How do you know that?" Lianna asked.

"How do you *not*?" Penny said.

"I'd say you shouldn't miss it, especially since you're already here," Lianna said. "And I do insist on you staying with us. The more the merrier!"

It was only when they were in a taxi on their way back to Lianna's apartment that Max began questioning the wisdom of bringing his mother and his girlfriend together. He hoped he wouldn't end up regretting this trip after all.

11

THE APARTMENT ON PLACE SAINT-ÉTIENNE FELT
different when Max entered it this time. Not quite like home,
but more like it. Just like Lianna didn't feel like Mom yet—but
she was more than a stranger.

She showed Penny to her small guest room and made it
clear that Max would be sleeping on the couch in the living
room. Penny requested a shower after her brief stint in prison
("Orange is the new yuck," she said), and Max and his mom
went into the living room.

"Tea?" Lianna asked.

"Sure," Max said.

"I think I only have oolong."

"I know."

She frowned.

"I mean, that's perfect."

He didn't tell her that a box of her oolong tea lived at the back of their pantry at home. He and his dad preferred coffee as their caffeine-delivery system, but neither had felt moved to toss her tea. Max had tasted it once. He'd hated it, but he wasn't sure if that was because the leaves were almost as old as he was.

Now when he sipped the hot beverage his mother brought him, he was sure: He hated oolong tea, even after adding enough sugar and powdered creamer to attract her notice. He dipped in a stale cookie from a questionable tin she'd found at the back of a cabinet. The combination made both the tea and cookie edible.

They had so much to say that they said nothing at all for a few minutes. Max was content—more content than he had been for a long time—just to be near her again.

He was also slightly distracted by the sound of running water from the bathroom, which reminded him that only fifty feet away, Penny was showering. Naked.

His mother's voice snapped him out of it.

"I'm very curious about why you were snooping around my place, Maxwell. Almost as curious as I am about how you found it." She snapped her fingers. "Hey. Are you hoping you'll spontaneously develop X-ray vision?"

Max turned to face her, realizing he'd been staring at the closed door of the bathroom while thinking about Penny. Lianna wore a bemused expression. He blushed.

To recover, he was a bit harsher than he meant to be. "I

think *you* owe me and Dad an explanation more."

"You must have a lot of questions," she said.

Max nodded. *Why? How could you? Where have you been all these years? Was it something I did?*

"Have you called Dad?" Max asked.

Stupid.

Lianna looked relieved. "No. I suppose I should?" She held her steaming mug between her hands like it was a life preserver keeping her afloat in the open sea. "Would Brad be surprised by what you did?"

"He'd be surprised that I got caught."

She pressed her lips together. "I see."

Anger flashed through Max for a second at her judgmental tone, which she certainly had no right to, but he tamped it down. Swallowed his anger and chased it with a sip of tea.

"Why 'Lee Hardy'?" he asked.

"Your grandpa and my best friend, Susie, used to call me Lee. And Hardy . . . that's my husband's name. My second husband." She gazed deep into her cup. "Or rather, my second *ex*-husband. We're divorced, but he's a local politician, so his name carries some advantages. Like when your son gets arrested for burglary."

"Oh," Max said. "Wow."

Wow that she had married someone else—Hardy must be that gray-haired man from the society photo Max had stumbled across before the police arrived.

Wow that she was using that guy's name for her personal

benefit. Max didn't have the heart or the strength to ask if their marriage had always been a strategic move or if she had actually loved him.

"I know how that sounds, but . . ." Lianna picked up a cookie and turned it over in her hands. "I liked having a brand new identity for a while, getting to start over. Everyone should be allowed to choose who they want to be."

"Did you ever miss your old life?" Max asked.

"I missed *you*. I loved being your mother. I loved our house and your father and the way we were a team. Sometimes I even miss Granville and having a simple nine-to-five day job, coming home to your dad's cooking, and reading stories to you while tucking you in at night.

"But this life is really good too, and I built it for myself. My work . . . I'm *helping* people."

"Who?" Max asked. "I know you founded Monde Libre, but what do you actually do?"

She scratched behind her right ear while squinting her right eye. "A lot of things. Lately we've been working a lot with stopping cyber violence against women. Abuse online, stalking, doxxing, that kind of thing. It's far more prevalent than people realize."

Max nodded.

"The digital world has been facilitating real-world dangers, including human trafficking."

"You mean like the illegal sex trade?"

"Exactly." Lianna pursed her lips. "There's a hidden website out there where people can buy, sell, or rent pretty much anything, including—"

"The Curtain?" Max asked.

She blinked. "You've heard of it? I've been investigating The Curtain for almost two years."

He stared at her. This couldn't be a coincidence. Ada had mentioned The Curtain and then Sharpe sent Max to his mom, who was also investigating it?

"How did you discover it?" he asked.

"Monde Libre provides trafficking victims with counseling, medical care, housing. We also encourage them to testify against their captors. I've interviewed dozens of women who have been sold through it. More than sixty-five percent of all sex trafficking happens via The Curtain." She frowned. "Unfortunately The Curtain protects the criminals using it too well."

Max nodded. He'd been reading up on The Curtain since talking to Ada and Sharpe, and the biggest issue was that the site somehow thwarted any and all attempts to index its content. International agencies had been devoting special task forces to target deep web markets and developing search tools to crawl the unexplored depths of the internet, but The Curtain was impenetrable.

Almost as if a major telecommunications company was devoting resources to deflect attempts to probe it.

This was just one of the reasons why The Curtain had quickly risen to the number-one black-market website.

"But you're also just treating the symptoms, not the disease," Max said. "You need to find the person or organization running The Curtain and shut it down."

"If only. If we knew who the Wizard is, we could go after him and save many more lives. My job would become a lot easier." Lianna sighed. "Max, I shouldn't have left the way I did. I *am* sorry about that."

"You shouldn't have left at all."

"But I don't regret that decision. If that makes me a terrible person . . ." She looked at Max and faltered. "Well, I'm a terrible person. Far short of mother of the year. But I am a person, and we all have to make our own choices and live with them. And out here . . . I've done a lot of good."

"For strangers. What about your own family?" Max hated himself the moment he said that. He had put his life on the line for plenty of people he didn't know and would never meet. He believed in what she was doing, but he couldn't help wanting what he wanted. He'd given up so much for others, and now he was finding out that he'd lost his mother for the same reason.

"Don't be selfish," she said.

Her words were a slap to his face. "We're all selfish. You say you left to go out and do some good, but you did that for yourself, because it made you the person you thought you should be."

I know what that's like, he wanted to say. Forget the proverbial sins of the father—Max was discovering he was more his mother's son than he'd ever realized.

"I was often tempted to call or write, but I thought it was better for you both if I didn't. Safer," Lianna said.

"Safer? What were you keeping us safe from? You have a supervillain archnemesis I don't know about?"

"There are plenty of ways to hurt someone that don't involve tying them up and dangling them over a giant vat of molten wax. I've made some waves. I didn't want you two to pay for my actions. Once you're a public figure, the media owns you. Which is why I divorced Roland. I've been trying to keep a low profile here under a different identity."

Roland?

"But we paid anyway, didn't we, Mom? Or should I call you 'Lee'?" he said.

"Maxwell . . ."

"You don't even know that I prefer 'Max.'"

"Max, then."

"Why did you work so hard to erase all traces of Lianna Stein?" he asked.

She jerked her hand, and tea splashed onto her fingers and the scratched oak table. "I was afraid."

"That Dad or I would find you?"

She shook her head. "I was afraid to find out what you thought of me after leaving. If you hated me, I would rather not know. I was worried that I would lose my resolve and try to come home. Part of me was afraid that you didn't miss me all that much—that your lives had marched on without me, and you were fine. So I concentrated on doing what I could for the people who didn't have anyone else to turn to. I knew your father would do a good job with you." She tilted her head. "He did, didn't he?"

"He's the best." Max folded his hands and pushed his palms against each other. "I don't hate you, Mom. I'm angry. I hate what you did, and I hated not knowing why. . . . But I also never stopped loving and missing you."

"Me neither. I've been so proud of you, Max. I couldn't believe it when you popped up on the news last year with that whole Panjea business. I'm sorry about your friend Evan."

Max swallowed some more tea and blinked back tears. "Yeah. I wish you could have known him."

"Sometimes the work we do gets dangerous," she said.

Max was pleased that she thought of him as an equal in her social-justice efforts.

"Sometimes it's *too* dangerous. You see that now, right?" she said.

"What?" Max straightened in surprise.

"Six people died to bring down Panjea. You were lucky." She held up her hands, palms out in apology. "What I'm getting at is, this is why I left. I had to go before our political activism went too far and Brad or I got arrested or hurt, or worse—someone targeted you."

"You were worried about *me*?" Max said.

Lianna twisted the silver bracelet on her left wrist with the thumb and middle finger of her right hand. "Your father and I used to organize rallies and peaceful protests. You might not remember—"

"You two were out a lot." Sometimes they were gone for

weeks at a time, leaving Max with his "aunt" Riley, who was not a real relative.

"Remember when Dad was in the hospital?" Lianna asked.

"From the hit-and-run?" Max asked.

She nodded. "We said it was a car accident, but he was beaten up at a rally. While he was taken to the hospital, unconscious, I was arrested. I spent the night in jail, not knowing if he was even alive."

Max fell back against the couch, stunned. He had never heard *this* story.

"The person who attacked him had been sending death threats for weeks—to our house. That's when I knew something needed to change. It was irresponsible for us to continue like that. We had to put you first, and I didn't want you to grow up without your parents."

Max snorted.

Lianna ignored him. "When I suggested that working from within the system could be just as effective, with less of the risk, Bradley felt betrayed. He said we'd be letting down too many people. I realized I'd been a bad influence on him—I had done too good a job of encouraging him to keep that life going. I didn't want to do the same thing to you, so I removed myself from the equation."

"The 'equation'? Life isn't a damn math problem." Max slapped the table. "Mom! What the hell. This is the worst apology I've ever heard."

Lianna narrowed her eyes. "I told you I'm not apologizing.

I'm just telling you what happened." Her words became cool and clipped. Max knew that tone of voice all too well; she was pissed. But so was he, and he had been saving this up for too long to stop now.

"You owe me so much more than some weak excuse for why you had to take off in order to protect me. You don't make those kinds of decisions for other people. We're adults, and we can make choices for ourselves."

"You were six," she said.

"I was *five*. But I grew up real fast after you left." He crossed his arms and stared at a yellow stain on the wall behind her head.

"Maxwell— Max. I needed to figure things out, what I wanted my life to be. I couldn't do that while I was still there with you and your father."

He rolled his eyes. "Oh, so you needed to go find yourself or something. I'm sorry we made that so inconvenient for you."

"Did you just roll your eyes at me?" Lianna smiled.

"What?"

"Nothing . . . I mean, I thought I had missed that phase of your life." She swept her fingers toward him. "The whole angry teenager thing, you know? Although I'm starting to feel sorry for your father."

Max couldn't help it: He laughed.

"I must have picked that up from Penny." He glanced toward the bathroom again and saw Penny standing there with a towel wrapped around her hair and another covering everything from her armpits down.

"Hey. Um, sorry to interrupt. What's your Wi-Fi password?" Penny asked.

"I don't have Wi-Fi," Lianna said.

Penny was stunned.

"You can plug in—" Lianna started to point to her desk.

"Never mind. I'll sort it out." Penny glanced at Max and adjusted her towel. "I think I'm turning in for the night."

"Uh, okay. Good night," Max said.

"Good night, Penny," Lianna said.

Penny walked away, shaking her head slowly in disbelief. When the door to the guest room had closed, another silence settled over the conversation.

"Just friends?" Lianna smirked. She *smirked*.

"It's complicated," Max said.

"It always is." She sighed. "You and I have a lot of time to make up for. But I'm glad you came here. Your turn: How did you find me?"

"Oh." Max hesitated. Should he tell her about Kevin Sharpe? Max hadn't even told Penny everything he'd said on the phone. And what about Ada Kiesler?

Max was ashamed to admit that he didn't think he should trust his own mother with that information, particularly with her ties to the French government. She also seemed a bit conflicted over his activism.

Plus, he'd lost his faith in her when she'd abandoned him.

"You know . . . hacking," he said. He wiggled his fingers in front of him like Penny had, miming typing on a keyboard.

Something clicked in her expression. "Penny's a hacker too? I've heard her name before. She was mixed up in Panjea."

"Yup. That's how we met," Max said. "We couldn't keep her entirely out of the news since she'd been kidnapped and all, but we didn't share everything about her involvement."

"That'll be a story for your kids one day." She grinned.

"Mom." How could she joke about that, while also making sure he and Penny were sleeping in separate rooms? Parents were so weird.

"Did she help you track me down?" Lianna asked.

"Sort of." Indirectly, she had. And if it hadn't been for her stunt with the TSA watch list, Max would already be back in the U.S. with no idea that his mother had been in France after all.

"I'll have to find out how so she can tell me how to cover my trail better." Max heard a phone buzz.

"Sorry." Lianna pulled out her phone—an old-school flip phone—and glanced at a text message. She paled. "That's terrible."

"What?" Max asked.

Lianna started texting. Focused on her business, whatever it was, she seemed like a different person again.

"A girl I've been working with. She needs me. I have to see her."

"You're going out?" Max asked.

"Just for a couple of hours." Her phone vibrated again. She peeked at it. "I'll be back soon and we'll continue this. . . ." She looked around. "Will you be all right here?"

"I'll be fine. I'm practically an adult now."

"Practically." Her eyes flicked toward Penny's room. "Be good while I'm gone?"

Max stopped himself from rolling his eyes. What, was she planning to call a babysitter for him?

"Yes, Mom," he said.

"I could be back at any moment. You won't know when."

"*Go.* I'm gonna get some sleep. I'm wiped."

After she left, Max sat on the couch until the teapot was cold, mulling over their conversation. He lost track of the time until Penny flounced down on the couch beside him.

In a damp gray tank top and purple panties.

Penny acted like it was no big deal, so he played it cool. Nothing he hadn't seen before. Even so. Hard not to stare.

Grow up, Max.

"So how'd that go?" She kicked her bare feet up on the coffee table and balanced her open laptop on her knees.

"Not great, not terrible."

"Vaguebooking."

"Sorry. I'm still processing everything."

"She seems nice."

"Yeah."

Penny cleared her throat. "So, I can't help noticing that we're finally alone. . . ."

"Oh? I thought you came out here to review more of Ada's files."

"That too." She closed her laptop and set it aside. Then she turned toward Max and raised her eyebrows. He grinned and leaned toward her.

Much hot, very kissing. Wow.

Penny swung a leg over Max's lap to straddle him and started unbuttoning his shirt.

They kept kissing until Penny pulled away. "Max?"

"Mmmm?" He opened his eyes slowly.

"You seem distracted."

"What? No, *you're* distracted." He reached for her.

"Nope." She slid off him and curled up on the couch. He sighed and pulled his shirt closed.

"Trust me. You're miles away right now." Penny ran her fingers through her hair. Her cheeks were flushed, and she looked annoyed.

"Okay. You're right. I'm in Berlin," he said.

"Berlin?"

"I've been thinking about Ada." Penny glared. "Her *mission*. Your mission. I've decided to help."

"Really?" Penny's face lit up. "I'm that good a kisser?"

"Yes, that's why," Max said. "No. Although you are a phenomenal kisser." He wished they could get back to that. But he had to say this first.

"Then what changed your mind?" she asked.

He told her about his mother's connection to The Curtain.

"So you think you can help her by shutting it down." Penny shrugged. "I guess I don't care why you want to work with us.

I'm just glad you are."

"There's something else, and you're not going to like this part."

"You're full of surprises tonight, Max. Lay it on me." She smiled mischievously.

"Before, when Kevin Sharpe called . . . he wants me to help *him*, to find out what Ada has on VT so he can prove that President Lovett isn't involved. Or to hide it if she is. He didn't want me to tell you. He said I couldn't trust you."

Max watched Penny's face nervously as he waited for her reaction. She didn't even blink. When she did speak, it was very calmly. He almost would have preferred it if she'd yelled at him.

"You trust *him*?" Penny asked. "Your nemesis?"

"That's dramatic," Max said. "I decided to wait until I had more information. Which I now have. I think Sharpe knows something about The Curtain and VT, and that's why he knew where to find my mother—because she's been investigating it. Ada is the key here."

"So you're going to play her to play him to learn what he's really after."

"No, I'll tell Mom the truth. There's that old saying: The enemy of my enemy is my friend. I don't like Sharpe, but if he's against The Curtain . . . if he's targeting Verbunden Telekom, maybe this time we can use *him*. You have to agree he's a good person to have in your corner."

"This sounds risky, Max."

"Risk is our business. And of course, I still don't know what you and Ada are actually up to. So who has the moral high ground here?"

Penny pushed Max back down into the couch cushions and climbed back on him, pinning him down. "Looks like I do."

"Now you're trying to distract me," Max said.

"You bet I am." She leaned down and kissed him. She really was a phenomenal kisser.

"Any objections?" she asked. Her dangling hair tickled his nose.

"Nope. But, Penny, at some point you have to tell me what's going on."

"Later. Much later . . ." She nuzzled his neck and slipped a hand inside his shirt. "On the trip back to Berlin. We have to go back to talk to Ada again."

"Mmmm . . . As you wish."

12

MAX WOKE TO THE SOUND OF SOMEONE CLEARING her throat. He looked up blearily at his mother, standing over him with her arms crossed.

"Mom!" Max struggled to sit up, but there was a weight on him. He pulled it off him—it was Penny's arm. She had been curled around him, between him and the couch cushions. They must have fallen asleep. He was relieved that at least they were both dressed—him more than Penny. They'd been making out, but that was all. She tried to snuggle into him, still asleep.

"I know what this looks like," he said.

"Do you?" Lianna sighed. "I'm not mad. I'm not even surprised. But I am embarrassed. . . . We have a guest." She nodded toward the door.

Max turned and saw a tall, dark-haired woman, not much

older than him, in his mother's hooded wool coat, clutching an oversize, stuffed beige purse.

"Hey," he said.

She looked at his mother cautiously.

"This is my son, Maxwell. Max," Lianna said. She repeated it in German.

"Ah," the woman said. "Nadia." He couldn't place her accent exactly, but it sounded Russian.

"Nadia's going to stay here for a while," Lianna said.

Max got up from the couch and ran a hand through his hair. "Oh. Um. What time is it?" Gray light at the window told him it was early morning and overcast.

"Eight thirty." She spoke to Nadia in German. Nadia glanced at Max again, then went into Lianna's room and closed the door.

"Sorry," Max said.

Lianna pressed her lips together. Max lowered his voice. "The Curtain?" he asked.

She nodded. "I'm making eggs. Still like them scrambled?"

"Well . . . can you do an omelette?" Max asked.

"*Absolument!* Omelette-making is a requirement for French citizenship."

"You're a French citizen?!"

"I've been living here a long time. But I'm an American citizen too."

"Wow. Okay." Max watched his mom crack an egg into a large blue mixing bowl. "I'll grab a shower."

She nodded.

When Max returned from the bathroom, Nadia and Penny were sitting on the couch with cups of tea. When they saw him, they giggled.

"Hi," Max said. "Good morning, Penny."

She yawned and rubbed the back of her neck. "We'll see."

He went into the small adjacent kitchen to see if he could help his mother with breakfast.

"You were out all night. Did you sleep?" he asked.

"Not much." Her mouth twitched. "I guess you didn't either."

"Look, Mom . . ."

"It's okay. You're seventeen now—"

"Eighteen."

She squinted. "Eighteen. Are you sure?"

"Aren't you?"

She paused. "Right. Yes. Eighteen. Anyway, you're old enough to make your own decisions, and when I was your age . . ." She poured the egg mixture into the pan.

"Let's not go there," Max said.

"Good idea."

His mother had brought home some groceries in a canvas bag. He finished putting them away and loaded the toaster with slices of bread.

"Penny seems great," she said.

"She is," Max said. "Really smart. If you somehow couldn't tell."

"Nothing wrong with showing how smart you are. Especially when so many people will try to ignore it."

"She's doing a lot to help people too. Not the way you do, but she seems to have it all figured out."

"You don't?"

"No," Max said. "I want to do some good, but it doesn't come as naturally to me. Penny says I should put myself out there more."

"Uh-oh," Lianna said.

"Uh-oh?"

She tipped the pan and gently lifted the edges of the omelette with a spatula.

"Mom," he said.

She lowered the flame on the burner and put down the spatula. She faced him. "It sounds like she's pushing you to do something you're not that invested in."

"I wouldn't say that . . ."

"Maybe, but I can see it on your face."

"You're right. I'm worried she's taking things to an extreme these days. She's very committed." .

"I know the type." Lianna smiled wryly. "Hey, take it from me: Don't let her overly influence your decisions. If you get in too deep, you'll regret it one day, and then you'll resent her for it."

"Are we still talking about me and Penny?" Max folded his arms.

"All I'm saying is, keep some perspective. Ask yourself why

you're getting involved. Is it important to you, or are you more concerned with what she thinks about you?"

"*She's* important to me." He glanced back at the women in the living room.

"I don't mean to cause any trouble between you two. I'm actually glad Penny's here. It might help Nadia to have someone closer to her age who also speaks German. She'll open up more."

"So she's from Germany?"

"No, but she's been living there, in a town called Kehl just on the other side of the border. About a ten-minute drive from here. She was brought there three years ago from Bulgaria."

Brought there. Max let that sink in. "She was trafficked?"

"Yes. She was only fifteen."

"And she's been selling . . . People buy sex with her through The Curtain? How did she get mixed up in that?"

"There are lots of reasons. Hundreds of thousands of them every year." Lianna seemed weary, but not from lack of sleep. "Nadia's story is unique, and it's just like everyone else's. I'm still getting the details, but it sounds like she's more than ready to go home. If we can get her back there."

"About that. Mom, I can't tell you why right now, but I've decided to return to Berlin with Penny."

Lianna froze and stared at Max. "Say again?"

"We're going back to Berlin. Penny . . . *we've* been working on something that might help expose The Curtain."

"Max, what have you two gotten involved in now?"

"I'm not sure yet. But we may be able to get that evidence you've been looking for to shut down The Curtain."

"I want that to be true, but . . . Max, I'm sorry. You can't go."

"Huh?"

"You were released into my custody."

"I'm eighteen!"

"That doesn't matter. You aren't allowed to leave France until your trial. Those are the terms of your release, and I vouched for you."

"*Mom.*"

"It's the law. Frankly, even if it weren't the case, I wouldn't let you go anyway."

Max narrowed his eyes. "You're playing the mom card?"

She sighed. "I just . . . We just reunited. I was hoping we'd get to spend more time together. Christmas in Strasbourg is lovely."

"Your eggs are burning," Max said.

Lianna looked down at the smoldering pan. "*Crotte!*" she said.

Max helped her start over with a clean pan. "We'll discuss this later," Lianna said.

"Right," Max said.

Lianna divided the omelette into four portions and scraped them onto plates. Max helped her carry them out to the small dining table in the corner of the living room. Nadia and Penny were acting like they were old friends.

Max had never seen her like this. Penny didn't make friends

easily, partly from lack of time, partly from lack of interest. And a large part from lack of trust.

Max and Penny didn't live close enough to spend time with each other's social groups, so the only other person he saw her interact with regularly was Risse. For obvious reasons, when Max was visiting them, Penny wasn't interested in having her little sister tag along.

Penny had asked Max what he considered "normal." All he could come up with was what other people's lives were like and what people expected things to be like: Basically, what you saw on television. You had a girlfriend who didn't live seven hours away. You went to the movies or dinner or parties with your friends, instead of meeting up in encrypted chat rooms online. You talked about homework, classes, college applications, prom—not government conspiracies or people getting killed or sold into the sex trade. Your best friend from childhood was still alive, not haunting your nightmares with his graphic suicide.

You knew who your mother was.

Max didn't need his life to be a perfect Disney movie, but he didn't want it to be some weird HBO documentary either. There had to be a middle ground between "boring" and "fearing for your life."

Nadia shoveled the omelette down like she hadn't eaten in days, and looking at her, that might have been the case. Without his mother's coat, she seemed unhealthily thin. She wore a white baby-doll T-shirt over a black bra and skinny jeans, which all hung loosely on her. There was an ugly black-and-purple bruise on her right forearm, just above her wrist, and a round burn scar on the back of her left hand. Dark circles underscored her eyes, and her lips were chapped.

She caught him staring, and she looked away dismissively.

"I'm sorry." Max felt like he was apologizing for more than rudeness, as if he was accepting the blame for everything that had happened to her.

"Nadia is from a city called Razgrad in Bulgaria," Penny said. Lianna translated the English to German for Nadia. "But she hasn't seen it in three years."

"That's terrible," Max said. He concentrated on chewing his food, but it seemed tasteless to him. He glanced at Nadia. "How did you end up here?"

Lianna looked concerned, but Penny interrupted. "It's okay, Lee. Nadia doesn't mind talking about it. And Max should hear this."

Lianna translated for Nadia.

Nadia took a bite of eggs and chewed it slowly. Then she sighed, put down her fork, and shoved her empty plate away from her on the dining table. She picked up her mug and cradled it in her hands. She started talking. Penny translated.

"I was a foolish girl," Nadia said. "I spent all my days on the internet, talking with older men. I thought it was a way out of Razgrad, a way to see the world. Now all I want is to go home and see my parents and my annoying little brother again."

"We can call your home," Lianna said in English.

Nadia shook her head, her eyes tearing up. "Not yet. No." She looked at the bruise on her arm. "Not like this."

She went on. "I talked to this one guy on Panjea a lot. Often. Damyan. He said he was twenty-five. Said he had money. A nice car. He had pictures, so I believed him, and he was so pretty. Strong."

Lianna interrupted with a question. Nadia shook her head.

"He reached me first, said he saw my beautiful photo and had to know me. He lived in Sofia. After we had been talking on Panjea a few weeks, he invited me to visit him.

"I packed my clothes. I stole money from my parents for the bus ride. It was just a weekend, but I had this feeling I would not be coming back. I was very happy." She laughed, bitterly. "Damn stupid girl."

Lianna put a hand on Nadia's knee, speaking softly, urgently in German. Penny translated for Max: "This is what they do. They prey on young women. Tell you what you want to hear, offer to make your dreams come true. They're the ones who did wrong. You made a mistake."

Penny closed her eyes and took a moment to compose herself.

"She was just Risse's age when they took her," she whispered to Max. "It makes me so sad, and so angry, that this bullshit is happening and no one can stop them."

"People like Mom are trying," Max said.

"It isn't enough," Penny said.

Nadia continued, explaining that she had lived in Sofia for

three days with Damyan and thought everything was wonderful. He was attentive, generous, funny, and handsome, and he told her she was beautiful and they would have a bright future together. He never slept with her or even touched her. But then his friends showed up, and they all took turns with her while he filmed it.

Soon she was on her way to Germany, where Damyan forced her to visit more men for money.

"I tried to run, but they caught me right away. Damyan said if I missed home so much, he would bring my Petr to me. My brother. I did not want that life for him."

So she did everything they demanded of her. She went wherever they sent her, she never complained or resisted or tried to get help—until another girl told her about Monde Libre. Everyone knew someone who knew someone who had escaped, but this story sounded true, so Nadia risked her life to contact Lee Hardy. She stole money and a cell phone from her, knowing she wouldn't have much time before he discovered it missing and deactivated it, or worse, reported the theft to Damyan.

"Then I ran," Nadia said. "I called for help, and you came." She looked at Lianna gratefully, tears in her eyes.

What Monde Libre offered was a fresh start, protection from the men who had been holding her, and eventually safe passage back home. Nadia would testify against her captors, if they were ever arrested.

Max found himself literally sitting on the edge of his seat

as he listened to Nadia. And he'd thought *his* life was messed up.

"What do you know about The Curtain?" Max asked.

"Ms. Hardy already asked about that. I am sorry, I don't know it." She shrugged. "I know I am on some website. They took pictures of me for it."

"Did you ever meet anyone who works on the site?" Max pressed.

"Max," Penny said.

Lianna translated the question. Nadia laughed. "A teenager. A boy like you," she said. "The Internet Kid. He makes the website go."

"He's Bulgarian too?" Max asked.

"No. English." She shook her head. "From England."

"Does it make sense for the Bulgarians to hire a kid from the U.K. to operate their webpage?" Max asked.

"Or does he work for The Curtain?" Penny said. "I'll ask if she remembers anything else. Anything at all." She turned to Nadia.

Nadia did remember. The kid was a jerk. He tried to touch her once, insisting that he had the right to "try the goods" for what he called "marketing research."

"She met him? When was that?" Max asked.

"On a boat a year and a half ago," Nadia said. "Damyan was taking me to meet the kid's boss. The kid happened to be on the same boat. I never knew where we were, but the boat was crowded; it was summer, there were a lot of tourists. There were other girls with us, all Damyan's." Nadia looked bitter. "We had to take a long train ride first, then the boat. We visited some little island covered in big fans."

"A little island with big fans?" Max said.

Nadia shrugged. "The boss interviewed me on another boat. Giant yacht, very fancy. I thought I could maybe get away from Damyan if I made his boss like me more, but he didn't choose me. They say he asks to see all the girls in person, to make sure the photos Damyan used were real and remind them who's in charge. Quality control? That's what he called it. We girls made a lot of money just to show up, take our clothes off for him. He took a couple of them into another room. Another woman there was watching us. No, maybe watching Damyan and his men. She was the one who led them in and out of his room."

"What were they doing?" Penny asked.

"I didn't ask questions, but . . ." Nadia raised her eyebrows. "You know. One of the girls, her name was Georgi. She didn't say what happened in there, but I saw the red marks, and later the bruises, even though she tried hiding them."

"What did the woman look like? The one working with the Wizard?" Penny asked.

"Wizard?" Nadia asked.

"The boss man."

"She was very short. Maybe . . ." Nadia stood and placed her hand at her shoulder height, indicating she was about four feet ten inches tall. "Chinese, I think. Big eyes. Pretty, but no chest or butt. She looked professional: black hair in a bun, white blouse, gray pants. Glasses."

"Did you get a good look at the . . . boss?" Max asked.

Nadia puffed out her cheeks and held her hands out in front of her, fingers touching.

"He was like Dyado Koleda!" she said. She laughed.

"Dyado Koleda?" Max asked.

Penny and Lianna looked at each other. Neither knew the translation.

Max pulled out his cell phone. The battery was low because he'd forgotten to charge it last night, but then he'd been distracted. He opened his translation app and repeated, "Dyado Koleda."

The screen displayed: SANTA CLAUS.

"Santa Claus?" Max asked. He put his hands on his belly and said, "Ho, ho, ho?"

"Yes! Heavy. Large." She puffed out her cheeks again. "He was wearing a red silk robe. He had white hair, bushy eyebrows, big droopy mustache. But no beard."

"What happened to the Internet Kid?" Max asked.

"After he got off that first boat with us, I did not see him again." She sighed. "He was a pig, but he seemed . . . sweet? Maybe inexperienced. The women made him embarrassed, even though he had already seen our pictures. He spent most of his time looking at his phone. Some of the girls pretended to be jealous of his phone, thinking he could help them."

Nadia yawned wide and apologized.

"We should let Nadia get some sleep. She had an exciting night." Lianna covered her own yawn. "I could use a catnap myself."

"We're going to check out this famous Christmas market anyway," Max said.

"We are?" Penny asked. "Sure, I'd love to. Nadia can have the guest room."

"Thanks," Lianna said. "It's convenient that we don't even need to put on fresh sheets."

Penny raised her eyes and pressed her mouth into an innocent smile.

"Thank you, Nadia," Max said. "Thanks, Mom."

Max and Penny piled the dirty dishes in the sink. They repacked their bags and headed out into the cold, bright morning. It was a short walk to the Christmas market, and they strolled at a leisurely pace. If Penny hadn't been so busy texting on her cell phone, Max would have reached for her hand. He did stop her and insist on taking a selfie.

"Are you kidding me?" Penny asked. "I may have to break up with you."

But she went along with it and even posed romantically with him. Just before Max clicked the shutter, she licked his ear, resulting in a hilarious photo.

"You have to send that to Risse," Penny said.

"Already am." They must have looked quite the couple, both preoccupied with their phones as they walked side by side.

"What do you think of what Nadia told us?" Max asked in a low voice.

"I think we shouldn't waste our time going to another Christmas market. We should get back on the road and see Ada as soon as possible."

"I agree," Max said. Unfortunately, the French police and his mother had prohibited that.

"You do?" Penny asked.

"Yes. But walking around the market gives us another chance to see if we're being followed. Don't look now, but we are. Check the photo I just texted you and Risse. Zoom in on the upper left, over your shoulder."

Penny did, and saw the same thing Max had. The woman and man who had chased them in Berlin—Clove and Volvo— were ambling up the other side of the street, about forty feet behind Max and Penny.

"What? How are they here?" Penny asked.

"I don't care. I'm more interested in losing them."

"We'll ditch them in this crowd, head back to the car, and drive away before they can catch up."

Max nodded. He could wait until she was safely at the car before he told her he wouldn't be joining her. If he had to, he could distract Clove and Volvo so she could get away unobserved. He took Penny's hand.

They didn't even pretend to show interest in the market this time; instead, they focused on putting as many people between them and the other couple that was trying to catch up.

When it seemed they had finally given their followers the slip, Max and Penny jogged north to Rue des Clarisses, where Penny had parked her car during their stakeout of Lianna's apartment yesterday.

Max saw the vehicle first. His pulse raced. "Oh, hell. Penny!"

Penny shrieked and ran toward her car—what was left of it.

The front of the vehicle was scorched black and gray, remnants of pink paint blistered and pitted. Once he was close enough, Max smelled the acrid odor of burnt plastic, hot metal, and ash. The front seats were a charred mess, and the side windows were broken or had blown out from the heat. Max tapped the frame of the vehicle with his fingers. Cold. The fire had burned itself out a while ago.

Tears streamed down Penny's face, and she was shaking. Max put an arm around her.

"This wasn't an accident," she said.

Max looked down the row of parked cars. Fortunately, the fire had been contained in Penny's car. "Maybe we should have paid for parking."

She glared at him.

"Too soon?" he asked.

"That sounded suspiciously like an 'I told you so.'"

"Never! Not me." Max held his hands up.

"I know this happens sometimes around here—"

"Seriously?"

"It's a thing, usually around New Year's. But my car's the

only one that was burned on this block. This feels personal."

"I wonder if our favorite spies had anything to do with this," he said. He hoped Risse would have some luck tracking down Clove's and Volvo's real identities from the photo he'd sent her.

"But why? To prevent us from leaving?" Penny asked.

"Or they're just being dicks." Max kicked a melted tire. "I guess you're taking a train back to Berlin."

He liked that idea. It was more public. What could happen to Penny on a fast-moving train with all those other passengers around?

"You're not coming with me?"

Max hesitated.

What was actually keeping him here? The court order restricting him to France was serious, but secrecy was key—the whole idea was to get to Ada in Berlin without being noticed. He could return to Strasbourg in a day or so, and the police would never need to know.

As for his mother . . . She had been acting like a good mom—whatever she thought that meant—ever since they had reunited. Max had played along, but she had given up the right to tell him what to do when she'd walked out of his life. Maybe it was time to return the favor.

"Let's go," Max said. *Before I change my mind again.*

His mother might not even miss him that much, or right away. They'd only been together for a day, and she would be preoccupied working with Nadia. That had to be easier without him around.

"I guess we're heading to the train station then. Unless you want to borrow another ride . . . ?" Penny spread her hands at the other parked cars in the small lot, like a game-show hostess.

"I don't do that sort of thing anymore. Anyway, I love trains!" Max said. You didn't have to stay in your seat the whole ride. There was plenty of space in which to get some exercise, walking up and down the train.

"Do you need to retrieve anything from the car?" he asked. Max looked skeptically at the trunk, with its blistered pink paint. He doubted Penny could recover anything useful from the devastated automobile.

"No. I carry everything important with me in my bag and my brain." She patted the roof of the car. "So long, Bessie. You shall be avenged."

13

LESS THAN A MINUTE AFTER THE TRAIN TO BERLIN
pulled out of Gare de Strasbourg-Ville station, it came to an
abrupt stop, sending Max, Penny, and the other passengers
lurching forward in their seats.

"That's not good," Max said.

The train trembled and groaned, but it didn't move so
much as an inch forward. Then the lights flickered out and
the train went completely quiet as the air conditioners stopped
running.

"Bah!" Penny closed her laptop. "Wi-Fi's not working now
either."

"Maybe they need to reboot the train," Max said.

The speaker system crackled with static and a woman's
voice spoke in a soft, apologetic tone. Max almost understood
it, but the English translation soon followed.

"This is the conductor. We are having technical difficulties. All trains are being held in position until further notice, and we may be recalled to the station. Please stand by. We hope to continue moving shortly."

Penny tapped at her phone's screen. "Eurail trains are stopped all over."

"So it isn't a mechanical failure," Max said. "And no one's targeted our train in particular."

They had been painstakingly careful to check the station for anyone following them. Penny had walked up and down the length of the train looking for their old friends Clove and Volvo, and Artoo and Threepio, in case they'd somehow anticipated their plans, while Max scanned the platform. Once she gave the all clear, he had jumped on board at the last possible moment and kept an eye out for anyone else doing the same. As far as they knew, they were finally moving undetected.

"Software, I bet. If the system crashed, they can't track where the trains are or direct them. This kind of thing is getting all too common these days." Penny squinted over her phone and kept reading. "Better to sit still than risk running into another train at full speed."

Max smiled. "Wouldn't it be funny if someone came around asking, 'Is there a hacker on the train?'"

"Ha. Would you volunteer? The thing is, their first impulse would be to blame this on hackers, not ask them for help." Penny pulled out her laptop. "Actually, maybe I *can* do something."

"I was kidding," Max said.

"So was I." She stuck out her tongue.

The lights came on and air hissed into the cabin. The train lurched and then started moving again.

"You didn't . . . ?" Max asked.

Penny held her hands up and away from her keyboard. "Not me. Nope!"

The other passengers cheered, but their applause soon died down when they realized the train was going in the wrong direction.

The conductor gave another update over the loudspeakers. Penny didn't wait for the announcement to be repeated in English. "We're returning to Strasbourg," she translated.

"Terrific," Max said. He wondered if it was arrogant to assume this was all happening because of him. Would they have to board another train and take their precautions all over again?

"Maybe hackers *are* involved," he said. "The grounded Oceanic Airlines flights last month, the messed-up traffic signals in London. Now this."

Penny picked at the flaking polish on her fingernails, not looking at Max. "Nah. If hackers were involved, they wouldn't pass up the chance to gloat a little. But no one has claimed credit for those incidents. I bet someone was only fooling around."

It was weird how she could joke with him and then shut him out in almost the same beat. It was weirder when they

shared a romantic moment, but ended up seeming even farther apart. Was she having second thoughts about their relationship?

Was he?

Maybe the secret he suspected she was hiding was that her
feelings for him had changed.

"I don't know. It seems too intentional, hitting transit systems that way. Some people were actually hurt."

"And what do you think these hypothetical hackers are
trying to do?" she asked.

"Testing the infrastructure of vital systems? If all these
things happened at the same time, there'd be chaos. I feel like
something big is coming," Max said.

The train pulled back into Strasbourg station at a crawl. It
shuddered to a stop.

"When did you start worrying about 'cyberterrorism'?"
Penny snorted.

"Not terrorism. But cyber *warfare*. That's real. It's already
happening."

Penny shook her head. "Things aren't always connected
that way. Coincidences do exist in life."

"If you dig deep enough, everything *is* connected."

"Now you're getting metaphysical. This is a *physical* problem. These computer systems and networks are tragically old;
some are still running Windows 3.1. They're unreliable. The
whole infrastructure has to be replaced with something more
stable," she said.

"Easier said than done."

"Maybe not." Penny flicked a nail.

"You've given this some th—" A shrill, repeating chord played from Max's pocket: *DA! DA! DA! DA!* It was even more startling in the strangely still train car. He fumbled for his phone and sent the call to voice mail without checking the screen.

"Jeez!" Penny said. "Is that from *Psycho*?"

"Yeah."

"Who gets *that* ringtone?"

"Mom," Max said.

"Twisted," Penny said. "Like! But what's going on with you two? Why does she deserve that?"

"Other than abandoning her family?"

Penny sighed. "Get over it."

"Excuse me?" Max said.

Penny turned in her seat to face him. "Max. You found your mom. Don't mess this up now. Did you look for her because you wanted to punish her for leaving, or do you want her in your life?"

"I missed her."

"And now you don't anymore?"

"I guess . . . I still miss her. I don't know who 'Lee Hardy' is."

"She doesn't know who you are yet. Your mom isn't the same person who left thirteen years ago. Focus on finding out who she is now. Look, I'll be honest—"

"That's a nice change."

"Hey. Don't make this about *me*." Penny poked him in the chest with a finger. "I'm trying to help. Listen, when you told me you were looking for your mom, I was worried."

"That I wouldn't find her?" Penny's father had disappeared after her mom divorced him, and she hadn't had any luck tracking him down either. She seemed to have come to terms with it, but he knew Risse still periodically ran checks to see if anything new had turned up.

"No. I was afraid you would. You aren't the kind of person to give up, and you're more capable than you give yourself credit for.

"Plus we had your back. I just didn't know what would happen. Your mother missed you too. Despite what she says about not wanting to apologize, she does regret what she did, because it hurt you and your dad. Lee is trying. She wants to be your mom again. She wants to be your *friend*. Don't you want to give yourselves that chance? Good friends are hard to come by."

Max sat silently. He was stunned.

"Thanks," he said.

"That'll be five cents." Penny extended an open hand.

The only change Max had on him was the fake nickel with Ada's files on it. "Will you accept a kiss instead?"

She raised an eyebrow. "Cheap kiss. But sure, why not?" She closed her eyes and puckered up.

Max leaned in and kissed her. She smelled like mint, just

like he did, since they'd used the same shampoo back at his mom's. Penny slid a cool hand under his T-shirt and pulled him closer, biting on his lower lip playfully, hungrily. The arms of their seats got in the way. Eventually they disentangled. The train car felt several degrees warmer.

"Did you get your money's worth?" he asked.

"The American dollar is weak against the euro right now. You owe a little more."

Max shuddered involuntarily. Even joking about exchanging money for a kiss seemed disrespectful after hearing Nadia's story.

"What?" Penny asked.

"Hold on. You remembered my mom saying she wasn't going to apologize for leaving, but you weren't there. Did you bug me or something last night?"

Penny cupped a hand around her ear. "I may have dropped some eaves. When in a surveillance state . . ."

Max shook his head. *"Penny."*

His phone rang again. Max skipped the call and switched it to vibrate.

"So why aren't you taking calls from *Mommie Dearest*?" Penny asked.

"She didn't exactly give me permission to go to Berlin. In fact, she explicitly forbade me from leaving."

"You're *grounded*?" Penny laughed.

"Sort of. I'm not allowed to leave France until after the trial."

"You're running away? Seriously? After you came all this

way to find her?" Penny threw up her hands. "Idiot."

"She ran away first." Max scowled. "She doesn't really get how complicated my life has become."

"It sounds like she gets it perfectly," Penny said. "You wanted a mom, well . . ."

"Your mom's different."

"Oh, she's different all right. She's always working, so she can't pay that much attention to me, and she's more focused on Risse these days anyway, figuring she can still be 'saved.' She thinks I'm at some computer camp in New Hampshire that will help bring in some money, so she couldn't wait to send me off."

"She must miss you, especially now?"

"When your mom has to work on Christmas and you still can't afford presents or a nice meal, it's just another day."

Penny was getting worked up. She turned her head away. "'Scuse me. I'm gonna call Risse."

Penny got up from her seat in a hurry and headed up the train car. Max watched her go. It was easy to forget that Penny had a troubled home life, because she always had her act together. He had never considered how his quest to find his missing parent would affect her; here he'd succeeded, and as she'd pointed out, he was screwing it all up. Never mind that he was sneaking off to Berlin to help Penny. Or was he?

Max's phone buzzed. If it was his mother, he'd answer it this time. But no, it was a text message from Risse: Go after her, dumbass.

Max smiled. "Thanks, Risse," he said.

He stood, scooped up his bag, and started toward the front of the car.

But as he sidled into the aisle, he saw a short Caucasian man with brown hair who was standing there quickly look away. He was wearing an ugly Christmas sweater, red and green with blocky reindeer profiles. He fiddled with a duffel bag in the overhead luggage rack. Max was pretty sure the man had been looking at his seat until Max had gotten up.

Max was also pretty sure that this was Artoo, from the Christmas market.

Without missing a beat, Max headed toward the man, pretending to be focused on his cell phone. As he passed him, he brushed against the man's side and felt something firm strapped to his left side, under his armpit.

A gun.

"Pardon," Max muttered. If he'd been as skilled as Enzo, he could have lifted the man's wallet at the same time and found out who he was, but he was glad he had learned enough to detect the gun. That and a bulletproof vest would keep him from getting shot.

The man ignored Max and slipped into his seat, beside a bald black man in a black turtleneck. He had shaved, but this was their other pursuer, Threepio.

Max's heart pounded. He rushed through the train car, now needing to find Penny for a different reason. Sweat trickled down the back of his neck.

Two cars up, he met Penny hurrying her way back to him.

"We have a problem," Max said.

"I know," Penny said.

They both paused in surprise.

"You first," Max said.

"Conductors are checking tickets and passports," Penny said.

Max groaned. "And I don't have mine."

Once you were in Europe, you didn't always need a passport to cross borders between countries. Max had gambled and lost.

"Okay." Max looked around. "Okay," he said again. "Follow me."

Max made his way toward the far end of the car. Outside the lavatory, he pulled out a black Sharpie and the sign Enzo had made for him back at the airport reading 503-ERROR.

"Good idea. That should make it easier for them to identify you," Penny said.

Max flipped the card over to its blank side and handed it and the marker to Penny. "Can you write 'Out of Order' in French and German?"

Penny gave him a skeptical look, but she scribbled on the cardstock:

OUT OF ORDER!

HORS SERVICE!

AUSSER BETRIEB!

"I was very tempted to write 'Out of order in French and German,'" she said. "How are you going to tape up the sign?"

Max poked around inside his bag until he came up with an

old Bugs Bunny Band-Aid.

"That's very official-looking," Penny said as he peeled the backing off.

Max smiled. "'Gee, ain't I a stinker?'" He folded the Band-Aid into a loop, sticky-side out, and stuck it to the back of the card. Then he slapped it onto the faux-wood door of the lavatory and slid it open.

"After you," he said.

He followed Penny inside and pressed against her back so he could close the door.

"Oh!" she said as he bumped her from behind.

He closed the latch to lock the door. There was only enough space for him to stand by the door, facing the toilet, with the small sink on his left. Penny wedged herself into the corner between the toilet and the wall. She turned to face him, one foot up on the closed toilet-seat cover.

"We can't hide in here for the whole trip," Penny said.

"Shhhh." Max closed his eyes for a second, suddenly light-headed. "Have I ever mentioned that I hate small spaces?" he whispered.

"You're claustrophobic?" she asked, matching his volume.

"If you have to apply a label to it." He nodded, then groaned as the motion made him feel nauseous. "Yes."

"Here, switch places with me."

Max and Penny managed a weird, delicate sort of dance as they swapped positions, requiring Max to climb up on the toilet as she scooted by him. He sat and wiped his arm across his forehead. He was in a cold sweat.

Penny ran cold water and soaked a paper towel.

"Thanks," Max said.

"This isn't for you." She crouched and squeezed the water out onto the floor by the door. It spilled out through the narrow crack into the train car.

"That should do it," she said.

The air freshener and hand sanitizer didn't completely mask the bathroom-y smell, and to Max's embarrassment, he actually did need to pee. But that was not an option at the moment—just another thing to keep his mind off of.

"That was quick thinking," Penny said.

"That's why they pay me the big bucks," Max said.

"I just have one question."

"Shoot."

"Why am *I* hiding? I have my passport, and no one's looking for me."

"That isn't exactly true," Max said. He told her about seeing Artoo and Threepio again.

"They must have boarded when we returned to the station. Who are they?" Penny's voice rose.

"Shhh."

"Sorry," she whispered.

"They probably aren't French police. They could have arrested me on sight for attempting to leave the country."

"Unless they want to see where you're going, and who you're talking to."

"They have to be from Verbunden Telekom. They must be on to us."

"I don't see how. More likely they're working for Kevin Sharpe," Penny said.

"We're still in Strasbourg. Maybe we should switch to a different train, or find another way to Berlin." She checked her phone. "Train service has been restored. More importantly, Wi-Fi is back too."

Max's phone dinged with another text message, this time from his mother: CALL ME.

"Do you think your mom would have reported you missing?"

"I hope not. That's a sure way to send me back to prison until January. Or longer."

"How badly does she want you to stay away from—" Penny held up a hand. She put a finger over her mouth and nodded her head toward the door. Max fell quiet and leaned his ear against it. He heard someone say, "*Fahrschein und Reisepasse, bitte.*"

"Ticket and passport," Penny mouthed.

Shit. This was never going to work.

Max's heart pounded as the voice worked its way toward them. *Fahrschein und Reisepasse. Fahrschein und Reisepasse.* His eyes roved around the tiny lavatory wildly, looking for some last-minute escape route. No window, no ceiling hatch. One exit, and no way he could get past whomever was out there and run away. Where could he go on a moving train?

The voice stopped outside the bathroom and he heard

someone mutter into a walkie-talkie. He jumped when three loud knocks landed on the other side of the door, right over his ear.

"Hallo? Hallo?"

Max bit his lip. He stopped himself from laughing when he imagined calling, "Out of order!"

Then Max heard a very normal sound that suddenly seemed more terrifying: the jingle of keys. They were going to open the door.

The jingling stopped. The conductor was talking to someone on the other side. Max strained to hear, but they were speaking in German. He glanced at Penny. She shook her head.

Then two pairs of footsteps walked away. Max took a deep breath.

"Don't hog all the oxygen," Penny said. She suppressed a giggle. "That was close. I wonder what happened?"

"Let's go find out." Max was hyperventilating.

"Not yet."

"I can't stay in here." Max's voice started rising in a panic.

"You're okay." Penny took the damp paper towel and wiped Max's forehead with it. He closed his eyes. The coolness and the touch of her hand helped calm him down. Then he felt her lips on his, quickly chasing away his fear of small spaces.

"Keep your eyes closed," Penny said. She kissed the side of his neck gently, working her way down. She sat on his lap and he put his hands on either side of her waist.

"Feeling better?" she whispered in his ear.

"Understatement," Max said.

He lost track of time in the frenzied choreography of hands, lips, breath, touch. They pushed and pulled and pressed against each other until they were both sweaty and flushed and raw. It felt so good it almost hurt.

"We're moving fast," Penny said.

"You think?" Max said.

"No. The *train* is moving fast." She pushed her hair back and straightened her blouse.

"I think it has been for a while," Max said.

She checked her phone. "We're already thirty minutes out from Strasbourg. So much for getting off."

Max snickered.

Penny splashed some cold water on her face and tried to straighten her hair.

Once they were more or less presentable, Max pulled open the door and took Penny's hand as they left the bathroom. An elderly man in the seat across from it looked startled, then winked conspiratorially. Max took the OUT OF ORDER sign from the door and folded it into quarters.

They went back to their car. Max paused at Artoo and Threepio's seats and let Penny go ahead of him. She looked at him worriedly.

"Excuse me. Do you speak English?" Max asked.

"Yes," Artoo said cautiously.

"Do you know what all that commotion was back in Strasbourg?"

"The conductor was looking for someone," Threepio said.

"Did they find them?" Max asked.

"No." Artoo smirked. What was that supposed to mean?

"Okay, thanks."

"You're welcome." The man said it slowly, deliberately, like the two words were significant. That was Dramatis Personai's catchphrase. These two couldn't be involved with the group, could they?

Max started to turn away, and then he hesitated. "Do me a favor: Tell Kevin Sharpe that I don't like being followed. If he wants my help, I don't want to see you two again."

The two men looked at each other.

"Good day," Max said.

He joined Penny in their original seats.

"Was that a good idea?" she asked.

"We'll see." He glanced over at the guys again. "The weird thing is, I think one of them talked to the conductor outside the bathroom and got him to leave us alone."

"Why would Sharpe's henchmen help us?" Penny said.

"They wouldn't. Unless he wants me back in Berlin."

"Now *I'm* nervous about this," Penny said.

Max had somehow missed two more calls from his mother. She had left a message saying she was sorry, but she had to notify the police that Max was missing. There would be hell to pay when he finally called her back.

"Great. The police are looking for me, thanks to my civic-minded mother," Max said. "And they know I'm trying to get to Berlin."

"But they don't know you're on this train," Penny said. "I can work with that."

She opened her laptop and ignored him for twenty minutes. Then she closed it and smiled smugly.

"I've just booked a dozen train and bus tickets for you, with departure points from Strasbourg and towns within the distance you can run, with multiple destinations outside France. They'll think you're just trying to get away, and they hopefully won't be looking for you right away in Berlin."

"How did you hack the transit systems so quickly?" Max asked, impressed.

"I didn't have to hack anything, actually. But I did use some borrowed credit card numbers."

"You know how I feel about that . . ."

She frowned.

"Never mind. Nice job." Max leaned back in his seat, suddenly exhausted.

And the real fun wasn't going to start until they reached Berlin.

14

THE NEXT MORNING, THE CROWD OF PROTESTERS
outside the Chilean Embassy's building was the largest Max
had seen there: easily a dozen people on opposite sides of the
doors advocating for Ada to go free or for her to go to prison.

Max didn't want to put on the horrible Krampus mask
again. If he was going to be Ada's spokesperson, the face of
her movement for a safer internet, he wanted to start now.
But he wasn't supposed to be in Berlin, so he had to keep his
identity hidden. That's what Max hated most about this kind
of business: the need for secrecy and lies. Even now, he didn't
know what Penny and Ada were really up to, but he hoped that
would change today.

There were also a couple of news vans parked in front
of the embassy, behind the police cars. As Max and Penny
approached, a man with a microphone, closely followed by a

cameraman, intercepted them at the door.

"Excuse me! Are you Maxwell Stein?" the reporter said.

Max faltered. *What the hell? How do they know I'm under the mask?*

"You have the wrong person," Penny said, her voice muffled behind her mask. "He just has that kind of face."

"Mr. Stein, what is your business here at the embassy? Are you meeting with Ada Kiesler?"

"No comment," Penny said. She opened the door and guided Max through, inserting herself between him and the reporter.

"What do you think about Verbunden Telekom?" the reporter called as the door closed.

"They get points for persistence," Penny said. Once they were safely inside the elevator, she pulled off her mask. Her face was covered in a sheen of sweat, and her cheeks and forehead were red. Strands of hair floated around her head like a halo.

Max pulled off his mask and crumpled it up. "How did they know it was me?"

"I probably should have found a mask that didn't look so much like you."

The doors dinged and they stepped out.

"Someone tipped them off," Penny said. "But they don't have proof it was you. They were following a hunch and hoping it would pay off. *Reporters.*"

Penny had a low opinion of the media, which she usually

expressed whenever Max's ex-girlfriend Courtney, a blogger, came up in conversation. This was as close to showing jealousy as Penny got.

Max had his own problems with the media: He knew and valued the power they had to not only tell a story, but to shape it. He only wished he wasn't a part of their news cycle so often. They just didn't respect boundaries between public and private in their all-consuming desire for getting the scoop and getting ratings, treating every piece of information as their right—and they hadn't appreciated Max drawing comparisons between them and the NSA to that effect.

Sr. Ortiz was too busy to greet them this time, so a young aide checked their IDs and then escorted them to Ada's room.

Ada smiled when she saw Penny and Max. "You came back! Prithee, what news dost thou bring from the world?"

"Max found his mom, got arrested for breaking into her apartment, and violated a French court order to return to Berlin," Penny said. "We were followed from Strasbourg on the train by a couple of guys who were apparently packing heat. And . . ." She glanced at Max.

"Kevin Sharpe called me," Max said.

"Interesting," Ada said.

"He wants everything you have on Verbunden Telekom, especially where its activities involve the U.S., and he wants it before you make it public so he can do damage control."

"Obviously we don't trust him," Penny said quickly. Max put a hand on her arm.

Ada stared at them. "You've been busy."

"So what's new with you?" Penny asked.

"You haven't heard? Sr. Ortiz has been ordered to revoke my political asylum by the end of the week."

"What? They can't do that!" Penny said.

"He'll do me the courtesy of delaying as long as possible, but unless we act soon, I expect I'll be dead before Christmas." She stated this matter-of-factly.

To her credit, Ada wasn't as bummed or frightened as Max would have been in her shoes. She seemed resigned to her fate—she'd dressed the way he was used to seeing her on TV, in a suit, hair done, makeup on, as though preparing her public persona once more.

"VT is powerful, and this is all starting to look bad for President Bachelet. She already has a low approval rating in Chile, and most people think she should be more concerned with problems at home. I can't blame her for cutting me loose, and in fact, I'm grateful she's hosted me here as long as she has," Ada said.

They settled around the small conference table and the feast of Indian food that had just arrived for Ada's lunch.

"We can help you sneak out," Max said.

Penny smiled. "Yeah!"

"Thank you. I'll consider it. But I always knew this was a very real possibility. I just want to expose VT's crimes and secure the internet. After that, whatever happens to me won't matter."

Germany was notoriously bad at protecting whistle-blowers; they had no formal law in place, and Ada's case would be at the mercy of the courts. Considering VT's political and economic clout, there was no question that she would end up in prison—if she survived that long.

"We'll keep fighting the good fight," Penny said.

As they ate, Penny and Max caught Ada up on everything they had learned about The Curtain from Lianna and Nadia. Increasingly, it looked like connecting VT with the dark web marketplace would be impossible for even a corrupt politician to ignore, and VT wouldn't be able to pressure any news organization into burying the story.

If only they could find that proof in Ada's files. Even spending every spare moment going through them, with thousands of documents to review, it could take weeks or months to check them all. It didn't help that most were in German.

"I can't believe your mother is Lee Hardy," Ada said. "I almost contacted her myself because of all her work to expose The Curtain, but she's difficult to get ahold of."

"No kidding," Max said.

"I decided to wait until I could give her something solid. I guess social justice runs in the family."

"I'm a hacker, not a doctor, but I'm pretty sure genetics don't work that way," Max said.

Still, he could see his parents' influence on him and his values and the kinds of things he could do—and thought he could do. Even with his mother out of the picture for most of his life, he'd heard stories about her exploits from his dad. Bradley Stein was wistful more than he was bitter about his ex-wife, and he romanticized the things they'd accomplished together. On some level, he had felt that he'd been holding her back, and was certain that no matter where she was in the world, she was making a difference for someone. Which had all been small consolation to a little boy who wanted his mommy to tuck him in at night and to hear her stories firsthand.

Ada was able to shed some light on one mystery: She only had to glance at a photo Max had taken of Clove before she could tell them who had been following them all this time.

"That's Valentine Labelle, a reporter for *La Vérité*, a French tabloid. She's asked me for an interview repeatedly, but her previous articles have been all pro-VT, so I've been putting her off," Ada said. "She found out you were coming here, Max, and clearly thinks there's a story there."

"Great," Max said. *Valentine, huh? I think I prefer Clove.* "Couldn't she just, you know, *talk* to me?"

Penny cleared her throat. "You're notorious for telling off reporters yourself, Max. She's probably trying to put the story together without your cooperation. What does a tabloid care about facts, ethics, and journalistic integrity?"

"I'm afraid Penny's right. Valentine posted those photos of you outside the embassy the other day," Ada said.

"Photos? What photos?" Max asked.

"I can't pull them up online, of course, but they're everywhere on television. I'm sure they'll be in the next issue of *La*

Vérité too. They show you and Penny leaving the building, talking to the police. The quality is terrible, but it's you."

"They photographed us when we took off our masks . . . ," Max said.

Penny elbowed him.

"I didn't know someone was going to take our picture!" He threw the Krampus mask across the room. It landed behind the couch with a soft squelch.

"Always assume someone is taking your picture." Penny sighed. "At least Labelle isn't dangerous."

Max laughed. "Of course she's dangerous. Irresponsible journalists always are. Ironic that she works for a paper called 'The Truth.' I guess that guy with her is her photographer."

He felt silly now for thinking that Volvo had been carrying a gun. He'd only shot Max with his camera, but the right picture could ruin someone's life as surely as a bullet.

"What about those other guys who were following us?" Max said. He described Artoo and Threepio. Ada drew a blank.

"And they were definitely carrying guns," Max said.

"Now *they* sound scary," she said. "Sharpe's people?"

"I assumed so, but I'm not sure now. I didn't think he had those kinds of resources anymore. When I mentioned his name, they recognized it, but I didn't get the impression they're in contact with him," Max said.

"I hope they're with him, because if they aren't, then VT or the Wizard are on to you two as well." Ada fell silent, her anxiety and worry plain on her face.

"We haven't seen them since the train. Perhaps because they already knew where we were going," Penny said.

"It's hard to believe, but I think they helped us back there," Max said. "Why would they do that if they want to kill us?"

"Because you're harder to get to in prison," Ada said.

Max swallowed. That was a terrifyingly sensible conclusion.

"This is getting more serious than I thought." Max looked from Penny to Ada. "If I'm going to help you take down Verbunden Telekom and The Curtain, and I want to . . . If our *lives* are on the line, then I need to know what this is really all about."

The two women exchanged a look that told Max he'd been right to be suspicious.

"Oh, boy," he said. He had wanted to believe that Penny wouldn't hold back something major from him, but now he was worried.

"I don't like ultimatums." Ada set her mouth in a hard, straight line.

Max crossed his arms. "That wasn't an ultimatum. This is an ultimatum: If you don't tell me everything, I'll take what I do know—still considerably a lot—to Valentine Labelle and let her figure out what you're up to. Then everyone will know the truth, and *The Truth* will set me free."

"Max!" Penny said.

Ada cursed.

"You're the one who wanted me here," Max said. "Now tell me why. Last chance. *What* the hell are you doing?"

Penny murmured something so softly he nearly missed it.

"Sorry. It sounded like you said, 'fixing the internet,'" Max said.

"Pretty much." Penny glanced at Ada. "I know, it sounded strange to me too, at first. But it's legit."

"I'm really fascinated by how you're going to 'fix the internet.' In the first place, don't fix it if it isn't broken."

Penny gaped at him. "Is that a joke?"

"No, really," Max said.

"Then you're either oblivious or delusional. The internet is *so* broken!"

He shrugged. "Just don't read the comments. Never read the comments."

"I don't mean that aspect of it. I mean, yes, it's broken because there are so many asses online and people are awful. But the tool itself . . . Panjea was just part of the problem. The whole thing is a farce."

"Privacy and security are nonexistent, and at this point, if everyone hasn't already adopted encryption and started running Tor, they aren't going to. It's a lost cause," Ada said.

"Nuke it from orbit, burn it to the ground, it's the only way to be sure," Penny said.

"Whoa. But we need the internet," Max said. "You haven't been online in weeks so you hired hackers to basically send emails for you, Ada." He groaned. "That's not why you hired hackers, is it?"

"Hear us out," Ada said. "You're partially correct. We do

need *an* internet."

Max narrowed his eyes. "Tell me more."

"Okay, so you know internet start-ups?" Penny said.

"Yeah?"

"Well, we're working on a 'start-up internet.' The Internet 2: Electric Boogaloo," Penny said.

"What makes the sequel better than the first one?" Max asked.

"We know so much more than we did in the early days of the internet. The net wasn't designed, not exactly. It evolved. Engineers and programmers planned it, but they were dealing with a changing, growing thing. They cobbled it together with chewing gum, wire, and good intentions. A Frankenstein monster of sorts," Ada said. "Now we have the opportunity to address the many failures and improve on the original model. We can design it as a perfect system."

"We can rebuild it. We have the technology. We can make it better than it was before. Better, stronger, faster," Penny said.

"It would be open source, separate from the private interests and resources of businesses out to profit from it. And consequently outside of the control of any one government," Ada said.

"Those businesses are the whole reason the internet even exists in its current form," Max said.

Penny looked scandalized.

"Playing devil's advocate," Max said. "For better or worse,

the internet was developed with corporate and government dollars, and it's growing because of them. What you're talking about sounds like a pipe dream."

Penny smiled. "Pipes are exactly the problem—where does internet traffic go? How do you get it there?"

"Intertubes?" Max said. "How can hackers help with that?"

"Don't forget, we hackers can build as much as we can break down. Sometimes we have to do both," Penny said.

"But still . . . getting a bunch of hackers to make an *unhackable* internet? That's . . ."

"Brilliant?"

"I was going to go with improbable, but the two aren't mutually exclusive."

Penny was clearly excited about this, more excited than he'd seen her about anything, ever.

After what went down with Panjea, after all her concern over how to keep fighting without putting her or Risse in danger, it was great that she had found a new passion. It sounded like this was a positive one, and relatively harmless—because how were they going to establish an infrastructure for a new internet, let alone get people to adopt it? People didn't even like it when their *web browsers* changed.

"So what have you really been doing at VT, *Emmie*?" Max asked.

"What they hired me to do: pen testing. But I'm going above and beyond a bit. I've been tracing all the connections between the internet exchanges VT controls through their subsidiaries.

Since they process all but a quarter of the world's total internet traffic, it's kind of like mapping out the internet itself."

"My dad has TeleGeography's Global Internet Map on our basement wall," Max said.

Ada laughed.

"What?" Max asked.

"TeleGeography relies on corporations and telecoms to report information about the cables and internet exchanges they manage—voluntarily. VT has been withholding or downright lying about most of that information. It's all in my files," Ada said. "No one is sorting through the financial and legal trails to determine who actually owns these exchanges."

"Then how are you doing it?" he asked.

"I have access to where all that data gets processed, and I've been using VT's own systems to scour the internet looking for where that data goes, kind of like the Carna botnet," Penny said.

Max remembered the web-famous animated gif capturing twenty-four hours of online activity all over the world, called the Internet Census 2012.

"You would need a huge botnet to accomplish that," Max said. He would know. As 503-ERROR, he'd controlled a fleet of around half a million computers with malware that allowed him to take them over and execute DDoS attacks with the push of a button.

Max had deployed it for the last time to force Panjea's servers to shut down briefly last year. That had seemed like a good

note on which to fully retire it, but he hadn't done his due dil-
igence and removed his malware from the infected computers.

Something itched at the back of Max's brain. He tried to
dismiss it as a ridiculous idea, but he couldn't shake the notion
once he'd had it. She would probably just laugh.

"Penny . . . You didn't use *my* botnet for this investigation,
right?"

He waited for her to laugh, roll her eyes, give him a con-
temptuous glare. Instead her eyes darted away, guilt written as
clear as plain text on her face.

"It's not like you were using it for anything," she muttered.

"Oh my God."

"It was just one of several we were using. Don't worry, it
wasn't harming anything. Just pinging computers and report-
ing on the path the data packets took through VT's systems."

Max stood up. His jaw was tight with anger. "I can't believe
you. You're doing the thing we're supposed to be fighting
against—spying on people."

If the authorities linked his old botnet to something this
big, Max would find himself on the TSA's no-fly list for real.
And soon after, prison.

"I'm a hacker." Penny sniffed. "I do whatever gets the job
done."

Max paced. "The real question is, why have you been doing
this? Once you know how data is being pushed around the
world . . ."

"We can change the map. We'll cut VT out of the picture,

and data will be forced along different paths," Ada said. "More trustworthy paths."

Max's skin crawled. "If VT manages more than seventy-three percent of the world's internet traffic, you can't remove them without making the whole thing fall apart."

"At first," Ada said. "But it will sort itself out over time."

Max had a surreal moment where he couldn't figure out whether this time he was working with the good guys or not. VT might be collecting everyone's data for nefarious purposes, but Ada was talking about shutting down the entire internet to protect everyone's privacy. That would be like a doctor killing the patient to treat an illness—technically they wouldn't be sick anymore, but only because they were dead.

The only consolation was that they were only talking about an extreme hypothetical, like when you say, "Wouldn't it be nice if war didn't exist?" You could come up with all the plans in the world to make that happen, but you couldn't actually do anything about it on such a large scale. Few things were as big as the internet.

Even with a map to help visualize how an email went from a computer in New York to a computer in New Delhi, showing the undersea cable it traveled and the specific internet exchanges that told it where to go, it was hard to actually wrap your brain around it. And if you, say, tried to cut VT's systems out of that route by literally attacking their servers and cables with an axe, it would take far too long to have much of an impact. Even a coordinated effort—lots of people with axes at all the right places at the exact same time—those facilities were too well protected for someone to take down more than a handful before you were stopped. Thank goodness.

So then what? Bombs?

Penny watched Max closely, as if she was waiting for him to figure it out. She and Ada hadn't sounded like this was a hypothetical situation at all. They already knew where to hit VT, and Ada was confident they would succeed. She had been speaking in absolutes: "We'll cut VT out of the map." The internet will fall apart at first, "but it will sort itself out over time." Not *could*, not *would*. *Will.* How were they going to do this?

Software.

Ada had a bunch of hackers working for her. What could they do? What could *Penny* do?

What had Penny already done?

"Border Gateway Protocol," Max said. His tone betrayed both the awe and horror of the concept.

Penny snapped her fingers. "He's got it!"

The Border Gateway Protocol, BGP, was how computer networks identified themselves on the internet: where they were and how to communicate with them. On the internet, that information was *everything*. All those tubes and hubs linking computers all over the world were useless if you didn't know where their data was coming from and where it was going. Having GPS and a map in a city didn't do you any good if you didn't know the address of your destination.

The problem was, BGP was self-disclosed. It worked on the honor system. You could claim to be whatever you wanted, and everyone else would accept it at face value and direct their network traffic accordingly. In one case, a technician in Pakistan accidentally changed the routing information for You-Tube; instead of blocking the site from Pakistan, he made it unavailable to everyone, everywhere. Shockingly, the system really was that fragile.

Which kind of proved Ada and Penny's point about the whole thing being broken.

Exploiting this weakness in BGP had long been talked about as the doomsday scenario for the internet, and now Ada and Penny were talking about bringing about the netpocalypse.

"I know what you're thinking," Ada said.

"Because any sane person would be thinking the same thing," he countered.

"I'm sure this all sounds . . . I don't know, villainous. Are we monologueing?" Ada shook her head. "But we've found a better way. Truly. As quietly as VT has been buying up internet real estate, we've been establishing a peer-based computer network that will take up the slack when their systems are disrupted. We've used botnets like yours to install software that makes personal computers capable of directing data around the world, without centralized exchanges to route the traffic. Without companies like VT. We're eliminating the middleman."

"Did you ask people for permission before hijacking their computers for this?" Max said.

"The main reason users don't adopt a better system is because they think it's too hard. What's simpler than doing it for them?" Ada said.

"How would someone opt out if they don't even know this program is on their computer?" Max ran his hands through his hair. This had to be some kind of nightmare, except his nightmares were only about one thing anymore. He looked at Penny. "You know this is wrong."

He wasn't sure which would be worse: If she knew it was wrong and was participating anyway, or if she didn't see anything wrong with it.

Penny averted her eyes. He glared at her, feeling the pressure of rage building inside him. *Look at me*, he thought. *Don't be a coward. Penny, look at me!*

"We'll let the people decide if this is wrong or right," Ada said. "We plan to use the exploit just once. All those networked computers will form a backup communications system for emergency services."

"Emergency services? Why would we need that?" Max asked.

"If the internet stopped working right now, it would be more than an inconvenience. Never mind binge-watching Netflix, sending email, downloading porn. . . . Most communication these days happens over the internet. That even means our phones! Without the internet, there'd be no way to contact the fire department or 911. Our backup internet will keep those vital systems operational." Ada had the cool, matter-of-fact voice of someone delivering a well-rehearsed PowerPoint presentation.

But this wasn't some showy TED talk or a theoretical discussion at a hacker conference. Max pictured airplanes crashing into each other, dropping flaming wreckage down onto the cities below. Trains running off their rails in spectacular explosions. People dying.

And still Penny was silent, letting her boss take the lead.

"Penny! You can't even look at me after lying to me constantly for the last few days?" Max shouted. "After everything we've been through together? What else have you been hiding?"

Penny slowly raised her eyes, like she was waking up. She looked at Max sympathetically. Defiantly.

"Have you only been pretending that everything's the same between us?" Max asked more softly.

"Haven't you?" she asked.

Max stared at her face, wondering who was behind the mask that still looked so much like the woman he thought he knew. Had she ever taken off that mask for him, really? Maybe she'd been wearing it so long, it was impossible to remove. Or maybe it was masks all the way down.

He wouldn't spend any more time on her. He turned to Ada.

"'If the internet stopped working . . . ,'" Max said. "That's a big 'if.'"

Ada smiled. "*When*. We're going to stop it ourselves: a proof-of-concept test run that will open everyone's eyes. Once the whole internet goes down for even five minutes, everyone will soon realize just how tenuous it is. People lost their minds when Panjea went dark. This will really make them think."

"Meanwhile, every search query that isn't related to an emergency service will redirect them to a repository of the files stolen from VT. There's no way anyone will be able to make them go away," Penny said.

Max bowed his head. "You said we inspired this idea, Ada?"

"*You* did," Ada said.

Crap.

Max rubbed his eyes wearily. "You're going to wipe out the internet—"

"Temporarily," Penny said.

"Even so. You're attacking it to show people how vulnerable the internet is to attack? Then what, it'll all go back to the way it was? Like nothing happened?"

"Hopefully it will get people to take notice, and no one will ever be able to replicate our experiment. Or if they do, we'll be prepared," Ada said.

Max collapsed onto the couch. "I have to think about all this."

Ada shot Penny a worried look.

He'd been all set to help Ada get the word out on VT, but this was much more aggressive, much more illegal—and potentially much more harmful. He couldn't be the spokesperson for

Ada's free internet if he didn't believe in what she was doing.

Scratch that. He did believe in her intentions. The idea of decentralizing the internet, basically taking it back to its humble roots on a grander scale, had been building up steam lately. On a fundamental, hypothetical level, Max supported it, especially after the revelations about the NSA and Panjea. But it had always been a grassroots initiative, a gentle suggestion.

Engineers had been inventing the technology and software that could make it possible, but despite successful crowdfunding efforts, it hadn't progressed. Because not enough people cared or were capable of making it so.

Ada's mission might not be his, and her methods certainly weren't, but it could actually work. If it did, she would force the world to take action in the way they hadn't after the efforts of Assange, Manning, Snowden—and Stein and Polonsky.

He knew why this appealed so much to Penny. She wanted to change the world, make it a better place. This could accomplish that.

Maybe Max was thinking too small again. Verbunden Telekom, The Curtain . . . They were just symptoms of a bigger disease. In Ada's new world order with a distributed internet, places like The Curtain could only exist if enough people wanted it to.

If Max considered himself a responsible global citizen, wasn't it his duty to step up when needed? The internet belonged to everyone. If he truly thought this was a crime that would do more harm than good, wasn't it up to him to report it?

He didn't like the idea of not being on Penny's side this time. Especially because he wasn't sure he could beat her and her team of legendary, elite hackers. She'd already demonstrated that she could put Max on the TSA watch list. What if she turned all her skills against him?

At the look on Max's face, Penny's softened. "Max."

"No wonder you didn't tell Risse about this." He waited to be sure that Risse hadn't also been lying to him; he didn't think he could handle that too. Penny shook her head. "Do you think she'd go along with it?"

Penny looked like he'd slapped her. She hesitated. "Yeah, because I'm her sister. That's why I'm not going to tell her. Neither of us is telling her." She stared at him. "I don't want her involved."

This could go all wrong, and they would all set a new record for the length of prison sentences for hacking. Forget that—if people died because of this stunt, they could be tried for manslaughter or murder, by every internet-equipped nation of the world. Yet knowing those risks, Risse would still join Penny's army.

Penny and Ada were making huge, irreversible decisions for other people, but they had given Max a choice.

He'd already done his service for his country and had barely survived with his life and freedom. His physical life, that is—he had sacrificed his privacy in order to protect that of others. He now lived his life as a public figure. Not too long ago that would have been appealing; after all, he'd reveled in the attention he got as a star athlete at Granville High.

The trade-off was that his actions would always follow him. He wouldn't be able to apply for college, seek employment, or even go on a date without people knowing—or thinking they knew—who he was.

"When do you plan to pull the plug?" Max asked.

"We're stepping up our timeline, given my imminent incarceration. And the possibility that you'll try to stop us." Ada smiled apologetically and shrugged.

"Okay," Max said.

"Okay?" Penny asked.

"Here's the deal. You have information about Verbunden Telekom that at best proves they've been acting in bad faith to control and monitor the bulk of internet traffic, and at worst that they are directly sponsoring illegal activities on the deep web. I think our play should be using the information you've gathered to prove that they're running The Curtain and take it down."

Ada shook her head. "That's small potatoes."

"It's a stepping stone. Besides, if we target The Curtain first and expose them, your life won't be in danger anymore. The narrative we'll tell is that VT are the bad guys, and you'll get everyone on your side. And then . . ." Max swallowed. "You can run your 'proof of concept' and pin it on them too."

Ada and Penny were quiet for a while. A smile slowly spread on Penny's face.

"That's fiendish, Max. I'm surprised, impressed, and

honestly a little turned on right now," Penny said.

Max ignored her. "Ada, you'll explain that you saw this coming because of your files, and when you weren't able to warn people, you came up with a plan for your backup system—using VT's own systems against them. You'll be a hero."

Ada licked her lips. "This is all sounding possible. We'll have to discuss it with the others."

"How many other hackers are involved?" Max asked.

"Enough to do the job right," Penny said. Chills went down Max's spine.

He practically felt sick now, but he needed Ada and Penny's help to stop The Curtain, and he hoped that before Ada destroyed the internet, he could talk some sense into Penny and convince her to give up this insane scheme. And if he didn't . . . at least she wouldn't be caught and punished, if Ada could be trusted not to implicate her too.

There was also the nuclear option: Max could follow through on his threat and warn the media before Ada could take action. Maybe share his information with someone more reputable than Valentine Labelle. In fact, if he could prove Ada was able and willing to disable the internet, that alone might accomplish her goals—wake people up to the need for a plan B if the internet should fall—without risking any lives or causing incredible economic damage. But for that to work, he would need Penny to stand with him; only she knew all the details of Ada's plan, and he'd hate to put her in the crosshairs like that.

It was going to come down to this: Could Max do the right

thing without considering his feelings for Penny?

In light of all this, what *were* his feelings for her? And what was the right thing?

Max's phone played the *Psycho* music. Ada smiled. The embassy aide hadn't bothered to ask them to turn off their phones this time, and in all the excitement, Max had forgotten. *Rookie mistake.* Well, if anyone had been listening to their conversation, they'd certainly gotten an earful, and maybe someone else would stop Ada for Max.

"Just answer it already!" Penny said. "It's his *mother*," she said to Ada.

Max swiped the unlock icon to the right to answer the call. "Hey, Mom. I bet you're pissed." Penny shot him a sympathetic look.

"Uh-oh. Having trouble with your mother already, Maxwell?"

Kevin Sharpe.

15

MAX SQUEEZED THE PHONE TIGHT.

"What are you doing with my mom's phone? What have you done with her? Is she all right?"

Penny's brow furrowed in confusion.

"Your concern is touching. You really do care about others, Maxwell. That's what I admire most about you," Sharpe said.

"Stop messing with me, Sharpe," Max hissed. Penny's eyes widened. Ada stood up and leaned forward with both hands on the table.

"Relax. As far as I know, your mother is fine," Sharpe said. "I may not be a hacker, but I can manage something as simple as spoofing another phone number on caller ID to protect myself—and to be certain to get your attention."

"You had my attention. Now I'm hanging up."

"Wait!" Sharpe actually sounded panicked. "Please."

Please?

"What?" Max said through gritted teeth.

"Have you considered my request? Did you find out what Kiesler and your girlfriend are really doing?"

Max glanced at the women. "Yes. But how did you find out about it?"

"Never mind that. To quote an old friend of yours, the question is: 'What are you going to do about it?'"

"No. You don't get to do that. Don't you dare bring up Evan." Max trembled with anger.

Ada stepped toward Max. Penny put a hand on her arm and shook her head.

"My apologies. Let's get down to it, then. Kiesler is leaving the Chilean Embassy any day now, which means soon she'll be in prison, locked away where no one can help her—or gain access to the data she has. Did you find the information I need?"

"You mean evidence that VT is responsible for The Curtain?" Max asked.

Sharpe was silent.

"That's what you've been interested in all along, isn't it? That's why you knew where my mother was and sent me to her," Max continued.

"Lee Hardy has been on VT's radar for some time. She's one of the few people who haven't been intimidated or bribed into silence on The Curtain, and so far she's come the closest to figuring out how to attack it. When I learned you two are related . . . Well, I can see where you get it from."

"Why didn't you just tell me all that to start with?" Max asked.

"I thought you might not go to Strasbourg, no matter how much you wanted to see her, and I wanted you to become personally invested in shutting down The Curtain. I assume we're on the same page now."

"I think so," Max said. "But I'm still trying to read the fine print."

"There's no more time. Meet me at the Brandenburg Gate tomorrow morning at ten. Bring everything you have connecting VT to The Curtain, and President Lovett to VT."

Sharpe is coming to Berlin?

"These files will be public soon enough. Why do you want them so much?" Max asked.

"Even forty-eight hours' notice, with a chance to review the extent of the evidence, will allow the great public-relations machine to spin the story."

"Or bury it," Max said. "No deal." They needed the release of Ada's files to have the maximum impact possible. Controversy and outrage all fed into that, and Sharpe wanted to soften the blow so Lovett wouldn't look so bad. Again. Max wanted to take her down as much as he wanted to destroy The Curtain.

Penny gave Max a thumbs-up.

"I admit, I'd be worried if you had agreed," Sharpe said. "Knowing you, you would have had a scheme to turn the tables on me, or hand me false data, or something clever like that. This way, you'll be properly motivated to bring me those files."

Max's phone dinged with a text message.

"That's a link to a live video stream," Sharpe said. "Open it."

Max opened the text message—also spoofing his mother's phone number—and found a short link with randomly generated characters. He hesitated for a second before he clicked on it. His phone scanned a file for viruses before displaying the option to play a video. He authorized the video app and saw a night-vision camera high over a city, moving. One of those quadcopters with a GoPro that were so popular on YouTube?

The camera flew over houses, streets, and trees. It began descending. As it got lower, Max tried to figure out where it was. It wasn't Europe, so it was probably back in the States. Definitely not Granville.

He'd been there before, he was certain. The camera was only a couple hundred feet high now, closing in on a dilapidated split-level house.

When Max recognized it, a lump formed in his throat.

"No," he said. He frantically waved Penny over to his side.

Puzzled, she rushed over and looked at the screen as the camera hovered close enough to look through an upstairs window, through which several computer screens glowed. Then it zoomed in to show clearly what was being typed on the green-on-black monitor: A private Dramatis Personai chat room. It pulled back and focused shakily on the girl sitting at the computer in a sports bra: Risse.

Oh no. Oh, shit.

Penny gasped. She grabbed for the phone, but Max was already switching on the speakerphone.

"You bastard," Max growled. "Leave her out of this."

"You're the one who involved her. I've had my attention on the Polonsky girls since last year, thanks to you. Since then I've collected plenty of evidence about Clarisse's illegal activities."

"You're blackmailing me into helping you?" Max said.

"I won't expose Clarisse Polonsky's extracurricular activities on the condition that you deliver Kiesler's files to me. In addition to your promise to cease all hacking and fade quietly into obscurity, your friends Penny and Clarisse must also give up their illegal activities, or they will be prosecuted."

Max made eye contact with Penny. Her face was red with fury, her lips pressed tightly together. She shook her head.

"You don't even have any power," Max said.

"I still have some resources. When I get back to the U.S. with Kiesler's files, President Lovett will reinstate me as her advisor—if she wants her office to survive the damning evidence linking her to one of the most vile sites on the internet."

"You're going to blackmail *her* too, just to get your job back?"

"That, and to prove a point."

"You're such a jerk, Sharpe."

"Maxwell, I'm actually trying to help you out. I know Penny will never agree to let you share those files with me even an hour before they go public. But I'm giving you the perfect excuse: You have no choice. I expect she'll go along with it to protect her sister's secret and her own freedom."

Sharpe was right. He was making things easier for Max on that front. At least he knew what Sharpe's true motivations were.

"Brandenburg Gate, tomorrow morning, ten a.m.," Sharpe said.

Max kept his eyes on Penny. She looked at Ada and then back at him. Her shoulders slumped in defeat. She nodded.

"Okay. I'll bring the files," Max said.

At least Sharpe had picked a public place with lots of witnesses. Where it was easy for someone to hide and record the whole thing. Max was going to have to play along, but this wasn't over. Sharpe thought he'd pressured Max into cooperating, but he'd only pissed Max off. He was going down.

"And call your lackeys off," Max snapped. "I don't want to see them following us again."

"Who?" Sharpe said.

"Those guys that followed us to Strasbourg and back. I guess they didn't give you my message," Max said.

"I didn't—" Sharpe fell silent for a moment. "You mentioned me to them by name?"

"Yeah."

Sharpe sucked his teeth. "Change in plans, Max. We're meeting today. Three o'clock. The east side of the Brandenburg Gate."

"Fine. Let's get this over with."

"We're out of time. Be there, Maxwell."

Sharpe hung up. Max fought the urge to hurl his phone across the room.

"Max, he knows about Risse." Max had rarely seen Penny so shaken up. The only thing stronger than her sense of justice and her temper was how much she loved—and worried about—her younger sister.

Max put an arm around her, and she leaned into him.

"We have to warn her," he said. "Tell her to destroy evidence and lay low. Get out of Roseburg if she has to."

"I should go back. I need to be there for her," Penny said.

"You can't do anything to help her back home," Max said. "This is where it's all going down. We know where Kevin Sharpe is going to be this afternoon, and we finally have him right where we want him. If we stop him, he won't be able to hurt Risse or any of us ever again."

Penny raised her head from his shoulder. "You have something in mind?"

"Sometimes you have to help your enemies to help yourself." He smiled. "Or make them think that you're helping them."

"I'm sorry about your sister, Penny. What can I do?" Ada asked.

You've already done enough, Max thought. He wasn't sure yet if she was his enemy or not, but he was going to pretend to help her too, until he figured that out.

"We only have a few hours to power through the rest of your files to find what Sharpe is looking for. Let's not waste any more time," Max said.

16

MAX GOT TO THE BRANDENBURG GATE AN HOUR early for his meeting with Sharpe. He played the tourist for a while, strolling through the streets, committing them to memory and matching them up with the maps he had studied that morning.

The morning had also been spent debating with Penny and Ada about what to do. Penny was furious that Risse had come to Sharpe's attention and so worried about her sister that she was ready to fly home right away to go into hiding with Risse.

"I wouldn't blame you," Max had said softly.

"You didn't blame me last time either," Penny said.

"It was the right call. You wanted to protect her."

"It wasn't only that. Max, I was being selfish. Risse kept on helping you anyway, and it was a good thing she did. I might not be here if she hadn't. But when we try to protect other people . . . we're really just helping ourselves, aren't we? We don't want anything to happen to the people we love because we don't know what we'd do without them."

"You might have a point there," he said.

"And I can't very well pressure you to get involved in all this and then leave you to sort it out. . . ." Penny pulled off her glasses and wiped her eyes. "Besides, I want you to be safe too, you know?"

"The best way to help your sister is to get the upper hand on Sharpe," Ada said.

"That'll be a nice change of pace," Max said.

Ada had no problem with Max handing over a complete copy of her files to Sharpe. They would only confirm what he already knew, and as Max had told him, he wouldn't have much of a head start on the rest of the world in reviewing them.

Max had not mentioned that Sharpe knew about Ada's plan to disrupt the internet; he was holding that one close to the vest for the moment, until he'd had a chance to talk to Sharpe personally.

Once they stopped arguing about what to do, they worked together to plan for the meet up and pore through Ada's files for connections with The Curtain. Max also texted Risse on her crypto phone to give her the heads up that DoubleThink's secret identity had finally been compromised.

It took them long enough, she wrote. I'm not worried.

You aren't? he typed.

No, because you and Pen will fix this.

If only he had that much confidence.

Need any help with those files? **Risse texted.**

We still don't have internet access, and it probably isn't a good idea to transfer them over our phone's wireless network, **he wrote.**

Also owned by VT.

Correct.

Speaking of secret identities, I know who "Clove" and "Volvo" are, **Risse texted.** Image search FTW! She's a reporter named Valentine Labelle. She writes for La Vérité, a French tabloid, and she stars in their online video blog. The guy is Luc Moreau, staff cameraman, photographer, and video editor. I'll send you her phone number and email address.

Thanks! **Max typed. Even though Ada had already identified Labelle, it was useful to have her word corroborated, and now he knew who the guy with the camera was.**

The reward for good work is more work, **Max typed.**

He had glanced over at Ada and Penny working on their laptops across from each other at the table.

Can you get me everything available on Ada Kiesler? **he wrote.**

There have been a ton of profiles on her in the media lately. She's already been doxxed, **Risse wrote.**

That's the superficial, easy stuff, the kind of things anyone can find. I don't need to know where she lives, she's sitting fifteen feet away from me. **At that moment, Kiesler looked up and Max felt his face flush with warmth. There was no way she** knew what he was up to. He flashed her a smile, and she nodded and went back to work.

Max continued typing. I want to know who she *really* is. What newsgroups she frequents, which websites she visits, where she accesses the internet, everything.

Is Pen with you? Risse asked.

Yup. They're practically BFFs.

What is this strange new feeling I'm having? Is this jealousy? Risse texted. You're right—it is *so* suspicious that Pen likes her. She obvs can't be trusted.

Max almost decided right there to spill the beans on everything, but Penny never would have forgiven him. Which was a funny thing to be worried about because he didn't know if he could ever forgive her for what she'd already done.

It was more that he didn't want to do that to Risse, though he knew perfectly well that he might need to involve her later— and hope that she did the right thing instead of just sticking by Penny, if it came to that.

Fine, just humor me.

Okay, it's not like I have anything better to do.

Is that more sarcasm? She didn't used to be so sarcastic. That must have been some of Penny's poor influence on her impressionable sister.

Sadly, no. OK to bring in DP on this?

Max hesitated. After it had turned out that most of Dramatis Personai had been working for Panjea—in some cases unbeknownst to one another—he was reluctant to rely on them for anything. At the same time, the core group had seen a lot of turnover, and though Max didn't know many of them well anymore, Risse had become their de facto leader and he trusted her judgment. This was just what they were good at.

If you think it's necessary, he wrote.

Okay. I'll get on it.

Max glanced over at Penny. He felt a little guilty for recruiting Risse without checking with her sister first, but he didn't think she'd approve of him running a background check on her new hero, the self-appointed savior of the internet.

It shouldn't cause any harm at least, unless Penny and Ada found out about it.

You're the best, Max typed.

I know :D

Max avoided looking at the corner of Pariser Platz where he hoped Penny was situated. The hardest part of their plan was that he was unable to communicate with her, and he had to hope that she was going to be able to pull off her task.

Time to find out. As a distant clock chimed three o'clock, Max walked toward the Brandenburg Gate. He felt a chill when he spotted a man on a green bench to the right of the Gate in a long black trench coat and a plain black baseball cap. Max did a double take.

Kevin Sharpe looked very different from the man who had graced the cover of *Wired* magazine only a couple of years before. His face was pale, and he had a full beard, brown with silver streaks in it, and shaggy hair that hadn't been in contact with shears for too many months. He was wearing black Elvis Costello glasses with the frame repaired with clear tape; behind them, his eyes had bags underneath. This wasn't a disguise, though it was a very effective one—no, Sharpe had seen better days.

Max sat down next to him and adjusted his hood. Kevin Sharpe was the closest thing to a criminal mastermind he knew, and sitting next to him made his skin crawl. Max smelled the strong whiff of whiskey and cigarettes clinging to the man's shabby clothes. Even his trademark white tennis shoes had been replaced by scuffed brown penny loafers.

"'*Ich bin ein Berliner,*'" Sharpe said.

"If we're going to do some kind of code phrase, you should have told me," Max said.

"I was just remembering President Kennedy's famous speech here." Sharpe looked Max over. "So, we finally meet in person."

"I saw you once before, at my school."

"That night." Sharpe nodded.

"I thought you were watching me."

Recognition glimmered in his dull gray eyes. "You were online while we were jamming phones. Well, of course you were." He sighed. "If only I'd had you arrested then. Damn."

"Missed opportunities."

"Missed opportunities," Sharpe agreed. "I also ran into Baxter lurking around the control room before the debate. I should have checked everything over myself, but I underestimated him. . . ." He shook off the memory, like he was waking up from a dream. "I promised myself that would never happen again. Maxwell, take out your phone. Remove the battery. You know the drill."

As Max complied, Sharpe turned away and looked at the Brandenburg Gate.

"All those people taking selfies, they aren't even thinking about how amazing it is that they can walk across this plaza. The Berlin Wall used to be right over there." Sharpe pointed and swept his arm in an arc across the plaza. "It blocked off this gate until 1989, when it was finally opened for travel between East and West Germany. Seeing the wall come down on television . . . It's one of the things that got me interested me in politics."

"I'm not here for a history lesson, Sharpe," Max said. "I thought we were in a hurry?"

Sharpe ignored him. "President Reagan gave a speech right here, an impassioned plea to the Soviet Union to tear down the wall. He said, 'We welcome change and openness; for we believe that freedom and security go together, that the advance of human liberty can only strengthen the cause of world peace.' Think about that. Listen to those words. He could be talking about the internet today."

"I thought you didn't want Ada to tear down the internet," Max said. "You said I had to stop her."

"It's a terrible, dangerous idea. But like all such ideas, I can't stop thinking about it. Wondering if I'm just afraid, the way the Eastern Bloc was afraid to open the borders. I hoped that Panjea and VT could reshape the internet, and ultimately the world . . ." Sharpe sighed. "Forget it. You have the files?"

"Why else would I be here?" Max retrieved a USB stick from his pocket. He put it down on the bench between them. Sharpe casually picked it up.

"If I plug this into a computer, it's not going to be infected with some kind of worm, is it?" Sharpe asked.

Max glared at him coldly. "No, that's more your style."

"Good one," Sharpe said.

Was that enough of an admission of his guilt? No, it was too vague, and he'd already been cleared of any charges related to Panjea. *Keep focused, Max.*

Sharpe pulled out a small laptop. "Don't take this personally, but I have to be sure."

"Knock yourself out."

Sharpe plugged in the USB stick and started scanning the files.

"I have one other condition for keeping your friends out of trouble," Sharpe said.

"Why am I not surprised? What is it?"

"You have to sign a binding agreement that you will stay away from any computers and internet-enabled devices for the duration of President Lovett's term in office."

"I can't do that!" Max said. "How is that even possible?"

"Not my problem," Sharpe said. "That's the deal."

He closed the laptop. "Thank you. I have what I need, so it's up to you."

"You'll leave them out of this?" Max asked. "Forget they exist?"

"As long as they stay out of my way too. But if Penny helps Ada with her plan, no one will be able to protect her from spending the rest of her life in prison, least of all you. Not that you don't all belong in jail, Maxwell."

Max laughed. "And you should be in an adjacent cell. No computers for what? Another three years?"

"Seven," Sharpe said.

"You're that sure she'll get reelected, even after all these scandals?"

"Memories are short, Maxwell, and I'm very good at what I do."

"You want me out of the picture that bad?" Max asked.

"It's the cleanest way to make sure you stop interfering with internet policies and government business," Sharpe said.

That was almost an admission. It also sounded like a threat. If Max were to disappear or suddenly die, it would certainly look suspicious given his accusations against Sharpe. Not that it would be any comfort to Max.

"At least tell me one thing, and I'll sign whatever you want and stay out of your hair," Max said.

Sharpe looked amused. "You're going to sign no matter what, but I might answer your question, depending on what it is."

"Is VT really running The Curtain?" They hadn't been able to find the smoking gun yet, but maybe he could get something useful out of Sharpe.

"You and your curiosity. I knew you'd join in your mother's crusade." Sharpe tucked away the USB drive and computer and stood up. He reached into the right pocket of his coat. "I have a plane to catch."

Max jumped up. "Come on. It's not like I can do anything about it."

"That's true. And that would drive you crazy, wouldn't it? Knowing the truth but having to keep it to yourself, to protect the people you love."

"We looked through these files, like you asked, and we did find the proof that the U.S. has been working with VT, helping them to build up their internet empire by ceding control of key exchanges and companies. But we also found that VT was a big contributor to Lovett's political campaign, a silent partner, of course."

Sharpe pursed his lips, hands in his pockets. "Maxwell, stop. Don't say another—"

Max went on. "We also saw your name all over a bunch of contracts that weren't set to go into effect unless Lovett won the election and took office. Even though you were no longer part of the cabinet, it looks like those under-the-table agreements were honored. And we found something even more surprising, a name we never expected to come up in connection with VT: Panjea."

Sharpe seemed to visibly wilt. "Ms. Kiesler was certainly far more thorough than I hoped."

"VT was part of your plans for Panjea, wasn't it?" Max asked.

Sharpe murmured something under his breath. It sounded like, "Strike that, reverse it."

"Wait, what?" Max asked.

"You already know far more than is good for you, Maxwell. I won't put either of us in any more danger by confirming or denying your speculations. Are you coming or not?"

"But we haven't even gotten to The Curtain yet," Max said. "Did you know about it, or suspect it, when you got into bed with VT? Did you care that Lovett was spending money most likely earned through selling drugs and sex online?"

Sharpe's eyes flashed dangerously. "Good luck, Maxwell. I'm going now."

"Fine." Max stayed put. "I bet you knew, but you never told her, and now you're trying to get ahead of the story and turn yourself into the hero. How?" Max snapped his fingers. "You wanted to turn them in yourself, link them to The Curtain, claim the credit to get your job back. But you ran out of time."

Sharpe looked around, and Max imagined he was actually *afraid*. Sharpe put a finger to his lips.

Max shook his head. "We're going to shut down The Curtain, and if you or Lovett were involved, everyone will soon find out. You won't get out of this one."

"Good luck," Sharpe said again. "I mean that sincerely; you

won't be able to stop The Curtain unless you find the Wizard, and you know how that goes: Nobody sees the Wizard. Not nobody, not no—"

Sharpe stopped midsentence, an astonished expression on his face. He clapped his right hand to his chest like he was reciting the Pledge of Allegiance, and red seeped between his fingers in thick streams.

17

"HOLY SHIT!" MAX SAID. HIS PULSE SPED UP AND TIME slowed down as he realized what was happening. Stupidly, instinctively, he took a step toward Sharpe, hand outstretched.

Sharpe pulled his hand away from his coat and stared at his bloody palm. "I'm a jelly doughnut." He chuckled to himself.

He staggered backward and slumped onto the bench, leaning forward like a puppet without a master. There was a tiny hole in his coat. The dark fabric was glistening wet, the red hard to pick out against it. For a moment, Max felt like this was all happening on TV, like he was watching a movie. Completely out of his control. Panic, rage, and fear hammered his senses.

Then Max remembered he was out in the open. He dropped to his knees, barely registering the pain as they hit the cold, hard bricks, and he glanced all over the open plaza. Tourists were still milling around, blissfully unaware that there was a shooter, that a man was bleeding out right in front of them.

Like you could figure out where the shooter is, Max thought. There were buildings on both sides of the plaza, and the sniper could be at any of those windows with a clear shot. *Take cover, idiot.*

"Sharpe?" Max hissed. If he was still alive, he had to get down.

Sharpe lifted his head slowly. He coughed and red mist clouded the air with his breath, splattering his beard like a Jackson Pollock painting. He gurgled a word, too low to make out. *Wizard?* Max leaned closer.

"You're gonna be all right," Max said. He just had to apply steady pressure to stop the bleed—

A neat hole appeared in Sharpe's forehead. Dead center. He toppled backward and fell off the bench. He didn't move again.

Max screamed. He scrambled behind the bench and looked around wildly. The people around him began shouting and screaming and stampeding. Footsteps pounded away from the Gate.

Shit, man. Max stared at Sharpe's lifeless body, trying to wrap his head around the fact that he was looking at a dead man, only a couple of feet away. The blood pooling beneath him on the stones steamed in the cold air.

Shit shit shit.

He hoped wherever Penny was that she was taking cover too. He didn't know if he should stay put or start running.

In the distance, sirens. Max pulled his hood back and wiped sweat from his brow. His fingers came back streaked red. Sharpe's blood. He wiped his hand furiously on his jeans and then swiped his sleeve over his face.

All this was just like the night Evan had killed himself, only this time Max had been right there, feet away from Sharpe, and he still couldn't do anything. In his nightmares about Evan's death, Max sometimes handed his friend the gun, sometimes blew his brains out himself. Would he relive Sharpe's murder from now on?

He had zero love for Sharpe and not much in the way of sympathy. The man was a manipulator and a murderer. But screw poetic justice. Being killed was more than he deserved, more than *anyone* deserved.

Max trembled as he stared at his faint, bloody fingerprints on the light denim of his jeans.

The files! Max's fingerprints were on the USB drive in Sharpe's pocket, and that would connect him to both Sharpe and Ada. He had to get it back and get out of there.

He fought the almost overpowering urge to run. Still crouching, he crept closer to Sharpe's body. He reached into Sharpe's coat, grimacing as he touched warm, slick blood, fighting his gag reflex at the coppery stench. He jumped when Sharpe's throat gurgled. His lips were painted crimson, resembling a garish clown smile.

Max fumbled around until he found the inner pocket, holding his breath. He grabbed the USB drive and Sharpe's computer, while he was at it. He wiped his hands on Sharpe's coat. Then he noticed that Sharpe was holding something in his left hand.

Max pried open Sharpe's limp fingers and found a dumbphone with a call still in progress. The phone number had a Berlin area code, and the call had been running for ten minutes and fourteen seconds, which meant the person on the other end had heard their whole conversation.

Max lifted the phone to his ear. It was still warm from Sharpe's grasp.

"Hello?" Max said.

There was a long moment of silence, then a woman said, "*Auf Wiedersehen,*" and hung up. The screen fritzed and went dark. Max pressed the power button, but nothing happened. It had been bricked. There was a chance Max could retrieve some data from it if the SIM card hadn't been wiped.

A shot rang out. Max ducked, and the ground in front of him geysered as a bullet hit a paving stone. He had dropped the phone. As he reached down for it, he heard another gunshot and the phone exploded.

Why can I hear the gunfire now? Never mind, he had to run.

Max turned and bolted for the Brandenburg Gate, recalling the details of one of the escape routes he had memorized earlier. He heard two more shots and then he was down, lurching forward and catching himself painfully on his hands and elbows. At first he thought he'd tripped over something, until fire suddenly burned in his left leg.

I was hit, Max thought.

Get up. Get up. Get up, get up, get up.

Max pulled himself up and tried to take a step. He immediately fell again and rolled onto his side, clutching his wounded leg. Below the knee, his jeans were soaked with blood, the heavy fabric clinging to his skin. He clenched his jaw and got back up.

Running was out of the question, but he half hopped and half limped to the safety of the columns in the northern wing of the Brandenburg Gate. He used them to keep him on his feet and provide cover, darting from one column to the next. Next to a door in the side of the building was a blue sandwich board labeled RAUM DER STILLE, with the translation: ROOM OF SILENCE. Max twisted the handle. Locked.

He stared through the glass and saw the frightened faces of people hiding inside staring back at him. A young woman in a I ♥ BERLIN T-shirt crept toward the door to unlock it for Max. The glass panel beside his head cracked loudly, pierced by a bullet. The Good Samaritan dropped to the ground, twitching. Her shirt slowly turned red. More screams.

Oh, God. Sorry, Max thought. He had to keep moving.

He reached the main portion of the Gate. Just past each of its six columns was a wall, dividing the Gate into five short corridors. Max joined the others huddling in the middle of the northernmost section and leaned against a wall.

His heart pounded and he couldn't catch his breath. He was

drenched in sweat. Somehow, he still had Sharpe's computer clutched under his right arm, but one corner was crushed.

Max leaned down and pulled up the leg of his jeans. He saw spots as the pain flared up. He blinked back tears and examined his leg. It was slick with blood, the wound throbbing in time with his heartbeat. People nearby gasped and whispered. A little boy's cell-phone camera flashed.

"Really?" Max growled.

He couldn't tell how bad the wound was, but if the bullet had hit bone, it would be excruciating, right? An artery, and he'd be dead. Lucky.

He was dizzy and nauseated. He slid to the ground, back braced against the wall, and pulled off his right sneaker; the left was already squishy with blood gushing into it from the wound. He pulled off his sock and tied it around his calf, squeezing it as tight as he could. He nearly blacked out.

He pushed his shoe back on and rolled down the cuff of his jeans. He tested his weight on his left leg. *Better.* It hurt like nothing he'd ever felt before, but he had to keep moving. He had to get away from there and off the streets. He had to get to Penny.

18

MAX GRITTED HIS TEETH AND TURNED HIS SCREAM into a low growl. He was sitting on a closed toilet seat in a bathroom at Hostel Caligari while Penny administered what passed for first aid.

"Shhh," Penny said.

"This . . . really . . . hurts . . . ," Max said through gritted teeth.

"It's just a little peroxide. You're lucky the bullet went clean through, or I'd have to dig around in there to remove it."

Max was overjoyed that he didn't have a bullet lodged in his leg, but had, essentially, "just a flesh wound."

"The downside is I have two holes in me instead of one."

She poured peroxide on the exit wound, and Max squeezed his teary eyes shut and held onto the toilet-seat lid with both hands. This time he whimpered.

"So does Sharpe, but you're much better off than he is," Penny said quietly.

"I *know*. He died right in front of me. God," Max said. "And someone else got shot while I was running away. I don't know what happened to her."

The memory of Kevin Sharpe being shot just a foot away from Max was enough to get him to briefly forget his pain. Very briefly, because Penny began daubing at the wounds with gauze and an antibiotic ointment.

"Are you sure you know what you're doing?" Max asked.

"Of course."

"You've never done this before, I assume."

"No, but I watched some videos on YouTube."

"That's not very confidence-making," Max said. "You're going to have to decide whether stuff on the internet can be trusted or not."

"I never blindly trust anything online. Always corroborate with independent sources. I wish everyone did that before forwarding the latest shocking 'news.'"

"I have to admit, I'm both surprised and not-surprised that there are videos explaining what to do if you get shot."

"Most of them say you should go to a hospital, which I'm inclined to agree with."

"Don't need a video to tell me that much. Ow!" Max howled as Penny poked a finger into the entry wound.

"Sadly, not an option. Not with everyone out there looking for you right now. And a gunshot wound, in general, is an indication that you've been involved in something not entirely legal." She poked him again.

"Why would you do that? Stop!" he cried.

"I'm just wondering if I should suture this or something."

Max eyed the needle and thread next to Penny's impromptu first-aid kit. After she found Max, pale, sweaty, and shaking, at their prearranged rendezvous point, the hostel, she had gone out for supplies. She'd been careful to spread out her purchases over several different stores in different neighborhoods, so it took her much longer than Max had felt was reasonable.

Penny stood and washed her hands in the sink. "I'd better check," she said.

She opened her laptop and started searching. After a few minutes, Max grew impatient.

"Um, I'm bleeding out here," he said.

Penny glanced over. "Sorry. Hold on. You just need a tight bandage. Meanwhile, you should see this."

She turned her laptop toward him, tuned to streaming video from BBC News. She started applying gauze and bandages while he watched coverage of Sharpe's murder.

The news was running a grainy video recording of Sharpe and Max sitting on the bench in Pariser Platz, talking. It was on a loop, always stopping just before the first bullet was fired, while the anchor provided a running commentary.

"Where did they get this footage?" Max asked.

"Mysterious unnamed source is mysterious," Penny said.

"*Kevin Sharpe, former security consultant and campaign*

*manager to United States President Angela Lovett, was seen
with a young man, identified as Maxwell Stein, at the Brandenburg Gate in Berlin this afternoon, just moments before he was
fatally shot."*

"It looks like this was filmed at a long distance, zoomed in,
from high up," Max said. "Drone?"

"Could it have been the sniper?" Penny asked.

"Maybe. But why film your own crime and deliver it to the
media?"

The video was replaced with a press photo of Sharpe, the
famous one that was used for everything, showing him in the
gray turtleneck he'd worn almost like a uniform before he'd
gone into hiding.

*"Maxwell Stein was flagged early this week at Charles de
Gaulle airport—"*

"Thanks again, Penny," Max said.

She sighed.

*"He was also recently arrested and charged with breaking
and entering at a building in Strasbourg, France. He is wanted
by France's Police Nationale for violating the conditions of his
release by fleeing the country."*

"Great," Max said.

Max's picture appeared on the right—the same crappy
school photo they'd been using since his trouble with Panjea last year. Why was the media so lazy, using the same old
images instead of putting in a little effort to get something
decent from his public social media profiles? Not that it was

in their best interests to make a fugitive look presentable. Max was tempted to send them a selfie, except that would make it easier for people to recognize him.

The photo was replaced with a pixelated blown-up image of Max from the video, where he happened to be looking left, in the direction of the camera.

"*Anonymous sources say Stein boarded the train to Berlin in Strasbourg, France, yesterday in the company of a woman named Penny Polonsky.*"

"Craaaaaaaap," Penny said.

"*Stein currently has short black hair and was last seen wearing a black hoodie and blue jeans.*"

"Ah," Penny said. "No mention of you being injured."

"Damn. Now I need a disguise."

"I suggest going in drag."

"You're always trying to get me in a dress."

"Only because you have such sexy legs. Though they look better when they haven't been punctured by metal projectiles." She stopped what she was doing and stared down at the blood on her hands.

"Penny? You okay?"

She looked up at him, her eyes wide. "Am *I* okay? Jesus, Max. You were shot. You could have been killed." She held up her hands. "What the hell are we doing? You should be at a hospital."

"You did great." He stood and tested his weight on his bandaged calf, suppressing a gasp from the pain. The muscle was sore and tight, and the wound felt like someone was twisting a knife inside his leg when he tried to move, but with some effort, he could walk without limping. "See? No problem. Thanks."

Penny watched him quietly before absentmindedly saying, "You're welcome." She cupped her hands under the faucet, letting reddish water spill out into the basin. Her hands shook. In the mirror over the sink, he saw that her eyes were closed.

"Stein is considered armed and dangerous, wanted as a suspect in the murder of Kevin Sharpe. If you spot him, do not engage, but contact your local law enforcement immediately."

"Wait, what?" Max asked.

"What?" Penny's eyes flew open. She spun back to face her computer and stared at the screen.

"Oh my God," Max said. "How can I be a suspect? I shot him without a gun at point-blank range? Don't they have labs who can test for that stuff?"

"You're being set up for some reason. Screw this, too slow." Penny wiped her hands dry on her jeans and tapped the keyboard to open a new browser tab. "Social media's much faster."

She scanned the posts that were updating almost too quickly to keep up.

"Looks like you're a hashtag again. Hashtag MaxStein, and the surprising return of hashtag 503ERROR. Some news outlets have already connected us to Ada because we were photographed there. So the embassy is even more crowded than before with media, protesters, and police. I don't know how we're going to get back in." She glanced at him. "That was going to be our next stop once you were feeling up to walking. But maybe we'd be better off laying low for a while. Get your disguise together here before people recognize you."

Penny gathered up their supplies, passing a bottle of aspirin to Max. He swallowed two of the bitter pills and tucked the bottle into his sweatshirt pocket.

They left the bathroom. The hostel was filling with noisy travelers returning from their day's adventures, but they were all congregating in the small cafeteria lounge, buzzing about the shocking news developments. What an exciting time to be vacationing in Berlin! It was scary imagining there was a cold-blooded killer on the loose. Some were babbling about how they'd changed plans to visit the Brandenburg Gate this afternoon. They could have been right there when it happened!

Max kept his head down as they headed for their room. Penny closed and locked the door.

The bunk beds reminded him of soccer camp, a lifetime ago. Penny raced for the lower bed. "Dibs!"

"Penny," Max said. He pointed to his injured leg. She shrugged.

He eased down next to her. The mattress was as saggy, lumpy, and creaky as he had expected. He figured he would be spending another sleepless night anyway, due to the nightmares he was sure to have.

Penny balanced her laptop between them on his right knee and her left.

"If they have video of me with Sharpe, then they must

know I didn't shoot him," Max said. "And there were so many eyewitnesses."

"Right." Penny spent a couple of minutes surfing around online. "This network is so sloooowwwww. . . ." She lowered her voice like a recording winding down.

"When you're using free Wi-Fi, you get what you pay for," Max said.

He was worried about VT or the authorities tracking Penny's web searches to find him, but as long as he was the top news story, their queries shouldn't raise any flags.

"This is all that was officially released," Penny said. She opened a video she had just downloaded and skipped to the end. The footage ended just before Sharpe was shot in the chest.

"Convenient," Max said.

"Not for you," Penny said. "Max, I think someone's framing you."

"Or at least trying to distract me and make things more difficult. What about your recording?" Max asked.

"I just have audio, but I have the whole thing."

"You kept recording through all that?" Max was impressed.

"Please. I'm a professional." Penny opened her video-editing software and an audio wave form displayed on her screen. "I'm not as good at this as Risse, but . . ."

She started playing the surveillance video from Max's meeting with Sharpe.

"*Ich bin ein Berliner,*'" Sharpe said.

"If we're going to do some kind of code phrase, you should have told me," Max said.

Max leaned forward to get a better look. "Wow. You synced the audio with it!" The recording was tinny and faint. Penny had been situated on the opposite side of Pariser Platz with the best long-range listening device that money could buy in Berlin on short notice, which was still very good in a city of spies and secrets.

"'Ich bin ein Berliner,'" Penny said. "I am a Berliner. Although some people mistakenly translate it as, 'I am a jelly doughnut,' because grammar."

Oh. So that's what Sharpe had been referring to when he was shot. "He was quoting President Kennedy."

"Yeah." Penny switched to an open Wikipedia page and read from it. "'All free men, wherever they may live, are citizens of Berlin, and therefore, as a free man, I take pride in the words *Ich bin ein Berliner!*' That was in June 1963 at the Brandenburg Gate. Five months later, JFK was assassinated in Dallas."

She skipped ahead in the video.

"I underestimated him. I promised myself that would never happen again. Maxwell, take out your phone. Remove the battery. You know the drill."

Max smiled. Even Sharpe hadn't counted on him being bugged from a distance. The master of surveillance had been watched and recorded from two separate people at the same time.

She skipped ahead to about where the video cut out, where she had left a still frame of Sharpe and Max standing in front of the park bench.

"You and your curiosity. I knew you'd join in your mother's crusade. I have a plane to catch."

"Come on. It's not like I can do anything about it."

"That's true. And that would drive you crazy, wouldn't it? Knowing the truth but having to keep it to yourself, to protect the people you love."

"We looked through these files, like you asked, and we did find the proof that the U.S. has been working with VT, helping them to build up their internet empire by ceding control of key exchanges and companies. But we also found that VT was a big contributor to Lovett's political campaign, a silent partner, of course."

"Maxwell, stop. Don't say another—"

Penny paused the video. "He's not trying to hurry you up. He's warning you." Max nodded. She pressed Play.

"We also saw your name all over a bunch of contracts that weren't set to go into effect unless Lovett won the election and took office. Even though you were no longer part of the cabinet, it looks like those under-the-table agreements were honored. And we found something even more surprising, a name we never expected to come up in connection with VT: Panjea."

"Ms. Kiesler was certainly far more thorough than I hoped."

"Nice bluff," Penny said. "If only we really did have those files."

"They could be in there. Sharpe seemed to believe it," Max said.

"VT was part of your plans for Panjea, wasn't it?"

"Strike that, reverse it."

"There it is. Sharpe was working for VT at some point," Penny said.

"And for Lovett. Little conflict of interest there. Do you think if his overlords were upset with how that went down, they'd want to punish him for it?" Max asked.

Penny held up a finger and scrubbed the video forward a little.

"I bet you knew, but you never told her, and now you're trying to get ahead of the story and turn yourself into the hero. How? You wanted to turn them in yourself, link them to The Curtain, claim the credit to get your job back. But you ran out of time."

"That's when Sharpe looked genuinely frightened and seemed to realize he was being watched," Max said.

"And a short while later . . ." Penny pressed a button.

"You won't be able to stop The Curtain unless you find the Wizard, and you know how that goes: Nobody sees the Wizard. Not nobody, not no—"

That's when the video cut out. The audio continued with that last moment frozen as a still image.

"Holy shit!"

"I'm a jelly doughnut."

"Sharpe?"

Then there was Sharpe's last gurgled word.

Max held up a hand. "Pause it. What did that sound like to you?"

"Hard to say," she said. "'Wizard,' I think. He's stuck on what he was saying before."

"That's what I heard too." Max tapped his lips with a finger. He mouthed the word. "Wizard."

"Wait, this is my favorite part," Penny said.

"You're gonna be all right."

Penny paused it again.

"That's sick, Penny. I don't even know why I said that." He shuddered at the memory of the whole experience. "What if we release this recording?"

"That doesn't help you. You never got him to really admit to anything, and there's no audio evidence that you weren't involved in his murder."

They let the video play through to the end. Penny artfully intercut cell-phone photos and video snippets that people had uploaded of Max after Sharpe was shot the second time, when they finally noticed what was going on.

He doubted these photos would do anything to clear his name of the murder either. Never mind that Max wasn't holding a gun and was taking cover himself. Forensics would reveal immediately that Sharpe had been killed from a distance, but would Interpol mention that publicly? One way or another, they wanted Max brought in for questioning, and there were still those charges in France.

Max was struck by a sudden, horrible thought. He leaned over and replayed a portion of the video. Penny started to jerk her computer away—she hated it when people touched her tech without asking—but she relented when she saw how worked up Max was.

"I knew you'd join in your mother's crusade."

"I have to warn my mom. She could be in danger too. Because I had to go bragging about how we're going to shut down The Curtain," Max said.

"It all goes back to that site," Penny said.

"All roads lead to Oz. . . . You can find killers for hire on The Curtain."

"So Sharpe's old boss decided to silence Sharpe permanently when he became even more of a liability."

Max covered his mouth. "Oh no."

"What?" Penny said.

"This is my fault."

"How?"

"Those guys who followed us on the train. Artoo and Threepio. They seemed surprised when I mentioned Sharpe's name, and he claimed they didn't work for him. I didn't believe him, but what if they worked for VT, and I tipped them off that Sharpe was in Berlin and in contact with me?" Max closed his eyes. "I led them right to him."

"You don't know that . . ." Penny didn't sound too sure herself. It made sense to him. "And then they decided to frame you rather than kill you?" she asked.

"I think they tried to kill me, and when I got away, framing me is the best they can do to get me out of their hair."

"You're the perfect scapegoat. Yesterday's hero is tomorrow's villain. We're hackers, with no respect for authority. No matter what we do, that's what we'll always be. And you have a personal vendetta against Sharpe."

"But I didn't want him dead. Oh my God. Oh my God. He's dead because of me." Max leaned over and pressed his hands to his head. "I didn't take this seriously enough. I—"

"Max! Let's look at the bright side."

"What's that?" Max asked.

"That means they see us as a threat. So we're close!"

"Yay."

Max suddenly felt very tired. He hated being used when he knew it was happening, but it was worse when he didn't know who was manipulating him, for what or why.

The only winning move is not to play. Max could turn himself in, like removing his piece from the game board, but then he would also be giving up any chance at future freedom, or vengeance. He couldn't leave all this on Penny, and he doubted anyone else would put themselves out to prove his innocence.

"There's another bright side. Sharpe is gone. Hopefully he kept his info on Risse to himself," Penny said.

"Hopefully."

Penny bowed her head, thinking. "Do you remember anything about that woman listening in on Sharpe's phone?

Was there a weird sound in the background? Did she have an accent?"

"She only said two words: 'Auf Wiedersehen.'"

"Good-bye," Penny said.

"Then the sniper took a shot at me."

"Think the sniper was the woman on the call?"

"Or they were in contact with the woman. There was a short delay."

"You know, Richard Rhone conducts all his business through his personal assistant, a woman named Apsara Siri-wanich. How did she say it? Was it conversational, or ominous, or with a sexy phone voice? 'Auf Wiedersehen.'" Penny used a low, suggestive tone, eyebrows waggling.

"That's your idea of a sexy phone voice?" Max asked.

Penny blushed. "Shut up."

"It was abrupt. Kind of . . . businesslike. But now that I think about it, I do have her phone number."

Penny slapped Max on the arm. "Next time, lead with that! What is it?"

"Four nine, four seven two five, one one three eight."

Penny typed it in. "No hits, but the area code is for . . . Helgoland? Where the hell is that? Let's see if anyone's home."

Penny pulled up a phone app on her computer and dialed. "I'm calling from one of my disposable numbers, so they can't trace it back to us."

The line rang, then three harsh tones sounded and a recorded woman's voice said, "*Kein anschluss unter dieser nummer.*"

"The number's been disconnected," Penny said.

"A dead end," Max said.

"What else you got?"

"Well . . . how about the fact that the first two shots were inaudible, but everyone heard the others?"

"You're suggesting there were *two* snipers?" Penny said.

"No?"

"That's overthinking things. Maybe they had already removed the silencer, then when they decided to kill you too, they didn't have time to replace it."

"And *I'm* overthinking it?"

"Still just one sniper though. That's simpler. Or maybe it was intentional: The later gunshots drew everyone's attention to you right away."

Max nodded. "Yeah."

"Where's Sharpe's laptop? Maybe we can salvage something from that."

Max grabbed it from the desk and powered it on. Despite the crushed and cracked corner, it still worked.

The machine didn't have any way to connect to the internet: no wireless radio, no network jacks. It also was configured to erase everything but its basic Linux operating system whenever it was shut down.

"Bah!" Max said, shoving the laptop away.

"It's all right. We'll figure this out." Penny put a hand on Max's thigh. They both suddenly realized that they were side-by-side on a bed in a private room, close enough to feel each other's heat. They leaned toward each other—and then Max drew back abruptly. Penny's face showed the surprise he felt that he didn't want to kiss her.

Max couldn't think about her the same way anymore, knowing about her master plan and how she'd been manipulating him. He still needed to convince her to change her mind, and he didn't want anything else complicating the situation right now.

"Well, time to face the music!" Max picked up his phone. "I'm more worried about calling my mom than getting arrested."

"You're calling your mom. Now?" Penny's voice betrayed her disbelief.

He shrugged. "I just saw someone die. *I* almost died. . . . I need some time," he lied.

"Max, what's gotten—" His phone started ringing in his hand. *Psycho.* Saved by the bell.

Penny covered her ears. "Will you *please* change that ringtone?"

"That's eerie. Maybe mother's intuition isn't a myth." Assuming someone else wasn't spoofing her number to track Max down.

"Maybe she's been listening in," Penny muttered.

"Ha." Max breathed in and out to prepare himself, then accepted the call.

He was expecting to get an earful. His mom had good

reason to be angry: He had lied to her, run away, avoided her calls, and gotten mixed up in a murder investigation.

But he hoped for a more emotional reaction, perhaps a tearful inquiry about his well-being. He hadn't wanted to worry her, but after her absence for all these years, it would be a clear sign that she cared.

"Mom?" he said.

"Don't say anything. Is your phone encrypted?" she demanded.

"Uh . . ." Max was stunned into continued silence.

"If it isn't, hang up right now," she said.

Max recovered. "My phone's encrypted! Of course it is. But . . . why is yours?"

Penny raised an eyebrow.

His mom sighed in relief. "It's only common sense these days. Many of the people I deal with require complete confidence that they and their information is safe. Are you okay?"

"I'm . . ." He looked down at his bandaged leg. *Later.* "Yeah, I'm fine."

"Good. And Penny?"

"Her too."

"In that case, what in the world were you thinking, running off like that?" his mother shouted.

Max grinned.

19

LIANNA STEIN DIDN'T DISAPPOINT IN THE concerned-parent department. But she was also very, *very* pissed at Max. It didn't help his case that had he listened to her, Kevin Sharpe might still be alive, and there wouldn't be an Interpol Red Notice out for Max's arrest.

But that was the situation they were in, and his mother was very adaptable. She had followed Max to Berlin and was staying at the Hotel Reichenbach. She offered to help and give him the chance to explain why he couldn't turn himself in—which she and *his father* agreed was the most sensible solution.

If his estranged parents were talking and agreeing with each other, Max knew he was in trouble. So he consented to a meeting, with some careful precautions to make sure Lianna wasn't followed or being used to get to him, and that she wasn't trying to trick him out into the open. He didn't like to think that about her, but he wasn't taking anyone's loyalty for granted anymore.

Now Max was sitting in a small café in West Berlin watching the entrance of the Hotel Reichenbach across the street, looking out for other people doing the same thing. Penny sat beside him, engrossed in a chat with Risse on her laptop.

Max and Penny's disguises were each other; they had dressed in cheesy matching outfits. Blue I ♥ BERLIN T-shirts, puffy black parkas, baggy jeans, white sneakers. Max had a bulky backpack that they used to carry their equipment, and Penny had a camera around her neck. Max wore a straw fedora that covered most of his hair, and their remaining medical supplies had come in handy: Penny had taped gauze and an eye protector over his left eye, bandaged the bridge of his nose, and artfully painted fake bruises over his forehead and cheek to further thwart facial recognition software. A pinhole in the eye shield mitigated his restricted vision, which was inconvenient for a stakeout.

To her credit, Max's mom hadn't pulled the "I told you so" card, so he didn't bring up again the fact that she had abandoned him and his dad first, which now felt like what it was: a cheap shot.

It turned out his mother was as skilled as he was in communicating more by saying less, so voicing their mistakes was as unnecessary as apologies. Later. Maybe.

Max glanced at Penny. He'd been thinking a lot about what went wrong between Bradley and Lianna. Max's father had a brilliant but very literal mind. He had flashes of inspiration that made him an excellent programmer, but his strength was attacking a problem head on, relentlessly, until he succeeded or failure was assured—at which point he lost interest entirely and moved on to the next thing. It was an admirable quality in his line of work, but it was a poor way to approach relationships with people.

Max's mother, on the other hand, was less technical-minded, but more imaginative, ambitious, and compassionate. She looked for ways to connect to people the way that Bradley looked for connections between data and code. She dealt with challenges by looking at the situation differently and, when necessary, changing conditions for a more favorable outcome. Running away wasn't giving up—she never gave up. Running away was just part of her process, as frustrating and hurtful as that might be. For someone who cared so much about others, she was apparently capable of being enormously selfish.

Max, as it happened, was both his parents' son—with the same raw talents and the same flaws. He had never really appreciated that, because for many years he had been more focused on comparing himself to Evan. Now Max realized that his attempt to distance himself from the hacking world, and consequently his best friend, had been like running away.

Max's mother exited the hotel. She paused in front of the sparkling glass doors and donned a pair of oversize sunglasses, then turned to her left and walked toward Lietzenburger

Strasse at a leisurely stroll, eyes downcast to read her phone's screen.

Max leaned forward and tilted his head to get a better viewing angle down the street. No one appeared to be following her.

"Mama bird has left the nest," Max said. "Clear skies."

"We agreed we weren't doing that," Penny said, eyes still on her computer as she typed.

"*You* agreed, but I still think it's a good security measure. Anyone could be listening."

Penny snorted.

"Come on," Max said.

Penny sighed. "Fine. Angry bird is tweeting again."

"Huh?" Max asked.

"Does a baby bird cheep-cheep?"

"What are you talking about?"

"The worm the early bird gets," Penny said, in her best Yoda impression.

"Now you're just being silly."

"Sorry, I thought that's what you wanted."

"Never mind. What's this about angry birds?"

Penny lowered her voice. "I've just heard from H8Bit and the rest of the crew. They were able to check in with Ada online."

"How?"

"The Berlin Firewall was turned off."

Max scratched above his right eyebrow. "That's weird. They didn't hack in?"

"They were hacking it, using the data I pulled from the ports at the embassy and my access at VT, but what they were trying shouldn't have worked. I've looked it over and over, and it couldn't have restored connectivity. But it's all systems go now."

"It's a trap," Max said. "VT wanted it to look like your hackers got through the firewall."

Penny pecked Max on the cheek. "Just what I was thinking!"

He ducked away from her kiss, and she gave him a strange look.

"Interesting timing," Max said. "Right after my conversation with Sharpe about Ada and The Curtain, they're making it easier for her to release her files and communicate with her partners."

"Making it easier for them to monitor her and figure out what she's doing," Penny said. "They all came to the same conclusion, and we won't be communicating online with Ada again unless we can guarantee full encryption on both ends and in transit. Which, of course, we can't with VT controlling the pipes. In the meantime, H8Bit and dorkph0enyx are standing by."

"For what?" Max asked.

"You know. The thing." She raised her eyebrows. "The *thing*."

Right. The thing: Ada's plan. "You mean Operation Undo."

"We're not calling it that. Why does it need a name?" Penny said.

"So we don't have to keep referring to it as 'the thing.' Anyway, why so soon?"

Penny frowned. "Ada's worried we're going to get arrested, and she needs us to be free to explain what's happening to the media."

"Nice vote of confidence," Max said. "The embassy is still kicking her out, even though they have access to the internet again?"

"I guess so. Probably they just want to cut her loose and get those crowds away from their building. Can you blame them?"

"When are they doing the thing?"

"*We* are doing it, uh, when I tell them to," Penny said.

"Huh?"

"Ada put me in charge because she's incommunicado. The others are waiting for me to give the order." She shrugged. "I guess because we're on the front line, and she knows we're still trying to track down The Curtain."

"Penny. That means *you'll* get the blame. She's passing the buck. I don't believe her!"

"I'm responsible either way. She couldn't do all this without my help."

"She could have found someone else," Max said.

"*Dislike.*"

"You know what I mean. It would have taken, like, six other hackers to replace you, but actually being the one who decides to go through with it, and when . . ." Max shook his head.

"Good save. But you're right. This is a big deal." She bit her lip. "Is it such a terrible idea?"

"Penny! Really?"

"I was so sure before, when we were just *talking* about it. But . . . What should I do?"

"This isn't my decision. Maybe it's time you sought the opinion of someone you trust completely. We could use her help on tracking down The Curtain anyway."

She gave him a pleading look. "Max. *No.*"

"She's your sister. She deserves to know. You can't protect her forever." Max hesitated. "Or are you avoiding this because you're ashamed?"

"Screw you," Penny said. But she looked more thoughtful than upset with him. He was getting through to her.

"Risse wasn't nearly as freaked as we were about her identity being out. She can handle this. She can handle a lot more than you give her credit for. Tell her what you've been working on."

Penny sighed but returned to her private chat with Risse. It went on for a long time, Penny practically pounding the keys in full-on "someone is wrong on the internet" mode.

Max texted with Enzo while he waited. His friend had seen the news about Sharpe in Paris, and he wanted to make sure Max was all right. Apparently the Beaumonts had already been interviewed by Interpol regarding Max's stay with them, and Enzo's computer had been confiscated. Shortly afterward, they'd been approached by Valentine Labelle, the reporter from *La Vérité*, but had refused to be part of their story. Enzo was certain they were all being followed.

Max sighed. Once again, he'd put his innocent friends in danger, and there was little he could do to help them, other than turn himself in.

He realized the café was strangely quiet, except for the soft pop music playing over the speakers. Penny had stopped typing and was staring listlessly at her screen.

"What did she say?" Max asked.

"She's on your side, of course," Penny said.

"Aren't *you*?" Max said.

His phone buzzed. A text from Risse this time: She's out of control. We've never disagreed so completely before.

Other than Panjea? Max wrote.

True. That's when it started.

It must be hard. You're growing up.

Pfffpt. Tell her that.

Just kidding. I mean, adulting. ;)

Terrible.

Penny was still typing beside him. Aren't you still chatting with P? he texted.

You know I'm good at multitasking.

Right. DT. DoubleThink.

I'm trying to convince her not to do it, but I don't know, Max. What do we do?

I don't know either. But it's up to P. I'm not going to stop her. I have enough problems to handle at the moment.

Good thing I've got your back. At least now I know why you wanted me to investigate AK. I'm sending you what I have now.

Max waited, but there were no further texts. He checked his email too. Nothing.

Did you send it? I didn't receive anything, he texted.

I sent you *everything* I found—which is nothing.

Nothing?

Other than what's on the public record, which by the way is limited to the official bio that's still on VT's site, there's nothing on Ada Kiesler. From what I can tell, she didn't *exist* before she started working there six years ago.

How can someone in a high position at a global telecom not have an internet presence? At all?

She could have used VT's resources to scrub her history? Or hired someone to do it for her with her access to their systems? I bet you can buy that service on The Curtain too.

Max drummed his fingers on the table. This was a stumper. But he'd read about Ada Kiesler's past. She was born in Singapore to American parents. Her family moved to Edinburgh when she was three and relocated to Oxford when she was fifteen. She attended the University of Hamburg and worked for several years as a consultant before getting the job at VT.

What about all those articles about her, after the attempted leak? Max typed.

They all share the same information from her bio. But I fact-checked everything and none of it is true.

No one bothered to look into this stuff before?

News organizations don't have the time or staff to do that anymore. Why wouldn't you trust something on the internet, on an official VT page? They must have assumed VT verified everything. She hasn't done many interviews, but the few I did find archived supported the official line.

Max had been keeping an eye on their surroundings, and he spotted his mother returning to the hotel from the opposite direction along Spichernstrasse, having walked around the block.

"Penny, the mama bird—I mean, she's coming back. Wrap it up. We have to move."

Max scanned the street again. The Saturday afternoon traffic looked perfectly normal. He didn't see anyone suspicious, and he hadn't seen the same person twice in the last few hours.

Okay, Max texted Risse.

Sorry, she said.

That was great detective work, Max wrote.

Need anything else?

Max hesitated. He didn't want to further pit the sisters against each other, but he didn't think Penny would go along with this.

Want a crack at these files? We need help narrowing it down to information about The Curtain, and especially identifying anyone who could be the Wizard. Your organizational skills are just what we need to process them quickly, Max texted.

Like you even need to ask.

I do need to ask. I'm asking for your help, but I want you to say no. P doesn't want you involved either.

Then I'm definitely in. :-P

Great. I'll send them to the usual place.

Under the circumstances, he would just have to trust transferring them to encrypted file storage. They'd be public soon anyway, and he doubted VT was interested in them anymore; they could have waited to ambush Sharpe where they could take the USB drive from him.

Keep working on changing her mind, Risse texted. Please.

Max's shoulders slumped. He felt bad about putting Risse in this situation, between him and her sister. He didn't know what he would do without them both.

I will. I'm sorry, he wrote. We've gotta go. For now, he and Penny were still a team.

Max tucked away his phone and stood up. "Penny. Game on."

20

PENNY LEFT THE CAFÉ AHEAD OF MAX AND crossed the two lanes of Nürnberger Strasse to the hotel's entrance. Once she had passed through its doors, Max exited the café and turned right, walking past the hotel parallel to the path his mom had taken. He crossed Nürnberger at the corner and continued straight down Lietzenburger for a block, all the while keeping his eyes peeled for anyone following him.

When he reached the next street, he made a left and walked past an apartment building. When he spotted the plastic keycard on the sidewalk, he stopped and knelt down with a grunt of pain. As he pretended to tie his shoelace, he palmed the card. He stood and continued down the road, making another left.

Near the end of Schaperstrasse, he cut through a line of bushes and worked his way behind Hotel Reichenbach to a little semi-enclosed courtyard. The back door was locked with a card reader.

A woman and a four-year-old girl stepped out of the door. The four-year-old courteously held it open for Max. He almost laughed, pocketing the unnecessary keycard. He smiled and said, *"Danke."*

"Bitte." The girl tilted her head and covered her left eye with one hand, mimicking Max's fake eye patch. Max winked with his visible eye and went inside.

His phone buzzed with a text message from Penny: 112. Max sent the room number to his mom and headed over there himself.

He knocked on the door: Three soft knocks, three loud, three soft. SOS. It opened and he darted inside.

Penny closed and locked the door. She had changed into a pink blouse and black capri pants.

"You changed." He pouted. "But I liked matching."

"The concierge is less likely to remember a businesswoman checking into his posh hotel than an idiot tourist in a kitschy T-shirt."

Max stared at her blouse and the glimpse of white lace underneath it. "I think he'll remember you. You missed a button. Not that I'm complaining."

"Prude." Penny calmly fastened the naughty top button. "If the concierge enjoys the view, he's more likely to give you a room with a view *you* want, even if it hasn't been visited by housecleaning yet. Sorry for the mess." She pulled her hair up and applied a hairclip. "I hate the game, but damn I'm good at it."

Someone knocked on the door: Loud, soft, loud soft. Pause. Loud, loud, soft, loud. *CQ.* Popularized as "seek you," the wireless code was shorthand for the French word *sécurité.* Safety.

Max started to peer through the peephole with his left eye, but then he remembered his disguise. He switched to his right and saw Lianna Stein through the fish-eye lens. She was nervously looking up and down the hall.

Smooth, Mom, Max thought. *I thought you were better at this.*

He unlocked the door, and she stepped inside quickly.

"Hi, Mom." Max smiled.

She gasped. "Oh my God, Max! What happened to your eye?"

"Whoa, calm down." He pulled away the bandage. "It's fake." He blinked his left eye rapidly as it adjusted to the bright light.

She studied his face skeptically and reached up to gently touch his forehead with cool fingers. "The bruises too?"

"Makeup," Max said.

"Jesus." She wrapped Max in a hug.

"I'm fine." He pulled away.

"Except for the bullet holes in his leg," Penny said.

Lianna turned to Penny. "I'm glad someone can find this funny. I suppose this is all your handiwork?"

Penny nodded.

"Thank you for looking after my son," Lianna said.

"No problem. He needs all the help he can get, and I'm kind of fond of him too."

"Who called who for help?" Max muttered.

"Max, what on earth are you wearing?" Lianna said.

"That's part of the disguise too."

"I should hope so."

"It made more sense before Penny changed."

His mother looked around the room, her gaze lingering on the lone king bed with the rumpled sheets.

Don't be such a mom right now, Max thought. "We just got here, like, ten seconds ago."

"Hmm. Were all these precautions necessary? Our phones are encrypted, and I don't think I was followed," she said.

"Necessary? Hopefully not, but better safe than sorry," Penny said. "Besides, it was fun."

Max and Penny had argued about whether he should meet his mother in person in Berlin. Penny had suggested that they couldn't trust Lianna because she didn't truly grasp the scope of what they were up against. His mother only wanted him to be safe, and to her, that meant turning himself in and defending his innocence. Max suspected Penny was being that way on principle, because he didn't trust Ada.

But his mother had already come all the way to Berlin looking for him, and she'd demonstrated that she did understand the seriousness of what they were up against. "I'd rather trust my own mother than a stranger," Max had said, once again expressing his apprehension about Ada, and by extension, her lead hackers, H8Bit and dorkph0enyx.

"Isn't your mom a stranger though?" Penny had said pointedly.

But Penny chose her battles and once she was on board, she was one hundred percent behind him. They'd worked out the plan to secure a ground-floor room facing the courtyard under one of Penny's many pseudonyms not known to Kevin Sharpe or VT, Susan Hilton, in case Lianna was being monitored after all.

"Are you ready to tell me what's going on?" Lianna asked.

Max glanced at Penny for confirmation. She nodded. Lianna noticed the exchange but didn't remark on it.

"You'd better get comfortable," Max said.

She sat down on the desk chair and he settled next to Penny on the bed. He floundered, wondering where to start.

"First of all, let's just get this out of the way. Unfortunately Penny wasn't joking about the bullet holes."

Lianna turned away from Penny's laptop screen, where she had been skimming some of Ada's VT files. Max and Penny had taken turns catching her up on events; she had asked questions at first, but as they went on she grew quieter and quieter. She hadn't said anything at all for the last ten minutes. Max wondered how she was processing everything. Did she believe them?

"This . . ." Lianna licked her lips. She gestured at Penny's computer. "*This* is what you do?"

Max and Penny shrugged.

"'We do what we must because we can,'" Penny said.

Lianna nodded thoughtfully. "I was right to get out of this kind of thing."

"Aside from your work to expose The Curtain," Max said.

"Aside from that." She flashed a brief smile.

"Kevin Sharpe was familiar with your work. Did you ever meet him?"

She shook her head. "That poor man." She looked at Max. "They almost got you too."

"That 'poor man' killed a bunch of people, including Evan," Max said.

"I know . . ." Lianna sighed. "But that was a terrible way to go."

Max kept his mouth shut.

"How did you get interested in The Curtain anyway?" Penny asked.

"It's responsible for the majority of the sex trade in Europe. That includes legitimate sex workers, yes, but also people who have been forced into it. Those are my clients, the people I've been trying to help."

"People like Nadia," Max said.

"Yes."

"How is she?"

"Okay, getting better. She's still scared. But she's in a safe place. May I?" Lianna gestured to Penny's keyboard.

Penny blinked. "No one ever asks for permission."

"It's only polite."

Penny still hesitated a moment. "Sure. Go ahead."

"I assume this is already configured for I2P . . . Yes. Thought so." Lianna began typing, but she stopped right away and hit the Backspace key to erase what she'd written.

"Oh—" Penny began to explain.

"A Dvorak keyboard! Haven't used that in years." Lianna resumed typing.

Penny leaned close to Max and whispered. "I'm totally girl-crushing right now. Your mom is cool."

A few minutes later, Lianna leaned away from the keyboard.

"What's that?" Max asked. The screen displayed a soft red-velvet background.

"That's The Curtain. 'You will never find a more wretched hive of scum and villainy.'"

Max's mom liked *Star Wars*? Or maybe Bradley had forced her to watch it every year on May 4, like he did with Max.

"You're on the Deep Web?" Penny asked.

"Not for criminal activity, of course. Not everything on it is illegal. Lots of people have good reasons for wanting to have business transactions without being tracked or marketed to. But I've been exploring the darker bits for my work."

She opened a new window that looked a lot like eBay, only all the listings showed women in lingerie offering various services. Max leaned over to study the screen, then caught Penny glaring at him.

Lianna offered her seat at the desk to him. Max scrolled

through the listings.

"Some of these women are your clients?" he asked.

"Yes. I've been trying to get the European Union to investigate and shut it down, but unless they have proof that it's being run from their jurisdiction, they can't act."

Max started checking out some of the other marketplaces available. He pointed one of them out to Penny: "Assassins." One of the subcategories was "Sniper."

"This is a real one-stop shop," Penny said. "And it has great UX design."

"Do you really think VT is operating it? How do we prove it?" Lianna asked.

"That's the tricky thing." Max memorized the .i2p URL so he could get find The Curtain's hidden eepsite again later. "We've been reviewing Ada's files looking for a connection, but there are still thousands of pages of text to go through. Our friend DoubleThink is helping out. They're fast and organized—"

"Ridiculously organized," Penny said.

"—but it'll still take them a while to study the patterns and people involved."

"Time you don't necessarily have," Lianna said.

"Pretty much," Max said. "The problem isn't even with The Curtain itself. Like you said, not everything on there is illegal. But this sex trafficking . . . the weapons, the killers, all those criminal services. Someone is sponsoring them. If VT is behind it, chances are it goes all the way to the top."

"Which means Richard Rhone, CEO and founder of Verbunden Telekom," Penny said. "You think Rhone is the Wizard?"

"Or he knows who the Wizard is," Max said.

"I've never found much about Rhone," Lianna said. "If he's authorized this site, he's just as accountable as the Wizard."

"So how do we find someone who has no online presence and never appears in public?" Max switched over to another browser and searched "Richard Rhone."

"As far as I can tell, he's never been photographed in the decade since he formed Verbunden Telekom. Not even at major press events like the acquisition of Cerulean S.A., which doubled their reach to the other side of the globe. Or for their charity concert for Free Water. Even when news broke about Ada Kiesler's leak, he only issued a written statement," Max said.

"What about photos from before VT?" Penny asked.

"The only thing out there is at least thirty years old. From almost before the *internet.*"

Max enlarged the photo, which was so low-resolution it ended up looking pixelated with lots of jaggies.

It showed a heavyset man in his twenties with short, black wavy hair, a wide red tie with yellow polka dots, and a buttondown shirt with the sleeves rolled up. He was chomping on a cigar, one eyebrow cocked.

"He looks like Orson Welles," Lianna said.

"Who?" Penny asked.

Max shook his head. "*Citizen Kane?*"

Penny gave him a blank look.

"*Touch of Evil?*" Lianna said.

"*The Third Man?*" Max said.

"Are those . . . movies?" Penny asked.

"Holy crap. Evan is rolling over in his grave right now," Max said.

"Where is this picture from?" Lianna asked.

"No idea. Image search isn't finding any other pictures of him—just more head shots of Welles." Max smiled. If you wanted to foil facial recognition, it helped to resemble a celebrity. "Conspiracy theorists online think Rhone doesn't even *exist*. Like, maybe that isn't his real name, or he's actually a group of people," Max said.

"That sounds pretty shady," Penny said. "I'm calling it. He's totally the Wizard."

"But his isolation also makes him difficult to indict for VT's crimes." Lianna slapped the desk. "He has to be a person, whatever his real name is. If he's changed it or has been using an alias, one has to wonder *why* he's so hard to find."

"Whoever he is, when we release Ada's files, he's going to have a lot to answer for. Even more so if we can definitively link him to The Curtain," Penny said.

"Which does us no good if no one knows how to reach him," Max said. "He'll just disappear with the money. Like, disappear even more than he already has." He drummed his fingers on the desk. "Sharpe said the only way to end The

Curtain was to find the Wizard. Whether or not he and Rhone are the same person, finding Rhone is the key."

"Which also takes care of VT. Killing two birds with one Rhone!" Penny grinned.

Max and Lianna glared at her.

"I'll see myself out." Penny walked toward the door.

Lianna looked concerned. "Max, you can't seriously be thinking of going after someone that high profile."

Max flashed her a confident smile. "We've already gone after the president of the United States."

"And lost," Penny said, leaning against the door with her arms crossed over her chest.

Max's smile faded. "Rhone is arguably more powerful than President Lovett, but no one could have a lower profile. The only contact information listed for him is his corporate email, which you can be pretty sure he never checks himself, and an office phone. Before VT, there's virtually nothing on him."

Just like Ada Kiesler.

"How does someone like that get investors and start the world's biggest communications company?" Penny asked.

"Maybe when VT hires people, they erase their past? Like in *Men in Black*," Max said.

"Is that part of some new benefits package?" Penny pushed her mouth to one side. "If so, sign me up."

"Ha," Max said. "Too bad you're just an outside contractor." But he could imagine plenty of people who would be interested in erasing their internet trail. The first generations of internet users had been at a disadvantage—no one could have known just how much your online reputation would stick to you as you grew up, got jobs, formed relationships. A lot of the early stuff hadn't been well archived, but for many since, the internet had become too good at remembering everything. Today it was all too easy for even unskilled people to doxx others and ruin lives on a whim. In fact, the European Union had recently given people the power to request their links be removed.

Maybe Ada had the right idea: They should burn it all to the ground and start over from scratch. Learn from our past and build a better, more useful tool that put everyone on the same footing.

Lianna flinched and covered her left ear with a hand.

"Mom?"

She looked up. He only caught the fear in her expression for a moment before it smoothed over and hardened into resolve.

"We have a problem. Someone just busted into my room on the thirteenth floor," Lianna said.

Max only now noticed that she had a small Bluetooth earpiece in her left ear, which had been hidden by her hair. She tapped her phone to transfer the audio to the speaker. They heard people clomping around, knocking things over and shouting, "Bathroom clear! Closet clear! Bedroom clear! There's no one here, sir."

"You've been monitoring your phone through an open line this whole time?" Penny didn't often sound impressed, but

Max's mom had just leveled up in her estimation. And in his.

"I'd better go," Max said. He and Penny packed up their computers.

"Max, don't. If you explain everything to them the way you did to me . . ."

"We've been through this kind of thing before, Mom. These guys aren't the type to listen to a couple of kids," Max said.

"Someone's been feeding them the wrong information on Max," Penny said. "They consider him an armed murderer. He has to get away from here."

"Come with us, Mom," Max said.

She shook her head. "No. I'll try to talk to them . . . distract them while you get away. And I'll be here if you end up needing legal help. Do be careful, Max."

Max hugged her.

"Try to keep him out of trouble, Penny," Lianna said.

"That doesn't seem likely if we're going after Rhone," Penny said.

"If we can figure out where he is," Max said. After all, he couldn't even find his *mom* on his own.

The speaker crackled. "Sir! This phone's live! Open line."

A clatter as someone picked up the handset. "Hello? Who's there?"

Lianna unmuted the phone. "Oh, hello. I'm sorry, you just missed me." She muted the phone again and shrugged.

"What? Where's Maxwell Stein? We know he entered this

hotel," the voice said.

"How did they find us? We were definitely not followed," Max whispered.

"I bet there are guys out in the lobby too," Penny said.

"We aren't going through the lobby, remember?" Max opened a window and stuck his head out. "Courtyard's empty. Let's go. We'll sneak out behind the hotel."

"Honey, you can't run." Lianna nodded to his injured leg. "I'll go out and talk to them to buy you more time." She switched the phone back to her earpiece and stood up.

Max was already halfway out the window. He grimaced as he swung his bandaged leg over the sill. This was going to hurt.

"Thanks. I love you," Max said.

"I love you too," Lianna said. "Go!"

Max watched as she tapped her earpiece and murmured something to the angry government man twelve floors above them. They certainly knew she was up to something, but their confusion would hopefully help Max and Penny give them the slip.

"She'll be fine!" Penny shoved Max out onto a patch of brown grass.

21

IT WAS UNLIKELY THE GOVERNMENT AGENTS WOULD make the connection between Max, Penny, and the room registered to Susan Hilton until they reviewed all the security footage from the hotel. By then, Max and Penny would be long gone.

Max led the way and set the pace as they emerged outside and headed off toward Nürnberger Strasse, taking them away from the bustling tourists drawn to the famous Kurfürstendamm avenue shops. He struggled to walk briskly, and he was developing a slight limp; while their disguises had helped them blend in before, a tourist and a businesswoman made a more incongruous pair. Passersby were noticing and would probably remember them.

Penny kept glancing behind to make sure they weren't being followed, while Max navigated the streets, taking quick turns and crossing traffic just before lights changed, always putting distance between them and the Hotel Reichenbach and his mother.

A white-and-blue car marked POLIZEI came around the corner ahead of them and turned down their street, lights flashing.

"Shit," Max said. He nudged Penny to the right. Farther down that street, another police car was heading right for them. He turned back, and yes, there was a third police car.

"We're surrounded. How do they—" Max suddenly noticed that groups of people around them had stopped walking and were now chattering and looking up behind them. Someone pointed.

Max followed their gazes and saw a small black quadcopter hovering a hundred feet above the intersection. Light glinted off the round camera mounted under it.

"W-T-F! A *drone's* been following us?!" Penny said.

"It must have been watching the hotel and my mom." Max and Penny had been looking for people in cars and on foot, avoiding surveillance cameras on the street and in the hotel, never thinking to look to the skies. Drones, satellites, everyone could be watched, if you had access to the right toys.

"Is that even legal?" Penny asked.

"I doubt that applies." Max looked around furiously. Two police cars were heading for them from the south, one from the north, and from the sound of sirens in the distance, more were on their way. How were they supposed to ditch their own personal camera, unless they went—

"Underground!" Max said. "Where's the subway?"

Penny spotted the entrance to the U-Bahn at the same time Max did, back the way they had come. She grabbed his hand. "Run!"

Max nearly fell after running a few steps, but she helped keep him on his feet and he recovered. He pushed through it, pretending it was the last stretch of a 5K race.

His leg screamed in agony, and he couldn't be sure he wasn't screaming too. The pain made him angry, and the anger produced adrenaline, and he could do this. *I can do this. I can do this.*

Though they had been neatly cornered, their sudden movement toward the subway entrance took the police by surprise. The cars squealed to a halt several feet behind Max and Penny. One car tried to reverse and smashed into a taxi. Cops jumped out of the other vehicle in the middle of the street, sending another car veering wide to avoid hitting the open passenger door and setting off a chain of honking horns adding to the blaring sirens.

"Stop!" shouted the cops. Max didn't. They were nearly there.

Out of the corner of his eye, he saw the drone actually dive toward them—*that* had to be illegal—before the operator realized that was pretty stupid. The drone hovered just over the stairs.

The stairs. Clattering down them hurt more than running,

but then Max hopped onto the railing and slid down, down, down. That was better, until he landed. Pain. *Keep running.*

He only glanced at the ticket vending machine. *Screw it.* He caught a flash of yellow out the corner of his eye: a train was just pulling into the station. He didn't care where it was going; they had to be on it.

Penny ran beside Max.

"Go!" he grunted. "You can make it!"

"Nope," she said.

Then she seemed to think better of it and put on a burst of speed. She was fast, and she had excellent form.

She darted through the closing doors of the train. *Yes!* At least she'd made it.

Max slowed and considered his options. Run upstairs to the opposite platform and hope to catch a train in the other direction?

"Hurry up!" Penny called.

She was holding the doors open. Max forced himself to run at his top speed, heedless of his injury, and he burst onto the train, tumbling into Penny's open arms, both of them cushioned by annoyed straphangers.

"Sorry!" Max said breathlessly.

"Verzeihung!" Penny said. "We're running late for an appointment."

As the doors closed again, two police officers came running onto the platform. They looked at Max. Max looked at them. They spoke into their walkie-talkies as they watched the train pull out of the station. One of them flipped up his middle finger in frustration. This wasn't over.

"The next station is Wittenbergplatz," he said.

"You and your freaky memory," Penny said.

"There's a map right above your head." They were on the U3 line bound for Nollendorfplatz. He held onto a yellow pole to take some of the weight off his bad leg.

"They might have someone waiting for us there or trying to board, if they can scramble in time. It's only a few minutes away. I say if there's another train waiting when we pull in, we get on it. If we're lucky, we'll catch one just as it's leaving," Max said.

They were lucky. The second train headed back the way they'd come. When it pulled into their original station, they both turned away and pressed their way to the other side of the car to duck down behind commuters. While the doors were open, they heard cops shouting orders to one another. The doors closed, and Max breathed easier.

"One of the cops got on the train," Penny whispered.

"Great."

"Are you okay? Do you need to sit?" An elderly black woman with gray curls leaned toward Max. An American tourist, judging from her heavy Boston accent.

"Thanks, I'm okay," he said.

"You're *bleeding*," she said.

The warmth spreading on his calf was blood seeping through the bandage and soaking his jeans.

"It's not mine," he said cheerfully.

The woman leaned back in alarm.

"He's kidding," Penny said. "A dog bit him. We're going to the hospital now."

"You poor thing," the lady said.

Still kneeling, Max slipped off his backpack and pulled out his hoodie. He put it on and zipped it up. It would have to do on short notice. Maybe the cop was looking for a tall boy in a blue shirt.

"We have to split up. You go sit over there, and I'll stay here. They're looking for us as a pair."

Penny nodded.

"Unless something happens, get off at Heidelberger Platz. That's four stops. Meet me by the ticket machines."

"Okay." She took a deep breath. "Okay."

Penny headed to the far end of the car. The train pulled into a station, and the cop jumped out to look up and down the length at all the passengers who were exiting. By the time he had gotten back on, Max and Penny had settled into seats.

Max put his bag on the floor and leaned it against his leg to hide the growing bloodstain in the dark denim. He closed his eyes and pretended to be asleep.

He woke with a start. He'd been so exhausted, the motion of the train had lulled him to sleep after all. He looked around wildly. Penny was sitting with white earbuds in her ear, nodding her head to music. The cop had moved to another car or disembarked at some point. Their station was coming up.

They got off and reunited at the ticket machine. "That was close. Where are we going?" Penny asked.

Max looked at the map of the Berlin U-Bahn. "Let's get two all-day passes. We can work our way to the outskirts of the city for now, but I think we might be safer down here than on the street right now. We'll keep switching trains for a while."

Riding the underground turned out to be an effective way to keep moving, and since they didn't know where they were going, no one else could figure it out either. There were perhaps more cops at the major stations than usual, but they avoided those and sat at opposite ends of the train car, communicating through their phones on a local, private network Penny set up.

They often had internet access too, which allowed Max to work through Ada's files with Risse.

Since downloading them, she'd been plowing through the files to the accompaniment of two seasons of *Law & Order*. She had already organized them in a similar database to the one she'd used when they sorted through Evan's Panjea payload from last year. Why start from scratch when you can reuse something? The best thing was, it allowed her to search the contents by keywords, allowing her to quickly review everything connected to Kevin Sharpe, The Curtain, and Richard Rhone.

Now that Max had access to that database, the tedious work of opening documents and skimming their contents was going much more quickly.

Penny plopped into the seat next to Max.

"What are you doing over here?" he asked.

"The car's empty except for us."

Max looked up. There was a hard edge in Penny's voice.

"Uh-oh," he said. "What's wrong?"

Penny opened her laptop. "I decided to transcribe the audio recording we made of you and Sharpe, to really study it. Something jumped out at me this time."

"Okay, shoot." He winced. "Too soon, right?"

Penny read from the transcript on her screen. "'I thought you didn't want Ada to tear down the internet. You said I had to stop her.' I can't believe I missed this before, but you told Sharpe about our plan? And you were planning to stop me?"

Max took a deep breath. *Oh, boy.*

"I may have mentioned it in passing," Max said.

"Max."

"Penny, he already knew you two were up to more than you claimed. He told me I couldn't trust you."

"Since this is the first I'm hearing about it, I guess you didn't trust me. But you trusted him."

"I wouldn't say that." Max pinched the bridge of his nose. He had the start of a killer migraine. "He planted a seed of doubt, that's all."

"And has that seed grown?"

"Uh . . ."

"That sounds like a coward's 'yes.' What the hell, Max?"

"Well, Penny, your scheme is, to be brutally honest, absolutely bananas. I've been trying to figure out how to make you see that," he said.

"The whole world is bananas! This is one way to get things back on track. The fact that we even have something like The Curtain shows how far gone the internet is."

Max? Risse wrote in her chat window.

Not now, he typed.

"Of course I agree The Curtain has to be taken down, but—"

Penny threw up her hands. "Who left it up to you?"

"Excuse me?"

"You were saying Ada's, like, some kind of internet dictator, making this decision for everyone in the world, but you're doing the same thing. First Panjea, now The Curtain."

"But . . . they're *evil*," Max said. "Someone has to do something."

"So you're just upset because it wasn't your idea? Because Ada's doing something that you couldn't—no, *wouldn't*—do?"

Max laughed. "Not at all. I don't want to kill the internet. I'm trying to protect it."

"That's what Sharpe thought too." Penny glanced at her screen. "'I hoped that Panjea and VT could reshape the internet . . .' See, he thought that the problem with the internet is that it made it too hard for governments to protect their people—so it was in their best interest to monitor everyone all the time, without telling them. For their own good. Here he's quoting Reagan, of all people: 'freedom and security go together.' They're right, but not the way they think."

Hey, **Risse typed.** Max? What's going on?

Your sister is tearing me a new one, Max thought.

Max raised his hands in surrender. "I know all this. It's me, remember? I believe in the same things you do."

Penny shook her head. "Not so. We've always disagreed on our methods. You don't approve of half the things I do."

"Penny, I think you're amazing—"

"But you do think I'm a criminal."

"I think sometimes you go a little too . . . You cross the line."

The tricky thing about hacking: You could apply your own sense of morality to your actions and look for gray areas in the law, but most of what you were doing was still illegal—even if the government making those determinations was also abusing the internet. Two wrongs didn't always make a right.

Penny ran her hand through her hair. "I'm surprised this hasn't been more of a problem before now."

"We've just been avoiding it," Max said. "You went dark on your activities because you didn't want us to have this argument sooner."

She nodded. "Where does that leave us?"

"With a mission to accomplish."

"No. Where does that leave *us*? You've been as cold and distant as Pluto since we left the embassy."

Max looked away. "I don't know."

"See? That's what I'm talking about."

"Can we deal with that later? It's more important that we agree on Operation Undo right now. Penny, it's too dangerous. I know it's just an experiment, a way to wake people up, but . . . It isn't you I don't trust, it's Ada and her hackers."

"*She* isn't evil," Penny said.

"Maybe not. But people make mistakes, and what if this backup internet she's set up doesn't work the way she thinks? What if you take the internet offline, and we can't return things to normal?"

"We don't want things to go back to normal, but I know what you mean. I've been looking over every detail closely." Penny licked her lips and nodded. "It'll work. You'll see. This is what we need: a democratic internet that can't be used to hurt the people who rely on it. We've lost the freedom right along with the security, but it's time to take back the net."

Max smiled. "That's a better name: Operation Take Back the Net. Sounds like you've decided to go through with it then?"

"Yeah. I'm just not sure when."

"Well, hold off for a little bit. We're still using the internet to search for Rhone."

Max glanced at his computer and saw a string of impatient and loopy chat messages from Risse:

Hey, listen!

Max?

Max.

MAX.

MAX!

MAX!!!

Your name's starting to look weird the more I type it. Max Max Maxmaxmaxmax.

Ew. Are you guys fooling around? Pen isn't answering her chat either.

Never mind, don't tell me.

Ugh, why do I have such a good imagination?

Max's phone vibrated. Risse was calling.

"Finally!"

"Hi, Risse." Max pressed the speakerphone button. "You're on speakerphone with me and Penny."

"Hey, sis," Risse said. "So I just had this brainstorm, okay? We haven't been finding anything about The Curtain, and that's when I realized that's what we should be looking for."

"We should be looking for nothing?" Max said.

"Oh! Great idea, Risse," Penny said. Naturally she caught on well before Max did. She and her sister were like two parts of the same brain.

"What?" Max said.

Risse took a breath. "I started thinking, so, you have this big secret, what would you do? You would try to hide it. The way people hide things is they delete or omit them. But something like The Curtain—it's big. It requires resources and personnel. There should be traffic, expenses, and revenue. All the things you'd expect from a thriving business. If it was at VT, it would have to be disguised as something else, something that doesn't fit anywhere. So I reviewed all their reports."

"She audited VT," Penny said.

"Other people had already audited VT, and Ada happened to grab the last five years of reports. I just found what other people missed, or more likely were paid to overlook. Then there was Project Scrybe. That seemed like a good place to start."

"What about it?" Max asked.

"Anything related to Scrybe was hidden too, but it still had to be accounted—that's how VT was billing the government agencies they were building it for. So I looked for items tagged with a project-reference number that didn't match anything else. Loads of servers, development teams—"

"Can you give us the 'too long, didn't read' version?" Penny asked. "Our train stop is coming up." They were planning to switch trains again at Warschauer.

"That's what this is," Risse said. "It sounds easy to you, but it took me two days to sort through all this."

"It doesn't sound easy. We've been looking at the files for almost a week. Ada's had them for more than a year. Take your time to explain," Max said.

"Within Scrybe, there were discrepancies. One: Computer servers that were supposedly replaced, but broken units were never returned and refunded. Two: A block of IP addresses that were reserved but never officially assigned. And three: Staff—programmers, managers, and support people who are on the payroll but not formally assigned a billing code. This is all a compliance nightmare, as you might expect."

"A secret, secret project?" Max asked. "Where does it get its funding?"

"That's not as interesting as where its profits are going. There are significant, unaccounted-for income streams being disbursed throughout VT's operations. More than enough to cover whatever this is."

"They have more money than they should," Penny said.

"Yes. But the real clincher is that Scrybe is hardcoded to ignore specific IP addresses on queries. Everything in that range might as well be invisible."

Penny pumped her fist in the air. "I love it! VT sells a tool to crawl the Deep Web, but of course it protects their biggest business—the servers hosting The Curtain."

"Which means the U.S. and German governments aren't necessarily supporting The Curtain itself," Risse said. "They may have been trying to discover it too, using Scrybe. Only they didn't know that VT was actually running it, and their money was going right back into the very illegal operations they were trying to stop."

"Sharpe was onto them," Max said. "Even though these agencies weren't actively supporting The Curtain, it will be embarrassing when the news gets out because of how much work they do with the U.S. and European governments. No one's going to look good coming out of this."

"Excellent job, Risse," Penny said.

"Damn. Mom's calling me. I'd better go," Risse said.

"If you can send me those IP addresses, we'll take it from here."

"Done and done."

"Oh, and tell Mama I said hi and I'll be home soon. I love you both," Penny said.

"You could call and tell her yourself, you know."

"I'm too busy saving the world," Penny said.

"*Again.*"

"I know, right? So tiresome."

"Anyway, stay frosty, guys. Risse out."

Max pocketed his phone.

The train car filled with light as it left Hallesches Tor and emerged from a tunnel onto an elevated track. Max blinked. Through the window across from him, the sun was setting over Berlin, and he felt the warm glow rekindle some hope in him. They were closer than anyone had ever gotten to tracking down the servers running The Curtain, VT's best-kept secret.

Actually, that was VT's second-best secret—the first being Richard Rhone himself.

They pulled into Schlesisches Tor station. Penny turned and looked out the window. "Beautiful!"

Max watched Penny snap a photo of the station and then the view as it passed over Warschauer Bridge into the eastern part of the city. Penny turned back around, looked up "Schlesisches Tor" on Wikipedia, and started reading. He liked seeing her happy, forgetting the burden she was carrying for even a brief moment.

Max pulled out a notebook and a pen and opened to a fresh page.

"What's that for?" Penny asked. "Writing things out helps me think," he said.

At the top he wrote: EVERYTHING WE KNOW ABOUT THE CURTAIN. Then he stared at the blank page.

"Yeah, that's super helpful," Penny said.

The train pulled into the station. "End of the line," Penny said. "Did you know that this was the first station built on Berlin's elevated S-Bahn line?"

"Fascinating."

The train car quickly filled with passengers, none of whom paid Max or Penny any attention.

"Start of the line too," Max said.

She packed up her laptop and tugged Max toward an open door. "Come on. Let's check out the rest of the station and switch back to the underground."

"Hold on." Max found a bench and sat. "Can I see that transcript you made?"

"Okay." Penny opened her laptop again and looked around the emptying platform. "We're kind of in the open here now."

"Just a second." He skimmed over the transcript to just before Sharpe died. "'You won't be able to stop The Curtain unless you find the Wizard, and you know how that goes: Nobody sees the Wizard. Not nobody, not no—'"

"'Not no-how,'" Penny finished.

Max nodded. "Then you have his last word as 'Wizard.'"

She shrugged. "Sounds like it."

"But it doesn't follow. What if he's saying *Richard*?"

Penny's eyes widened. "That could fit too. It's so garbled."

"He knew he was dead, and he was identifying both his killer and the identity of the Wizard behind The Curtain. Richard Rhone, like we figured."

"Sharpe was shot right after he said it. If he was in the middle of pointing his finger to Rhone, that would be the time to finish him."

Max wrote R.R. = WIZARD at the top of his page, followed by INTERNATIONAL MAN OF MYSTERY. He underlined MYSTERY.

"We do know someone who's seen the Wizard though. Nadia, and the other girls being sold on the site," Penny said.

"She said he looked like Santa Claus. So that's what Rhone looks like now." Max wrote that down. "She also met an English teenager who runs their website." Max wrote: PRO-GRAMMER? HACKER??

"She saw a woman working with the Wizard," Penny said.

"And there was a woman on the other end of Sharpe's phone who was listening in on our conversation." Max wrote: WHO IS THE WOMAN? Then he added her phone number and wrote: HELGOLAND.

"Nadia said something funny about the location. They had to take a boat to get to an island with 'big fans,' and they met the Wizard on a yacht," he said. "Helgoland is an island."

"Archipelago," Penny said.

"Close enough. And it has a wind farm just offshore."

"When did you go to Helgoland?" she asked while typing. "And why?"

"I've been to a virtual version of it. Helgoland and its surrounding waters are in a ship-simulation computer game. A couple of years ago, Evan showed me a level map modded to use LEGO bricks and minifigs."

"So you've been to a *LEGO* version of it?"

"It was called 'Hey LEGO Land,'" Max said.

He smiled at the memory of steering a plastic LEGO boat on search-and-rescue missions with Evan. The real Helgoland served as a base for the German Maritime Search and Rescue Service.

"Look." Penny showed Max a photo of a large three-bladed wind turbine rising from the ocean, silhouetted against the horizon. "A big fan."

Helgoland's other claim to fame, its wind farm, firmly placed the quaint and historic locale on the cutting edge of renewable energy.

"I'd bet you a bitcoin that Rhone is at Helgoland," Penny said. "It's remote, private, but still only three hours from the German mainland. It has its own government and low tax rates. Seems like the perfect place for a businessman with something to hide. And criminals. The only problem is, VT doesn't even cover that area. Internet access is spotty and slow at best. Hardly what you would expect from a technology and media giant like Rhone, and an odd place to run an online marketplace from."

"It's clear he likes to keep a low profile," Max said. "And maybe the fact that internet isn't provided by his own company is intentional. I think we should check it out."

"We still have to find him," Penny said.

"It's a small island, right?"

"Only about eleven hundred people."

"If Rhone lives there, someone has to have seen him. We're gonna need a car," Max said.

"We're driving to an island?"

"It's too risky for me at the airport, and even the train is out of the question. We can take a ferry from the mainland."

Penny smiled. "Since you have a mom now, do you think we can borrow her car?"

"As long as she hasn't been arrested. You don't want to just steal one?" Max asked.

Penny elbowed him gently. "I'm reevaluating some of my life choices," she said. "You call your mom, and I'll get H8Bit and dorkph0enyx started on tracing The Curtain's servers. Once we know where they are, we can take them offline." She clapped her hands. "Oh! No, wait. I have an even better idea."

Max lost Penny to her laptop. He studied their notes on The Curtain, and slowly a plan to find and apprehend Rhone began to form.

22

RICHARD RHONE MAY NOT HAVE CARED ABOUT THE privacy of Verbunden Telekom's customers, but he was dead serious about his own. Getting to the island of Helgoland required a five-hour drive from Berlin to Cuxhaven on Germany's northern coast, which Max spent in the backseat of his mom's red Citroën DS3, beside Penny.

Nadia rode in the front passenger seat; the only way she would agree to revisit Helgoland with them and identify Rhone was if Lianna accompanied her—which worked out, because Max's mom had refused to let Max out of her sight again. Given that taking down The Curtain had become Lianna's life's work, he couldn't argue with her. And it felt good to be going after the site's dark Wizard together.

By the time they reached the docks at Cuxhaven, Penny had told them plenty about their final destination. Situated in the North Sea, twenty-nine miles off the German coast, Helgoland was actually made up of two small islands that together covered less than one square mile. They had been one landmass until 1720 when they were separated by a storm.

"Helgoland is technically only the larger island. The smaller one is called Düne," Penny said.

"'The spice must flow,'" Lianna said.

"It doesn't say anything about a spice trade here," Penny said. "It mostly serves as Helgoland's airstrip, and there's a lot of sand."

Lianna sighed. "Try cross-referencing 'dune' with 'melange.' M-e-l-a-n-g-e."

A short while later, Penny laughed. "Nice. I keep meaning to read *Dune*."

"We still have your copy, Mom," Max said. He didn't mention that every time he tried to read the well-worn paperback, or watch the film, he fell asleep.

"Wow," Lianna said. "I bought that at the Strand Bookstore on our honeymoon in New York City. I'm surprised that Bradley saved it. He's never been much for sentimentality."

"I saved it," Max said. "I have a lot of your old things."

He'd always thought those worn science-fiction and fantasy books had been from his mother's childhood, stuff she'd grown out of as she became an activist. But in the last few days he'd seen how much they were still a part of her; she was even more of a geek than Max or his father. Some things don't change.

Max sneaked a sidelong glance at his mom, realizing that you can't really leave behind the people or things or experiences that define you—even if you try to start over and build a new life.

No matter how much he tried, Max would never be able to give up his hacking roots, not voluntarily, not even with a court order. His online identity, 503-ERROR, wasn't a mask he had hidden behind; it was a part of his true self.

Maybe that was what Evan had been trying to tell him when he sent him all those media files of the television shows, films, and music he loved. *Some hacker you are, Max*, he thought. *It took you a year to decode his final message.* "This is me," Evan was saying. "And I am you." Evan was always going to be an important part of Max's life.

He bet Evan and Lianna would have loved talking about their favorite stories. When all this was over, Max hoped he'd have that chance with her, and that he'd get to see more of the complex picture that made Lianna—Lee Hardy—who she was. Not an activist, not a mother, not a pop-culture nerd, not a hero, but all those things at once, and apparently much more.

She glanced over at him. When she saw him watching her, she smiled.

"So what's your favorite book?" Max asked her.

The rest of their trip flew by as they talked about everything but what they were going to do when they reached their destination, both of them trying to cram thirteen years into a few hours.

Helgoland seemed like an ideal place to run a multi-billion-dollar illegal-trading site. It was once a haven for pirates and spies on the open seas, as well as a German naval base in World Wars I and II. Today it was a popular tourist spot and destination for people looking for tax- and duty-free goods, a kind of real-world, wholesome version of The Curtain. The tax haven probably attracted plenty of white-collar businesspeople like Rhone.

It was also difficult to get to. Once they reached Cuxhaven, they still needed to board a ferry that would take them three hours from the mainland, what the locals called a "butter ferry"—a *butterfahrt* being a shopping trip on a boat. They had to leave Lianna's car because automobiles were actually largely banned on the island. Bikes, too, except for local law enforcement.

"A three-hour tour. A three-hour tour," Lianna intoned ominously as they crossed the metal gangplank leading into the MS *Helgoland.*

"Stop that," Max said, knowing that she couldn't help it.

Penny gave them a quizzical look.

"*Gilligan's Island,*" Max and his mom said at the same time.

She laughed. "You watched my DVDs?"

"Unfortunately," he said. "Why did you own those anyway?"

"I used to watch it with your grandpa."

Max expected something drab and utilitarian inside the ferry, but instead they found elegant furniture, atmospheric lighting, and trendy interior design.

"This is like a floating hotel," Penny said. She snapped photos with her phone to send to Risse.

They oohed and ahhed their way deeper into the ship. The MS *Helgoland* was clearly meant to carry hundreds of passengers; it almost seemed endless. But as it was winter, only a couple of days before Christmas, there were few other passengers besides them. It would be easy to find a private place to talk.

Max led everyone up a steel-and-glass spiral staircase to an atrium. They stood in front of the wide windows, admiring the stunning, slightly terrifying, view of the open sea.

"She's here," Penny said glumly. Max looked over at a set of ramp-like steel stairs and saw Clove—no, it was Valentine Labelle and her shadow, Luc Moreau—emerge from the lower deck. A small, surprised sound escaped from Nadia's lips, and she stepped back to hide behind Lianna.

Risse was the only fan of Max's idea to include the journalists, but Max knew that this was the right thing to do. He'd been pushing off the media for too long, forgetting that under the right conditions, there was no better ally. Provided they weren't all completely mistaken about Richard Rhone being on the island, and his involvement with The Curtain.

Max had also realized that it would take more than him and Penny to comb the island looking for Rhone, so he'd decided to "crowdsource" their efforts. Since Rhone wasn't on the internet, they had to take their investigation to the real world, the places he frequented.

"Mr. Stein." Valentine shook hands with him.

"Have you been following us?" Max joked.

She laughed. Valentine and Luc didn't seem nearly so scary now that he knew who they were, and they were hopefully on his side.

"I wasn't sure you would be here," she said.

"Thanks for coming. And call me Max."

"Of course I came. You mentioned an exclusive with Ada Kiesler. I hope that's still the deal."

Valentine surveyed the rest of their motley group. Max introduced Penny, Lianna, and Nadia.

"This story is so much bigger than Kiesler," Max said. "I'll wait until you get the cameras rolling to go into details, but if I'm right, we're going to uncover the man behind The Curtain. All you have to do is follow us with the camera, get our story, and don't miss anything. You'll have our full cooperation for interviews, photos, whatever. Anything you need to make this compelling."

Valentine nodded at Luc, and he started unpacking his video and recording equipment. She pulled a small notepad and a pen from her purse. "So I assume this has something to do with Kiesler's files on Verbunden Telekom?"

"That's an understatement," Max said. "You can have all those files too, if your paper isn't afraid to release that information to the public."

"My paper is called 'The Truth' for a reason. If they aren't on board with this scoop, I have my own blog, which sometimes rivals it for views. Don't worry. I do have your permission to report on everything I witness honestly, regardless of how it reflects on you?"

"That would be refreshing," Max said. "Please do."

The ship trembled with the vibration of its engines. They were off!

23

IT UNNERVED MAX TO BE OUT THIS FAR FROM LAND; he'd never been on the open ocean before. He much preferred being on solid ground, preferably ground that didn't rock, rise, and fall with turbulence. He was a strong swimmer, but that ocean water had to be freezing this time of year, if it came to that.

After he'd spent an hour telling their story to Valentine on camera, Max passed things off to Penny and then paced around the ship. His injured leg still twinged when he put weight on it, but he needed to be moving after sitting for so long. He showed every crew member he encountered the only picture he had on his phone of Rhone and asked if they'd seen or heard of anyone named Richard Rhone on the island. They were all regular staff, so if he ever took the ferry, someone would have to recognize him. How could it be that no one even knew who Rhone was?

When Max asked people whether they'd seen Santa Claus, most of them laughed and said they had to get back to work.

Pretty soon they spotted a tall column of reddish rock in the distance, a landmark named Long Anna on Helgoland. Not long after that, beyond the natural formation, they picked out Nadia's "big fans": massive white windmills rising from the ocean about thirty-five miles off the coast.

"Do you still have my copy of *Don Quixote* too?" Lianna asked Max.

"Yup."

"Have you read it?"

"Nope. It's really long. Why?"

She squinted out at the ocean. "You've heard the phrase, 'tilting at windmills'?"

He nodded.

"In one scene in the book, Don Quixote mistakes windmills for giants and attacks them. You can imagine how that goes. I guess I'm just wondering if we're going to find our enemy here or not," she said. "Or is he really a windmill?"

Their ferry couldn't get too close to the island or it might run aground, so Max, his company, and a large group of other passengers transferred carefully into another, smaller boat— stepping out over a shifting gap between the vessels—that took them to the harbor. Luc kept an open barf bag pressed over his mouth as the vessel rose and pitched with every swell of water. Valentine sighed and took over with his camera, snapping a rapid succession of shots of their group, the ferry, and the island.

Waves crashed all around them, quickly drenching them in frigid water. Now Max knew why there were so few people traveling to the island in the dead of winter.

Helgoland was tiny enough that Max could see its entire length as they approached. Above its striking red striped sandstone cliffs, the terrain was flat. It was sparsely developed along the coast, with more buildings concentrated toward the center, none more than a few stories tall. Farther out to sea, back the way they had come, storm clouds gathered on the horizon. They had arrived just in time.

The passengers disembarked on the quay, which was lined with dozens of huts in varying shades of red, blue, and orange. The tourists from their boat made a beeline for these quaint shops before the rain hit, while Max's group sought shelter from the biting wind under the roof of the port building that listed the ferry schedules. Valentine and Luc stood apart, the latter keeping his DSLR camera focused on them while she held a boom microphone over their heads to try to capture clear audio in the gusting wind.

Max took in a deep whiff of the freshest air he'd ever breathed. The ban on automobiles had kept it clean. He could run for days on air like this, if it wasn't for his injury.

"There aren't a lot of things to do here," Max said. He figured it would only take someone a couple of hours to walk around the entire island.

"I'm shocked," Penny said.

"I think the best approach is for us to do the tourist thing. Stop by the museum, visit the aquarium, get friendly with the locals and ask them if they know or recognize Richard Rhone. You all have a copy of the only photo we have of him, and Nadia's description of the man we think is the Wizard." They nodded. "Nadia, if you see *anyone* you recognize: the Wizard, his assistant, or the web guy, let me know."

Penny translated for her.

"You got it," Nadia replied in English, rubbing her arms for warmth in Lianna's oversize coat. She had picked up the phrase recently from Penny and used it as often as she could.

"Mom, can you go up to the hotel and see about reserving some rooms for us? This may take a while, and we'll need a base of operation."

"Absolutely," Lianna said. "I bet they're chatty over there too. They probably know everyone on the island. After that, I'll take Nadia to the docks to see if she recognizes the Wizard's boat?" She gave Nadia a questioning glance. Nadia hesitated, and then she nodded.

Max turned to Penny. "You find a coffee shop with reliable Wi-Fi—"

"Ha! Here?" she said.

"I know. Whatever passes for reliable on the island. At least you don't have to worry about interference from VT—according to your maps, no data from here passes through servers they control. When you're online, connect with, uh—" He glanced at the camera recording his every word. "Connect with DoubleThink and your hackers, and see what you can do about disabling The Curtain. With any luck, the Wizard will place a service call to his webmaster, and we can track *him* down."

Penny saluted. "What will you be doing?"

"I'm taking this door to door. There are only eleven hundred people here, but I'm gonna knock on as many doors as we can." Max looked up. There were a lot of houses on this lower level of Helgoland, known as the Unterland, but there were a lot more up there: the Oberland. This place reminded him of a game map from one of his RPGs. And this was going to be about as much fun as grinding, fighting low-power minions just to level up for the imminent boss battle.

"Assuming we don't find Rhone right away, we'll meet in the lobby of Hotel Rickmers Insulaner in four hours to compare notes," Max said.

He turned to Valentine, unsure if he should address her directly while they were recording. She could always edit it out later.

"What do you want to do?" he asked her.

"I'd like to spend time with everyone as they go about the search, but for now, I'm sticking with you," Valentine said. "But I'm not knocking on any doors."

"Great," Max said. She was going to keep following him after all. Well, he'd asked for it.

"Okay. Remember, let's stay in touch with our encrypted texts. Good luck, everyone!" he said.

They split up.

24

WALKING AROUND THE RESIDENTIAL NEIGHBOR-
hoods of Helgoland with Valentine, Max imagined they'd been
transported to the 1950s. Most of the island had to be rebuilt
after being bombed in World War II, so few houses dated to
earlier then 1959; but more than that, it was quiet, harmoni-
ous, and it felt *safe*. The people of Helgoland lived life simply,
at a slower pace. For the first time in a long time, Max didn't
feel like his every move was being watched—ironic, because he
was constantly under the scrutiny of Luc Moreau's lens.

Better still, because many of the people of Helgoland didn't
spend much of their time online, no one recognized Max as
either a fugitive or a key figure in the Panjea scandal; if they'd
read about him recently in the newspapers delivered from the
mainland, they must not have paid attention. It was easy to
discount everything outside of the island, even in the rest of

Germany, as being in another world, someone else's problems. "Not my circus, not my monkeys," seemed to be the general attitude toward current world events.

Unfortunately, none of the people they talked to recognized Richard Rhone either, from his ancient picture. More than one elderly person commented, "Isn't that Orson Welles?" No one could tell them if anyone like him even lived on the island, let alone where they could find him.

By the time the storm finally slammed into Helgoland with gale-force winds and heavy rain, the only thing Max and the others had to show for their afternoon's work were snapshots of some local attractions: the lighthouse; St. Nicolai Church's pyramidal clock tower; and, Penny's favorite, a small bronze bear that faced Berlin and marked its distance from Helgoland, 456 km. She named him Bearlin.

They compared notes over dinner in the hotel's charming Galerie restaurant, so named for its collection of paintings depicting Helgoland's history.

"Everyone here is so helpful though," Lianna said. "It's lovely here."

"It's creepy," Penny said. "I didn't think places like this actually existed."

"I'll finish visiting houses tomorrow," Max said, trying to hide his disappointment.

"We knew it would take a while," Lianna said.

He nodded. "Does *anything* look familiar, Nadia?"

Nadia paused her chewing while Penny repeated the

question in German. "No. I don't remember. I was taking something for seasickness, so I only remember the visit to the Wizard's boat, but not where or how we got there."

"It would have to be at the marina," Penny said.

"There are several marinas," Lianna said. She frowned. "If it's even still docked. Nadia, when were you here last?"

"In the summer. Early July, I think?"

Max groaned. "So he might winter somewhere else entirely."

Penny stroked his hand soothingly. "We should know as early as tomorrow morning, when the first ferry arrives. Tonight H8Bit and dorkph0enyx are pulling the plug on The Curtain's servers. We traced the IP address to an unlisted server in Rotterdam."

"They're in the Netherlands?" he asked.

"Affirmative. And guess who actually owns the Rotterdam Internet Exchange?"

"Verbunden Telekom," Max said.

"Affirmative again! They bought it three years ago. Silently."

"That's about when The Curtain first appeared," Lianna said.

The waiter returned to take their dessert orders, and they all switched back to innocuous conversation about their holiday. As the waiter camer around the table, Max pulled out his phone.

"Excuse me, but do you recognize this man?" He flashed the picture of Richard Rhone. "He would be about thirty years older, and heavier, with a white beard."

He didn't know why he bothered. Rhone was a ghost.

"Let me see . . . ," the waiter said.

Max was so surprised, he broke his rule and handed over his phone. The waiter studied the photo. "Yes, I think so."

"Really?" Max said.

"He comes in here at least once a month. Usually with a young woman. An Asian woman."

Max glanced at Nadia. She nodded.

"I haven't seen him in a while," the waiter said. Max's hopes crashed.

"The woman though." The waiter handed back Max's phone. "She's here more often, sometimes with a guy about your age. In fact, she stopped in earlier today, but she left in a hurry when the storm started."

That was when Max and his group had arrived. They'd just missed her.

"Do you know where either of them live?" Penny asked.

"I believe she's up in Unterland." Along with hundreds of other people.

The waiter shrugged. "The old man, he's got money. I think he lives on his yacht. Moves around a lot." He glanced over at a glass door leading to the outside patio, obscured by a waterfall of rain. "Not much fun to be out there tonight."

"Do you know their names? Does he pay with a credit card?" Max asked.

"Cash. Always cash. He calls her Sara? But I don't recall his name." The waiter furrowed his brow. "Sorry. Are they in some kind of trouble?" He looked worried that he had already said too much.

Max indicated Valentine Labelle. "Just looking to interview them for a reality TV show. Please don't mention we asked about them. We'd like it to be a surprise."

"I get it. One of those hidden-camera shows?" the waiter asked.

"Something like that," Max said.

It was the tiniest of leads, but it told Max that at least they were on the right track.

The next morning, Max and Penny went to Café Forseti as soon as it opened. Penny insisted that it had the strongest Wi-Fi signal on the island, so The Curtain's webmaster was bound to show up. The café also had the strongest coffee Max had ever tasted. As promised, H8Bit, dorkph0enyx, and Penny had succeeded in taking the dark web marketplace offline—and people were paying attention. Most assumed the Feds had brought it down and conjectured that an arrest was imminent, and the U.S. government hadn't made any official statements confirming or denying their involvement. Max imagined them scrambling to figure out what had happened as well.

Valentine sat at a nearby table, observing them. She had hidden a wireless camera in a plant by the door to record footage without being obvious about it; Luc had gone with Lianna and Nadia to canvas the rest of the residential neighborhood.

It was still gray with a light drizzle outside, but the worst of the storm had blown over.

Around midday, as they pored over the transaction logs copied from The Curtain's server in Rotterdam, a gawky white man, in his late teens or early twenties, arrived. He had long, curly brown hair, a scraggly goatee, and mirrored sunglasses.

Without even ordering a coffee, he sat at a table facing Max and Penny and opened a beat-up laptop. He pushed his sunglasses up on his head and started typing.

Penny messaged Max. Is this is our guy?

Could be. Can you see what he's working on? Access his screen?

Penny shook her head. He has it all locked down. Not proof he's a hacker, but he at least knows what he's doing, and he's careful. Look at his computer. That's an MSI Whitebook. Just a shell. He built that laptop himself, or paid someone to do it.

Hard-core, Max wrote. Even Evan had never bothered to make his own laptop from scratch, though he had often done a fair amount of customization and tinkering to get things exactly how he liked, typically erasing the stock Windows operating system and installing his favorite flavor of Linux.

Very, Penny typed. I'm impressed already.

She rubbed her hands together and resumed typing. Showtime! I'm sending something interesting to your screen.

Is it safe for work? ;)

Open it and see . . . if you dare. Mwa-ha-ha.

Max approved her link, which she had named "naughty-4maxxx," and a window popped open displaying a terminal Penny shared from her laptop. A series of commands and numbers were scrolling down it.

You're packet-sniffing the shop's Wi-Fi router, Max wrote. She had installed an analyzing tool that was logging all the data transferred on Café Forseti's network. If the other hacker accessed any sort of admin interface for The Curtain, they had him. How did you set that up?

I asked? I told the owner, a lovely elderly woman named Zelda, that a hacker has been using her network to commit crimes.

She believed you?

It happens to be the truth! You aren't the only one who can be charming, you know. She has a grandson my age that she wants to introduce me to. Also, I told her she could be held responsible for any crimes committed using her equipment. Look, he's trying to connect to The Curtain's IP address.

Max kept one eye on his screen and the other on the hacker, who was typing with the focus and frenzy of someone engrossed in challenging work that they love. Penny explained that he was trying to find the server logs at the internet exchange and trace what had happened to block The Curtain. Meanwhile, Max snapped a photo of the hacker and ran an image search online, but he came up empty.

"Frak me," Penny said.

"What?" Max asked.

Penny looked up at him, angry, seemingly without even

recognizing Max for a moment. Then she nudged her eyebrows and nodded, gesturing with her eyes down at her screen. She typed.

The Curtain's back online!!!

Already? Max asked.

I know!

How'd he do it? Max looked at the hacker. He was smiling at his screen.

Backup servers, Penny wrote. He's redirected traffic to a mirror of the site. I figured they would have at least one fail-safe, but I thought it would take longer to set up.

Well, we have what we need. We can link him to The Curtain. We can use him to get to Rhonc.

Penny shook her head furiously, ignoring Max. She was typing faster. The other hacker looked up at her, his smile fading from his face. Then he looked at his screen in disbelief. The sound of his keys joined Penny's in a strange, clicky duet.

Max watched the data flow across his screen, trying to interpret the numbers as reality, the push and pull of Penny and her opponent's private hack-off.

"Got you," Penny muttered.

The hacker slapped the table and jumped up.

"Enough!" he said. "No more games. You don't know what you're messing about with."

English accent. Check. He was the young man Nadia had encountered on her first trip to Helgoland.

Penny leaned back in her seat. This time she was all smiles.

"What did you do?" Max asked her.

"The Curtain is down again. Permanently," she said.

"You knew it was us?" Max asked the hacker.

The hacker laughed. "I recognized you two the instant I walked in. Aaaand . . . you were talking over chat while sitting a foot apart."

"Then why didn't you turn around and leave?" Penny asked.

He shrugged. "I can't outrun Max Stein."

He picked up his laptop and strode over to their table. "It's brilliant to meet you." He extended a hand to Max.

Max stood and shook his hand. "You have a name?"

"I have many identities. Call me Omega13." He turned to Penny and winked. "After what I just saw, I want to propose to you, Penny Polonsky."

"Not interested." She reached up and shook his hand. "Sit with us."

As Omega13 pulled over a chair, Max texted Omega13 to Risse.

"Care to join us too?" Omega13 said to Valentine, who was a few tables over, pretending she wasn't listening.

Max waved her over. She carried over her chair and sat across from Omega13.

"Valentine Labelle, *La Vérité*," she said.

Omega13's already pale face turned ghostly. "A reporter."

"Guilty." She smiled.

For the first time, Omega13 looked concerned. The

seriousness of his situation was starting to sink in. He shifted in his seat.

"If I had to be caught, I'm glad fellow hackers did it, particularly you two. There's some honor in that," he said.

"So. Omega13. Is one of your other names 'the Wizard'?" Max asked the gentleman hacker.

Omega13 laughed. "I s'pose you don't know everything."

"We know enough. You're responsible for maintaining The Curtain. Even if you're just a puppet and the Wizard's pulling the strings, who do you think is going to take all the blame when he's caught?"

"Can't prove I have anything to do with it," Omega13 said.

"We can. We have the coffee shop under surveillance. Video cameras and a packet sniffer that show you're at least an administrator of The Curtain. If you help us find the Wizard, you'll be helping yourself," Max said.

"I'm sure you've committed lots of other crimes, ye of many names. If you don't help us, you'll go to jail for a very long time, mister," Penny said.

Omega13 tossed up his hands. "What can I do for you?"

"You'll cooperate?" Max asked.

"I'm a merc. I work for the highest profit, and I do whatever it takes to win."

"We aren't paying you," Max said.

"You're paying with the greatest currency: my life. Chances are, if I don't go on record with you while I can, I'll end up dead. This is my new insurance policy."

"You're saying the Wizard kills people to protect The Curtain?" Max asked.

"He has done at least once. He hired an assassin through the site not long ago. Then I heard about that poor bloke on the news." He tipped his head toward Max. "Your timing's solid. I've been having an attack of conscience of late, and that murder got me thinking about an exit strategy."

"You were aware that the Wizard contracted a killer?" Max asked. *And you didn't try to stop it,* he thought.

"I'm aware of every transaction on The Curtain. Thanks to a little script I've got going in the background."

"Do you have logs of all those transactions too?" Penny asked. "Including the Wizard's?"

"Natch. I've got copies of it all, even what I was explicitly ordered to delete—stored offline, honoring the spirit of the thing. The best protection is collection: Grab as much info on other people as you can."

"You have a bright future at GCHQ," Valentine said.

"They couldn't afford me," Omega13 said.

A text message arrived from Risse. Nada on Omega13. If he's a hacker, he hasn't been bragging about his exploits. Pic didn't—

The rest of Risse's text message was truncated, but Max gathered she hadn't had any luck figuring out Omega13's real name either.

"So you'll give us what you've collected and speak on the record about your involvement?" Max said.

"If you can meet my three conditions. First: Don't ask me to turn myself in or reveal my identity. I don't do that sort of thing. That means you promise not to use my face and you disguise my voice if you use your surveillance video."

Max looked at Valentine. She hesitated, then nodded.

"Splendid. Second: Get me back to mainland Germany before Sara finds out I've talked to you," Omega13 said.

"Sara?" Max said. "Apsara Siriwanich, Rhone's assistant?"

"Same. But I wouldn't call her an assistant to her face. She doesn't bring coffee or take notes. Make no mistake: She's dangerous."

Max texted the name to Risse.

"You knew Rhone created The Curtain, Omega13?" Penny asked.

"He had the notion, but he didn't *create* it. I did. From scratch." Omega13 cracked his knuckles.

"Good for you." Penny scowled. "What's your third condition?"

"Third: You knocked the backup server offline, and I can't even connect to the internet anymore. Tell me how you did it, love." Omega13 got that dreamy look in his eyes again. Max couldn't blame him for being impressed with Penny and her skills.

She smiled. "A magician never reveals her secrets. But we can trade information. You tell us everything first, and I'll consider sharing how we did it."

Valentine pulled out her notepad. "This is where I come in,

thank you. Mind answering a few questions?"

Omega13 flung his fingers out theatrically. "Can't promise to tell you 'everything,' but fire at will."

Slowly they learned some details about Omega13 and his work. The hacker had first become involved with VT five years ago, when the company was beginning its major efforts to gain more leverage over the internet—both by controlling the routes data passed through and the information itself.

He came to their attention after hacking into their email system and stealing some of their sensitive communications. Instead of releasing them to the public like Ada had, he offered to sell them back to them—and Rhone countered with a job offer. Omega13 was hired to manipulate information on the internet, primarily by erasing all traces of data that Rhone and his executive staff didn't want to be available.

Omega13 was instrumental in covering up VT's shady activities and acquisitions; one of his first assignments was to clean up the online records of his bosses and scrub Rhone's existence from the internet. Eventually he headed a team of hackers monitoring data about VT, including Ada Kiesler's leaks, before Omega13 had transitioned to "special operations," primarily involving The Curtain. Presumably, he'd covered his own trail pretty well.

"Are we nearly done here? The next ferry leaves in twenty," Omega13 said.

Penny typed something on her laptop. Max glanced at her message as it popped up on her private network:

Are we really cutting this clown loose?

We're going after the big guy. As long as we have his testi-
mony on video and his records from The Curtain and his time at
VT, we don't need Omega13, **Max wrote.**

Yeah, I don't want to turn in our own either. :-/

"Sure," Max said. "You can go, after you do one more thing
for us."

Omega13 glowered at Max.

"Tell us where to find Rhone," Max asked.

"Easy enough. Helgoland." Omega13 shrugged. "Can't narrow it down any further, sorry. He does his business on a yacht
in international waters, but I don't know where it docks."

"Name of the yacht?"

"Never noticed."

"I'm guessing 'never noticed' isn't the name of the yacht,"
Max said.

"No."

"Where does Sara Siriwanich live?" Max asked.

"In Unterland, near the pier. But I've never been to her
house, no matter how many opportunities I give her," Omega13
said.

Penny rolled her eyes.

"We usually meet at the Rickmers Galerie Restaurant, or
when it's very urgent, she comes here directly to look over my
shoulder. So helpful. She called me in today to get The Curtain
back up. We're scheduled for dinner at Restaurant Atlantis at
five, so you know it's serious. I hate to miss their lobster."

"How do we know you won't turn around and warn Sara about us?" Penny asked.

"I need to get as far from her as possible before she finds out, or I won't be going anywhere. As I say, it's long past time I walked away from all this. As of now, Omega13 exists no more." He pulled out a cell phone and slid it across the table to them.

"This is how we contact each other for Curtain business. I don't have any other way to reach Sara. The transaction log is inside. The password . . ." He grabbed Valentine's pad and pencil and scribbled something. He slid it over to Max: hArcD8KRBbWvW4Qa.

"Got it." Max removed the phone's battery and pocketed them both. They had Omega13's confession, his phone, proof that he worked for The Curtain and Verbunden Telekom, and records of all the illegal transactions carried out in Richard Rhone's name—including the hit on Kevin Sharpe. And they knew where Rhone's right-hand person, Sara Siriwanich, would be that night, so Max could hopefully follow her to her boss.

Omega13, whatever his name would be after he walked out of the coffee shop, stood.

"Right. Your turn, love. How did you shut down The Curtain?"

Penny glanced at Valentine. "You can read all about it in *La Vérité* on Christmas," she said.

25

MAX WAS PRETENDING TO SHOP IN A SUPERMARKET near Restaurant Atlantis when Lianna's text message dinged on his phone: She just walked in.

The attached picture loaded sluggishly, an out-of-focus shot of a plate with a half-eaten steak and mashed potatoes. Beyond it, much clearer, was the woman Nadia had described, only her hair was in a ponytail and she was wearing a red cardigan over a peasant blouse and black jeans.

Max forwarded the photo to Risse. He hadn't heard from her yet on his request for info on Apsara Siriwanich, but he hoped this image would help in her search. If they were lucky, there could even be a photo of her with an uncredited Richard Rhone—but probably not if Omega13 had gotten to it first.

Let me know when she's leaving, Max texted back.

Ten minutes later, the text came. She's paying for her coffee. She is *pissed*.

Language! he texted. On my way.

Max put down his shopping basket, which was filled with random things he'd grabbed to look busy.

Be careful.

Always. He inserted his Bluetooth earpiece and switched it on. It connected to his phone.

Huh. Then try to be *more* careful than usual, Lianna texted.

Yes, Mother. <3

Max headed out into the chilly night. The rain had stopped, but it was still misty out, and the temperature was dropping rapidly. The forecast called for snow by morning. It seemed likely that Helgoland, at least, would enjoy a white Christmas this year.

The cold worked its way through his thin layers of clothing. He drew his hood up and shoved his hands into his pockets as he walked briskly toward Restaurant Atlantis, guided by the delicious aroma of cooking lobster. He'd committed the cardinal sin of grocery shopping—or pretending to shop—on an empty stomach, and he was paying the price for it.

Max was startled to see Sara hurrying toward him on the street. She was shorter than he'd expected, and she moved gracefully, like an athlete. He wondered what her sport was. She was slender and fit. Gymnast? Maybe a ballerina.

He lowered his head as they neared each other and hoped she wouldn't recognize him. If she'd arranged the hit on

Sharpe for Rhone, she certainly knew what Max looked like, though she likely wouldn't be expecting to find him here.

Sara was so focused on getting where she was going, she didn't notice him, even though his sleeve brushed against hers. His fingers twitched. Enzo would have had her phone or wallet by now.

She's heading for the coffee shop, he realized.

He texted a warning to Penny and spun around to pursue Sara. She was already almost out of sight in the dark, wet night. He picked up his pace, drawing a sharp breath at the pain in his leg. He was pretty sure he knew where she was going, but he was worried about what she would do when she got there.

He was nearly there when Sara emerged from the coffee shop, confusion plain on her face. Max ducked into the shadow of an antiques store, closed for the night. Rainwater dripped from an awning and splashed on his cheek.

Sara stood on the threshold of Café Forseti, silhouetted by the glass door and the light from within the shop. She dialed a number on her phone and listened, motionless. Then she started yelling.

Max couldn't make out what she was saying, but he imagined she was giving Omega13 an earful.

Max's Bluetooth headset played a tone followed by the word "Penny" in a robotic monotone. He tapped the button on his earpiece to pick up the call.

"She was just here," Penny said.

"She's still there, standing outside the door. I'm watching

from across the street." Max kept his voice low, not that Sara could have heard him over her screeching voice.

"She spoke to me. Asked if I'd seen Omega13—not by name, of course. I told her I'd seen him before, but that he'd gotten agitated by something on his computer and taken off in a hurry. That's close enough to the truth."

Sara hung up and stalked off. Max trailed behind her.

"She's moving again. I'm gonna follow," he muttered.

"Be careful," Penny said.

He sighed. "Of course."

She snorted and hung up.

He followed Sara all the way back to Restaurant Atlantis, where she checked again to make sure Omega13 hadn't arrived. Her next stop was a nearby pub. Max's ID probably would have gotten him in—the legal drinking age in Germany was sixteen—but he didn't want to risk Sara spotting him. So he skulked just around the corner, growing colder and damper by the minute.

Fifty minutes later, Sara left the pub and continued on her way at a leisurely, slightly unsteady, pace to the residential neighborhood of Unterland.

Damn.

She isn't going to the waterfront. I guess she isn't meeting Rhone tonight, **Max texted Penny.** Looks like she's headed home.

Maybe she met him at the bar? **Penny wrote.** Or she has another way to contact him from there.

DAMN.

Max looked back at the pub. Should he go back or keep following her? He wished Valentine wasn't so insistent on staying out of the story herself—she only wanted to observe. It would be great if she or Luc would go observe the pub to see if Rhone was there, or had been there. Instead they had decided to film their interview with Nadia. Even if they couldn't catch Rhone, there was still a powerful human-interest story there, and the media coverage might do her and other trafficked women some good.

Max kept following Sara until she let herself into a house on Friesenstrasse, after fumbling with her keys for a couple of minutes. Inside, a light went on upstairs, and he saw her shadow pass by the shade a few times. He felt creepy watching her window, but he stayed until the light went out.

He made sure he could identify the house again and headed back to the hotel to thaw and grab a few hours of sleep. Then he was back early the next morning.

Max had new respect for the various people who had followed him in the past; this was hard work. He'd have to tell Valentine and Luc that when he saw them later. They had gone with Penny to the Helgoland police station to present their evidence against Rhone, so he could be arrested as soon as they found him. Max wanted to be there, but he supposed he could watch it all on video later.

It turned out Sara was a jogger too, and she really liked going up and down the Grand Staircase connecting Unterland

and Oberland. A run that would have barely been a work-out for Max before had him sweating and clenching his teeth against the pain in his trembling leg. What would he do if it didn't heal properly and he couldn't run anymore?

The rest of Sara's morning routine took her back to Café Forseti for breakfast: scrambled eggs, dry toast, coffee. Max went in for coffee while she was working on her laptop, trying to get online. The Wi-Fi was down.

Good job, Penny, Max thought. *Keep them guessing, force their hand.*

He wondered if there was another hacker en route to deal with The Curtain being down; how many others were involved in operating it? They had to be completely screwed without Omega13.

It wasn't until late afternoon that Sara made her way to the South Marina. A few snowflakes drifted down and tickled Max's cheek as he watched her walk up and down the pier. She was now acting extra cautious. *Did she spot me?*

Finally, she approached one of the larger yachts and boarded it. The name in cursive black letters on its side was *Nowhere Man.* That had to be their guy. It flew the ubiquitous green, red, and white Helgoland flag over its bow. Very Christmassy.

Max snapped some photos of Sara on the deck of the *Nowhere Man* and sent them on to Penny and Risse. It wasn't like Risse to go so long without responding to him, and normally throughout the day she sent him lots of random things about celebrity news and the TV shows she was watching. He checked his text history again, to be sure. Nothing from her since yesterday.

Max texted Penny. Hey, have you heard from Risse?

Sure. She's fine. She's taking my advice to lay low for a bit, Penny texted.

That wasn't like Risse either.

Good work locating the boat, Penny texted.

Right. The boat. Rhone.

The *Nowhere Man* slowly drifted away from the dock. Max groaned.

Make that *identifying* the boat. It's leaving. Soon we won't know where it is.

They conduct all their business at open sea, right? Doesn't matter. We can confirm that it docks in the same place, or find out where else it might live.

Can't the cops do that?

Yeah . . . About that. Hold on.

Max's earpiece dinged. *Penny.* He switched it on.

"What happened?" Max started walking toward the hotel as the *Nowhere Man* motored out of the marina.

"The cops can't do anything without a warrant. They can't get a warrant without probable cause, and they can't prove that unless they know for certain that Richard Rhone and/or the Wizard is on that boat," Penny said.

"What!" Max said.

"The good news is, they've reached out to our old friends at the FBI, agents Ocampo and Egwu, the team that investigated Panjea. They've been building separate cases against Rhone and The Curtain for a while now, and they'd be thrilled to merge them into one. Tidier paperwork. They are so excited about Ada's files, which I sent to them. So excited! But . . . they can't move on this either until we confirm his identity. And they can't bring him in unless his boat is within twelve miles of the German coastline; it has to be close to either Helgoland or the mainland."

"So they want us to literally do all their work for them, then they can swoop in to put the handcuffs on and take all the credit. Unbelievable," Max said. "Do they want Rhone's head delivered on a silver platter too?"

"Ew. No. Anyway, they didn't say as much. Anything we do to help their investigation would be considered 'extralegal.'"

"You mean illegal."

"You say potato, I say tater tot," Penny said.

Max's stomach rumbled. "Please don't mention food right now." He gazed out at the ocean. The vast, unyielding ocean.

"Does that mean we could face criminal charges?" he asked. Max was already in enough trouble with the law.

"I'm sure they'd try to protect us," Penny said.

"You trust them?" he asked.

"If we get them Rhone, they'll be heroes. Grateful heroes. If we screw up, if we have this wrong, I bet they'll make the most of the situation and we'd be behind bars. So, you know, don't fail."

"All we have to do is get close enough to Rhone to positively ID him, and bonus points if we can prove he's the Wizard?"

"Yes, but if we can catch him in the act of committing a crime, or attempting to commit a crime, we'll have a rock-solid case against him and VT, and The Curtain will be no more."

"Well, we should do *that* then. Why not?" Max sighed. "As long as they're asking us to lasso the moon . . ."

"I do have one idea, but you aren't going to like it," Penny said.

He laughed. "Why break our streak now?"

26

MAX STEPPED OUT OF HIS HOTEL-ROOM BATHROOM, feeling more self-conscious than he had in his entire life, which included all the awkwardness of puberty.

His shoulders were a little too broad for the gray blouse Penny and his mother had picked out for him, but it was okay as long as he limited his arm movements. The black pencil skirt *just* managed to fit around his waist, but he was all the wrong shape for the rest of it. He'd shaved his legs—not fun!— and skipped stockings, so his legs were freezing, and there was no hope of him fitting into flats. They found some Crocs for him at the same shop where they'd picked up the brown wig that endowed him with frizzy shoulder-length hair.

As for other endowments, Max kept pushing up his bra, which was stuffed with tissues from the unisex restroom.

"Stop that," he said as Penny straightened his fake boobs.

She scrutinized the overall effect. "Hmmm. This is a little strange for me."

"How do you think *I* feel?" he said.

Penny's expertise with makeup even made Max look twice in the mirror. Maybe he'd finally hit on the perfect disguise. After twenty minutes of practicing standing and walking, the women declared him not a complete disaster.

"I just got used to having my son back, but now I have a daughter," Lianna said.

"Ha-ha," Max said.

"Wait until Risse sees this." Penny snapped a photo with her phone.

"Is this actually going to work?" Max asked.

"You'll get on the boat this way, but I don't think you'll fool anyone for long," Lianna said.

"I just need to get the Wizard out in the open so Nadia can identify him." Luc would be standing by with his camera and a telescopic lens to both capture the moment on video and allow Nadia to get a clear look at him. Meanwhile, Penny would be using her long-range listening equipment to capture audio just as she had for Max's interview with Kevin Sharpe. Hopefully this meeting would turn out better.

Nadia shrugged and said something. Penny laughed, then translated. "You are not the worst man in drag I've ever seen, but you aren't the best either. You are the Wizard's type though. He likes tall, strong women with large breasts."

Max slung his mother's purse over one shoulder. He'd

often wondered why many women carried giant purses like this, seemingly loaded with everything they could ever need. But now he was glad it was large enough to fit his laptop— which was loaded with everything he could ever need.

"If anything looks off, call the police," Max said.

"Off? What do you think could happen?" Lianna asked.

"Rhone's gotta be, what, in his fifties? I think I can take him. Besides, we're on a freaking island. There's nowhere for him to run. Once I confront him with what we know, he'll know the jig is up."

Max straightened his skirt. "Let's finish this."

Max walked up the little ramp leading from the dock to the *Nowhere Man*. No one confronted him. Nadia had said Rhone's office was in the master cabin, so Max made for it. He stood in front of the door, nervous. He shifted to the left a little to give Luc's camera a better view and then he knocked lightly.

A minute passed. Max knocked again. No answer.

As he reached for the handle to see if it was unlocked, the door opened. A broad, muscular man in a white polo shirt and white slacks stood there. He was as tall as Max. He smiled and stared at Max's chest. *Charming.*

"Hello there," the man said.

He did sort of look like Santa Claus, if Santa had been working out and getting plenty of sun. Close-cropped white hair, all the more striking in contrast with his dark, weathered face. Ruddy cheeks and a bushy white Mark Twain mustache.

Why had Max assumed that Rhone would be overweight and out of shape? Max subtracted years from the man's face, imagining him with dark hair and in a nice suit. Orson Welles.

"Are you Mr. Wizard?" Max softened his voice and pitched it slightly higher.

Rhone gave a hearty belly laugh. He even sounded like Santa Claus. "It's just the Wizard. What's your name, honey?"

"Damyan sent me. I am Maggie Carmine. His new girl." Max fluttered his fake eyelashes. "*Vesela Koleda.*"

He had picked out one of the latest additions to the offline archive of The Curtain that Penny had downloaded, a woman who had some facial similarities to Max.

"'*Vesela Koleda*'?" Rhone repeated.

Max glanced down demurely. Rhone was wearing black sandals, which somehow worked with his business-casual ensemble. "It means Merry Christmas in Bulgarian."

"How old are you?"

"Seventeen," Max said.

Lianna had advised him that although the age of consent in Germany was technically fourteen, sex with someone under the age of eighteen in an "exploitative situation" was still very illegal.

"Mmm," Rhone said. He glanced around them, scanning the docks behind Max. "It's freezing out here. Come on in, sweetheart, and we'll warm you up."

Max hesitated. This seemed to be working, but he needed to catch Rhone while he was off guard, and preferably still being recorded. He couldn't do that behind a closed door.

"Don't be shy now. Come *along*," Rhone said. He reached out and grabbed Max's wrist firmly with a large, meaty hand. He pulled Max inside.

It was warm, and the air was heavy with the smell of cigars, whiskey, and popcorn. Max almost laughed when he saw the large screen TV in the corner was playing *It's a Wonderful Life*. But it was the colorized version, what Evan always called "the abomination"—and a sure sign that Rhone was evil.

Max yanked his arm away, and Rhone looked astonished when he lost his grip. Max massaged his sore wrist. The red marks slowly faded from his skin.

"So you are the man behind The Curtain?" Max dropped his purse carefully just inside the door.

Rhone glared at him.

No, he was staring *behind* Max.

"Don't say another word, Mr. Rhone. This is a setup." A woman's voice.

Max turned to see Sara standing framed by the still open doorway. He had just enough time to register that she was really pretty when he saw her fist coming at the corner of his eye, and he was suddenly sprawled on the deck in the fetal position. The right side of his head hurt and his ear rang.

He blacked out for a split second, then found himself on hands and knees on the floor, blinking his eyes rapidly to clear the spots dancing across them. Someone had vomited in front of him.

Max scrambled away and up. The back of his blouse split. He touched his right temple and felt a cut there.

He spun around a couple of times, looking for Sara.

"Apsara Siriwanich?" Max said in his normal voice. "I thought you were a personal assistant." He coughed and spit.

"Labels are so limiting. I have a lot to offer," she said.

"You're a *guy*?" Rhone bellowed. "Sara, what's going on? Do you know . . . him?"

"This is Max Stein, sir." The way she said "sir," it sounded like she spelled it *i-d-i-o-t*. "Don't worry, I'll take care of this."

Sara advanced and kicked out at Max. He instinctively deflected the kick with an arm. It felt like he'd been hit by a steel pipe.

"You've been following me, Max," she said.

"Oh. You noticed that."

"You and your friends have been asking a lot of questions. You should have stuck with computers. They're less dangerous."

"I don't know if that's true."

"Less deadly, then."

Max shrugged. "You'd be surprised."

He backed up and she jabbed at him again. She moved so fast, it was like watching a video that was skipping frames. He dodged the blow, but took another to the same side of his head. Then a kick to his left ribs. He was reasonably sure she'd cracked one. He had a hard time breathing. Moving. Thinking.

"What . . . what do you call that fighting style?" he asked.

"Muay Thai." She adjusted her stance: head low, fists raised, feet planted apart.

"It's impressive," he gasped.

He took a roundhouse kick to the stomach and crumpled. He writhed on the floor and flipped onto his back, in sheer agony.

As she moved in, he rallied enough strength to launch himself forward, tackling her to the floor. She rolled him off of her fluidly, pretzeling his legs painfully in hers and locking them into place. She slashed down at his collarbone with her left elbow, and he gasped from the pain. His eyes drifted to the right. Rhone was watching the whole fight with a fascinated, terrified expression on his face.

"Sara, that's enough, don't you think?" Rhone said. "You're going to kill him."

"That's the idea. You don't know who this is?"

Rhone shook his head.

"You really need to get out more. Max Stein is the kid who shut down Panjea last year. The German police want him for the murder of Kevin Sharpe. So what do you think he's doing here?"

"He killed Sharpe?" Rhone said. He glared at Max. "You?"

Max lay on the floor for a moment, throbbing all over with pain. This conversation wasn't making sense. *Rhone* had put out the kill order on Sharpe.

Sara said something about The Curtain being down and

Omega13 running off with three million dollars in bitcoins. She mentioned Ada Kiesler and Interpol. "We're ruined," she said. "It's over. This is damage control."

But Max couldn't piece it all together. Their voices were fading, along with his vision. He passed out.

27

MAX WOKE UP TO FIND HIS FACE AND SHIRT SOAKED.
Richard Rhone was leaning over him, cradling an empty paper
cup in both hands, which were cuffed together.

"Get up," Rhone said.

Max bolted upright and regretted it. He had a monster
headache, and the edges of his vision were soft and dim. His
stomach lurched and he fought the urge to throw up. Again?

He groaned.

His head felt like his brains had been scooped out and
replaced with cotton stuffing. He was bruised and raw all over.
Dried blood crusted the left side of his face, and he couldn't
open his left eye. The right side of his mouth was swollen, and
he probed a loose tooth with his tongue. His chest burned, and
his left shoulder grated in its socket when he moved his arm.

"You okay?" Rhone asked. "Stay with me." He snapped his

fingers in front of Max's face a few times. That was annoying.

"I've been better." Max's voice was so thick, he didn't recognize it as his own. Rhone sported a black-and-purple bruise across his forehead and a bloody nose.

"What happened to *you*?" Max asked.

"My lovely assistant tendered her resignation." He massaged his jaw. "Or she enacted a corporate takeover. It's probably splitting hairs."

Max pressed his hand flat against the deck. It was vibrating very gently.

"We're moving?" he asked.

"Sure are."

"No!"

Max pushed Rhone aside and staggered toward the door of his office. He jiggled the handle. Locked.

Max peered through the porthole, but all he could see was the reflection of the cabin lights. He pressed his face to the cold glass and shielded his eyes—beyond them was darkness. Vast, terrifying, deadly, pitch-black. It was all around them.

Max experienced a moment of vertigo and started breathing faster, fogging the window. He yanked harder on the door and regretted it when fiery pain erupted in his shoulder.

"She locked us in," Rhone said.

"Where are we going?" Max asked.

"Out there." Rhone raised his cuffed hands and flapped them vaguely north. "The open sea."

Max slumped against Rhone's desk. He just needed to take

it easy for a second, organize his thoughts. "What's Sara up to?"

"She's escaping while we die out here. If we somehow survive, she'll be long gone and out of our reach."

"They'll send rescue boats," Max said. "My friends were watching from the marina. And they'll catch Sara when she gets back to Helgoland without us."

Rhone shook his head. "It will take Search and Rescue a long time to find us. Sara altered our course randomly several times before she directed us away from land. The longer we're out here, the harder it will be to pinpoint our location. In the meantime, we don't have any food or water."

"Why didn't she murder us more directly? Not that I'm complaining."

"That would have required her to throw us overboard or strangle us with her bare hands. More humane in the long run, perhaps, but not her style. Better to let a storm or starvation do the dirty work for her."

"Why's she trying to kill *you* anyway? Doesn't she work for you?"

"Because I tried to stop her. Sara despises weakness, especially in herself." Rhone shook his head. "Let's start over. Obviously you aren't Maggie Cartwright."

"Carmine," Max said. He pulled off his wig, which was skewed but had stayed on. He gasped when he found out why: the dozens of tiny hairpins Penny had used to secure it to his head, which came out painfully.

"She said your name is Max?" Rhone asked.

"Max Stein. And you're Richard Rhone, aka the Wizard."

Rhone hesitated. "Yes, I am."

"You're the CEO of Verbunden Telekom and you created The Curtain."

He slumped his shoulders. "Yes."

Now they were in business. Max had their guy—for what good it would do him. Before Rhone could be arrested and charged for his crimes, they had to get back to land safely.

"Does this ship have a lifeboat?" Max asked.

"It does. But Sara took it."

Crap. Max swallowed. "How long have we been out here?"

"A few hours, I guess."

"And you haven't tried to get out of here yet? That's the first thing we have to do." Max pulled himself to his feet. He swayed. Rhone held out his cuffed hands, but Max shrugged off the help. "Where's the key to this door?"

"She took all the keys." Rhone spread his hands as far apart as he could as if to say, "What can you do?"

What *could* they do?

From the rocking of the boat and the distant rumble of the engine, the yacht was still sailing straight out into the ocean. How much fuel had they burned, and how far had they come already? Even if they could turn it around, would they have enough to get back? Every moment was taking them farther from land and making it less likely that they could return safely.

"We have to get to the cockpit. Turn this boat toward the mainland." Max stared at the locked door, wishing he still had Enzo's lockpicks.

He rummaged around in his purse, looking for anything that would help.

"My phone is gone," he said.

"Sara took it."

"So we can't call for help or be tracked by GPS."

"It probably wouldn't have worked out here anyway."

Max pulled out his computer. "But she left me this?"

"No Wi-Fi on board," Rhone said. "We used the marina's. Not that it's ever been reliable. The bad weather knocked it out completely yesterday."

Max smiled. That was Hurricane Penny.

He flashed back to Penny putting together his disguise, securing the wig so it wouldn't slip off. He practically dove for the wig he'd abandoned on the floor. He pulled out a few of the hairpins and studied them. *This could work.*

He used his teeth to strip off the smooth, round ends, exposing the sharp, flat metal tips beneath. He spit out the bits of plastic and knelt in front of the door. The smell of vomit was stronger here, making him nauseated on top of everything else working against him.

"You're a tough guy to find," Max said while he fiddled with the lock on the door.

"That's the idea. Better to let the board run things."

"But aren't you in charge of VT?"

"I founded the company, but it didn't become profitable until our trustees stepped in. I've always been more of a dreamer than a businessman. We had to make back a lot of money I lost, and we needed massive amounts of revenue to fulfill our five-year strategic plan."

"To take over the internet."

Rhone grunted. "Gaining a controlling interest in the infrastructure of the internet. So I set up The Curtain."

"The Board of Trustees knew about it?"

"Absolutely. All they care about is the number of zeroes in their salaries. That's all anyone cares about. That and getting laid, am I right?"

Max narrowed his eyes.

"Anyway. The Curtain became my main focus, and I became the Wizard. They set me up at Helgoland and gave me Sara to handle most of the day-to-day stuff: the boring meetings back in Berlin, site management. I'm not very detail oriented."

He didn't sound apologetic or embarrassed, just very matter-of-fact. Rhone was a person who knew exactly who he was and what he wanted, and he was fully comfortable with it. He owned his strengths and his weaknesses. Max kind of envied that Rhone had such awareness of his identity, so he didn't mind too much that he was about to burst the man's bubble.

"CEO, the Wizard—those are nice titles. But if you look at your job description, you'll see your real role at VT, your true value, is as a patsy," Max said.

"Excuse me?"

"The board doesn't want you out of the spotlight to protect you. They didn't give you a yacht at Helgoland so you'd have time to concentrate on running The Curtain. They're protecting themselves. You're the Wizard! You're the person who takes the fall when all this gets out. Everything you've done, all the files Ada has collected, make you out to be a lone operator in this."

"But Sara . . ." Rhone frowned. "She does most of the work. Truthfully, she's more of my partner than an assistant."

"She doesn't work for you. You didn't hire her; the board did, right?" Max asked.

Rhone nodded.

"If you look at *her* job description, she's more than an assistant or a bodyguard. She isn't a partner, she's your . . . handler. She keeps an eye on you and she keeps you under the board's control." Max stopped what he was doing to stare at the man. "Jesus. You had no idea. You're a scapegoat, Rhone. The board could do whatever they want knowing that if they ever got caught, they would blame everything on you. You're going to prison."

Rhone's head was bent over his cuffed hands, folded together like he was praying. Rumpled, bleeding, and bruised, he looked somehow smaller. He seemed lost in more than the literal sense of them not knowing where their boat was.

Max almost felt sorry for him, if he weren't such a despicable excuse for a human being. He deserved everything coming for him—except dying.

"I'm more concerned about our immediate situation. Worrying about anything else is pointless. Can you get us out of here?" Rhone asked.

"I'm trying." He returned to working on the door. He was getting closer. . . .

A pin snapped. Max cursed and flicked it away. He took a fresh one and bent it into shape.

Rhone covered his face with his hands. He took a deep, shuddering breath. *There we go.*

"How did you find me?" Rhone asked.

"My friends and I are hackers. We're good at finding things that don't want to be found. But we probably wouldn't have succeeded if you hadn't ordered Sharpe's assassination."

There. *Almost.*

"No!" Rhone snapped his head up. "No. I didn't do that. Sara suggested it once, and I said absolutely not. We don't do that. I told her to deal with him another way."

"But you let people hire killers through The Curtain, and that's what Sara did. I spoke to her right after Sharpe was killed. She led us here."

"She said *you* killed Kevin."

"Rhone, she's *evil.* She lied."

The lock clicked. Max twisted the knob, and the door opened. Cold air blasted him in the face. Snowflakes drifted into the cabin.

Rhone's eyes bugged. "How'd you do that?"

"Practice." Max pulled himself to his feet slowly. Slowly . . . "And luck," he grunted.

Rhone held up his cuffed hands. "Now get these off of me," he barked.

"I don't think so," Max said. "I'm gonna check out the cockpit." He slung his purse's strap over his chest like a bandolier, nestling his computer securely under his elbow.

Rhone climbed back onto his feet. "I'll take you."

They stepped out and discovered they were sailing through a blizzard. A foot of snow blanketed the deck, which was rolling softly in the choppy waves.

"*'The weather started getting rough, the tiny ship was tossed . . .'"*

Thanks, Mom. Max had that damn theme song stuck in his head now.

"Fantastic," Max said. The wind whipped the sound of his voice away into the night.

"This isn't good!" Rhone shouted, Captain Obvious of his own ship.

Max scooped up a handful of snow and sipped at it, trudging after Rhone and praying he didn't pitch or slide over the side, into the crashing waves.

28

WHEN MAX SAW THE DEAD CONTROL PANEL IN THE cockpit, he imagined the headline: "Media Magnate Richard Rhone Lost at Sea."

The lights on the console were all out. Max pulled a lever and pushed a button, but nothing happened. He could at least see that they were traveling northeast at 6 knots, about seven miles an hour, which placed them about twenty-one miles out from Helgoland. On their current course, they would run out of fuel long before they reached land.

Max explored under the console. It wasn't a matter of needing the ignition key or hot-wiring the engine; the wires had been pulled out of the instrument panel, rendering it useless. The radio had also been disabled. Sara was thorough, and she didn't care that when the boat was eventually found, it would be clear that it had been sabotaged.

The headline: "Murder at Sea! CEO Rhone Found Dead." Maybe a subhead for Max, "World's Most-Wanted Hacker Also Discovered, Deceased."

There was a slim chance of them running into another vessel out there that could help, but there was also a chance of them running *into* another ship.

Max studied the damaged instruments. Maybe he could rewire the yacht's running lights to flash an emergency beacon to any nearby ships. The ship had a marine computer to manage its systems, but there was no way to interface with it. Given more time, Max might be able to figure it out, but time was one of the things they didn't have.

Wait.

Max practically jumped up, making the boat spin around him. He caught himself before he fell and took a moment to regain his balance and breath. He didn't have to Google "concussion" to know there was something wrong with him.

He grabbed onto the console to steady himself. It wasn't just his head injury—the boat itself was tilting from side to side in the crashing waves. *Who knows what course we're on now?*

"Maybe you should lie down," Rhone said.

"I'll lie down when I'm dead. Which hopefully won't be for a good long while." He pulled his laptop out of his purse. Sara probably hadn't bothered to take it or toss it overboard because she didn't think he could do anything with it on a boat in the middle of the ocean, without internet. Under normal circumstances, she'd be right. But Max had something she didn't know about: Evan Baxter.

Max fished around for his network cable at the bottom of the purse. Never leave home without it.

"You can't email for help," Rhone said. "No signal for miles and miles and miles. Hey, what's with that creepy smile?"

"Get me back down to the instrument panel." Max found his legs weren't working the way he wanted them to anymore.

Rhone grabbed on to Max's arm awkwardly with his cuffed hands and gently eased him to the floor. He felt Max's sweaty forehead.

"You have a fever," Rhone said. He propped Max up next to the instrument panel, and Max pulled off his shredded, blood-stained blouse and struggled with the bra.

"Here." Rhone reached around and unfastened the clasp in back. "There's one thing I know how to do. Even with hand-cuffs on."

Max busied himself plugging his laptop into the network port of the instrument panel. He closed his eyes for a second, and jolted awake when Rhone shook him violently. No, that was the ship rocking in the waves.

"Still with me?" Rhone asked.

"Barely. I should have tried to take your cuffs off after all. I'm not sure I can do this." Max opened his laptop and accessed the encrypted folder, moving slowly because his vision was doubling. He focused harder.

Rhone watched with interest as Max navigated through the folders of what Evan had called his HAX-Files: a collection of all the useful tools he had programmed, contributed to, or downloaded over the years. They were part of the massive data dump he'd sent Max posthumously last year—via Penny's friend H8Bit.

Max had only a vague sense of what he was looking for, but it didn't take him long to dig it out. He opened the folder named "hackerf1337." Hackerf1337 was an organization of hackers who gathered on a boat each year to code up new tools for ships—and exploits.

Max explained to Rhone what he was doing, what he hoped to do, just in case he passed out again. Rhone followed along as Max ran the program called SIM.

Just like you could hack a car's onboard computer to control it with a laptop from a vehicle, or remotely through its online software, SIM was designed to give you another way to control a boat via a marine computer. It used a graphical interface ripped from a popular simulation-training program to access its navigation and automatic-steering functions.

Max blinked and looked away from the screen. He dialed the brightness down to its minimum, but the glow still hurt his eyes, and his headache was getting worse. He rubbed his eyes and closed one of them, squinting at the screen with the other.

Without an internet connection, Max couldn't download the latest updates and patches, which improved compatibility with newer boats, but he hoped he had something that would work anyway. The program scanned *Nowhere Man*'s computer and came up with a close match: version 1.77 of the software instead of 2.44. He applied the software and let the progress bar creep along.

"What's happening?" Rhone asked.

"I'm trying to regain control of this death barge."

"Don't call it that."

Max laughed. "Death barge. Death barge. Death barge."

He was losing it, just like Kevin Sharpe had at the end. Why was dying so funny? It was like some big punch line.

The progress bar hit 98 percent and flashed the word ERROR in red. He slapped the side of the console in frustration.

"No go?" Rhone asked.

"Eh." *Close enough.* Max crossed his fingers and hit the engine-stop button.

Ten seconds later, he thought he couldn't feel the rumbling of the engine in the floor anymore or hear its mechanical whirr. But he felt like they were still moving. Inertia.

"Did we stop?" Max asked.

"We did! You did it!" Rhone said.

Max covered his ears. "Shhh."

"Sorry," Rhone whispered. "What do we do now?"

"How much gas do we have?" Max asked.

Rhone peered over the console. "Not enough. Quarter tank? We probably used twice that getting here, wherever here is."

"Okay." Max fiddled with the other controls on his virtual dashboard. He fired up the engine again and slowed the speed to 1 knot. Too late, he realized he could only slow down, not speed up. Reverse didn't work, and they couldn't turn left. Was that port? But he could bring the ship about to starboard; like a UPS truck, this baby could only make right turns.

"'All I need is a tall ship and a star to steer her by,'" Max said.

"It's still snowing," Rhone said. "Can't see a damn thing out there."

"Which direction are we pointing?"

"Uh . . ." Rhone checked the compass. "Due south."

"Good enough," Max said. If they kept in that direction, they might make it to one of the East Frisian Islands off the North Sea coast of Germany. But once they ran out of gas, they'd just drift wherever the ocean current took them. "Do you have any signal flares?"

"Yes!"

"Shhh . . ." Max closed his eyes.

He heard Rhone fiddle with something at the back of the cockpit. When he returned, he balanced a red flare gun and a box of flares in his cuffed hands. And a first-aid kit.

"I could kiss you," Max said.

"Thanks, but you aren't my type."

"That's not what you thought when we first met." Max looked at the remains of his Maggie Carmine disguise scattered across the floor of the cockpit. It was suggestive of a different wild night than the one they were spending together.

Max loaded the flare gun and handed it to Rhone. "Keep firing those at regular intervals as we head back in the general direction of Helgoland. Someone should be out there searching for us."

Max pulled the first-aid kit over to him. All he needed now was YouTube to figure out how to patch himself up.

Which of course made him wonder: Would he ever see Penny again?

29

THE REST OF THE NIGHT PASSED IN A BLUR. RHONE forced Max to sit out on the deck where the cold air, blowing snow, and splashing waves helped keep him awake. Periodically, Rhone fired a flare that lit up the endless black water around them.

At some point, the engine sputtered and died, finally out of fuel. Rhone continued firing flares as they drifted with the waves. The snow tapered off, and the boat stopped rocking. There was a break in the clouds, and Max squinted up at the too-bright stars, trying to pick out constellations, counting the satellites as they passed, hoping that one of those lights might be a passing plane or a rescue helicopter.

Finally, their supply of flares exhausted, Rhone settled down on the deck beside Max, picking at the lock of his handcuffs with a hairpin from Max's wig. Broken pins littered the area.

As grayness seeped around them and the sun broke over the horizon, rescue finally came.

"Is this the *Hermann Marwede*?" Max asked when they were brought on board what he assumed was Helgoland's search-and-rescue vessel.

"No, we're the *Den Lille Havfrue*, out of Esbjerg," said an astonished crewman, a boy about Max's age.

"Esbjerg? Where's that?" Max asked.

"Denmark."

"How did you know to look for us?" Max asked.

"We didn't. You drifted into our shipping route."

Max glared at Rhone. "You said we were going south."

"You can't blame me for taking a shot at getting away." Rhone looked at the burly crewman who held fast to his right arm. His handcuffs still dangled from his left wrist.

"I could have died before we were rescued," Max said.

"We both could have. But we didn't."

"Are you hurt?" the crewman asked Rhone.

"I'm okay, but I could use a drink."

"Then I'm taking you to the brig." He jerked his head at his companion. "Bring the kid to Emil."

Emil turned out to be a doctor, Emil Ibsen. He examined Max in a cramped sick bay belowdecks.

"If your boat hadn't run out of gas, you would have made it close to the Danish coast before too long," Dr. Ibsen said.

And Rhone would have escaped, though Max wasn't sure if he could have swum to shore with his hands cuffed, which was probably why he'd been so focused on getting them off. Max certainly couldn't swim in his condition. He had barely made it to the doctor on his own feet.

Dr. Ibsen tsked over Max's injuries. "Thank God we found you when we did. I need to order an MRI when we reach the mainland, but it looks like you have at least a mild concussion."

"The mainland? Like, Denmark? You aren't taking us to Helgoland?" Max asked.

The doctor looked concerned. "You need emergency medical care, Mr. Stein. Besides the head injury, you have massive traumas all over your body, two broken ribs, and a bullet wound that's showing signs of infection. I've radioed ahead, and we're trying to reach Helgoland to let them know we've got you. Their distress call about your missing boat never reached us, but communications are a mess right now, and the increased radio traffic is clogging our bandwidth."

"Why? What's been going on?" Max asked.

Dr. Ibsen studied him. "I guess you wouldn't have heard yet. The internet's down."

Max squinted. "I don't think I heard you right."

"It's true. The internet has not been working since yesterday."

Oh no, Max thought. He was too late.

"It's been over twelve hours! I'm sure someone is working on bringing it back up." The doctor shook his head. "It's been quite an adjustment."

It wasn't just the medicine that was making Max numb. He

heard his voice, seemingly coming from far away. "Emergency services are working?"

"Yes, thank God. How did you know?"

Damm it, Penny. What have you done?

"Has anyone claimed, uh, credit for taking it down?" Max asked.

"We don't have much information, I'm sorry. It seems like everything has been shut down by this. The world runs on computers these days, it's all networked. No network . . . Poof!"

Max nodded and had to grab the table for support.

"Don't do that," Dr. Ibsen said. "What about that fellow you arrived with? What were you two doing on a boat out there in this weather?"

"His name is Richard Rhone, CEO of Verbunden Telekom AG."

Dr. Ibsen whistled to show he was impressed.

"He was also one of the people running an online black market, which I suppose has finally been shut down for good," Max said.

That was unquestionably a good thing, the outcome they had been hoping for. But Max feared the cost had been too great. Was the internet salvageable? Could Kiesler's plan for the next internet work? He hoped so. It had to.

"Good. Crooks on the internet have been selling meds and drugs at outrageous prices to people who shouldn't be taking them without supervision." Dr. Ibsen scowled. "Hope he gets what's coming to him."

"Believe it or not, underneath all the selfishness, greed, and moral decrepitude, he's kind of a nice guy," Max said.

"They always are," Dr. Ibsen said.

"You might want to radio ahead to your port as well, so the police can take him into custody. Just tell them you've captured the Wizard, you're here with Max Stein, and they should contact Interpol."

"You're Max Stein?"

Max almost nodded again, but he caught himself before bringing on another crippling headache. "Yes."

"I did hear about you, before. Won't they arrest you too?"

"Oh, probably." Max sighed.

"All right, I'll take care of everything. Sleep now."

That was the best idea Max had heard in a long time.

When Max opened his eyes again, he was handcuffed to a hospital bed by his right wrist. He tugged at his restraints.

"Max," Lianna said from a chair beside the bed. "Sweetie, are you all right?"

He smiled weakly. "Hey, Mom. Got a hairpin?"

"I'm afraid not."

The blinds in his room were drawn, but it looked like it was daytime outside. Even the dim light was enough to make Max feel like daggers were poking from behind his eyeballs.

"This is so strange. I've been sitting here remembering that whenever you got sick, I sat in your room just like this and read to you," Lianna said.

"I remember," Max said.

"I hadn't thought about that in years."

"How long have I been asleep?" Max asked.

Lianna puffed out her cheeks. "Merry Christmas?"

"Oh no! Today? Crap." Worst. Christmas. Ever. "Where are we?" Max asked.

"Ribe County Hospital in Esbjerg, Denmark."

Max noticed just how tired she looked. She'd been crying.

"Hey. Hey, Mom. I'm fine. I am fine, right?"

"You should be. A concussion, bruises, and scrapes. Fractured ribs . . ." She sighed. "I am the worst mother in the world, aren't I?"

A week ago, Max would have thought so. "No. Because you're here." She took his hand.

The door opened, and Bradley Stein walked in carrying two paper cups. "She isn't the only one."

"Dad!" Max struggled to sit up, but his mother placed a hand on his chest and gently made him lie down.

"Dad, I can't believe you're here!" Max glanced at Lianna. "You see him too, right? I didn't suffer serious brain damage?"

"I'm not an illusion," Bradley said.

"An illusion would say that," Max said.

"I couldn't miss Christmas with you." Bradley handed Lianna one of the cups.

"I didn't even know you had a valid passport. Hey, is that coffee?" Max asked.

"Not for you." Lianna sipped it. "Ahhhhh. I needed that." She smiled.

"Alicia Beaumont called me after Kevin Sharpe was killed." Bradley shot a significant look at Lianna.

"Get over it, Brad. We've been busy here," she said.

"I can see that." He sat down in the chair beside her and crossed his legs. "Anyway, when I *finally* heard what was going on, I got on a plane. It was a good excuse to get away from nosy reporters back home. I made it on one of the last flights out."

"Out of San Fran?" Max asked.

"Out of the *United States*." Bradley ran a hand through his hair. Was it possible that his hair had more gray since Max had last seen him, only six months before? "Max, all the planes are grounded. Without a functional internet . . ."

"Oh, shit," Max said. He glanced at his mother. "Sorry."

"No, that was entirely appropriate. 'Shit' doesn't really cover it," she said.

Max looked around the room—slowly. If he turned his head too fast, the room kept turning.

"You look terrible, kid," Bradley said.

"Why do people like telling me that?" Max asked. "I think I look pretty good for someone who was shot, used as a punching bag, and abandoned to die at sea."

Lianna pulled a compact mirror out of her purse and handed it to Max. He studied his reflection.

"Wow. I look terrible," he said.

Bradley leaned forward, holding his cup between both

hands. "Max, you almost died. Twice."

"I prefer to think of it as barely not dying."

"Always the optimist. I'm happy you're alive, but this was a close one. I'm really angry with you." He tipped his head toward Lianna. "At both of you. When you're feeling better, we're going to have a talk about this."

"Fair," Max said. "Mom, have you heard from Penny?"

"She's here too, but only family is allowed to visit."

Good. So Penny hadn't been arrested.

The door opened, and Penny and Enzo darted inside.

"But what do rules matter to hackers and thieves?" Lianna threw up her hands.

"Max!" Enzo said.

Max winced.

"Oops," the boy whispered. He tiptoed over to the bed.

"What are *you* doing here?" Max asked. "I mean, it's awesome to see you, but . . ."

"The only way to get to Denmark from Paris was to drive," Bradley said. "With computer systems down, renting a car was out, so I asked to borrow the Beaumonts' car. Enzo insisted on coming along, and then his mothers had to come because it's getting seriously post-apocalyptic out there, and . . ." Bradley sighed. "It was a loooong drive. Lots of roads are closed and traffic lights aren't working."

"Thanks for making the trip," Max said.

Seeing his mother and father in the same room again . . . Max couldn't have asked for a better Christmas present. Well, maybe if they had been brought together under different circumstances.

He struggled to sit up. Lianna adjusted the bed to a reclining position. He already felt a dull ache at the back of his head, but he ignored it.

Penny came to his side and tentatively took his hand. He tensed at first but then relaxed, curling his fingers around hers.

"I had the craziest dream," Max said. "You were there. And you, and you." He turned to his mother and Enzo.

"Ha-ha," Penny said. "The nightmare isn't over yet."

Max narrowed his eyes. "So I hear. The internet...? *Penny.*"

She raised her hands. "It was the only way."

"Bullshit. When did you do it?" Max asked.

"At Café Forseti, when we were facing off with Omega13. He got The Curtain back online so fast. VT had backup servers everywhere. That's when I knew that the only way to bring it down, to get him to talk, was to bring it *all* down."

"That long ago." It must have taken time for the full effects to become evident. The problems texting Risse, the spotty Wi-Fi. All part of the death throes of the internet as it fell apart piece by piece and struggled to keep the data flowing.

"Why didn't you say anything? How could you keep this from me?" he asked.

"I was trying to fix it, Max."

"So I wouldn't find out?"

"You had enough to worry about. I thought I could make

it all right." She took a shaky breath. "I couldn't. I can't. Not by myself."

Max swallowed. *The internet is gone.*

"It was supposed to be a test. Five minutes, tops," he said.

"That was the plan. By the time we were done with Omega13, I realized something was wrong. The internet never went back online." She scowled. "Ada gave H8Bit and dork-ph0enyx different orders. She never bothered to tell me that when I gave them the signal to pull the plug, it was going to be permanent. Fortunately, the backup systems she promised were legit. We avoided some of the injuries it could have caused and made sure people got help when they needed it."

"*Some* of the injuries?"

"Max, people got hurt." Penny blinked back tears. "People died. A lot of people. Trains derailing, car accidents. Planes coming down." She shuddered. "I feel terrible. I don't know what to do."

She looked almost as bad as he did. Her eyes were bruised from lack of sleep. Her face was more drawn, and she even looked thinner. She was haunted the way he'd been for so much of last year. He wanted to comfort her, but . . . He pulled his hand away. She bit her lip and stepped back.

"Ada played you," Max said.

"She played us all." Penny paused, perhaps waiting for an "I told you so." Or hoping for Max to say it wasn't her fault.

That wasn't going to happen.

"I guess this makes Ada Kiesler the world's first recorded

cyberterrorist," Max said. "Ruining it for whistle-blowers everywhere."

"She's taking the blame. Or the credit, if you want to look at it that way," Penny said. "She turned herself in right after Rhone was arrested."

"We got him?" Max said. That was something, but it didn't feel like a victory anymore.

"He's facing a whole bunch of charges: money laundering, computer hacking, distributing narcotics online, conspiring to distribute narcotics, human trafficking, prostitution, statutory rape, engaging in a criminal enterprise. And, oh yes, murder."

"He didn't put that hit on Sharpe. He's actually a decent guy, for a criminal." But now Max and Penny were technically criminals too, and how much more damage had they done to the world in trying to stop him?

"Rhone's cooperating fully with the investigations into Verbunden Telekom," Penny said.

"What about Sara?"

"Luc got video of her attacking you and the boat pulling away," Lianna said. "We alerted the German Maritime Search and Rescue Service, and police were waiting to pick her up when she returned. But she never did. They found a lifeboat from *Nowhere Man* on Düne. I guess she had another way back to the mainland from there."

"She's the one who had Sharpe killed, against Rhone's wishes. She's been keeping an eye on him for Verbunden

Telekom's board." His eyes widened. "What about the board members?"

"Police are still sorting that out," Penny said. "They've scattered. It's easier to hide with everything that's going on now, and their usual ways of finding people don't work anymore. They're also hunting Omega13, but I think he'll be a tougher target."

"Supposedly he ran off with three million dollars in bitcoins from The Curtain's clients," Max said.

"That could be, but more than *seven* million is missing," Penny said. "No wonder he didn't mind helping us. We just added to the distraction while he got away."

Max bet Sara had carved out a piece of the pie for herself when she realized The Curtain was going down.

"We'll see how valuable that currency is with the internet gone," Max said.

He held up his handcuffed wrist. "Why am I under bed arrest?"

Lianna frowned. "Well, you did break a lot of laws, actually, not least of which is leaving Strasbourg while the primary suspect of an active investigation. I'm trying to pull some strings to get most of the charges dropped. My ex-husband—the second one—is calling in some favors. I think we're going to be okay. You're already being called a hero for bringing in Rhone. Everyone wants to talk to you—the media, FBI, CIA."

"A deal is a deal. Valentine Labelle has an exclusive," Max said.

"The special print edition of *La Vérité* sold out this morning, by the way. That's huge on Christmas Day," Lianna said.

"It's like *Newsies* out there, kids selling newspapers on street corners and shouting the news," Lianna said.

"Not singing it?" Bradley asked.

"Give it time," she said.

"Oh, yeah! Happy Christmas, Max!" Enzo said.

"Happy Christmas," Max said absently. He yawned. "How can I be tired when I've been sleeping for two days?"

"You've been through a lot, and I haven't even heard all the details yet. All right. Everybody out," Lianna said. "You two don't want to get caught in here."

Enzo and Penny grumbled but they moved toward the door. Enzo slipped out of the room, but Penny looked back at Max sadly.

"Ada got what she wanted. What *we* wanted," she said.

"Did she? She got everyone's attention, but how can people be talking about this? There are no more blogs, no chat rooms. Jesus, no *email*. We can't change anything if we can't talk to one another," he said.

Penny nodded slowly.

"No kidding. We're back to print papers and broadcast news," Bradley said. "And I'm out of a job now, so no hurry getting back home, I suppose. Which works out, because we're grounded."

"I'm out of work too, for the moment," Lianna said. "I'm okay with that, considering."

"What I mean is, everything Ada said has been right so far, so her plans for the replacement internet, maybe that'll work too. If we just give it a chance?" Penny said.

"You still believe in her?" Max asked.

"I have to," she said in a small voice. "If I want to see Risse again . . ." She straightened and smiled confidently. "We'll get this sorted, Max. Together."

He turned to look at the flowers by his bed, a bouquet of red roses tucked into a plastic water pitcher from the food cart. They could only have been there for a day or two, but they were already withering.

"I hope so," Max said.

30

BY THE TIME MAX WAS RELEASED FROM THE hospital a few days after Christmas, he'd already been visited by dour-looking Interpol agents concerning The Curtain and his role in apprehending Richard Rhone. The matter was far from over, but thanks to Penny's audio recording of his meeting with Sharpe before he was killed and Valentine and Luc's videos, Max was at least cleared of being a murder suspect.

Unfortunately, he still needed to present himself at court back in Strasbourg just after the New Year for breaking and entering at Lianna Stein's apartment building. The gang got together for a meal together at a restaurant in Esbjerg called Sand's, to say good-bye before they would all part ways the next morning. The Beaumonts were of course returning to Paris, to avoid Enzo missing any school.

Limited train service was operating again throughout

Europe, one of the signs of a slow crawl back from the abyss. So Penny was heading back to rally Verbunden Telekom's elite team of hackers, not to keep The Curtain running, but to help her reboot the internet. The clock was ticking; techheads around the world were picking up the pieces of the internet and having a very serious discussion—via excruciatingly slow dial-up modems and a Taiwanese bulletin-board system— about how to put them back together, and whether they should or not.

IT professionals, infosec experts, and hackers were investigating ways to use the existing infrastructure for the internet—the intact connections, like the fiber-optic trunk lines—to resurrect the web the way it was before, perhaps with some minor improvements.

But to realize Ada's dream of completely revising the way the internet was maintained, rather than return ownership and power to the hurting telecom companies, Penny would have to work fast. The only thing slowing progress was the difficulty in coordinating efforts to save the internet—without the internet.

The key seemed to be in hacking into those already func- tioning emergency systems, and Penny had both the means and the moral righteousness to do just that, as safely as possi- ble. The last thing she wanted to do was cause any more deaths.

Meanwhile, Max would be heading to Strasbourg on another train with his parents. If it was anything like the cab ride to the restaurant, it would be an interesting experience.

"Back me up here, Brad," Lianna said.

"Listen to your mother, Max," Bradley said.

"But all I've been doing is resting," Max said.

"And writing op-ed pieces for various newspapers from your sickbed, even though you're under doctor's orders to avoid screens—" Lianna said.

"I've been dictating my posts to Penny," Max protested.

"—and give your brain a chance to rest."

"Fat chance of that. He's terrible at following orders," Bradley said.

"He's much too selfless to worry about the permanent physical damage he could be doing by pushing himself too hard," Lianna said.

"He gets that from you," Lianna and Bradley said at the same time. They stared at each other.

"That was weird," Max said.

Bradley paid the driver in traveler's checks, and then they walked to the corner entrance to Sand's. Max trailed just behind his parents so he could see them both walking side by side. Even though they were probably having another one of their quiet, civilized arguments, he grinned like a little boy.

He didn't know what his family was going to be like from there on out, but for now, they had been reunited. Just like living without the World Wide Web, they were simultaneously returning to their roots and embarking on new ground.

The handwritten sign on the door read CA$H ONLY. No explanation needed—everyone knew that plastic and mobile payment systems weren't working. But it was ironic, considering that most Danish banks didn't even print or carry cash anymore.

Max limped into the restaurant, ignoring the pain from his still-healing injuries. He hated that he wouldn't be able to run or use a computer for at least another month, but he was working on ways to keep himself busy. Writing those articles, for one. Valentine was lobbying to get him a weekly column in *La Vérité*, and he was considering starting his own podcast, if and when the internet recovered.

"We're getting your tables ready," the hostess said. "Would you care to wait at the bar? It should only be a few more minutes."

Penny was already at the bar with a drink and a laptop. She was dressed as she'd been the first time he'd met her, in a bright pink parka.

"Hey," he said. "What are you working on?"

"A dark and stormy. Rum, ginger beer, lime juice."

He raised his eyebrows.

"What? I'm of legal drinking age here." She sipped at her drink. "I love Denmark."

"I was referring to your computer," he said.

"Still trying to fix my mistakes," Penny said. "What good is saving the world if you can't Tweet about it afterward? We need to reopen the lines of communication, or we'll really be in bad shape." She closed the computer. "But it's going to take a lot of people to make this work."

"Anything I can do?" Max asked.

Penny gave him a dubious look. "I thought you'd want to sit this one out, spend some time with the family, be normal."

"I have to do something. It's not just because I'm already involved, but I realized that there are a lot of people out there who aren't being heard. Part of the problem is that so many people are actively being silenced, and there's also too much noise on the internet drowning them out.

"You and Ada were right, to a point; we took a wrong turn somewhere. The internet hasn't fulfilled its potential yet. It's time I also step up and speak out. I'm not going to self-censor anymore."

"I'll drink to that. Welcome back to the fight." Penny raised her glass.

"I still don't think any one person should determine what the internet is going to be. But I want to start a conversation everyone can join." Max picked up a menu and looked it over.

"What can I get for you?" asked a bartender.

"Just water." Max sat down next to Penny and turned toward her on his stool. "As long as we're both stuck in Europe for the foreseeable future, we may as well make the most of it. I already have a full schedule of TV interviews for the next couple of weeks, assuming I don't get imprisoned." He figured if he couldn't spend a lot of time behind the screen for the moment, he might as well get in front of it.

"You're going all out. Your mom's a bad influence on you," Penny said.

"Says you."

"I just hope you know what you're doing."

For the first time in a long while, he did. He could do more to persuade people to think about privacy issues with a funny story and a big smile than he ever could pounding at a keyboard. Internet or no internet, no more hacking. No more secrets.

Max turned and looked toward the front of the restaurant. His parents were admiring the colorful pictures adorning the walls and sneaking not-so-furtive looks at Max and Penny.

Penny touched his arm so he turned back toward her. "Max, are we good?"

"I don't know," he said.

Penny took Max's hands in both of hers. Her fingernails were decorated with 8-bit hearts. The one on her left pinky was half red and the others were empty.

"I love you," she said.

"I . . ." *Just say it, Max.* He sighed. "I don't trust you anymore."

She pulled her hands away. "Okay. I deserve that. We'll work on it."

"We'll work on it? Like fixing our relationship is the same as . . ." He waved his hand at her computer. "Fixing the internet?"

"We have a lot to work on, but I think it's worth it. Don't forget: the internet is all about relationships. It's going to take teamwork to build the internet we want to see, and it'll take both of us to get back to where we were. If you're up for it."

"Not where we were," Max said. "We can't go back. But maybe we can make things even better."

"Challenge accepted."

They leaned toward each other—

And were interrupted by a loud, exaggerated smooching sound behind them.

Max turned. "Hi, Enzo."

"Jeez. Get a chat room, guys. Oh, right—you can't." Enzo hopped onto a stool and spun around. "Too soon?"

"Sorry for the interruption," Alicia Beaumont said.

"He does that to us too," Ophélie said.

Penny closed her eyes and blushed.

Bradley came over and hugged Alicia and Ophélie. He had mastered the art of the double-kiss greeting in no time at all.

"Our tables are ready," Bradley said.

The rest of the evening passed with delicious Danish food and the delight of several conversations happening at once, sometimes talking over one another, often around one another, and sometimes weaving together in surprising parallels.

Over a decadent dessert of hot chocolate sponge cake and coffee, Max came to a decision.

"Pen, can I borrow your laptop?" he asked.

"Max," Lianna warned.

"Just for a minute," he said.

Penny entered her password to unlock it. Max plugged in his USB drive.

"I wanted to show you all what I've been working on. So there won't be any more surprises," Max said.

"So we can prepare to bail you out of prison, you mean?" But Bradley leaned closer to the screen with interest.

"That too." Max explained that he'd been trying to coordinate interviews with everyone involved in The Curtain story, including Nadia, using the telephone, of all things. "We need to keep the media focused on the people affected by VT, the victims of the internet."

"I'm proud of you," Lianna said. "Even factoring in the multiple arrests."

"Especially because of them," Bradley muttered.

"I've also prepared a statement for dead-tree media." Which was the only media for the moment.

Penny scrolled down and started reading. "'Forget what I think about all this: The Curtain, VT's crumbling monopoly, the lack of privacy, the role of our governments in allowing this all to happen . . . Instead, ask yourselves what *you* think about it, and how *we* let this happen in the first place.

"'I have a question for you: Now that you know the truth, what are we going to do about it? How do we stop this from happening again, with whatever rises to take the place of the internet? How can we do better next time?'"

"That's marvelous," Ophélie said. Alicia smiled.

"Hear, hear," Bradley said.

After dinner, Max and Penny took their time walking back to her new car—he didn't ask her where she'd gotten it, but she had her ways.

"Do you think this is what Evan wanted?" she asked abruptly.

Max thought for a while. He wasn't sure if she was referring to everything they'd done to bring down VT and The Curtain, or Max and Penny being together. Maybe it was all that and more.

"Evan loved the internet. He always wanted to make a difference. Make the world a better place . . ." Max shook his head. "So no, I don't think so."

"No?"

"Because the world is much worse off without him."

Penny smiled sadly. "But it's not all bad."

"No, and it's getting better. There's still hope for a shiny tomorrow." Max slipped his hand into hers. "We live in interesting times, Penny Polonsky."

"Can't wait to see what happens next. Bring it."

They walked hand in hand toward that hopeful but uncertain future. Max might not know what it would bring, but he was certain of one thing: He and Penny were on the same side again. Now that they finally had managed to come to a middle ground in their goals, and what they were willing to do to achieve them, he thought they could face anything together.

Even the end of the world as they knew it.

ACKNOWLEDGEMENTS

IT TAKES AN INCREDIBLE TEAM TO OVERTHROW an evil corporation, even a fictional one. I couldn't have asked for a better group of storytellers with which to tackle Verbunden Telekom than my partners at Adaptive Books.

I have wanted to work with Jordan Hamessley for years, and I'm glad this project finally brought us together. Thank you, Marshall Lewy and Kristy King, for helping to bring Max, Penny, and Risse to life in *The Silence of Six* and then launching them into an even bigger, more personal adventure. With kissing. Thanks also to those at Adaptive who work in the shadows . . . I may not know your names or faces, but I see what you're doing, and your hard work and support is appreciated. You all deserve generous raises.

Merci to Alyssa Masor for our European travels and for

the last-minute translation help. All mistakes are mine and Google's.

Finally, thanks to Ben Turner, who told me about phone phreaking and other hacks in a gym class long, long ago and taught me nearly everything I know about computers—mostly, not to be afraid of messing with them. Sorry about any technical mistakes in this book, but I'm still learning.

E. C. MYERS is the author of the Andre Norton Award–winning *Fair Coin* and *Quantum Coin*, young adult science fiction novels published by Pyr, and the acclaimed young adult thriller *The Silence of Six* from Adaptive Books.